RICH GIRL,
POOR GIRL

EILEEN RAMSAY

ZAFFRE

First published in 1996 in the United Kingdom by Warner Books as *Butterflies in December*

This edition published in Great Britain in 2017 by
Zaffre Publishing
80–81 Wimpole St, London W1G 9RE
www.zaffrebooks.co.uk

A CIP catalogue record for this book is available from the British Library.

Paperback ISBN: 978-1-785-76222-2

Also available as an ebook

1 3 5 7 9 10 8 6 4 2

Typeset by IDSUK (Data Connection) Ltd
Printed and bound by Clays Ltd, St Ives Plc

Zaffre Publishing is an imprint of Bonnier Zaffre,
a Bonnier Publishing company
www.bonnierzaffre.co.uk
www.bonnierpublishing.co.uk

RICH GIRL, POOR GIRL

Eileen Ramsay grew up in Dumfriesshire. After graduation she went to Washington D.C. where she taught in private schools for some years before moving to California with her Scottish husband. There, she raised two sons, finished her Masters Degree, fell in love with Mexico, and published her first short stories and a Regency novel. The family returned to Scotland, where Eileen continued to teach and write and to serve – at different times – on the committees of the Society of Authors in Scotland, the Scottish Association of Writers and the Romantic Novelists' Association. In 2004, her novel *Someday, Somewhere* was shortlisted for the Romantic Novel of the Year award. Eileen is currently Chair of the Romantic Novelists' Association.

For more information, visit www.eileenramsay.co.uk

Also in the *Flowers of Scotland* series by Eileen Ramsay

The Farm Girl's Dream (previously published as *Walnut Shell Days*)
A Pinch of Salt (previously published as *The Broken Gate*)
The Crofter's Daughter (previously published as *Harvest of Courage*)
A Lesson for a Lassie (previously published as *The Dominie's Lassie*)
The Convent Girl (previously published as *The Quality of Mercy*)

For
Mr and Mrs James Harrison McGlothlin
from No. 4

1

Washington, D.C., 1888

THAT YEAR THERE was a particularly fine Indian summer. For those foreign residents of this capital city who had alternately burned and sweated profusely during July and August and who could not afford to leave for cool cottages on Cape Cod, it was doubly welcome. Mind you, here in the old colonial city of Georgetown with its splendid trees, relief from the usual breathless days could be obtained. Lucy Graham lay back in the swing beside the man she loved more than anybody or anything in this whole world and idly watched the blue sky appear and disappear behind leaves. Just round the corner the Bliss Estate with its friendly name, Dumbarton Oaks, ran from high ground all the way down to the waters of Rock Creek. A bridge from the Dumbarton Oaks side straddled the clear waters of the creek and gave access to Virginia: home of fine horses, gracious living and, of course, several presidents starting with George Washington.

'Maybe I should have put Washington first,' thought Lucy idly, 'before the horses.'

She spoke for the first time in several somnolent moments. 'Have you ever met anyone who was born and bred in this city, Father?'

Colonel Sir John Graham lay back in the garden seat beside his daughter and considered the question.

'No,' he finally said. 'Can't say I have. Everyone at the embassy is a foreigner. All the politicians, too, come from other states.'

With his heel he set the swing in motion again, and father and daughter drifted back and forward under the massive trees watching the sun chasing its beams in and out of the leaves above them. They revelled in the time that they could be alone together. Beside them, Amos, Lady Graham's general factotum, finished sweeping the afternoon's drift of leaves while he listened to their gentle well-bred Scottish voices. He loved the sound and paid little attention to the content, unless it was directed at him. It would never have occurred to him to say, 'Look at me, colonel, sir. I been born here, and my daddy and my daddy's daddy.'

'Not many more days of sitting outside, Lucy.'

It was September and already chill winds were blowing down from the north.

'Mother will be pleased. She finds swinging with one's own father a complete and utter waste of time.'

They laughed together.

'Not that I agree with her,' Lucy went on lazily. 'Poor mother. To be stuck with a bean-pole for a daughter.'

'A delightful bean-pole.' Colonel Graham stopped the swing and looked measuringly at his daughter. 'You have my height, Lucy, but your mother's looks and her grace. I can't understand why this garden isn't swarming with teenage boys sporting boating blazers and carrying tennis rackets. There are enough of them in the diplomatic community.'

'I inherited your brains too,' said Lucy flatly. 'I cannot simper.'

'You refuse to simper.'

'I cannot chatter.'

'You refuse to chatter.'

'Would you have me different?'

'Not me, my darling child. A woman like you, Lucy, is rare as a butterfly in December.'

A butterfly in December. How sweet he was, and how poetic for a soldier. She looked at his clear-cut profile.

'We must look for a collector of rare butterflies,' she said lightly and watched him laugh.

'Auguste Arvizo-Medina?'

Lucy started up from the swing in mock horror. She was enjoying this repartee, knowing perfectly well that they could not speak so boldly and openly if Lady Graham were present. 'Good heavens, no. Would you have me mother of at least five fat babies in as many stultifying years?'

'He says he is fascinated by you.'

'I would bore him to distraction when I refused to turn into a brood mare. I should have been a man, Father, and then I could have, could have . . .'

'Followed me to military college?' The colonel spoke the words lightly, rather as though he and his daughter shared some absurd joke.

'Rather to Oxford.'

There, she had said it. Lucy looked at him from under her eyelashes, but there was no shock on his face.

'It's not the way of our world, my dear. Don't despair.'

'American women go to college, Father.'

'My dear child. I will not have my only daughter labelled a blue-stocking and, besides, there is something so unfeminine about the college girls we have been obliged to meet.'

'Perhaps because they have had to fight like men for a place they should have by rights, although you must agree that Americans have been so much more modern in their thinking than we Scots. It's perfectly acceptable for well-bred American girls to be educated. Mount Holyoke Female Seminary must have been in existence for almost fifty years – and there's Vassar Female College, and Wellesley, and Smith.'

'You're remarkably knowledgeable, Lucy,' said Sir John drily and decided to change the direction of the conversation; he was a brilliant strategist. 'You can still use that not inconsiderable brain.'

'How?' Lucy almost jumped from the swing and he registered, with appreciation, the compelling picture she made as she walked about the garden. 'By deciding how much chicken feeds two hundred guests, or how much cream is needed to pour over those peaches Amos gathered this morning? Women have brains, Father, and I have been luckier than most. Because of Kier, I am as qualified as any man to enter a university.'

She sat down again beside him and he set the swing into gentle motion. They did not speak but Lucy knew that her father, Colonel Sir John Graham, military attaché to her Britannic Majesty's embassy in Washington, D.C., had to be thinking, like her, of the son of their neighbour in Scotland. Kier Anderson-Howard had been Lucy's friend since early childhood. Having had a bad riding accident when he was twelve years old, for nearly five years he had been unable to continue his education in the public school system. Because his parents did not want him to be educated alone, they had invited their neighbours, Sir John and Lady Graham, to send along their daughter to share Kier's tutor.

A new world had opened for Lucy: Latin, Greek, Mechanics, German, Philosophy, Mathematics, a world

away from the History (abridged), French, English literature (censored), and Drawing, which was the bulk of what
Miss Bulwark had been able to teach her.

'That prissy girls' school where you were enrolled
would have collapsed from shock at your ignorance if you
had ever joined them, Lucy,' Kier had teased after their
first morning together in Herr Colner's classroom.

'I'm glad dear Mr Colner did not,' Lucy had said seriously and had gone on to astound herself, her friend, and
their tutor with the remarkable agility of her mind. By
the time Kier was pronounced strong enough to return
to Fettes to take the entrance examinations for the university, Lucy was as ready and as able as her schoolmate.
But in 1886, no one considered sending young ladies to
university with their brothers.

She had joined her father in his appointment to Washington, where she received long interesting letters from Kier who
did not try to spare her maidenly blushes – knowing she had
none – and told her about everything he experienced, first at
Fettes and later at Oxford University.

'What of Kier, then?' asked the colonel into his daughter's silence. 'You will come out next winter and then . . .'
He did not add that his daughter, even at sixteen, should
be thinking of a future with a good husband.

'Kier is my best friend,' said Lucy, and then, because he
was her father and she had always known that she could

tell him absolutely everything and anything and never be judged, she poured out her feelings. 'I love him desperately. I think I always have ... even before the accident, I mean. That changed everything. Not just my education but ... my relationship with Kier. That first year when he couldn't move, I did so much for him. I saw him in so many moods, dealing with pain, with fear, being sick. There's little romance left when someone has wiped up your vomit.'

She lost herself in her memories and her father looked at her in wonder. His sheltered, protected daughter cleaning up vomit! Her mother would faint at the very idea.

'I read to him in the afternoons sometimes when Herr Colner would rest. He was ill too, you know, some wasting sickness from years of privation: the Jews have never been well treated, have they? I wonder why that is? I hardly think God chooses to punish them for eternity for denying Christ.' Lucy shook away that thought impatiently. 'Anyway, Father,' she went on, 'Kier could not bear his mother about him – she fussed so, and wept constantly over his broken bones. It was easier to clean him up and dispose of his soiled nightshirts than to send for her. I cared deeply, but somehow I was able to do what had to be done for him with the minimum of hysteria. Still, I doubt that he sees me as a delicate flower; a butterfly, if you will.'

'He will see quite a change when we return home next Christmas. You will be sixteen; your hair will be up. Your flashing eyes will devastate him.'

Two years in one of the most sophisticated and richest cities in the world, albeit one that was still classed as a hardship post by Her Victorian Majesty's Government, had had quite an effect on Lucille Graham. Her father could hardly wait to see the effect she would create in London and Edinburgh salons.

'Sir John, stop filling the child's head with nonsense.' They had not heard Lady Graham glide elegantly out of the French doors, managing her skirts with a grace that Lucy would always envy. 'Senator du Pay and his son have called. Lucille, I would like you to meet the du Pays. They are very wealthy and, what is more important, very influential.'

'I'd like to meet them, Mamma. Max du Pay is the one with the matched bays.'

Lady Graham threw up her head – almost, thought Lucy wickedly, like one of those self-same horses. 'Not one word about horses.' Elizabeth Graham looked at her daughter, almost 'out', and all that was in her head was books, horses, and books again. Where had she gone wrong? John's influence. Not for the first time she wished that she had been able to give her husband the son they had both wanted. 'Go and tidy yourself, Lucy. Max du Pay is already at Harvard. He is used to sophisticated young women, not hoydenish schoolgirls who can think only of books and horses.'

Lucy went upstairs, but not to her room. She went to the circular landing where she and her father had their favourite indoor retreat. It was no more than an enlarged landing really, and was full of huge, comfortable, but decidedly unfashionable, armchairs, bookcases and dog baskets.

From the huge windows, almost as tall as the room, which flooded the staircase with light in all but the depths of the Washington winter, she could see the street and, more importantly, the horses Max du Pay was driving today. She caught her breath. Oh, such beauty!

'Aren't horses the most beautiful creatures God put on the earth, Digby,' she told the elderly Sealyham who had merely raised one eye by way of greeting. 'If you weren't too old you would adore to chase this pair; they're black as night and they shine like polished jet, like Mamma's mourning beads. Oh!'

She remembered that her mother was waiting for her and without doing a thing to her appearance, ran downstairs. She had time to stop and compose herself before entering the drawing room and, because she was late, the guests were already drinking tea and she had the opportunity to look at them before they saw her. She knew

Senator du Pay by sight, but she had never seen his son before. *What do they feed them on in the South?* she asked herself, for if her father and the American senator were tall, this young man was a giant.

He turned and looked at her and the oddest feelings ran through Lucy.

'Why, here is your little girl, colonel, sir,' drawled the young man and his eyes, as he looked at Lucy, registered her blush and laughed at her.

She lifted her head and ignored him completely.

'Senator du Pay. How do you do, sir. Father and I were just analysing your dissertation to Congress this week.'

The senator took her hand and tucked it into his arm as he led her to a seat in the window. 'My dear young lady. I can't believe such a beautiful young woman bothers her pretty little head with such dull stuff. Lady Graham, you British mothers are to be congratulated. Beauty, charm, and brains too. Why have I not met this delightful young lady before?'

Lady Graham revelled in the game the senator was playing; he and his son could tell the tale being told by the long hair dancing on Lucy's shoulders and catching the light from the candles already burning on the tables. 'Senator, you know perfectly well our daughter is not yet out.'

He pretended surprise. 'Why, ma'am, she will lay waste this city with her beauty as her compatriots once wasted it with their bullets.'

Lucy looked at him. She was not unused to such silly talk; it was the way all her parents' elderly friends flirted with her, but the senator's son said nothing and Lucy was intensely aware of him. He was laughing at her. Why? She put her nose – classically straight, thank heaven – even higher in the air.

'I will be too busy to take Washington, sir. Why, Father and I were discussing college this very afternoon.' Not completely true, but she would not have Maximilian du Pay look at her as if she was nothing but a silly schoolgirl allowed for a moment to a grown-ups' party.

'Together with Father's speech.' He laughed down at her, down. Lucy was used to looking into the eyes, if not over the heads of most men.

Why was he teasing her? He made her uncomfortable. Never, ever, had she been so aware of a man. She threw herself into the verbal fray.

'And many, many more important things.'

'Oh, shush, Lucy.' She had gone too far and even Father was angry. But he said nothing; that would come later.

'Lucille, would you go to the kitchen and ask Amos to bring those peaches we picked from the glasshouse this morning? I would like the senator to try them.' Lady Graham was ushering her daughter to the door. 'And then you go straight to your room, young lady,' she whispered as she opened the door.

Lucy almost ran to the kitchens. She was angry and embarrassed and she hated that supercilious, overbearing Maximilian – what a stupid name – du Pay. It was his fault that she had been rude. She would never, ever, ever speak to him again. He would beg but she . . .

From the kitchens came the sound of a crash, a scream, a muffled groan. Lucy picked up her skirts and ran. She opened the door and saw the cause of the commotion. Female, the young black maid, had obviously tipped over a kettle of boiling soup and it had splattered Amos as he was in the act of slicing some of the splendid peaches. The knife had slipped and buried itself, not in a peach but in his hand. Lucy did not even pause to think.

'Stop screaming, Female, and get me some water. Sit down, Amos, and keep your hand up.'

'This ain't no job for you, Miss Lucille,' whispered the old man. 'What will your mamma say?'

Lucy knew perfectly well what her mother would say, but she lied. 'She'd say that we should get you to a hospital as soon as possible. (Hospital: doctor. How did one staunch blood? Should the knife come out or be left embedded in the wound? Tell me, tell me.) 'Female, go to the drawing room and ask Sir John to come down.' She did not wait for the girl's flustered protests: 'The drawing room. I doesn't go in there when there's white folks there,' but calmly went on staunching the blood with a

12

cloth. 'Right now, Female.' The girl threw her apron over her head and ran.

'I hope she doesn't bump her head on something,' she said and in spite of the pain Amos grinned. 'She know her place, Miss Lucille, and it ain't in your mamma's drawing room.'

They could hear the servant girl shrieking out her story and in a minute or two the kitchen was invaded. Lucy ignored the du Pays.

'An accident with a knife, Father. We'll take him to George Washington, or would Georgetown be better?'

The four men, three white, one black, looked at one another, and one of the white faces flushed.

'It don't make no never mind, colonel, sir,' said Amos gently. 'I can't go to them fine hospitals, Miss Lucille; that's for white folks. I thank you for your help: she didn't swoon or nothing, colonel, sir. I can take care of it myself now, Miss Lucille. Female can sew it up with the thread she been using to sew up that chicken. The knife ain't cut nothing important, and now she's stopped screaming she'll do a good job. Won't you, Daughter?'

Female wiped her tear-stained cheeks and nodded. 'Pappy's learned me lots about wounds, colonel, sir, Miss Lucille. I'm sorry I yelled so; I just hates the sight of blood. How can you stand it, Miss Lucille? Ain't it indelicate in a young lady – and a white one at that – not to swoon?'

Lucy ignored everyone but her father. She was hardly aware of Maximilian du Pay leaving the room.

'It's bleeding badly. He should see a doctor. I just don't know what to do.' She turned to her father, the soldier. 'You must have dealt with wounds?'

'I got a ointment for bleeding, Miss Lucille,' said Amos before the colonel could answer. 'You'll see, I'll be fine tomorrow. Female'll go get her mother when she's done sewed me up and Abra will look to everything here.'

The young American came back, his indolence gone. 'I've arranged the carriage, Father. I'll take him to Freedmen's myself, with your permission, of course, colonel. It's 13th and V Street, I think? I've never been before.'

Was that a glance of admiration he gave Lucy? She could not be sure. More likely it was surprise, distaste even. Hadn't he heard Female say her behaviour was indelicate? Well, she didn't care. Look at them, look at them just taking over, putting the little woman back in her place. She followed the men out of the kitchen and wearily made her way up to her bedroom to await the tirade that was sure to come. She felt certain that she could write the script herself.

*   *   *

In the end, it was not her mother who came to her room but her father.

'Mother must be furious,' said Lucy lightly when she saw his set face.

14

'You amazed us both this afternoon, Lucy, and we've talked. Mamma loves you and she wants for you the things she enjoyed – a coming-out, new dresses, parties, dancing. But she is broad-minded enough to see that those treats don't interest you . . .'

'They do, Father, of course they do, but . . . not so much as . . . as doing something really special with my life.'

'I can think of nothing more splendid for a woman, Lucy, than being a good wife and mother,' said Sir John seriously, 'but we've decided – to use a horsey term – to give you your head for a while, till it's out of your system . . .'

A few weeks later, Lucy found herself a very young student at the very young Smith College for women in Northampton, Massachusetts. She decided not to think of Maximilian du Pay and the extraordinary effect he had had on her, and after a few months she forgot all about him and everything else that kept her from learning, learning.

She loved Smith; she loved New England. She both loved and hated being surrounded by so many people. Lucy had never been to school; her largest class had had one class-mate. Here there were dozens of bright, articulate, young women. Classes of five, ten, twenty girls were uncharted waters for Lucy and she set sail eagerly. Often, though, she had to steal away from the laughing, loving companionship and seek solace and a kind of inner rebirth. For this she would wander in the grounds among the age-old trees. At all times of the year, the college was lovely. In the autumn – the Fall as her American classmates called it – the grounds were breathtaking. How was it possible for leaves to turn those colours, and all with an intensity that she had seen nowhere before? Yellow, red, brown . . . but yellow, red and brown that had been ignited by a fire that was only to be found in these New England states. The trees burned their way into winter. The leaves crackled on the branches as they struggled to free themselves from their tenuous hold on life and they crackled under Lucy's soft leather boots as she wandered among them. She wrote long letters, weekly to her parents and monthly to Kier Anderson-Howard. She told him of her delight in the formal education for which Herr Colner had so ably prepared her. She told him of her pleasure in joining five, ten, fifteen alert brains in healthy argument and discussion.

I loved being educated with you, Kier, but I have just realized that because of that education, I have knowledge but no friends besides yourself and I did not know what I missed. I would not have it different, but now I am happy to catch up with my own sex. Already I have been invited to spend an exeat weekend with a classmate who lives in *New York City* and I have invited another, who lives in

Oregon – which, as you know, is about as far from Massachusetts as it is possible to go without falling into the Pacific Ocean – to spend the Thanksgiving holiday with us in the capital. What fun to introduce an American to her own historic buildings. Mirabelle, from New York, is to take me to the Opera and to dine in a *restaurant* with her huge family of brothers. How decadent I am become – exactly what Mother feared!

In a later letter she asked him what on earth she could do with the degree she would soon earn. Even to Kier, she could not mention the only real idea she had had, which was growing so strongly that it threatened to blot out everyone and everything. She felt that she was two different people: Miss Graham who lived in Massachusetts, and little Lucy who lived in Washington, D.C. Little Lucy went home at the holidays and did the things her mother wanted her to do, although the trip to Scotland and the presentation at court had had to be sacrificed on the voracious altar of further education. On her last Thanksgiving holiday from Smith, Lucy returned home like every other student but, unlike most students, she found herself heading for a recital at the Russian embassy.

They had almost been late. Female, Amos's daughter, had been announced to be in a *delicate* condition.

Female was unmarried and Lucy found herself fascinated and wanted to know the whys and the wherefores. Her unseemly interest in something that had caused friction between her parents – Lady Graham wishing to dismiss the girl and Sir John more interested in keeping excellent servants like Amos and Abra happy – had caused Lady Graham to remember Lucy's own wayward and unfeminine behaviour several years earlier; she had never really mentioned this, no matter how hard it was, but it had gnawed at her occasionally. Now she lapsed from self-imposed virtue a little.

'A girl in your position, with your advantages, should have nothing to do with such things, Lucille. I still can't bear to think what the du Pays thought when they found you alone in the kitchen with a black male servant . . . I'm quite sure their friendship cooled a little.'

'Mother, how can you ignore Amos's very presence one minute and the next be so conscious of it?' Lucy had teased.

'They found you doing what no well-brought-up young woman should even contemplate doing.'

'Florence Nightingale is a lady, Mother, and she did a great deal more than bind up a bleeding wound.'

'One admires Miss Nightingale. One does not necessarily wish one's only child to emulate her. Besides, she did it for our soldiers.'

'Oh, and of course none of them was black. I wonder if it would have made a difference to her.'

The colonel stirred on his seat. The quarrel between his wife and his daughter was becoming a little too heated. 'Lucille, your mother is right to concern herself with the opinion the world has of you.' He laid his hand gently on Lucy's satin-covered knee and she decided to argue no more.

'I'm sorry, Mother, but I'm sure you didn't want poor Amos to bleed to death. He is, after all, an invaluable servant.'

'And could have been looked after by other servants: that hysterical daughter of his, for instance, with the ridiculous name.'

'Feh-ma-lay,' smiled Lucy, drawing out the syllables the way their servants did. 'It's rather sad, actually, that they couldn't pronounce Female, couldn't read . . .'

'And where, by the by, was Abra during that incident?' Lady Graham interrupted, a sense of injustice gnawing at her. She had been quiet for too long; she would have a little satisfaction now, and Lucy had brought it on herself. 'Now that I think about it, I don't remember giving her time off mid-week.'

'We did discuss all this, Elizabeth,' the colonel put in. 'Remember, my dear, Amos had asked me when you were with your dressmaker. It seemed only fair; they do work such very long hours.'

Lady Graham sighed. Her husband would never learn how to treat servants properly; they would do exactly as they liked if she didn't keep a firm hand on the reins.

The carriage drew up at the embassy and Lady Graham was considerably cheered when she saw that her daughter was to be partnered with the very handsome and very wealthy Russian Count Fyodorov. She smiled complacently. Lucy could make a beautiful countess, if she so chose.

Lucy well knew what was going through her mother's mind, and because she loved her she decided to be good and to charm the count as best she could. There was another more compelling reason to shine with the Russian. Almost the first voice she heard as she entered the embassy was the low drawl of Maximilian du Pay and, what was worse, she found that he was to be seated very near her but, thankfully, on the other side of the table; she need not speak to him at all. She nodded stiffly, as if she vaguely remembered him but could not quite place him though would never for a moment be rude . . . and then decided to ignore him as best she could.

'I wish we were to have dancing after dinner, Miss Graham, instead of that dreadfully boring, and even more dreadfully fat, mezzo-soprano. I should insist that you dance every dance with me but, perhaps, while they prepare the salon for the entertainment, we could walk a little on the terrace. It is mild for November, no?'

'It is mild for November, yes,' agreed Lucy. 'If others are strolling on the terrace, count, then I am sure we may join them.'

'Not a good idea, Miss Lucy. I may claim the privilege of old friendship, may I not?'

Lucy was amazed. She had turned, as custom demanded, to the guest on her right, and had caught Max du Pay's eye. Obviously the odious man had been listening to her conversation. It is one thing to flirt with a handsome Russian, it is quite another to be observed doing it by someone one loathes, and especially when flirting is completely against one's principles. She blushed rosily.

'Charming,' he said. 'I had no idea that empty-headed, rich young women could blush any more.'

Lucy was furious and she forgot all her mother's rules for good behaviour. 'How dare you! You know perfectly well that I am neither wealthy nor empty-headed.'

He laughed. 'And being called empty-headed rankles more, I'll be bound. But as I was saying, Miss Smith College, don't stroll in the moonlight with the count. He is a most notorious philanderer.'

'I think I'm capable of taking care of myself, Mr du Pay. No one would be invited here who was . . .'

'Not *comme il faut*?'

'Not empty-headed . . . I mean who was empty – oh, stuff!' She heard the ridiculous words as she was speaking them and would have drawn them back if she could. He saw her predicament and laughed.

'You need have no fear to speak your mind around me, Miss Graham, although usually we Southerners prefer our women meek and mild.'

'How nauseating.' Again that unruly tongue.

'I do believe you are right, Miss Graham.' He laughed and turned away from her.

Since Count Fyodorov was still engaged in conversation, Lucy studied the American, safe in the knowledge that, since he was giving an inordinate amount of attention to the very sophisticated but married woman on his right, he could not see her. What had he been doing for the past year? He must be finished at Harvard. She had been to balls at that prestigious college twice during this heady year and had never seen him – had tried, oh, yes, she had, not to look for him. She had forgotten how tall he was and how fair. His hair, which was too long for fashion, was almost bleached by the sun, and his face and hands showed that he spent rather too much time outside in all weathers. She was so busy watching the man she had resolved to ignore that she almost missed the next move in the conversational game of bat and ball.

'I detest Maximilian du Pay and I adore charming Russians,' she said to herself and turned with a glorious smile to her dinner partner.

After dinner she found herself walking with him and several other people towards the glass doors that led to the terrace. Count Fyodorov solicitously wrapped her light voile scarf around her bare shoulders.

'You should wear ermine,' he said.

Lucy smiled. She could just imagine her father's face if she were to ask for an ermine cape. His diplomatic salary made up the sum total of the Graham fortune, and a military attaché's income did not stretch to ermine stoles for his daughter.

To her surprise, she found herself whisked behind an enormous urn and held tightly in a man's embrace.

'Miss Graham, Lucy, that smile. It tantalizes; how you are adorable,' he said and, to her amusement, kissed her ruthlessly.

This was not the first time that Miss Lucy Graham had been kissed and, really, she chided herself, 'You ought to be able to handle men better by this time.' She pushed the count away and laughed. It worked; it always did. Nothing deflated an enormous ego more than laughter. At least, it had always worked with the college men who haunted the grounds at Smith.

Count Fyodorov visibly controlled his annoyance. He bowed. 'Your servant, Miss Graham. May I escort you back to her ladyship?'

'I'll take her, count.'

'Not nice, Miss Graham,' said Maximilian du Pay in an amused voice as they watched the discomfited Russian walk away.

'You had no business spying on me, Mr du Pay.'

'Max, please, and I wasn't spying. You're lucky the entire diplomatic party did not witness your petty triumph.'

Petty triumph! Lucy could not believe it. She had been assaulted – well, not quite – and a second arrogant male called it a petty triumph.

'Don't bristle, for I won't say you look charming when you pout . . .'

'I never pout,' Lucy broke in.

'You led that poor man by the nose all through dinner, and then you act surprised when he accepts your invitation.'

Lucy flushed to the roots of her hair. Was there some honesty in what he said? A gentleman, however, would never have said it.

'I think we have nothing further to say to one another, Mr du Pay.' She would refuse his invitation to make free of his Christian name.

'Au contraire, Miss Lucy,' he smiled, 'but not yet. I decided, and I never go back on my decisions, that when you have grown up a little . . .'

He did not say what he had decided, but he bowed courteously and turned away and Lucy watched him, her mind in a turmoil. He was the rudest, most arrogant man she had ever met. She must make a real effort never to meet him again. She hurried back to the magnificent salon where seats had been arranged for the recital. Her parents had saved a chair for her and if they were surprised to see her unescorted they were unable to say anything.

In the carriage, on the way back to Georgetown, there were no such restrictions and, while her husband sat quietly in a corner, Lady Graham was able to allow a flood of recriminations to fall upon Lucy.

'Two of the most eligible men in Washington beside you at dinner, Lucille, and you throw away the opportunity.'

'Then you would have preferred that I submit to Count Fyodorov, Mother, pretend that I enjoyed his kiss.' She would not ask about Mr du Pay.

'Of course not, girl, but if you had not wanted it then it should never have happened.' Lady Graham sat back in anger and then relaxed. 'Oh, Lucy, you are very young. You know we have nothing but Father's salary. Count Fyodorov is related to the Tsar; his family is extraordinarily wealthy . . .'

'Then they should have spent a little more on his education,' said Lucy quietly.

Lady Graham pretended not to have heard. 'And he specifically asked for you at the dinner.'

'Definitely not a butterfly collector, Lucy,' said Sir John, and then when he felt rather than saw his wife's growing anger he turned to her and added, 'But you must admit, my dear, that Max du Pay seemed taken with our daughter. We have all been invited to join the Thanksgiving Hunt this year.'

The Thanksgiving Hunt! Lucy had not expected an invitation to one of the social season's most prestigious events. She conveniently forgot how much she detested the Southerner.

'Oh, how wonderful!' She clapped her hands together in excitement like a small child. 'Can we go, Father?'

'You will hill-top with me, Lucy,' Lady Graham answered for her husband.

Hill-topping: following the horses by carriage and watching their progress from the tops of hills. Great fun, but not so much fun as sweeping across the Virginia countryside on the back of a strong, spirited horse.

Lady Graham saw the disappointment in her daughter's face. 'Mrs du Pay has generously invited us to join her in her own carriage, Lucy. Every girl in Washington will be green with envy.'

'Except the ones on horseback,' Lucy mumbled.

Lady Graham sighed and ignored the mumble. 'The du Pays are one of the most important families in the South, and it is a great honour to be asked. And there is the ball,

Lucy. She will have to have a new gown, John; it will do for London too.'

'What did you think of Max this time, Lucy?' asked her father. 'Your first meeting had a rather unfortunate ending.' To his surprise Sir John saw his daughter blush.

'I didn't have too much conversation with him, Father.' Lucy was annoyed with herself. Senator du Pay was a personal friend of the ambassador and a good ally for Her Britannic Majesty's Government, and here was she crossing verbal swords with his son. 'He doesn't look like a . . . a . . . socialite,' finished Lucy for want of a better word.

'Rather unconventional: he's studying animal husbandry, but I think he's interested in art. I thought you would have liked him,' said Sir John. 'Never mind. You can adjust your thinking when you see him in his own setting.'

The rest of the journey passed in silence. Amos, as usual, was at the gates to meet them.

'Nice party, Miss Lucille?' he asked as he handed her down.

Lucy kept his hand in hers. 'Delightful, thank you, Amos, and how are you?'

'Lucille,' scolded Lady Graham when they had gone upstairs to prepare for bed, 'you really must not be so familiar with black servants. You treat Amos just the way you treated Annie at home, and she's been with us since before you were born.'

'I really can't see that his being black is relevant, Mother, and if Annie is part of the family in Scotland, then surely Amos and his family are part of our family here. Besides, I was merely enquiring about his health. Perhaps it's just that I've been away from home so much, but he doesn't seem quite himself. It's odd, Father, but his skin looks a little paler and there's a clammy feel . . .'

'Lucille, I have had quite enough of this unhealthy interest in Amos . . . good heavens, do you realize the man doesn't even have a surname?'

Lucy looked at her mother. How was it possible to love someone and be so annoyed and exasperated by them at the same time? She kissed her parents and went to bed. She would check up on Amos, quietly, in the morning.

The morning brought a posy of flowers from Max du Pay and a magnificent bouquet from the count. Perhaps even more exciting than the flowers was the note that accompanied the posy:

Should you care to ride in the hunt, Miss Graham, I should be delighted to provide a mount suitable for a thinking woman.

He was teasing; he had remembered their conversation but had conveniently *forgotten* that she had admitted to being both intelligent and poor. Sir John could not provide his daughter with a riding horse. But Max du Pay's horses . . . Lucy rushed to her mother's bedroom. Lady Graham was sitting up in bed looking delightful and quite young in a froth of pink silk as Lucy handed her the posy and the note.

'Aren't they lovely, Mother? I shall keep them in my bedroom.' She looked at her mother, who was smiling complacently as she read Max's note. 'There's a disgustingly vulgar bouquet from the count too.' Ah, that shot had gone home.

'Flowers from Count Fyodorov, Lucy. How very sweet.'

'A hothouse full of them. These are in such innate good taste, wouldn't you say, and I may accept the senator's offer, Mother. The horses must belong to him. Max is only a boy after all . . .'

She stopped at the look of consternation on her mother's face.

'A riding-habit, Lucy? We must get you a new riding-habit.' Lady Graham slipped from the bed, hurried across to her voluminous French wardrobe and began to rifle through the contents.

'Here, darling. We can get this altered.' She handed a dark blue velvet riding-dress to her daughter and looked at her carefully. 'Oh, Lucy, when are you ever going to . . . fill out?' she finished delicately.

'I'll look better in this than in the ball-gown Petal is making,' said Lucy as she held up the dress in front of her. Yes, dark blue was a very good colour.

'Petal should be working on the dresses now. Run upstairs and beg her to get this finished for Thanksgiving . . . only two days . . . and then you may write Max a note of acceptance, and change your dress. It's possible the count will call.'

Lucy picked up her posy and rushed upstairs to the attics where Petal, Lady Graham's dressmaker, was doing wonders with yards of pale green silk – not such a good colour as the blue, but better than insipid white. She had hardly had time to make her request when Female followed her upstairs to say that a gentleman had called. Amos usually announced visitors, but Lucy was too excited by flowers and gowns and, oh, yes, a magnificent horse 'suitable for a thinking woman', to wonder why he had not.

The next two days passed in a whirl.

'Why am I so happy?' Lucy asked herself several times a day as she stood in her petticoat while Petal tried somehow to make her look more girl than boy. The riding-habit suited her slim figure. Max would notice. 'I don't care if he notices. I haven't ridden in two years. I am excited by the thought of such horses and galloping, galloping, free of restrictions.' She lowered the green silk over her head.

'A dark Venus rising from the waves,' was Sir John's comment.

'Petal has worked wonders,' agreed Lady Graham, 'and only just in time.' She looked at her watch. It was already

Thanksgiving morning. 'We'll have Amos make up a basket for her to take home, and you must find a bonus, John.'

'The others are surely in bed, Elizabeth, and Petal must stay the night. She can't walk through the streets at this time of the morning. Come along, Cinderella, take off that beautiful gown and get some sleep or you'll be too tired to dance away tomorrow evening.' Sir John looked at his daughter, but Lucy was not listening to his banter. She stood, head poised like a deer who senses danger.

'I hear Female,' she said. 'Something's wrong, Father.'

She opened the door. Although it was so late all the lamps were still lit. 'You see,' she said triumphantly, 'Amos is still awake. He never goes to bed before we do.'

But it was Female who stood on the stairs, her voluminous nightgown disguising the bulge at her waistline. It was obvious that she had been crying.

'Ah so sorry not to be dressed, ladyship, colonel, sir. Ah been in bed, but Mammy says Pappy jist can't git moving although he sure done tried.'

'What's wrong, Female?' asked Lucy. 'We must go to their quarters and see, Mother.'

Lady Graham was furious. 'Female! How dare you walk around the public part of the house in your nightwear? Go downstairs and send your mother up here at once.'

Female burst into loud sobs and turned and ran for the servants' stairs.

'I'm sorry, Lucy,' said Lady Graham, looking at her daughter's angry face, 'but we must maintain standards. Please go to bed. Father and I will find out what's wrong and send for a doctor if need be.'

'I'd rather wait, Mother.'

Abra was a tall, slender woman, as neat at two in the morning as she would be at two in the afternoon. She came upstairs quickly.

'Amos has taken some kind of a turn, ma'am, Sir John. I'm sorry Female was in a state of undress. There ain't a brain in that girl's head.'

'What kind of turn . . . ?' began Lucy, but her mother was in charge.

'I will come to see Amos, Abra.'

She swept from the room and Lucy and her father sat down. They did not have long to wait, and one look at her mother's face told Lucy that Amos was seriously ill.

'I've sent Female next door to wake John-Joseph. He will bring some of their own people with a cart to take Amos to Freedmen's. I'm afraid he's seriously ill.'

'Surely we can do something. Get Professor Archibald . . . something?'

Professor Archibald was a close neighbour who was also on the staff at the nearby Columbia Hospital, a hospital established for the wives and widows of Union soldiers and sailors.

'At this hour of the morning, Thanksgiving morning, for a negro! You are so young, Lucy,' said her mother disparagingly.

Lucy refused to go to bed and sat in the drawing room and listened for the next-door servants to arrive. She did not notice how cold the room grew around her without the heavy diet of logs with which Amos fed the fire's insatiable appetite. She heard her father's voice and he went out – to do what, she did not know. It was only later that she learned that he had roused the coachman at the stables used by the Grahams, that he had driven to Freedmen's hospital and had sat, one white face in a frame of black ones, while Amos gave up the battle against his exhausted heart.

Sir John had found her in the drawing room, still in her sea green ball gown. He had shaken her awake gently and told her the news, only half expecting the terrible outpouring of grief.

'But Amos was only a servant, Lucy,' he had hazarded, in an attempt to understand. 'You hardly know . . . knew him.'

'I couldn't help him; I knew nothing, Father.' She lifted her ravaged face to him. 'It could have been you.'

And that, Lucy confessed to herself later when she was safely and anonymously back at Smith, one student among so many, was the real cause of her distress. Had it been her beloved father who had continued to function with the weakness in his arms, the clammy skin, the alternate hot and cool skin, and eventually on that last morning the tightness in his chest –' not a pain, Miss Lucy, he said he didn't have no pain' – she would have thought that perhaps he had eaten something that had disagreed with him, or that he had over-indulged. She would have sent at last for a doctor, one who would perhaps have come at two o'clock in the morning because Sir John was a fairly important part of the British Legation, and Sir John would have been taken to Georgetown Hospital, and perhaps . . . perhaps, he would have recovered.

'I will not give up the Thanksgiving Hunt at the du Pays for a servant,' said Lady Graham, who had kindly given Amos's family paid leave to bury husband and father, and who would willingly have accepted the hospital costs as one of the necessary expenses incurred by looking after good and valued servants.

There was no need for a family disagreement, however, for when the members of the family finally managed to get to sleep, they slept soundly through the hours of Thanksgiving morning and, in the afternoon, could find little for which to be wholeheartedly thankful.

'I'm sorry, Mother, I just can't go to a ball.'

'I don't feel much like dancing either,' agreed Lady Graham.

'Next year,' said Sir John.

But next year saw Lucille Graham in Edinburgh, Scotland, and there were so many beautiful and talented girls at the du Pays Thanksgiving Ball that hardly anyone missed her, hardly anyone.

2

Dundee, 1888

ROSIE SAT SHELLING peas and whistling. The whistling did not help her work but it kept Ma happy. If Rosie was whistling, she couldn't be eating the peas; or so Ma thought. Rosie actually had the eating of fresh young peas while keeping up a piercing chorus of whatever was playing at the Playhouse that week, off to a fine art. Mind you, she had to hold them lodged in her jaw for quite a while before she could take a breath and then swallow them all at once. That rather spoiled the pleasure of eating but it increased the pleasure of winning, and that, for Rosie, was the greater pleasure. Rosie liked to win.

There was a much more important battle on the horizon and Rosie was concentrating on that while her strong young fingers automatically prised open the pods and released the peas. If only it had been done before . . .

If it had been done before, she could talk about it and ask how it had been done. Then, armed with all that information, she could go to Ma and say, say what? Say, 'Ma, I'm not following every other member of this family into the mills, I'm going to get an education: I'm going to be a doctor so that no more bairns up this closie will die because we're poor and we cannae afford the doctor or the medicines.' But doctoring was for men, and universities were for men, and even though some lassies, and especially Rosie Nesbitt, were cleverer far than any laddie in the class, nobody would teach you Latin and Mathematics for those subjects were suitable only for men, and whoever had come up with a braw notion like that hadn't the sense he was born with. Rosie Nesbitt could read, write, spell, and add, better than any boy in her class. She had won a bursary at the age of ten that allowed her to attend the Harris Academy with all the nice, well-brought-up, well-dressed lassies from the West End of Dundee. One ancient teacher had even been heard to say that he had never come across a brain as gimp as Rosie Nesbitt's. But the powers that be – and all of them, wouldn't you know it, male – would not allow her a real education. Mind you, Scotland, that thought very highly of itself in terms of education, still barred women from its universities, but Rosie did not allow that small point to worry her. Something would happen: for Rosie Nesbitt something always did.

The idea came so suddenly and was so right, so sensible, that Rosie stopped whistling and nearly choked to death on her accumulation of peas. Old Wishy! She thought of the Classics master at the Harris, a bit like a hoodie craw – the children laughed at him in his threadbare old gown – but with a face that didnae fricht a child. At least, not Rosie Nesbitt. She had smiled at him that first day as she passed him on the stair, so pleased was she at being there in that old building, a bona fide pupil among all the toffs frae the West End. He had smiled back at her, a smile of genuine liking and approval, and had said, 'Welcome, my wee lass,' in that nice voice that wasn't a toff's voice but wasn't the sound of Dundee either. It sounded of education. Rosie almost hugged herself with joy at her brilliance. Why hadn't she thought of him before? She would pay him to teach her Latin.

There were plenty of ways of earning a few pence; she would just have to think of a few of them.

Rosie finished the peas and, quiet as the proverbial lamb, went in to help Ma with the rest of the dinner. Some dinner. Potatoes, mostly. Occasionally a bit of minced beef; sometimes fish, if the boys caught it.

'You're awfie quiet, Rosie.' Ma was tuned in to the moods of all her children and perhaps especially to those of this strange child, this cuckoo in the nest. 'Did ye eat too many peas?'

Rosie bristled; there was no way Ma could know. 'Did I stop whistling?' she demanded rashly.

Elsie smiled, a smile that wiped years and strain from her face. 'It's yer grannie thinks that's foolproof. Why did ye think she worked that out? Was it no me that ate peas years afore you were born, Rosie? Noo, whit's on yer mind, lassie?'

Rosie looked at her mother. How old was Elsie Nesbitt? Well, Frazer was near twenty and so she had to be at least thirty-five. Could you birth a bairn afore the age of fifteen? Elsie, Ma, had to be between thirty-five and forty years of age. She couldnae be more than forty even if she looked, what, fifty? It was too late for Elsie. Rosie's turn. Better just to tell her right out. 'I'm going to be a doctor.'

Elsie Nesbitt sat down hard in a chair and looked almost in awe at her fifth child. It had to be blood. The others weren't like this. Rosie's dad had not been one of her regulars; Rosie had resulted as the outcome of a chance meeting at the docks – a lad who spoke differently, who'd given her a rose instead of the two shillings he had promised. Now here was Rosie, already too big for her boots with a school uniform and a real schoolbag, talking about . . . oh dear God, what kind of a nonsense?

'It's not nonsense, Ma,' said Rosie as if she could read her mother's thoughts. 'Why should I no be a doctor? I'm clever. I like taking care of folk and I'm good at it. You aye said I was better wi' Grampa than onybody.'

'Och, lassie, that's a long way from getting all the book learning that makes a doctor.' Elsie had no real knowledge of higher education but she knew, as well as she knew the face of the girl in front of her, that the fulfilment of such a dream would take years . . . and money. Where could she ever get the money that was needed? By some strokes of divine providence, Rosie had aye managed to pay her way, and to see her stepping out of the door in the morning with her face washed and her hair brushed and a school-bag full of exciting books in her hand did her mother's heart good – but doctoring!

'Here, Rosie. Take a penny-halfpenny oot the jar and run doon for a bowl of potted meat; it'll go nice with the peas.' She had meant the money for two nice girdle scones from the bakery at the bottom of the stairs – sometimes the smells rolling up the closie on the wind were almost too good to be borne – but the meat was probably a better buy, more nourishing.

Rosie was already half-way down the stairs. Buying anything from a shop was an adventure. 'Ma's thinking on it,' she told herself. When Elsie changed the subject, it usually meant she was thinking.

She took her place in the queue outside the butcher's and waited, ignoring the other customers, her two sisters playing with their skipping-rope in the middle of the street, and the slabs of raw red meat. They held no interest for her; she had never tasted anything other than mince or boiling beef and her salivary glands agreed with Elsie – 'What you've never had, you'll never miss.'

No need to wrap up the wee bowl for the run back up the stairs. Rosie's mind kept pace with her steps. 'I've done it, I've done it.' Nothing was settled; nothing had been won; but she had brought her great dream out into the open and now it could grow. After all, it was only when flowers faced the sun that they really began to flourish.

Ma was still in the front room; she had not moved. Was she merely enjoying the unaccustomed peace of an empty room or was she still awed by the pronouncement from her third daughter? She turned from the window as Rosie catapulted into the room.

'I've been thinking on your plan, Rosie.' She moved to the huge oak dresser her grandfather had carved thirty years before and took out a patched but clean tablecloth which she threw over the scratched table top. 'Here, help me set the table; they'll all be in afore we know it – but I've been thinking that there's nae harm in trying for it. I heard a verse frae the pulpit once and it stuck in my mind. "Without vision the people perish." Well, I aye thought it meant a vision of angels and such, but it doesn't. You've got the vision all right, lassie, and we'll have to see aboot it. If I only kent where tae start.'

'With Latin, Ma. I need Latin, and I'll ask old Wishy tae teach me after school.'

'And whit would a bonnie lassie like you need with the Latin?'

With shrieks of joy Rosie and her mother rushed to throw themselves at the tall, windbeaten young man standing in the doorway. Frazer Nesbitt was Elsie's oldest son, and he had been gone over six months on a whaling expedition.

'I must have kent you were coming, laddie. Have I no just sent Rosie for potted meat?' Elsie was laughing and crying as she pulled her first-born into the room and forced him into the one good chair by the fire.

'And fresh peas, Frazer,' cried Rosie, who was now perched on her brother's knees.

'Aye, there's whit madam's no eaten. I'll make you a cup of tea, laddie. How long can you stay? You didnae get hurted in ony way, did you?' Elsie's questions rained down on the boy's head like the snows he had been glad to leave in the far north but, good-naturedly, he tried to answer all of them.

Rosie's grandiose plans sat and simmered like the soup on the back of the fire while Frazer talked and ate and talked again. Such places he'd seen; such people he'd met.

It was only after the others had come home – Lindsay, Leslie, and Murray from Baxter's jute works where they had started as half-timers and were now full time, and Donaldina and Granta, the wee ones, from their play in the street – and after they had all eaten and heard again and again the wonderful stories, and admired the strange carvings that Frazer had bought for a plug of tobacco from a man he called an Eskimo, that there was time to talk about Rosie again.

'And now, whit's this about Latin, Rosie? What would a wee lassie want with the Latin?'

'I want tae be a doctor, Frazer.'

Frazer did not laugh; neither did any of the other children. Elsie Nesbitt had always insisted that her children get as much education as circumstances would allow. Education was the way out of poverty; everybody knew that. Wasn't there a fellow called Carnegie who had started near as poor as themselves and now had suitcases full of money?

'And for doctoring you need Latin?' asked Frazer.

'Aye. I could easy win a bursary, when I'm big that is, but I need tae learn Latin and Mathematics and the Harris only teaches them tae boys.'

'You'll need private tuition, then,' said Frazer quietly and in such a matter-of-fact fashion that his mother stared at him, almost in awe. It never occurred to Elsie Nesbitt that it was something in herself that made these children different from the other children in the closie. Frazer had lapped up the learning too in the few years he had had at the school but, unlike Rosie, he had never set himself against circumstances but had gone out, as soon as he was able, to set about earning a living for himself, his mother, and the other children.

'I've a fortune saved, Ma,' he smiled. 'I aye fancied you in a smart new coat for the winter.'

'Ach, Rosie'll keep the hale gang of us in fur coats when she's a doctor – will you no, Rosie?'

Rosie stared at them both. She could say nothing. Words of gratitude were chasing one another around in her head but refused to find the way to her mouth.

'You can take the money to Mr Wishart the morn efter the school, Ma.'

But Elsie could not bring herself to confront a terrifying schoolteacher and, the next day, it was strong young Frazer who met Rosie as, almost sick with excitement, she left her last class.

'Whit if he says no?'

'I've ten pounds here in my poke,' said Frazer. 'That's near a half-year's wages for a teacher.'

Rosie looked up at him, almost as if she could not understand why the weight of such a vast sum of money had not bent him double.

'And after he says yes, Dr Nesbitt, there's still enough money to take you and Ma and me out for a fish supper and a cup of tea.'

Rosie clutched at his hand to steady herself. Latin tuition *and* a meal in a fisherman's café! She could not take much more. She almost stumbled along the corridor to the classroom of the Classics teacher.

Francis Wishart looked up from his marking when they answered his abrupt, 'Come.'

Whatever he had expected, it was not wee Rose Nesbitt and this tall weatherbeaten, old young man.

'Come in, Rose,' he said courteously. 'And this must be . . .'

'My brother, Frazer, Mr Wishart. He's a whaler,' finished Rose proudly. The teacher held out his hand to the whaler, who shook it in some surprise.

'What can I do for you, Mr Nesbitt?'

'It's Rosie. She wants to be a doctor.' Frazer looked into the older man's face but there was no scorn or derision there, only interest. 'She needs Latin.' He put his hand in the pocket of his rough jacket and pulled out a salt-stained pouch. 'I've saved my wages . . .'

'It was for a coat for Ma,' burst out Rosie and subsided quietly as Frazer looked at her in sudden anger.

'And you want me to tutor Rose for the entrance examination?'

Frazer looked at him in surprise. He was out of his depth now. 'Entrance, tae what? . . . sir,' he added.

'There's a medical school in Edinburgh for women.'

Edinburgh. Rosie and Frazer looked at one another. It might as well be on the moon. Rosie shrugged. Something would come up.

'Aye,' said Rosie. 'I mean, yes, Mr Wishart.'

Wishart looked ahead to the years of commitment.

'You understand what you are proposing, Rose? An hour of tuition one night a week and hours of private study . . . and for the next four years?'

'Yes, sir.'

'Four to five every Thursday. Other nights I have pupil teachers.'

'That will be fine, Mr Wishart.' Frazer gestured with the pouch.

'I'll give you the list of books your sister will need, and I'll update it as required. Buy your mother a coat, lad. I'll have free medical care from Dr Nesbitt when I'm in need of it.' He picked up his pen and dipped it in the inkwell on his desk. Rose and Frazer looked down at his bowed head.

'Till Thursday then,' said Rosie. 'Thank you, Mr Wishart.'

Out in the corridor, she walked to the front door, reserved for teachers and visitors, with her head high as befitted one of Scotland's first woman doctors. No one saw them leave and, rather to her regret, she went unchallenged out into the street.

'He's no going to charge, Frazer. Teachers must be rich.'

'I don't think so, Rosie. That one's good.'

'Oh, aye. Everybody's says he's the best Latin teacher; Greek too.'

Frazer looked down at his young sister sadly and then shrugged. She was very young and had lots of growing-up to do. He wished that he could be around to help her do it.

'Let's get Ma and take her out for her tea. Tomorrow I'll buy her a coat.' He stopped walking and caught Rosie's arm. 'Work hard, Rosie, and never let him regret what he's doing for you.'

'Or you, Frazer. I'll never let you down either.'

'Good lassie.' He gripped her tightly by the arms and stared down into her face as if he could see the woman behind the immature child. 'Doctor Rose Nesbitt. God in heaven, lassie, you've signed your life away and I pray I'm here to see it.'

'Ach, you will be. I'll invite you months before the graduation. Heavens, you'll be an auld man wi' bairns. You can bring them all, but dinnae let them greet and disturb the ceremonies!'

3

Edinburgh, 1891

IT WAS AS Lucy had expected. Father would force himself to be supportive. She realized, however, that not so deep down, just below the surface of his habitual control, he would have preferred that she follow the usual route of a young lady of her class. He took her side now, just as he had done three years before when she had stupidly lied to Max du Pay about her plans for going to college.

'Not a bad idea,' he had told his wife as they argued and tried to discuss, rationally, the future of their only child. 'Get all this nonsense out of her head. She'll settle down, you'll see.'

She had not settled down, and then the sudden and tragic death of Amos had made it all worse.

'It's almost as if she blames us,' said Lady Graham.

'Worse, my dear. She blames herself.'

'I was too interested in my new dress,' she had cried, 'and going to the hunt with Max du Pay. If I'd even looked at Amos, really *looked* at him, surely I would have known he was ill.'

'Stuff and nonsense!' said Lady Graham, who had a clear conscience. She had sent for help when her servants told her they needed it. She had not asked Amos to work when he was unwell; he was the one who had said he was just a little seedy.

And here they were, two years later, listening to Lucy voicing this totally unacceptable idea.

'I should have sent her to school in Bath. It was all those years studying with Kier.'

Perhaps it was, although Lady Graham, of course, had no real knowledge of how intimately her daughter had involved herself in the care of her friend. Nor did she really know how Lucy had felt that night when Amos suffered his last massive heart attack.

'Actually cost about the same as bringing you out, my dear,' Sir John said when he finally believed that his daughter was serious. 'So don't worry about anything. Just as long as you're really sure.'

'Oh, I am. It's been simmering away for years now.'

'It's absolutely ridiculous, John, and why you encourage your only child in such folly I can't imagine.' Lady Graham was not supportive. She tried again. 'Lucy, have you any idea what our people will say? It's totally unsuitable, so unladylike. You'll be cut, Lucy, cut completely by the people who matter. Decent women don't study medicine; everyone knows that. People will say you're fast or . . . worse. Think, Lucy, think. Do you really wish to become so . . . intimate with the human body, with all its . . . unpleasant functions?' Lady Graham could not find suitable words to clothe the horrors she felt sure were lined up waiting for her cherished, sheltered little girl. A girls' college had been one thing but this, this! 'And it's not as if you need to earn your living. You'll have grandmother's money and everything Father and I have.' Looking at the unhappy young face before her, she wanted to scoop up her child and run away with her to safety. She said the last thing she could think of in support of her position. 'You should be thinking of marrying. Who would want to marry a female physician, a woman who knows so much of . . . everything impure? Oh, child, please, before you find yourself completely ostracized. There's Kier, or what about Max du Pay? When you're here, he's here. You do like him, don't you?'

Lucy thought of Max, his calm, deep voice like honey on warm toast, his humour so like her own.

'I do like him. Of course I like him.' A sigh of stifled agony surged upwards again. 'He understood my feelings of inadequacy over Amos's death but . . . I haven't seen him very often lately.' She did not add that whenever she had seen Maximilian du Pay he had seemed to be in the company of one of his own Southern belles, and that he was obviously perfectly happy.

'You'll meet him often this autumn. I know his father wants him to work in his office. Now, Lucy, let's be sensible. We have delayed our furlough home so that you need not miss any of your classes at Smith, and I'm perfectly happy about the quality of education you have received there, but after graduation there must be an end to it. We will return to Scotland and you will be presented at Court.'

'If you can arrange it during the summer, I will be happy to comply, but my mind is made up: I'm entering the Edinburgh School of Medicine for Women. Please be happy for me.'

'Happy for you? Happy to see my only child spend her life amongst dirt and disease . . .'

'Eradicating dirt and disease, I hope.'

'You are underage. I refuse my permission.'

Desperately Lucy looked at her father. Well she knew that he was happier confronting an enemy battalion than his wife or daughter, but he did not let her down.

'She has my permission, Elizabeth,' he said sadly. Lady Graham looked from one unhappy face to the other. 'As usual, you have conspired together and now submit to me a *fait acompli*.' She moved towards the door, her silk skirts rustling on the polished wooden floor. 'But how am I to explain . . .' She stopped as Lucy half rose. 'No, Lucille, there is nothing more to say.'

Sir John rose to follow his wife from the room. 'Don't fret, Lucy. Mother is a hardened campaigner. Now you feel guilty. Next, Petal and her army of dressmakers will be busy with all the new clothes for our furlough. Dresses to show Kier and sundry other men your charms; dresses to make you think that it might be very pleasant to spend your life ordering more dresses and – what was it you said to me once, "trying to decide how much cream is needed for so many peaches".'

'There are no peaches in Scotland.'

'In the Anderson-Howard succession houses, there undoubtedly are. The next few months will possibly bring your hardest battles, child, and if you can defeat your mother without breaking her heart, then years of medical training should cause little difficulty.' He stopped at the door. 'But what of Kier?' he asked.

She had looked at the white door as it swung gently behind his departing figure. He had his way of campaigning too.

Now, six months later, she was being asked almost the same question, and this time by her mother.

'And Kier? You've been constantly in his company since we returned. What has he to say?'

'I plan to tell him this afternoon. I'm riding over for tea.'

'Let's hope he puts some sense into your head. Please be back in time to dress for dinner.'

Lady Graham stood up and left the room and Lucy longed to run after her. It would be so easy to capitulate, to throw her arms around her mother and to say, 'I didn't mean it. I'll be a dutiful daughter and find a husband,' but she could not do it.

As always her father, now relaxed and happy in his almost disreputable old country tweeds, read her mind. 'She'll come round, Lucy . . .'

'So you keep saying, Father.'

'I know her. She'll scold and fret and try to argue you from this chosen way, and you must admit it will be a hard life you've chosen, but she'll fight for you and your reputation like a lion. She'll be very proud of you once she's managed to turn her mind around, away from bride clothes and . . . baby clothes,' he finished softly.

'I want those things too, Father, but not yet. I need to be a doctor; I don't need to be a wife and mother . . . not yet. One day, some day.'

'Go and tell Kier.' Colonel Graham held her close for a moment. 'I am so proud of you, Lucille Graham, BA. I always have been, always will be, no matter what you choose.'

'Poor Father,' thought Lucy as she rode slowly across fields not yet ploughed. 'Deep down he's hoping Kier will change my mind. Am I hoping that too?'

As always she stopped at the rise of the hill to look down on Laverock Rising. Built and extended in the reigns of the Georges, it had been the centre of the huge estate on which the Grahams' more modest house also stood. A hundred years had seen the estate farms sold one by one until now, at nearly the end of the century, less than a thousand acres of owned land surrounded the great house but it still stood, even more beautiful as it settled its foundations yet more firmly into the rich Fifeshire soil. Soft light spilled from its windows, for it was a dull day, and Lucy felt welcomed and quickened her pace.

'You know where to find them, Lucy,' Kier's mother welcomed her, 'and won't I be grateful to you if you can prise them out!'

Kier and his father were in the room always called the estate office, although now only three farms comprised the estate. The room smelled of wood-smoke, tobacco-smoke, dogs, and a further indefinable smell that Lucy put down to a mixture of men and old paper and spilled ink. She loved it.

'How you ever find anything in this mess, I do not know,' she said by way of greeting and since that was how she had announced herself at any time in ten years, Kier's father answered as he always did. 'Why, we know where everything important is. I'll go and find your mother, lad.'

Kier too had stood up as Lucy entered, and as he held the door for his father Lucy wondered aloud at one of the questions that had fascinated her for years.

'You must be near a foot taller than your father, Kier. I wonder why that is.'

'He's pure Celt, Lucy,' said Kier as he cleared a place for her to sit by the simple expedient of swiping several ledgers from an armchair. 'I am a throwback to some rapacious Norseman. Come, sit down and tell me what's bothering you.'

Lucy sat as she was bid. How well he knew her, almost as well as she knew herself.

'I've come to a decision and I wanted you to hear about it first. I've told my parents, of course, but . . . you are my oldest and dearest friend. . . .'

'Good heavens, Lucy! What's wrong? You sound so formal and . . . are you all right? You're not ill or anything?'

'I've never been better. It's just that . . . I want to be a doctor, and I have already been accepted at the Edinburgh School of Medicine for Women.'

She looked at him as he received the rather bald statement, and for the first time felt that she could not read the emotions that followed one another across his handsome face. University had changed him, changed both of them.

'Rather you than me,' he said at last. 'God, Lucy, you scared me. I thought you were going to become a missionary or a nun or something. Well done! I didn't know there were any women doctors.'

'There aren't many. Universities in Scotland don't admit women. London admitted women to all degree courses three years ago, and there's now a medical college for women in Edinburgh. Actually there was a British lady doctor as early as 1849, one Elizabeth Blackwell, but she had to qualify in the United States where educational ideas are more advanced. Thanks to this college, however, there will soon be seven female physicians who have qualified in Edinburgh.'

'And you want to make it eight. Whatever for, Lucy? I always thought, well, one day . . . aren't you for presentations at court, and ballgowns and parties and too much champagne and "Here comes the bride", wedding trips to exotic places, and gummy little people dribbling all over one's best shirt-front?'

As he spoke Lucy saw it all, and she realized how different her experience was going to be, experiences instead of . . . no, no, before . . . I want it all, I want it all, her heart cried.

'Of course I'm interested in all that,' she said calmly and then added daringly, 'especially the gummy litle people, if they have the right father . . . but not yet. There isn't time for them yet.'

Kier smiled at her and stood up. He held the door open. 'Let's tell the parents. God knows what Mother will think. Not very socially acceptable.' He stopped. 'Gosh, Lady Graham?'

'Yes, her reaction was exactly as you picture it.'

'Oh, poor Lucy, but I can see her point. Besides, won't it take years and years?'

'Yes.'

He stopped walking and she had to stop with him. She looked up into his face.

'Hell, Lucy. Years. Have you thought it all out?'

'I've thought of everything, Kier.'

He smiled, the gentle sweet smile that reminded her of their shared childhood. 'Then I must be your strong supporter and your first patient.'

'You *were* my first patient.'

He laughed. 'And no bedside manner did you have. We must hope for an improvement, Doctor Graham.'

The awkward moment was over. Hand in hand they went to the cosy sea green drawing room where Lucy had spent so many hours with the ailing Kier.

'Mother,' he announced as they walked in, and Lucy listened to him and thought that perhaps she had never loved him more, 'you will never guess what our frightfully clever Lucy is going to do.'

The evenings arrived early in that part of Scotland. Kier rode back to The Larches with Lucy, for even a girl modern enough to contemplate becoming a doctor could not ride home alone in gathering darkness.

'I have the curious feeling I've lost something very precious,' he said, surprising himself more than Lucy, 'and I can't think what it is.'

Lucy's heart raced and she was glad the twilight hid the blush she could feel stealing over her cheeks. 'Everything is just the same,' she said calmly. 'We'll always be great friends.'

Kier said no more until they reached the stables. Unlike his own home, where at least ten servants were needed to answer the basic needs of the small family, no stable-boy rushed to unsaddle Lucy's horse and Kier did it for her automatically, just as he had done since she first put up her hair.

'How long will it take, Lucy?' He spoke quietly, but she had a strange feeling that a great deal depended on the answer she was able to give.

'Only a little while, three or four years, perhaps a little more if I want really worthwhile qualifications.' Lucy knew that she was not being quite truthful. 'I really don't know the answer myself,' she thought.

Kier heard her calm, almost deep voice through the darkness. How often had that same quiet, matter-of-fact voice steadied his nerves through the panics of illness and fretfulness? Three or even four years? 'I can wait,' he said and surprised himself, for he was not sure what he hoped for at the end of the wait.

Once she had made her opinion known, Lady Graham threw herself into the process of making years of medical schooling as easy as possible for her only daughter. Before they returned to Washington, D.C., she had found a good tenant for their beloved little house and had bought a small flat in a good area of Edinburgh.

'Annie will come with us, won't you, Annie, to look after Lucy while we're abroad?' Lady Graham spoke to Annie Bell, their maid-of-all-work who had been with her almost since Lucy's birth. 'The Archibalds, their new tenants, want you to stay on here, but I said you were part of the family, not a servant. You will come, won't you?'

And Annie went, although a noisy, dirty city full of smoking chimneys and horse-drawn carriages that bowled past her at . . . well, she wouldn't be surprised if they went as fast as five miles every hour, and horrid little boys with iron hoops that they spun clattering along the cobblestones, was not precisely where she would have liked to be. She made no judgement about Lucy. God had called her to a station in life where she was to look after her mistress and, to the best of her not inconsiderable ability, she would ensure that Lucy had a clean home, three decent meals every day and clean underwear – which she might well need if she were to be knocked down by one of those self-same carriages and taken to the very hospital down Leith Walk where she was going to do her practical work.

Lucy had a fair notion of the sacrifice the country-woman was making for her, and although she vowed to take her back to the country whenever possible – had they not an open invitation to stay with Kier's parents? – she realized very quickly that she was exactly where she should be and sacrifices would have to be made, by Annie as well as herself, for the greater good.

From that first morning, when she had walked into the lecture room and been warmly welcomed by her fellow students, she had known this was where she wanted to be. These few women were, she felt sure, the vanguard of an enormous army that one day would take the field against ignorance and prejudice. They were not all young; she was quite sure that the tall bronzed woman who sat so quietly waiting for the first lecture was at least thirty. Good heavens, half her life was over already and she was prepared to start to study. Lucy looked at her with respect and interest. What had brought her here? Perhaps she would never know, but it was enough that they were together.

She had had no idea of the enormous scale of illness and disease in the world. Illness caused by poverty, and there was too much of that; illness caused by accident or neglect; and the more frightening one, illness caused by ignorance. She threw herself wholeheartedly into medical training, everything she learned filling her with an almost unbearable excitement and desire to learn more and to help more. Letters from her parents, once more in the American capital, or from Kier at Oxford, called her back unwillingly from what was to her the real world. She answered them quickly, assuring her mother that Annie's cooking was as tasty and nutritious as ever and that, no, she had not had time to make herself known to Mrs This or Lady That yet, but she would, honestly, just as soon as she had a moment to spare. Her letters to her father and to Kier were different:

I am to have one hundred lectures in Anatomy from a Doctor Dewar, another one hundred lectures in Physiology from Doctor James, and so, academically, you will agree that there is nothing I will not know of the human body. What really interests me, of course, is why the body malfunctions from time to time and, much more important, what I will be able to do to set it back on the right track. I am thrilled to discover from Amy Wood Browne, a fellow student, that we are to enjoy fifty lectures in Practical Pharmacy from Doctor Jex-Blake, yes, *the* Dr Jex-Blake, the pioneer. Shall I sit in such awe of this wonderful woman that I shall be totally incapable of making a single note and shall fail her classes miserably? I am also to have, see how bold my language has become, Father, fifty lectures in Midwifery from this same idol. I think the subject interests me the least of all the wonders in store.

Her first lectures were in Physiology and in Surgery. Physiology was interesting. Her dictionary told her it was the branch of science concerned with the functioning of organisms. Dr James, the lecturer, made it almost holy, for was not the human body a collection of the most interesting and fascinating and yet secretive of all organisms? They went to the hospital down in Leith for their first lectures in Surgery. Amy Wood Browne was among the three students who silently collapsed and were unceremoniously helped from the operating theatre. Did Dr Cathcart even notice them as he continued dissecting? Lucy did not. The human tissue so revealed did not repel her, it engrossed her. She could not learn quickly enough.

She considered remaining in Edinburgh for the winter break. There was so much reading to do; her notes should be read and corrected. Hospitals could be visited. Goodness knows, a pair of hands that had some idea of what they were doing were very welcome, especially in the poorer area. Textbooks and clinical specimens were well and good and they could be examined over and over again at any time of the day or night, but people, real people, suffering people, that was where one really learned.

'I must remember always the person. I must not be so excited by symptoms that I forget the living, breathing body.' Healthy people had to be considered too. Kier's parents, who had renewed their invitation; her own parents, who wanted her to have a rest; and, of course, the most important person that Christmas was Annie, who missed the country and her family.

Lucy packed her suitcases and found space for a few textbooks. When they boarded the train at Waverley she was pleased that she had bought first-class tickets, for it was packed with holiday-makers. She had almost resented the break from what she was coming to consider the real world, but at last she began to feel that delicious sense of growing excitement that had always heralded Christmas.

'Lucy? I don't believe it. What absolute luck,' called a well-loved voice, and she found herself caught up in a strong masculine embrace.

'Put me down at once, you idiot,' she scolded as she tried to wriggle free from Kier's exuberant greeting.

He did not quite release her but looked down into her face. 'Gosh, it's good to see you. I have had the most appalling forty-eight hours. The wine at the Christmas

Ball gave me the most unbelievable headache. Did I drink too much, or was it the quality that was dubious?'

'Both,' said Lucy, pushing him away firmly and sitting down to meet Annie's aggrieved look. 'What else happened?' she asked.

'The train was like something out of the Inferno – too hot, and too many people squealing around.'

'Definitely too much to drink,' diagnosed Lucy. 'Does your mother expect you by this train? She said nothing in her letter.'

A wash of colour swept across his face. 'You will never believe, Lucy . . .' He stopped and she waited. 'I was going to a house-party; chap I met at school. They're all coming to me for the New Year. They think Scotland should be fun – "quaint", I think was the word she used. Anyway, his sister . . . I took her to the ball, and there she was, behind an urn, wrapped around some chap.'

Lucy, who had once found herself behind an urn, felt a sneaking sympathy for the unknown girl. 'Perhaps she couldn't help herself.'

'My very thought. But when I pushed him away and walloped him, she screamed at me like a little cat.' He glowered at her morosely and then laughed. 'Women,' he said. 'I'm giving them up!'

'I've given you the best guest room, Lucy dear,' said Mrs Anderson-Howard.

They had arrived at Cupar station to be met by Kier's delighted father.

'Welcome home, welcome home. There's a nice hot pig for your feet, Lucy, and a warm rug. Have you snug at home in no time. You sit up here with me, old chap. Fresh air might cure whatever ails you.'

'More likely kill me, sir.'

'Then all the more reason for you to sit up here and blow away the cobwebs and the tobacco smoke. We've had a powdering of snow, just enough to slow me down, but I'll be as quick as safety allows.'

And now here they were home, and Mrs Anderson-Howard had taken Lucy straight upstairs to a delightful bedroom where a coal fire blazed cheerfully. 'Such a surprise that you met Kier; I had not expected him till nearer Christmas. Dinner is ready as soon as you like, my dear, but there's just the four of us so no need to dress.'

Lucy, quite rightly, took this to mean that if she had diamonds she need not wear them, and she washed in the hot water brought up to her, uncoiled her hair and quickly put it back up again, and changed her wool travelling dress for a dark blue silk dinner-gown.

The soft lamplight in the dining room lit up the faces at the dinner table but not the corners of the large room, and Lucy was lulled into feeling that they were the only four people in the world. The talk went from one young person to the other and Lucy told as much of her medical training as she felt the older couple would find interesting, and Kier recounted what Lucy felt must surely be an expurgated account of his activities.

'He tells me things he does not tell his parents,' she realized and had a sudden overwhelming desire that this dinner-party could continue for ever, that she could really belong to the loving circle and not merely be a welcomed guest. 'Have I made a terrible mistake?' she thought sadly. 'Have I pushed him towards all these, no doubt beautiful and eminently suitable, young women he talks about? At least this Cynthia has blotted her copybook.'

But, although Cynthia of the urn did not come for the New Year festivities, it seemed to Lucy that the house echoed always with the laughter of others.

'What do they mean to him?' she asked herself sadly as she watched Kier flirt with each girl in turn, but the only person she could confidently ask about the strange ways of marriageable young men was three thousand miles away.

She returned to Edinburgh early in January. A letter from her mother had reminded her yet again of the visits she was supposed to make in the capital and Annie Bell, who had professed to hate the city, was definitely unhappy away from what she now saw as her own home.

When Kier took Lucy to the station to catch the London train, they were both quiet, perhaps restrained by Annie's presence.

'It's been a lovely . . .' They had spoken together and so they laughed, at last at ease.

'Will you come home for the Easter break?'

'No,' said Lucy quietly, 'and I won't come back in the summer either. Leith Hospital is allowing me to do volunteer work in the spring and I'm going to Rouen for the summer, to work in a hospital there.'

'Alone?' Kier was shocked.

'Don't be silly. There will be hundreds of patients and not a few real doctors and nurses.'

'You know perfectly well what I mean, Lucy. Your parents will never allow it. You're a girl, you're young: you need the protection of a brother, or father, or . . . well, a husband.'

The word dropped between them like a stone but Lucy managed to laugh.

'I've had enough trouble getting into training, Kier. A husband would certainly be an encumbrance I can well do without . . . at this point,' she finished softly.

'Damn it all, Lucy,' he said suddenly, and like poor Cynthia behind the urn, Lucy Graham found herself being thoroughly kissed.

'He must mean to marry you,' said Annie comfortably as a slightly dishevelled Lucy watched the young man stride away.

'He's going the wrong way,' she said.

'What did I tell you?' said Annie triumphantly and steered her mistress to the open door of their first-class carriage.

4

Dundee, 1892

In 1892, when Lucy Graham was finishing her first year of study at the Edinburgh School of Medicine for Women, Scottish universities opened their doors to women for the first time.

'There, didn't I tell you?' With frozen fingers Rosie Nesbitt stuffed the newspaper she had been reading inside her schoolbag and hurried home, her thin coat protecting her as best it could from the biting wind. It was all coming together. With the University of St Andrews a mere eleven miles away across the Tay, she need not live away from home. That troubling thought had managed to surface every now and again over the last few years. How was she to live in Edinburgh when she had gained entrance to the women's medical college there? It had never occurred to Miss Nesbitt that she would not win a place. If you were prepared to work, you could do anything in this exciting world. She could hardly wait for the new century. It would see Rose Nesbitt, MA, MB, Ch.B, most likely with distinction, for Miss Nesbitt was thorough. She had thrown herself into her Latin studies so well that dear old Wishy had insisted on teaching her Greek too. Rosie could not absorb enough and now, thanks to the generosity and far-sightedness of Sir William Taylor-Thomson who had left the residue of his estate to provide bursaries for students of either sex, and especially so that females might study medicine, she was working towards winning such a grant to St Andrews University. She would have to wait until she was nineteen to study medicine, but at least she could start on an Arts degree. If she came top in the combined entrance and bursary examination – and there was no reason why she should not – she could win an amazing twenty pounds a year. Then Frazer could afford to marry his sweetheart, Nancy, who had waited so patiently. Everything and everyone had willingly sacrificed themselves to Rosie's driving ambition. And, oh, how she would thank them and make it all up to them once she had qualified?

She raced up the stairs, for once so excited by the wonderful news she had to read to Ma that she forgot to watch out for daft old Tam, the 'flasher'. He had waited for her, as he did every night, and his sad genitalia almost withered away as she raced past without even seeing him. He settled back against the closie wall to wait for the next woman, and Rosie banged into the kitchen where Ma was painfully stirring the stew in the pot over the fire.

'Your back's bad again,' said Rosie, taking the spoon. 'Sit down and put your feet up. I'll make you a cup of tea and read you the paper. Where are the weans?'

'In the street. Mind you, it's that cauld with this bluidy snaw day after day that they're probably in somebody's hoose. Did ye no see them?'

Rosie straightened up. 'Ma, I'm so happy I didnae see old Tam and he must have been there waving defiance at me.'

They laughed wickedly at one another. In the past few years they had become more friends than mother and daughter. Elsie treated Rosie as if she were an adult and Rosie rewarded her by telling her everything, by sharing her learning, assuming rightly that her mother, though illiterate, was intelligent. Ma had even learned a word or two in Latin and Greek, in German and French.

'Come on then, lassie,' said Ma, gratefully gulping back the scalding hot brew, 'tell me whit's sae exciting.'

Rosie pulled out the *Dundee Courier and Advertiser* and unfolded it. Then she smoothed out the crumpled sheets and read out the article. ' "Tuesday, March 15th 1892. The Senatus Academicus of the University of St Andrews has agreed to open its doors in Arts, Science and

Theology to women students from next session onwards, and, although it rests with the university court to make arrangements in detail, women will henceforward be taught along with men. Next year the university will receive the sum of £30,000 to be spent by it in bursaries open to students of both classes attending the university, one half of this sum being devoted to women exclusively." There, Ma, what do you think of that? D'ye see what it means? Instead of waiting till I'm old enough tae get into the women's college in Edinburgh, or instead of leaving the country for an education – and heaven knows how we could have afforded that – I can bide at hame and take the train into St Andrews every day. Frazer can marry Nancy and get their ain bit. Losh, Ma, with just the two of us and the two weans, we'll be rich and there'll be that much room we could hae a lodger and you could stop working in the mill.'

Ma looked around at the shabby room that she had tried to keep clean and tidy through many years of bringing up her children on her own. 'A lodger?'

'We should hae done it when Frazer went tae the whaling or when . . . when pair Lindsay died.' Like too many children in Dundee's crowded tenements, Elsie's oldest daughter had died two years before from tuberculosis. 'Or we should definitely hae done it when Leslie got wed.'

Leslie, the next girl, a mill-worker like her sister Lindsay, had married two months before. She was five months' pregnant at the time, but there was no scorn or shame heaped upon their sinful heads for anticipating holy matrimony. It was the way of the world. It was cheaper to live separately and so young couples in love lived with their own families, or what passed for a family circle, until the imminent advent of their first child forced them to marry.

'I cannae think why I never thought on it afore,' Rosie went on, 'but at least now you can start to take things easier. A nice country laddie, we'll get, that's come to work at Cox's or Baxter's. He'll sleep wi' oor Murray when Murray's hame – and this year he's been awa' near as much as Frazer – and you'll probably see the back of him on a Sunday.'

'A nice laddie?' Ma grinned wickedly and, by doing so, looked years younger. 'A click for you, mair like. We'll hae ye marrit, and then where will all your fine plans go?'

Rose Nesbitt was not yet thirteen years of age, but in some ways she was already quite, quite old. 'There's no the laddie born that could turn me from my path, Ma, and I'll certainly no throw myself away on some mill laddie. I've no interest in men and how could I tell Frazer and even auld Wishy that I was giving up? Years Nancy's waited for Frazer and years Mr Wishart has spent coaching me. I'll no throw it back in their faces, not for the Prince of Wales himself.'

The thought of her daughter with Edward, Prince of Wales, was too much for Ma and even Rosie saw the funny side and they began to laugh. They stopped suddenly. Was it not just two months since the sad death of the prince's oldest son, the young Duke of Clarence, from the fearsome influenza, this killer disease that weeded out both the low and the mighty?

'You're a real joy tae me, Rosie Nesbitt,' said Ma at last. 'I'll think on a lodger; could be grand, but what about your studying? You're aye throwing the weans oot.'

'I'll be a university student, Ma. I'll do my studying at their grand library. Think on it. In nae time at all me, at the University of St Andrews!'

'My mind willnae accept it, lassie. Goodness, I wis thinkin' it wis a' arranged and ye've years at the skill yet.'

'Ach, Ma. Life's like building a wall. Ye pit one brick on top o' the next and ye dinnae think on it falling. Everything's going tae be great.' She stood up suddenly. 'I've had a grand idea. We'll go the first fine Sunday. We'll take the weans and a piece. There's sand there, Ma, and a ruined castle and buildings from books. Then when I'm there, every single day you'll be able to picture me walking through the arches in my grand red goon. Wishy says it's so rich and poor will look alike. Naebody kens that you've only the one skirt if it's aye hidden by a grand red goon.'

'Clever folk think on everything.' Ma was overwhelmed.

'I'll shout the weans for their tea, Ma. Noo, no a word about the surprise. I'll need tae find the money fer the train first, and the driver'll need to be able to see the way across the bridge through this damned snow.'

As with everything else Miss Nesbitt set her mind to, the weather began to improve. Rosie did without her lunch piece and so money was available for the train. Never had there been so much excitement in the Nesbitt household and even Nancy, Frazer's fiancée, agreed to join them.

'Whit a lot I'll hae tae tell our Frazer,' she said as she helped Elsie scrape dripping on the doorstep slices of bread. Nancy sighed a little, for she had popped in to see Leslie before coming into the next closie to join Frazer's mother. Leslie's swelling belly only reminded her that all she ever had of Frazer was kisses.

Elsie understood the sigh and she hugged the girl in a quick gesture of affection. 'It'll be all the better for the waiting, hen. Frazer loves you dear, and soon you'll wed and then you'll no be quite sae jealous of our Leslie when it's you having bairns like shelling peas, year after year. Where they come frae, I sometimes wonder.'

'That's what Frazer, well, that's why he says . . . well, he's an awfie guid man, Elsie.'

'You've nae need tae tell me, lassie. Is he no spending a fortune on our Rosie's education, books, exam fees, but she'll mak it up tae the both of you, and free medical attention for a'body up the closie. So, noo let's get wir pieces ready and off we go like toffs tae St Andrews.'

It was a day none of them would ever forget. Donaldina and Granta, Elsie's two youngest, were unable to talk for the excitement of being on the train but they made up for that as they rushed pell-mell, here and there, over the streets of the beautiful medieval city: Market Street, North Street, South Street, St Regulus' Tower, St Rule's, the castle with its horrifying tales of murder and mayhem and starvation in a bottle dungeon, the sands, the sands, the sands. Rosie and Elsie were content to touch the walls, to dream of the thousands of men and women who down the centuries had walked under these archways or through those doors or along this very beach. Nancy thought of her sweetheart somewhere on the ocean and dreamed of a honeymoon weekend with him here in this beautiful place that Rosie had shown her was easy, easy for anyone to reach and to enjoy. A train from Dundee rattles aross a bridge and through the kingdom of Fife and in two shakes of a ram's tail, as Elsie kept saying, they were there.

Never had bread and dripping tasted so good. Nancy had brought slices of dumpling and Rosie bought a bottle of lemonade and they all shared its sour refreshment. No one thought of shared germs, only of shared fellowship. Silently, in awe, they walked through the university buildings. Rosie taught the wee ones to avoid the sacred stones on which the student martyr, Patrick Hamilton, had breathed his last in the grip of cruel flame, and then, since she had scared them so much, she walked them, clinging tightly to her hands, along the walk where she told them every Sunday the red-gowned students would go.

'You can picture me here on a Sunday morning,' she said.

'How can we when you'll be at hame?' said practical Donaldina.

'I niver get out o' ma bed on a Sunday, Rosie,' confessed Granta. Granta was the silliest of all the silly names Elsie had given her children. Not one child, as far as she could judge, had the same father as another, and she punished the fathers by calling their children after them so that eveyone in the Hilltown knew who had fathered Elsie Nesbitt's latest bairn. Elsie had never married. She had kept herself and her parents alive by selling herself on the crowded streets of her home, and she had raised a large family of clean and healthy children in a remarkably clean home. Elsie Nesbitt had integrity and pride and, as her daughter Rosie knew, she also had brains.

Rosie looked at her mother now. She was a child, a grey-haired, wrinkled, stooping child, and very soon she would be a grandmother, and Rosie vowed that her future would not resemble Elsie's past.

Too soon it was time for the train.

'You'll be back loads of times, Ma,' she said. 'You'll get tae ken St Andrews as weel as you ken the Hilltown.'

'As long as you ken it, Rosie.'

'I'd like fine tae come back wi Frazer, Elsie. Whit a place fir a holiday.'

'Aye, Nancy. Ye ken, oor Rosie gets me that fired up I believe her grand thoughts. I wis ready tae believe she wis sterting at the university this year, but she's years tae dae yet. But she will do whit she says and she will get the grants. Can you imagine somebody geein' money jist so bairns can learn? There's good folk in the world or ma name's no Elsie Nesbitt, but whit I wis wantin' tae say is that Frazer'll no need tae worry aboot us and wi' Leslie marrit and Murray an apprentice and away most o' the time, I could easy tak a lodger and then, jings, Nancy, I'll be rollin' in it and I'll no need Frazer tae help.'

'You mean?'

'Aye, hen, there's nothing tae stop you and Frazer being wed.'

Nancy lay back in the questionable comfort of the Caledonian Railway's third-class carriages and the little girls fell asleep on the train. When they got out Elsie carried Donaldina and Nancy carried Granta up as far as Reform Street where they almost dropped them.

'That woke ye baith up,' said Rosie, now again as broad in speech as the rest of the family. 'They wis havin' the pair o' ye on. I'd hae left the baith o' them on the train tae Eberdeen.'

'Come on in by wi' us, Nancy,' suggested Elsie. 'I've a stane o' tatties waiting tae be fried up.'

'No, I'll no come in. I'll awa hame and tell my mither and I'll look in on Leslie. She was having a bit of bother this morning.'

'Oh?' Elsie, who had carried and delivered seven healthy children with the help of a few neighbours, was perfectly ready to see that childbirth was not easy for everyone.

'She's too fat,' said twelve-year-old Rosie unkindly but truthfully. 'Bert brings her sweeties and cakes on his way home from the works and she hasn't washed a dish since the day they got married. He does everything.'

'Frazer'll be like that,' sighed Nancy and went off to see the girl she hoped soon to be her sister-in-law.

When they got home, Rosie and Elsie scrubbed the two small girls in front of the fire. It was a Saturday night and no matter what else happened in the Hilltown on a Saturday night, Elsie Nesbitt's children had a bath and had their hair washed. Then Elsie fried the potatoes which she washed down with beer and the girls with hot strong tea.

'I'm awae tae ma bed tae, Rosie. Dinnae you stay up late wi' books. I don't ken whit it is, but that day in St Andrews has fair tired me out.'

Rosie agreed with her and so they were both sound asleep when Bert, Elsie's eighteen-year-old son-in-law, came flying up the stairs and knocked furiously on the door with a knock loud enough to wake any of the neighbours who was already asleep. Leslie had gone into premature labour and there was something wrong.

'Turn yer back, laddie, till I get my drawers on. There's nothing wrong jist acause she's a bit early, and hoo would you twa ken hoo early it is, onyway?'

'There's something wrang, Elsie, even ma mither says so.' Bert's mother was the best midwife in the area.

'I'm coming.'

They looked at the small figure in the big bed.

'You're no practising your doctoring on my wife, Rosie Nesbitt. You're no decent, wanting tae come tae a lyin'-in.'

'I jist want tae help.'

'Stay here and look oot fir the wee wans, Rosie. You're too wee and even had ye book learnin', unborn bairns cannae read and it's them that's in charge.'

Rosie was angry. Here was her first chance to witness a birth at first hand, her own sister, her own nephew or niece, and she was being kept away like a wee lassie.

'I wouldn't be feart,' she told the fire as she sat beside it in her gown and made the first of many pots of tea. She was not conceited or foolish enough to think that she could be of any help, but there were so many things she might have learned. How did the baby get out? She had far too true an idea of how it got in.

She was asleep when an exhausted and heart-broken Elsie let herself into the house.

'Our Leslie's deid,' said Elsie as her daughter sat up in the chair.

Rosie eased her mother into the chair and poured her a cup of the – by now, stewed – tea. Death. She had seen it before when Lindsay had coughed her lungs up in the big box-bed, when neighbours had died of age or infirmity, but death in childbirth? Oh, she heard of it often, too often, but not Leslie with her adoring young husband who gave her too many sweets.

'But how? She was well, she was strong, well-fed; it's two months since she did a day's work. Did ye get the doctor?'

'Oh aye, wan came eventually, along frae the infirmary, a nice laddie, seemed tae ken whit he was daein', though hoo a man kens is beyond me. Tam, Nancy's brither, is oot lookin' for Bert. He went screamin oot o' the hoos like a bogle. They wis jist bairns theresels.'

'Whit went wrang, Ma? Did the doctor ken?'

'Ach, lassie, whit questions. Well, all richt, if ye'll jist get tae yir bed and let me be. A bairn's supposed tae come oot heid first. Well, first a wee leg cam oot and they shoved it back in, and he put his airm in and tried tae turn the bairn, but its wee backside cam next and it wis too big and it ripped my wee lassie awful.' She looked down at her skirt in horror. 'That's my wee lassie's life's-blood. A mammy shouldnae see that. Och, lassie, whit noo?'

Poor Leslie. Poor Elsie. At 3.30 in the morning of Sunday the 22nd of March 1892, she cleaned up Rosie Nesbitt who had been violently ill for the first and last time in her medical career.

There were two tragedies that night. Young Bert, maddened by the screams of his young wife – he had refused to do as every other man in the closie did and seek solace in the pub from the pangs of labour – had run shrieking from her deathbed and thrown himself into the Tay, the river that was often Dundee's life-line and too often the source of death to the town's miserable. Leslie was buried with her child in the local churchyard and her husband was buried in unhallowed ground.

'That cannae be right,' thought Rosie, but wisely said nothing.

She continued cutting her brilliant path through the Harris Academy and even saw the rector begin to consider Latin and Mathematics – in a limited way, naturally – for brighter girls. Already she had made a difference.

Frazer never saw her win a combined university grant and bursary of twenty pounds per year. He never came back from his last voyage, never saw St Andrews, never married Nancy. His ship returned from its long voyage on May 20th 1893 and the captain had only letters, wages and consoling words to give his mother. Frazer's letters were very different from the tone of the various articles that appeared in the local press after the voyage:

Dear Mam,

We left Dundee on September 6th and went south. We sailed for weeks with nout to do but play cards and nout to see but the sea and sometimes other ships.

In three months we reached the Falklands. There's nout there but sheep.

It's mid December and we have found ice. It's now bluidy cold. We look for black whales.

No whale but seals. We've killed thousands. It turned my stomach. They're no feart. They havenae learnt tae fear and they lie and wait for the kickey. Their eyes follow me.

The captain says we are congenially occupied. We're killing penguins. We laughed at them, like funny wee men from London or grand places. They line up in rows and we walk atween them, whack, whack, whack. They taste good, like yon jugged hare I had one time at Nancy's. You wouldnae believe the ice.

I've been in the Brig. I wouldnae hit nae mair wee birds. If they'd fight us, snap, or bite. I havenae been eating. I couldnae eat penguin. We should sell them in Dundee, says the mate. They cost nout and they taste good, but when I eat, I see them standing waiting tae be killt. I'm rowing the boat because I want tae stay out of the Brig. The money's grand for this voyage. 10/- extra the month. I dinnae like the ice. The sea goes twa roads at the same time and you have tae watch oot for ice slipping past . . .

The captain gave Elsie her son's letters and his bible; Frazer owned nothing else. He also gave her the full £45 the boy should have earned had he completed the nine-month voyage, and he told her of the accident. The rowing boats had been in a channel where two currents met. Frazer's boat, heading south, had been grazed by an iceberg travelling north at three knots per hour. He had fallen overboard and his body had never been recovered.

'He was a good man, Mrs Nesbitt,' said the captain seriously. 'The men tried desperately to find him.' He did not add that it would have been useless even if they had found him, for he could not have survived in such temperatures.

Nancy waited for him for two years. Every time a whaler came in to the harbour she ran down to the docks and watched the men disembark. In 1895, just as Rosie was preparing for her final year at the Harris Academy, and just as one Lucille Graham, BA, was graduating with her first medical qualifications, Nancy emigrated to New Zealand. She travelled with her sister Jean who had married Rosie's other brother, Murray.

'You'll tell him where we are, Elsie. You'll tell him I'll never give up?'

Elsie watched her last young son climb the gangplank. 'I've lost four,' she thought, 'Four,' for when would she ever see Murray again? And there was Nancy. Did that make five?

At least for Elsie there was the dream of Rosie, the dream even Elsie was beginning to believe could come true. For Rosie was now a university student. She jumped out of bed every morning when the milkman arrived at 6.30 and just had time to wash, dress, grab a bap and eat it as she ran like a hare for the 7.10 train which would get her into St Andrews in time for a tutorial class in Maths, a condition of her acceptance, for Rosie, mainly self-taught in mathematics – another unsuitable subject for females – had done badly in the entrance examination. Often she cut her train-catching so fine that she had to be pulled into the luggage van by the guard, who would then proceed to air his views on education versus motherhood as a reward for not allowing her to miss the train.

Rosie was content not to argue with him in her awakening state and, besides, he said the same things every morning.

'What does a braw wee thing like you want with an education? Are you jist looking for a better type man? What good will all that book learning be when you're peeling tatties?'

Rosie knew that his views were only half serious. He just liked having someone to talk to, but his attitude changed when she roused herself one morning and told him that she would not be content with a mere degree. She was going to become a doctor.

'A doctor?' His eyes narrowed. 'And you look like such a nice wee lassie. Well, you can never tell.'

Like countless others, men and women, he had assumed that she was not a *good* girl because she wanted to become a doctor. Narrow, narrow minds, she thought, as she looked at the cold, set face and vowed to get up before the milkman. She had a feeling that from now on no friendly helping hand would pull her aboard and she would be left disconsolate on the platform. Nothing, nothing must keep her from her classes.

Rosie loved everything about university. She loved the walk from the station in the morning, in every weather. She walked around the golf course and never once wondered what it would be like to play golf, although someone told her that Mary Queen of Scots had actually played here on the ground on which she trod.

Occasionally she, a travelling girl, would meet one of the town girls, and they would walk together. There were three types of students at St Andrews. Those who lived in the university residences – there were, as yet, no residences solely for women – were top of the social tree. Then there were the town students who lived in lodgings, and the travelling students who came in every day by train or bus or farmer's cart. Attendance at all lectures was compulsory and a student could only sit examinations if he, and now she, could prove by production of a certificate that they had done all the course work. Rosie could not understand how anyone could contemplate missing one word of the drops of knowledge that fell so readily from the lips of learned professors. Constantly she pinched herself to assure herself that, yes, it was true, Rosie Nesbitt was a student at St Andrews University.

Apart from lectures, what she remembered most about her first few years was the singing. Students sang everywhere, not raucous rowdy songs, although many were silly nonsensical ditties, but folk songs, melodies from the theatre.

When a residence was built for women students, the warden invited Rosie for tea.

'I'm getting a name for myself, Ma. I'm known at the university, and this warden wants all the town and travelling girls to come along and have lunch at the residence. There's no common room, you see. I'm sure she's only worried that we're not having a hot meal.'

'How much?' Practical Elsie.

'9d.'

'A week?'

'A day.'

'My God, does the woman think we're made o' money? You go and have your tea, but don't let them rich people . . . whit's the word?'

'Patronize.'

'Aye, make you feel cheap.'

'Oh, they won't do that. Thank God for the gown.'

'Will you maybe have to take it aff in the hoos?'

'I'm great at pretending I'm too cold. Ma, don't worry. I'll see what she wants to discuss and I'll not stick my pinky up when I'm drinking my tea.'

Rosie took the train back to St Andrews. 'Poor Ma,' she thought. 'She thinks tea is a meal; she'll be hoping I get sausages.' Rosie had never been particularly interested in food, but she did like a good sausage.

She washed and ironed her *good* frock and washed her hair. She darned her stockings with tiny stitches and cleaned her shoes. 'Hell, hell, hell. I won't ever give a damn what I eat, but I will have leather shoes in all colours of the rainbow and hell, hell, hell' – this last as she looked at her one pair of gloves, too shoddy to take her hands to tea – 'gloves, silk gloves, leather gloves.' Did gloves look right with the gown that hid all other imperfections except the scuffed and well-polished shoes? Ladies always wear gloves. Do they? Do they not?

The warden of the new residence for female students was not wearing gloves . . . but then she was inside her house.

Miss Louden, herself a brilliant scholar, was aware of most of the worries besetting Rosie. She recognized the look almost of belligerence that disguised shyness and a fear of being pitied. Only too well she knew that in men and women the gown too often hid inadequate clothing draped on a too-thin body.

'I feel that it is very important that I get to know as many of the travelling girls as I can, Miss Nesbitt. I am aware of all the reasons that many young women have for not living in this residence.' She saw Rosie's proud head lift and the small nostrils almost flare. 'A natural desire for independence being foremost. Students who live in residence enjoy a completely different view of university life. I would like all the women of St Andrews to share that fellowship in some way.' She gestured to the table where an exquisitely embroidered cloth made a perfect backdrop for the porcelain plates with their beautifully arranged sandwiches, their delicate and delicious cakes and pastries. 'China or India?' she asked, and looked at Rosie whose mind was a complete blank. Before the silence became embarrassing she realized that Miss Louden meant the tea. My God, what kind of tea? The tea that comes full of stoor in a wooden box from the shop in the Pillars in Dundee. I know no other.

'I'm afraid I'm not a connoisseur, warden,' said Rosie and could have sworn that a look of genuine liking crossed that austerely beautiful face.

'I like mine hot and wet, and quite frankly rarely notice the flavour, but we'll try China and next time India perhaps. I hope you don't mind if I eat like a ravenous schoolboy, Miss Nesbitt, but I find that there are so many interruptions at luncheon that I very rarely have a chance to finish. Do try the roast beef. I swear Mrs McBride should have been a surgeon. See how thinly she cuts.'

Rosie took a sandwich. Roast beef. This is my first ever roast beef. I must remember everything for Ma and I must not like this woman. She wants something from me.

'You are hoping to do medicine, Miss Nesbitt. I wish you well. Sophia Jex-Blake is a friend of mine. You may have heard of her?'

How had she managed to eat three sandwiches? 'Doctor Jex-Blake. *The* Doctor Jex-Blake?'

'Yes. We fought together for the right of British women to get to university, Miss Nesbitt, not to have to go abroad as she did, and so you will see that the welfare of all female students is very precious to me, for her sake as well as mine.'

Rosie held out her cup, what a beautiful cup, for a second cup of the China tea. 'What do you want from me, warden?'

'You are very popular with the students, Miss Nesbitt. You look surprised. Are you so involved in your studies that you have not noticed?'

'Yes.'

The warden laughed, a tinkling, musical laugh. Rosie liked the sound.

'You have or could have influence with the travelling girls and the town girls – oh yes, of course I know the names by which you call yourselves. I would like you . . .' She stopped. She could see Rosie bristle. Silly child, silly child, I will not insult you by offering you a free meal. She pretended that she was checking the silver pot. *My God*, thought Rosie, *a silver pot with nothing in it but water.*

'I would like you to come, at least occasionally, for lunch in the winter. If you come, many of the other travelling girls will come, and the town girls. We will give a three-course luncheon, a different selection every day. Fish on Fridays, of course. Are you Catholic?'

Violently Rosie shook her head. 'I don't think we're anything.'

No disapproval. Just acceptance . . .

'We could arrange luncheon recitals, poetry readings, music. We might have guests, like Doctor Jex-Blake, or, who knows, the divinely handsome D'Arcy Thomson from Dundee. You do know about the Marquis of Bute, by the way?'

Rosie could not follow this quicksilver mind. 'The rector?'

'Yes, my dear. He intends to fund a medical school. He is dedicated to the development of medical and science teaching in St Andrews. But you must know, as a doctor manqué, why we are unable to complete medical training in St Andrews?' She waited for Rosie to acknowledge the correctness of her remark.

Rosie blushed. It had simply never occurred to her that she could not complete medical training at the university; she had been so glad to get a place in the Arts department. Medical training was not allowed for women before the age of nineteen, which would have been three wasted years.

'I was so grateful to have been accepted by the university, warden.'

Miss Louden nodded. 'There is no hospital within reach . . . for experience, Miss Nesbitt, clinical training. You must, if you are accepted, finish at Dundee. His lordship is building a conjoint medical school with the University of Dundee and funding it. £20,000 per year. There will be scholarships, one hundred pounds per year. I would imagine you will be one of its first students, Miss Nesbitt, if not its scholarship winners.'

One hundred pounds every year. God in heaven! With money like that a body could have a 9d lunch, three courses with fish on a Friday, every day of the week, and have money left over.

The warden stood up. Between them the plates were nearly empty.

'St Andrews is so beautiful, warden, that it is a joy to wander the streets during the lunch-hour. But in the winter . . . well, I could imagine that a hot lunch . . . occasionally . . . would tempt me from the wynds or the links.'

'You are a golfer?' Even more interest.

'No, but I love to walk along and smell the sea and see St Andrews rise up . . .' She stopped, embarrassed.

'It casts its spell on all of us, Miss Nesbitt. I will keep you informed of my luncheon programme.'

She offered her hand. It was white and soft, and the fingernails shone without the aid of polish. Rosie grasped it in her short, stubby, rough red hand and was surprised at the strength of the grip. Well, perhaps someone who ate sandwiches like a schoolboy did not notice such stuff as bitten fingernails.

What had that old recipe book said? Half an ounce of pure glycerine in a three-ounce bottle. Fill it up with distilled water and rub it into the hands every time you wash them and before they're quite dry. Easy, easy, to be well groomed.

'And I can at least stop biting my nails,' said Rosie aloud and rushed, exhilarated, to a late tutorial.

5

Edinburgh, 1893

IN 1893 HERMANN Dresser introduced a substance called acetylsalicylic acid. For years Lucy called it aspirin. It was a magic potion and doctors loved it. Doctors' lives and, of course, the way of the world changed with other news that Sir John gave his daughter in a letter from Washington that same year. Henry Ford had developed what he called a gasoline buggy.

> They say we will all take to the highways and byways in these noisy smelly contraptions, Lucy, but quite frankly, it will never be as reliable as a horse. I do not intend to buy one – that is, if the man is not a maniac and actually gets the thing into production. Your mother, however, insists on being the first diplomatic wife to have one, not, I would say – but who listens to a poor soldier? – the most diplomatic of manoeuvres.

Lucy laughed. A letter from her father was like a week's holiday, so refreshed did she feel after reading them. It was years since she had seen him. He would have no home leave for another year, and she had used her two long summer holidays in further study. She was reading the letter in Dublin where she was taking a summer class at the famous Rotunda Hospital. Moving from one hospital to another was as much of a holiday as she allowed herself. There was just so much to learn.

The letter continued:

I have some bad news for Mother's ambitions. I am to be transferred. Actually I am surprised that we have been left here so long. We are to go to Delhi. I was there as a subaltern and enjoyed the life very much. Will you visit? I know your mother will enjoy the social life once she has forgiven the Foreign Office for another hot posting. The good thing about it is, of course, that we will have home leave, and by the time you receive this letter all should be in train for our removal. Shall we take a hotel suite – I do not want to ask the Alexanders to move: they have been excellent tenants – or can your tiny flat accommodate us? What a wonderful Christmas we shall have.

Max du Pay continues to cut a swath through society. We cannot understand why he has not succumbed to the blandishments thrown his way. His mother is one of those fragile women who ask for nothing but always seem to get their own way, and there is a certain Southern belle of her acquaintance. . . !

What shall we bring you from these United States? I regret that we did not travel more here. I should have enjoyed a visit to the west coast.

Lucy read the letter several times and then folded it away. Max du Pay! When his face, a memory of his voice, had pushed itself into the forefront of her mind in these past years, she had ruthlessly thrust the memories away. Once she had thought . . . what had she thought? That she liked him, that he liked her, that perhaps they could be friends. 'When you have grown up a little,' he had said, but she had grown up and he had seemed deliberately to ignore her. There had been no other personal invitations to the du Pay Thanksgiving Hunt. Her parents seemed to have dined with the du Pays often, but when they returned the invitations when Lucy was at home, Max was always somewhere else . . . tiger-hunting in India, skiing in Switzerland, trekking in Africa, or already engaged with one charming Southern belle after another. And now one of the hunted seemed to have captured the great white hunter. Good luck to her. Who cared for Maximilian du

Pay? Her parents were coming, though Father had not said when they were to leave. She would write immediately to insist that they stay with her. It would be wonderful.

And so it was. November had been a dreadful month when a tempest swept across Scotland, destroying property and even life. The beginning of December too had been windy, with great trees being blown down in Perthshire. Now, as they approached Christmas, the winds had settled down and there were frosts, flutterings of snow and rain, rain, rain. 'Typically Edinburgh,' said Lucy as she clutched at her skirts and her umbrella.

The flat was warm and welcoming. Lovely smells came from the kitchen where Annie, delighted to have all her family together, was singing as she worked. Sir John lay in an armchair by the fire, his long legs stretched out to the flames, the *Scotsman* over his head.

'That is not the way to absorb the news,' said Lucy as she removed it and kissed his forehead.

'I'm living in a lovely dream, Lucy,' he said. 'Toasting my slippers by the fire, my daughter blowing in from school . . . sorry, college, my wife bankrupting me buying Christmas presents, steak and kidney pie, if I'm not mistaken, in the oven, that same daughter pouring me sherry . . .'

Lucy took the hint and filled a crystal glass with amber liquid.

'Join me, my dear.'

'I'll wait for Mother. I have some notes to write before dinner. Why does it always happen that just as I congratulate myself that I have sent all my greetings, two drop through my own letterbox from people I have forgotten about completely?'

Lucy left him and went to her room. Annie had drawn the curtains against the dark and cold, but Lucy opened them again. She loved to look at snow or rain falling against lamplight. She busied herself with her correspondence and after a while heard a horse-drawn cab pull up at the door. Lady Graham stepped out and then reached behind her for her parcels.

'What can be in that huge box?' laughed Lucy and hurried down to help her mother. Annie was there before her and the box had been spirited away.

Lucy felt twelve years old again. 'That in my room, that in the kitchen, that in . . .' The orders went on and on, a beloved part of Christmas past.

'Lucy, my dear. Has Father told you we are going to Fifeshire for New Year? I refused the invitation for Christmas, but there is to be a Hunt Ball and lots of young people and old friends of our own we haven't seen in an age.'

'Where?' asked Lucy but she already knew.

At New Year it would be exactly two years since she had seen Kier, although he still wrote – not so often as before, but every few months.

'Will Kier be at home?' She followed her first unanswered question with another.

'I expect the ball is to announce his engagement?' Lady Graham looked at her daughter's stricken face in some surprise. 'Why, Lucy my dear, you don't mind, do you?'

'Of course not.' His letters were full of Cynthias and Alices and Janes. Lucy had never believed they meant anything to him, and now one did and she heard herself tell her mother she did not mind and did not know whether or not she told the truth.

On Christmas morning, the big box revealed a sealskin coat with fur trimming. It was absolutely lovely and Lucy threw it round her shoulders and danced around the small drawing room.

'It is the most beautiful thing,' she said over and over again.

'It will see you through medical school, darling,' said her mother. 'That wool coat you're wearing is not nearly warm enough for Edinburgh winds.'

'Good gracious. I wore it in Washington,' laughed Lucy as she stood before a mirror admiring the fetching picture she made in the lovely soft grey coat.

'Ah, but Americans know how to heat their houses,' said Lady Graham, and frowned as her husband laughed at the irrelevance of her remark.

Lucy wore the coat on the journey to Fife and was glad to know that she looked her best as Kier handed her down from the train and kissed her with all his usual exuberance.

'I ought to have a sleigh drawn by reindeer to pull you home,' he said. 'I've put my name down for one of these new gasoline carriages though, Sir John. Have you seen one, sir?'

It was as if they had never been apart. It was always like that with Kier. He had been a big part of her life for so long and she could not imagine him belonging to anyone else.

'You have a large party this year, Kier?' she asked.

'Oh, you'll meet them all at sherry,' he said. 'Family, people I knew at Oxford, one or two from the regiment, their sisters, that sort of thing.'

That sort of thing. Not the remark of a lover. Make a diagnosis, Doctor Graham. Your pulse has been racing all the way from Edinburgh to Leuchars; it races just as fiercely before an examination. Your heart leaped when he kissed you; it did exactly the same when you met your father off the boat train. Diagnosis: you are delighted to see a childhood friend again. Oh, Lucy, be truthful. You are even more delighted that he has not told you about a special Cynthia.

He waited until they were all gathered in the drawing room for sherry before dinner. The room was as Lucy always pictured it: lit by soft lamplight, warmed by blazing logs, the furniture and carpets faded and worn.

'Lucy, I would like you to meet Sally.' He proffered Sally as if she was some rare species of butterfly for Lucy to admire.

'How do you do, doctor?' The voice was as timid and gentle as the girl herself.

Good God, she lisps, thought Lucy. *Whatever attracted him to a girl who lisps?*

'Hello, Sally,' she said. 'Just call me Lucy, please. I'm not a doctor yet.'

'Ooh, we have all been quite, quite terrified to meet you.'

Lucy looked at Kier, expecting him to catch her eye at the absurdity, but he was gazing down into the tiny face as if he was hearing the words of an oracle.

So that is love, thought Lucy. *I prefer to be rational and sensible.*

Brave words, but over the holiday period she did admit to a little pang of what . . . regret, jealousy? All the other young people seemed to be paired off, and the charms of the rather elderly clergyman who was the only unattached male did not appeal to Miss Graham. Several times, had she been vain, she could have made herself believe that Kier sought her out. He partnered her at dinner; he danced as often with her as with the fair Sally; he rode neck and neck with her in the hunt. Sally did not hunt. 'Too, too terrifying, and horses smell so.'

In a game of hide-and-seek she found herself alone with him on the nursery landing, as they crouched behind a dresser and waited for their pursuers to pass by. When it seemed that they were safe, Lucy went to rise from her cramped position but Kier held her down.

'Let's wait awhile, Lucy. I am determined to win the prize. Let's just sit here on the floor for a time. I must stretch my legs or I'll cramp.'

They sat in the half dark side by side on the floor, leaning against the dresser. They had hidden up here so many many times during their childhood, but this time it was different. She was intensely aware of him, the warmth of his arm, the length of his leg, through the thin stuff of her gown

'This is fun,' said Kier quietly.

Lucy nodded. She could not speak.

'Sally would never sit on the floor.'

'Her gowns are finer than mine.'

'Oh, I don't know.'

They sat still, listening to the laughter and the cries from downstairs.

'Not fair, not fair. Kier and Lucy know the house.'

'Lucy?'

There was something in his voice that told her what he was about to say was vitally important. She did not want to hear it; she must not hear it. She moved to get to her feet, but his hand on her wrist held her down.

'Lucy. How many more years?'

She could say, 'I will be a registered physician this year. I will have achieved that much,' but she could not. To throw it all away to marry Kier and follow the drum . . . Part of her longed for it, for the security of a warm, loving

103

relationship, but there would be no Dr Graham in the regiment. No Doctor Graham. That was the thing, the only thing. *I am so unfair to Kier. Let him go, Lucy, let him go, she told herself.*

'Three . . . at least. I must do practical work, and there are other courses. I want to take a course at the Rotunda Hospital in Dublin, in midwifery, you know. It is not my favourite subject, but Dr Jex-Blake's lectures were an inspiration, and if I am to set up general practice I must be as well qualified as any man, more qualified.'

'The regiment's going to India in the summer. Delhi. Isn't that a strange coincidence?'

'Very strange.'

'I'll be gone two years. You would like Delhi; you're used to a life on the move.'

Her mouth was very dry. 'I plan to visit—'

She got no further, for with a stifled moan he had pulled her into his arms. His mouth was on hers, not the brotherly kiss as at the station. This was searching, demanding. Was it the memories of childhood, the warmth of the holiday season, the mulled wine they had drunk in the drawing room a while ago . . . but Lucy answered his kiss. She too was searching, demanding. Her arms were around his neck and somehow they were full length on the floor and her body was on fire and she was desperate for the fire to be extinguished. She came to her senses when his hand found its way inside the low neckline of her dress, and she pulled herself away and stumbled to her feet.

'This is madness.'

'I am the one who is mad, Lucy.' She could see the effort he made to pull himself together. 'Forgive me,' he said and she was back in the sick-room of the fourteen-year-old Kier who had behaved abominably and thrown his medicine and his crutch at her and then begged so sweetly for her forgiveness. 'We must go downstairs,' said the man, Kier. 'I'll go first, give you a chance to . . . There is no excuse for my behaviour.' He half saluted and ran quickly down the stairs and she heard him calling lightly.

'Lucy? No, I have not seen her. Has she not been found ?'

Has she lost?, thought Lucy. *Had happiness been within her grasp? Should she have pulled it to her and kept it safe against all-comers?* She straightened her dress and smoothed her hair and went back to the party.

* * *

Her father came to her room on New Year's Eve as she dressed for the ball in a made-over gown that Lady Graham would not need in Delhi.

'You look charming, my dear,' said Sir John as he fastened her twenty-first birthday gift of pearls around her neck. 'The announcement is for midnight, Lucy. Are you able to wish him joy?'

'I wish him luck, Father.' She tried to sound light-hearted, even flippant. 'She will bore him to tears in a twelve-month.'

'Not if she gives him a child, Lucy. Kier is ready for fatherhood and will make a doting papa.'

Lucy laughed. 'What an absurd idea! Kier is a child himself.'

'He is twenty-three, two years older than you. And I have often found that it is more the desire for stability, for a wife and children to return to, that shepherds a soldier into holy matrimony, than deep, passionate love.' He handed her her shawl, another relic of Washington. 'I am glad your heart is not broken. I always hoped you might marry Kier, but if you do not love him . . .'

'Of course I love him. I always have but . . . oh, Father, I don't know. If I marry anyone that will be an end to my dream. I'm so very selfish. I want it all. Isn't that greedy of me? I want Kier . . . or someone . . . to wait until I am ready, and I do not want to marry for another three years. Even after that, I would like to go on to the university for an advanced degree. There is so much to learn and every day there are more and more discoveries. Perhaps I am not meant for a domestic life. I would find it . . . difficult to give up medicine for any man.'

'Then obviously you have not yet met the right man. For when you do, Lucy, when you know that this is the man with whom you want to spend your life, nothing, including the practice of medicine, will stand in your way.'

At midnight Mr Anderson-Howard wished the company a very happy New Year, but he looked discomfited, puzzled. Kier was nowhere to be seen and neither was Sally, whose parents looked even more discomfited than Kier's. There was a buzz of speculative talk among the young people and Lucy heard some of it.

'Of course they were going to announce.'

'He never actually asked her, you know.'

'She assumed, we all did . . .'

'He's going to India, for God's sake. No girl in her right mind would want to get engaged and then see her beloved go off to years in India.'

'But where is she?'

'You don't think they've run off, do you?'

Lucy's heart skipped a beat. Run off? She forced herself to kiss her parents, to chat normally to Kier's mother and father.

'You don't know what's happened, Lucy dear?' said Mrs Anderson-Howard. 'We were so sure, you see. He said he was going to ask her; I'm sure he did.'

'Perhaps they decided to wait until after India.'

'That'll be it. She's not like you, Lucy, used to trailing half-way across the world every few years. Oh, do make the musicians play, Archie. This is turning into a funeral tea.'

The musicians played, the waiters poured champagne, the young danced, their elders sipped the wine and talked and tried desperately to avoid the only subject they wanted to discuss.

It was nearly one in the morning before the door opened to reveal a flushed and windblown Kier and Sally.

'So sorry we're late,' said Kier cheerfully. 'We went for a walk and then found ourselves, blondes both, about to become your first foot of the New Year, Mother, so we went around the house tapping on windows till we could find a dark-haired footman to come out and lead us in.'

'The butler was frightfully fierce, Mrs Anderson-Howard,' said Sally. 'He attacked us with a cricket bat.'

'Not really, Mother.' Kier reassured his mother, who had half risen in alarm. 'Bless his fierce old heart, though, he did have it in his hand, ready to beat off the invaders.'

'Rather a strange time to go for a walk, Kier.'

Kier looked at his father. 'We had such a lot to talk about.'

'Snakes and things,' said Sally with another little shudder. 'Oh, Kier darling. Champagne!'

Lucy watched them for a few moments before excusing herself and going off to bed. Sally had recovered from her disappointment at not becoming an engaged woman. 'Snakes and things.' Kier had obviously filled the poor girl's head with a lot of nonsense about living conditions in the outposts of the empire. But why? Had it anything to do with that wine-induced moment of madness on the nursery stair? And it *was* wine-induced, wasn't it? He would not have kissed her so had he been completely sober. Lucy looked sternly into her mirror as she brushed her hair. 'If he asked you today, would you leave everything and go off with him to India?'

But Lucy Graham refused to answer the question.

6

Edinburgh, 1893

IN THE FORMAL setting of a house-party it was impossible for Lucy to avoid Kier altogether, although she tried. Her mind was in a turmoil. Part of her said that if Kier truly loved Sally he would not have kissed her, Lucy, on the nursery stair. On the other hand she worried that she might just have spoiled poor Sally's romance.

But she looked happy. She doesn't love him enough. He does not love her enough. I do not . . . Oh, the permutations were endless. Her racing blood told her that she had wanted more, much more, from Kier on the nursery landing. But was that love, or Christmas spirit, or wine, or frustrated spinsterhood?

If he loved her, truly loved her, he would not have frightened her with tales of life in India. If she loved him, truly loved . . . if I . . . oh, dear God, why is life so complicated?

'Hello, Lucy. I felt sure I should find you here.'

It was Kier.

Lucy turned from the nursery fire she had kindled herself – had she not done the same so often in the long ago – and looked up at him. He looked tired and pale. The ravages of a New Year holiday, no doubt.

'Sir John says you leave tonight.'

'My classes start soon, and there is so much for my parents to do. They are considering selling The Larches, you know. Did your father tell you so?'

'No.'

She did not stand up. He did not kneel down beside her

'Finance. India will be expensive. The Alexanders love the house and so it would seem sensible to sell.'

'Lucy, I love you.'

She continued to look into the flames. 'I know. I love you too,' she said softly.

He laughed but it was not a laugh, almost a cry of pain. 'This is where we should fall into each other's arms.'

What could she say?

'Lucy. I want a home and healthy little children playing in the orchard and creeping out at night to feed their ponies extra sugar-lumps. I want a wife . . . you – I have never ever really wanted anyone else – at my table, on my arm . . . in my bed.'

She stood up, the firelight throwing her shadow on the wall.

'In three years' time you will have had a chance to get all this out of your mind. You should have fulfilled whatever it is in you that longs for . . . for . . . what I can't, no man can, give you. I should make major about the same time. A perfect time for us to marry. I won't ask you to become engaged. For one thing, if you accepted me, it would be a dreadful humiliation to poor Sally; I'm extremely fond of her, you see.' He turned away from her and his voice was very quiet. 'Sometimes it's nice to be admired by someone who doesn't really know one, bumps and all as they say. And you know me so well. I have no secrets from you. But you, Lucy, you have always kept your counsel. We'll write, shall we? And then in three years' time, I shall come and all you will have to say is, "Yes, Kier. The time is right."'

She said nothing. The tears were flowing freely and oh so quietly.

'Oh, my love, don't cry. My soul tells me that you are worth waiting for, Lucy Graham.' He bent down and gently kissed her. 'Make it better, doctor,' he said softly and when she looked up he was gone.

Had the adults, the parents, made a pact? No more was said about Kier's engagement. Nothing was said about the fact that, for the first time ever, he did not see them off at the station. Lucy had her story ready but was not called upon to tell it.

She returned to her medical lectures and her parents eventually sailed to India. Her father sent her a straw hat from Firpo's at Aden which she hung on the wall.

'I shall wear the hat as I sail through the canal,' she told him in a letter.

But she never went to India. Lady Graham died from dysentery within a few months of arriving in Delhi. Sir John brought his wife's body back to be buried in the grave-yard of the wee kirk in Fife where they had been married and, after a few weeks' compassionate leave, returned to India. Lucy worked harder than ever, if that was at all possible. Why had medicine been unable to save her mother? There was so much to learn, so much to do.

The frontiers of medicine were being pushed farther and farther. Doctors all over the world, male doctors, were adding – daily, it seemed – to the understanding of the human body. Halstead explained his operation for mastectomy. Oliver and Schafer discovered the nature of adrenalin and, a year later, Röntgen discovered X-rays. Lucy read of every new discovery and she studied, in Edinburgh, in Dublin, in Rouen. She moved to Dundee and attended lectures given by Professor Geddes, and Professor D'Arcy Thomson. In 1896, when a little Dundee girl called Rosie Nesbitt was entering the hallowed portals of St Andrews University for the first time, and an anti-toxin against diphtheria was being introduced, Lucy Graham at last became a fully qualified doctor. She graduated MB, CM and was among the first woman doctors ever to graduate from a Scottish college. She put Kier Anderson-Howard, who had not been able to attend her graduation, firmly to the back of her mind. He was now in Africa, likely to remain for a while, and while he was there she did not have to think about marriage. And who would want to marry in this wonderful year when the whole world was spread out before her.

She could stay in Edinburgh and run a practice from her home or she could move. She had liked Dundee when she studied there. It was almost home, since Fife and the now sold Larches lay just across the Tay. It was immaterial, she told herself, that Laverock Rising was also just across the river. Quite bluntly she faced the fact that there would still be prejudice against her because she was a woman. The Anderson-Howard patronage would be useful to her, and there was the goodwill her own parents had built up in the area.

Sir John smoothed the rocky path which lay ahead of his daughter. 'I think you're right to go to Dundee,' he said. 'If you sell your Edinburgh flat, you should be able to buy the right address. Somewhere in the West End would be best.'

He could not stay long enough to see her settled, but instructed his lawyers to help her in every way possible. A house was to be found in a quiet residential street, preferably quite near the centre of town and the university. The lawyers went to work.

'This house offers excellent accommodation, Miss Graham,' said Mr Dryden, the senior partner in Dryden, MacDonald and Dryden. 'There are four floors, the first of which would be ideal for offices for the practice of medicine.' The distaste in his voice was so palpable that Lucy almost recoiled. 'The second floor makes ideal living accommodation; in fact, so it is with several of the neighbouring houses. Then the attics for servants, and the basement for the usual offices, kitchens, pantries.'

'Why is the house for sale, Mr Dryden?'

'I advised it. The owner lives abroad and has rented out the property for some years. He needs an income and wanted to ask forty pounds per annum, that is a five-pound rise in one year. I could not see the last tenant paying such an ambitious sum. On the other hand, should we sell the property, which needs little in the way of work, £420 invested sensibly brings in a handsome income and with no worries.'

'I should like to see the house.'

He rang a little bell and almost immediately an aged clerk entered in reply to the summons.

'Ask Mr Colin to come in, Herbert.'

Mr Dryden turned to Lucy as the old man shuffled out again. 'My nephew will show you the property, Miss Graham. Ah, Colin. This is Miss Graham and she would like to see No.4.'

Lucy looked up into twinkling brown eyes.

'This is an honour, Doctor Graham,' said Colin Dryden, with a very slight but noticeable stress on the title. 'My aunt, Mrs Dryden, is anxious to become your first patient. I have the keys, Uncle,' he said and held out his hand to help Lucy from the deep leather seat.

'You must be the second Dryden of Dryden, MacDonald and Dryden?' asked Lucy as they walked down the great stone staircase.

'Good heavens, no. That's my Uncle Ian. I appear nowhere at all on the family escutcheon and, if Uncle Alistair has anything to do with it, I never shall.'

'Oh, why not?' asked Lucy. She looked at him carefully as he handed her into a cab that had been waiting patiently, and liked what she saw. Only of middle height, so that she stood eye to eye with him, there was an engaging frankness about his roundish face.

'For one thing, I advocate the rights of women. Uncle Alistair thinks women should be in the . . . kitchen.'

'And your aunt?'

'Stays out of the kitchen . . . and everywhere else, as much as possible. She says, "Yes, dear," regularly and does exactly as she chooses. Seriously, she will make every effort to wear the accolade, *Doctor Graham's first patient.*'

'I have already had hundreds of patients, Mr Dryden,' said Lucy acidly. Medicine was not a joke. She softened, for he was so very anxious to please. 'Is there something wrong with her?'

'My dear Doctor Graham. What has that to do with anything? You are the social event of the season.'

'Are you sure you don't mean pariah?' Lucy interrupted.

The eyes twinkled at her again. 'The old biddies will be lining up in the street. There will be dowagers, young women from the upper echelon of society, female lecturers, students, maids.' The eyes became serious and Mr Dryden frowned. 'The men won't come.'

'Will they let their wives come, their children?'

'Some. Well, what do you think?' They had reached No.4, a tall, narrow white house with wrought-iron railings around the windows on the first floor. There was a slight air of neglect.

'The door needs a lick of paint,' said the young lawyer as if he could read her mind.

They walked up the outside steps and he put the key in the door. Inside, light spilled into the hall from a stained-glass window and danced around the black and white tiled floor.

It was the most extraordinary feeling but Lucy, who had spent most of her life travelling around the world, immediately felt at home. The house welcomed her. Mentally she shook herself, for she did not approve of people who accorded human values to inanimate objects.

She wandered around, seeing her mother's furniture arranged in the living areas, deciding where cabinets and tables and chairs should go in the offices. There was no doubt at all that she would buy the house.

'The kitchen is a joy, is it not? That range is very up-to-the-minute. See, it's an Eagle, and has the latest in flue construction, lifting fire and' – he kept the best till last – 'a reversing damper. Your cook will adore it.'

Lucy, who knew next to nothing about kitchens and even less of the mysteries of ranges, agreed with him but did not award him the satisfaction of telling him so.

'I shall have to see what my housekeeper thinks of it, but I believe we can come to an arrangement about the house, Mr Dryden. The location is certainly excellent, and no doubt the garden is quite pleasant.'

'Do you have a gardener, doctor? If not, we will be delighted to advertise for you. See, we can go out here through these French windows and the balcony of the main bedchamber also looks out over the gardens.'

Lucy looked in dismay at the overgrown flowerbeds and the barely recognizable vegetable garden. Originally, the gardens had met the needs of a large family.

'I may not be able to afford a full-time gardener,' she said with a frankness that almost made Colin Dryden wish he had the time and talent to care for it for her. 'Until I build up a practice—'

'A few hours each week should keep it under control. Do you need to see any of the rooms again today, or shall we return to the office?'

'I would like to show the house to Annie, my house-keeper. She has been with me almost all my life and deserves the courtesy.'

He understood. He bowed and, after he had carefully locked up, took her back to the cab.

Annie, who was staying with her sister in her home village of Cupar, refused to visit the house.

'I really should have given up some time ago, Miss Lucy, but I can't go on working. I promised your mother that I would look after you in Edinburgh . . .'

Lucy looked at the woman who had been with her for so many years in so many places. She saw a thin, wrinkled elderly lady: someone who had certainly earned the right to stop working.

'Oh, Annie, how selfish of me. Of course you must retire.' Lucy's mind was working feverishly. How would Annie live? She must see her way to making her a monthly payment. But from where was this largesse to come? 'Where will you live?'

'Here, with my sister and her man. I'll still see you, Miss Lucy, but it's time you got a young woman. I'll be all right here. I have the one hundred pounds your mother left me invested and . . .'

Lucy was about to protest, to say 'That was for your old age,' but this *was* Annie's old age. *I have taken her toil so much for granted she thought, and my parents. My poor mother . . .* She could not bear to think about her mother, who had not even had the satisfaction of seeing her unsatisfactory daughter graduate.

'I'll see that you are all right, Annie,' she said. 'You'll never want for anything.'

She took a fond and tearful farewell of the woman who had laboured conscientiously for years and years, in hot climates and cold, to see that her life ran smoothly. Clothes were soiled: Annie washed them. Food was ready whenever Lucy chose to eat. Not a particle of dust was allowed to lie unchallenged. An evening dress, thrown carelessly over a chair after a night's dancing, was returned, cleaned and pressed, to the wardrobe, ready to be worn again.

Lucy caught the train back to Dundee and her mind went in tandem with the click-clack of the wheels.

I have no housekeeper: more importantly, I have no patients. My grandmother's money will furnish my office and Mother's money will keep me until Christmas. I must make Annie an allowance. I must get a gardener or my weeds will upset all my neighbours. So first I must place an advertisement in the Courier *and* Journal.

'An announcement that Doctor Lucille Graham etc. etc. is now practising at 4 Shore Terrace will probably be more helpful in the first instance than a request for a maid-of-all-work.' Colin Dryden made the suggestion as Lucy sat in his book-littered office and drank coffee.

'This cubby-hole, dare I call it an office, reminds me of my childhood,' said Lucy lightly, so at ease with the young solicitor did she feel. 'All it needs is tobacco smoke.'

'Filthy habit,' said Colin Dryden dismissively. 'My father smoked constantly and I'm sure it contributed to his early death. Don't you agree – or are you encouraging me to buy a pipe?'

'I don't know enough about it, but a Professor Potts did find a marked incidence of ...' – she stopped the word 'scrotal' just in time – '... a cancer among chimney sweeps. The carbon, he thought.'

He smiled. 'Well done, a doctor who listens. Usually medical men are so dismissive. Now, shall we send the announcement and the advertisement?'

Lucy decided to ignore his sweeping judgement of the medical profession. 'Yes, please.'

'And will you dine with me this evening? The ladies' dining room of my uncle's club is suitable.'

Lucy had often dined with groups of other students during her years of study, but perhaps because most of the men were too hard up, or perhaps because they were all working too hard, she had not made any intimate friendships. Even when she had gone to a ball or a party with Kier, it had been as part of a group. She felt as nervous as she had done on the day she put her hair up. But it did not occur to her to decline.

'I would like that,' she said simply.

'Good. I shall brave Mrs O'Brien at half-past seven. In the meantime I shall place these advertisements.'

Lucy's thoughts as she walked swiftly back to her boarding-house were not of her career or the size and upkeep of the house she had so rashly bought, but of what to wear. The late summer evenings were still warm and so an Indian shawl for her shoulders would be nice, but which dress? In the end, there was no decision to make. Most of her clothes were packed in trunks and the only evening gown she had with her was a half-mourning gown she had had made after her mother's death. It was lilac, and she congratulated herself for the colour suited her. The neckline was not very . . . not too low.

'If I remove that little satin frill around the neckline and sew it very neatly . . . and then Mother's little gold chain with the amethyst teardrop . . .'

Lucy Graham banished Dr Graham and set out to be frivolous.

What an amusing companion Colin Dryden turned out to be. He had a fund of stories about his student days and his early years in his uncle's office. Perhaps they were so endearing because he was laughing at himself, never ever at anyone else.

'My aunt, by the way,' he said as they sat in the lounge waiting for their after-dinner coffee, 'says that she feels the most dreadful migraines approaching Dundee from the south-west. They should arrive just about the time your office opens.'

'Is she as frivolous as you, Mr Dryden?'

'Oh, eminently more so. If she likes you, and I know she will,' he added with a look that caused Lucy to turn her head away from the intensity of his gaze, 'she will have everyone who is anyone rushing to sign on Doctor Graham's list.'

'I want to take care of the sick, Mr Dryden, not overfed, underworked matrons who are suffering from ennui.'

'Oh, they will adore to be cured of ennui. It will be the disease of the century.'

'A Doctor Rehn in Frankfurt has just sutured a heart wound. Do you realize what that means?' Lucy asked him seriously and, at once sober and serious, he shook his head.

'Doctors will begin to operate on the heart itself. The bounds of medicine will soon know no limits. In Italy they have found that if a substance called chlorine . . .'

She stopped as he looked puzzled, and blushed with embarrassment. As always she had the bit between her teeth. 'I'm sorry. This must be boring for you.'

'No, not at all. Your face lights up with enthusiasm; your eyes flash; even your hands speak.' He stopped as she looked away again. 'Sorry. What is chlorine? I've never heard of it.'

She laughed and they were at ease again. 'I was hoping you wouldn't ask that: I'm not too sure myself. It's a gas, one of the halogens, smells terrible but if, according to the Italian research, it is added to water – and don't ask me how – it kills germs. Just think. Typhoid wiped out all over the world, literally overnight. What next? Dysentery? Cholera?'

'How good is it at hunger and poverty?'

'So there is more to you than laughter?'

He looked pained. 'Sometimes laughter is the only pill that works, doctor.' He reached across and grasped her hands and she did not pull away. 'There are sick people here in Dundee, Lucy. Don't think about Germany and Italy; we need you here.'

He was so young, so sincere, and yes, it was very pleasant to be admired.

'Your law firm has just sold me a house that cost me a king's ransom. I must stay in Dundee to pay for it . . . but I need patients.'

He smiled at her. 'They'll come.'

But they did not come. Day after day Lucy sat in her newly decorated and furnished consulting room and waited. She visited the hospitals and introduced herself to the various heads of department; she was known to many of them already from her years at Dundee Medical School.

'Our patients are sent by their own doctors, Doctor Graham, or they are too poor to afford one. We will recommend . . . should the opportunity arise.'

Opportunity. She found herself almost hoping for an accident in the street so that she could rush to the aid of the injured and thus make herself known. Kier's mother invited her to lunch and to dinner several times and, in this way, she met many prominent and wealthy people, but they did not rush to her rooms.

The attitudes of several of the women she met in this way were interesting and sometimes ambivalent. They thought her terribly clever and brave to have spent so many years fighting her way into the closed world of medicine but, oh no, they could not possibly consult her themselves.

'Why did you want to study medicine, Miss Graham?' was an often asked question, and the answer was always the same.

'I want to help the sick.'

'There is great discussion in Dundee, and I'm sure elsewhere, about the advisablity of having only fully trained nurses in hospitals,' said Mr MacDonald of Dryden, MacDonald and Dryden, who, in this small world of society, was well-known to the Anderson-Howards. 'Is that not women's place in medicine, Doctor?'

At least he awarded her her hard-won title.

'It is a place, Mr MacDonald, but there is a very special place for a woman doctor, a unique place. Women bring special skills to medicine . . .'

'To nursing, surely. Their God-given role of nurturing, caring?'

'In the field of medicine for women, Mr MacDonald, a woman is surely better qualified than any man.' She tried to make her arguments simple, perhaps too simple. 'Merely by virtue of being a woman, she has empathy and understanding.'

'A properly qualified and trained physician, Doctor Graham, will surely have the same understanding of the more intimate functions of a woman's body as an unmarried woman.'

There it was again. Unmarried women should be gentle little flowers. The practice of medicine was indelicate and robbed them of their femininity.

'You do not have to have experienced childbirth to understand it, Mr MacDonald.'

'An unmarried woman should know nothing of these matters, and moreover, Doctor Graham, a decent woman should not want to know of them.'

There was nothing more to be said but, as luck would have it, that strange unwritten law that allotted twenty minutes to the partner on either side was working and Lucy was able to turn her burning face away from his appalling rudeness. She could hardly concentrate on the conversation of the young man on her other side and he was so tongue-tied that he dried up completely, and each of them sat in misery until the dessert course was brought in and he, at least, could seek solace in a chocolate meringue.

That her embarrassment had been witnessed by others was made obvious by the solicitude with which Kier's mother poured her coffee.

'My dear,' she breathed sympathetically and moved on.

'May I sit down, Doctor Graham?' The woman who stood before her was expensively if not fashionably dressed in a pale green silk gown that hung on her too-thin frame.

'I am Mrs MacDonald,' she introduced herself, as if afraid that Lucy would prefer her to sit elsewhere.

'Do please sit down,' said Lucy and smiled at her.

The woman still stood, twisting a silk handkerchief in her long thin fingers. 'Some men find progress . . . difficult, Doctor Graham. Have you found this to be so?'

'Some men, yes,' Lucy agreed.

Mrs MacDonald seemed to gather herself together as if she needed courage. 'It is quite wonderful that you have come to Dundee. I hope you will be very happy and successful,' she said and, turning on her heel, walked rapidly away.

The party finished early since so many of the guests had to catch the last ferry across the Tay, and Lucy was glad that she had refused the Anderson-Howards' offer of hospitality.

'I hope you will be successful.' Mrs MacDonald's words rang in her ears as she watched the shores of Fife slip away.

'I hope so too, Mrs MacDonald, I hope so too,' she said to herself.

7

Dundee

EXACTLY ONE WEEK after she officially opened her new consulting rooms, Doctor Lucille Graham found a housekeeper, a gardener, and her first patient, and they all came to her through the good offices of Mrs MacDonald.

The patient came first. The MacDonalds' nursemaid had a backache and her mistress sent her to see what the new young female doctor would advise.

'The advice is to stop carrying heavy loads, Mhairi,' said Dr Graham after she had given the young woman a thorough examination. 'How old is the baby?'

'Well, Archie's three and then the twins is two and the baby's six months.'

'No wonder,' thought Lucy, 'that Mrs MacDonald is so thin and pale and that her overworked nursemaid has an aching back.'

'The twins must be walking?'

'Oh yes, doctor, but they get jealous if the mistress is feeding the baby, and they want to be babies, and then little Archie wants to be a baby and . . .'

'And you give in to them?'

'Well, it saves yelling. They yell, and the master doesn't like that and the mistress gets upset and starts to cry, and that's not good for her milk, is it?'

'No, but neither is it good for you to be carrying heavy children around, children who are perfectly capable of walking for themselves.'

'The mistress thought maybe . . . you being just qualified . . . you would know of some pill . . .'

Lucy looked at the anxious face. A pill. Everyone was looking for a pill that would cure everything.

'Perhaps, since there are so many small children . . .' She stopped for a moment, remembering Mrs MacDonald's age. 'Are there other, older children?'

'Oh yes, miss, I mean doctor. Margaret is eleven and Alice is nine.' Mhairi smiled with pride as if she herself was the mother of so many children. 'I think we're really pleased that the twins are boys . . . three of each, we have now.'

'A fine family,' said Lucy wryly. 'And the girls are in the nursery too. Perhaps a little more help . . . ?'

Mhairi looked quite shocked. 'Oh. The master says his own mother raised eight perfectly healthy children with no help at all.'

Lucy thought rapidly. A five-year gap between the older girls and the next child; that probably meant at least two miscarriages. No wonder Mrs MacDonald was so pale and worn-looking; too many children, one after the other. Before the body had had time to recuperate from the demands of one pregnancy, another child was on the way. How she wished she could do something to regulate that. There were the rather bizarre methods she had heard a little about: vinegar-soaked sponges inserted in the vagina, for one. She could hardly see the fastidious Mrs MacDonald resorting to that. And what of Mr MacDonald's part in all this? He did not like to hear his twin sons yelling. Their crying disturbed him and he got annoyed. Poor Mr MacDonald!

Lucy sighed. Such was the way of the world.

'Try to avoid carrying heavy loads, Mhairi. If you must lift the children, bend your knees and don't bend over from the waist to pick them up. I don't know why that helps but it does. Tell Mrs MacDonald that hint too. And perhaps . . .' She stopped, suddenly appallingly aware that she knew absolutely nothing about the minds of small children, of any child. 'Perhaps you could make getting up and down stairs a game for the twins and Archie. A race to see who is the fastest or perhaps,' she groped desperately back to her memories of her father in her own nursery, 'perhaps they could play at being frogs hopping about . . .'

To her amazement Mhairi's face lit up. 'Or tigers, Doctor. The mistress read them a tale about a tiger from foreign parts and they liked it.'

Lucy stood up. 'Yes, that's a good idea. Capture the imagination.'

'Oh, I will, doctor. I feel better already.'

Lucy sat for a few minutes looking at the door which had closed behind her very first patient, a delighted patient. Would that it would ever be so! She remembered Annie and a friend from her childhood. 'What a little blether Miss Sarah is,' Annie used to say wonderingly as they sat at the nursery tea-table.

Well, Annie. I did a bit of blethering myself just now and I sincerely hope it worked. Sir Ronald Ross may have identified the cause of malaria and that would be a great help were I in India, but I'm not. I wonder how Sir Ronald would deal with nursemaid's back – my first ailment.

No patient followed Mhairi through the door. Doctor Graham wrote up case notes. She almost blushed to call it a case but, no, she chided herself, the ailment is very real to poor overworked Mhairi.

Shall I ever be overworked? she thought as 5 o'clock came and she made her lonely way upstairs to her living quarters. She looked in her pantry and there on the stone shelf, the tried and true method of keeping food cold and fresh, was the piece of beef she had rashly bought for her evening meal. 'I really don't know quite what to do with you,' she told it and reached further along the shelf for the remains of the cheese that she had had for lunch.

That did not look too appetizing, even with the addition of a lovely piece of crusty bread and a rather tired apple.

'I'll melt the cheese,' thought Lucy, 'if this stupid unobliging, terrifically modern up-to-the-minute range with its reversing damper hasn't reversed itself again and gone out.'

The meanest of her patients, had she had any, would have been shocked to see how much cold or undercooked food the wonderful new lady doctor was eating. Doctor Graham was not overburdened with domestic skills.

'Blast!' There was no warmth at all from the great iron monster that took up so much room. Lucy looked at it. Could she bear to try to light it again? Would it stay lit till the morning and thus make a nice hot cup of tea a possibility?

She heard the front door-bell and half sighed as she ran upstairs to answer the summons. It might just be a patient? It was not.

'Doctor Graham. Mrs MacDonald sent me. My name's Isa Murray and I need a job.'

'Come in, won't you, Miss Murray.'

'It's Mrs, Doctor, and I hope that won't make a difference. Mrs MacDonald thought with you it might not.'

Mrs MacDonald? Why was the woman making so much effort? Was it because, as a loyal wife, she could not straight-forwardly apologize for the arrogance of her husband but would do so in other ways.

'I was in service before my marriage, doctor, to Mrs MacDonald's family. I know how to mind fine furniture and I'm a good plain cook. I've even been lady's maid and can sew small stitches. But I have a husband and won't be able to stay nights. We have a place near the mill.'

'Your husband is a mill-worker?'

'Was, Doctor. It's done something to his lungs and he can't work in the mills no more. We wanted to do farm work up the Carse, but he couldn't manage like, not full time, and we'd not get a tied cottage. I've been doing a bit here and there. I was doing Mrs MacDonald's silver and she said as there was an advertisement . . . I would stay really late when you were entertaining, Doctor.'

Lucy had always thought deeply, and would always think very hard before she reached an important decision, but this once she made an immediate decision and it was one she was never to regret.

'Mrs Murray, I need someone in the house very much and I need them right now. The garden needs attention. You can see from the window here, it is not too large and has been well planned. The top floor . . .' She stopped. The floor was a warren of empty rooms.

'We have our own bits and pieces, doctor,' put in Mrs Murray eagerly. 'If that was what you were wanting, like. Donald's a good man and works hard when the coughing's not on him.'

'Phthisis,' thought Lucy. 'Or perhaps it is the effects of inhaling jute hour after hour, day after day.'

'Has he worked in a garden before, Mrs Murray?' she asked.

'When he was a lad, like, doctor. He's from the Carse, raised in the country. He only came in to make a better living from the jute and he was a good worker. He'd do the garden beautiful, but it would have to be in his own time.'

'I'll show you over the house and then you can go home and discuss it with Mr Murray.'

To Lucy's everlasting embarrassment, her new retainers turned up with their possessions on a hand-cart borrowed from a friend who was a carter.

'I should have hired the removal company for you, Mrs Murray.'

'Oh no, doctor, we couldn't be beholden. The neighbours will see we're clean and respectable, and that's what counts, isn't it? I'm sorry if we've disgraced you.'

'Clean and respectable.' That was what was important. And that they were not beholden. Very well, thought Lucy.

Let her grand neighbours think what they liked. 'Let me give you a hand, Mrs Murray.'

The rather austere face softened into a smile of singular charm. 'That wouldn't be right, doctor. Off you, and I'll make us all a nice cup of tea when we're done.'

There was not much to unload and soon Donald and his friends were setting up the bed and arranging the lovingly polished bits of furniture, while Mrs Murray bustled around in her kitchen, returning again and again to touch the surface of the magnificent but, to Lucy, frightening range.

'Mrs MacDonald had one of these. So easy, and it makes bread beautiful, and heats water and the kitchens.'

Lucy did not confess that she had not found it easy. 'We'll go to Draffens tomorrow, Mrs Murray, and get you a uniform for answering the door. I put some aprons in a drawer in the kitchen. You'll know which ones are which.'

'Oh yes, doctor, and it's Isa, doctor. I'd like for you to call me by my name.'

'Very well, Isa, but not in front of patients.'

Isa smiled again. 'That's right and proper, doctor.'

Lucy went to bed that night after eating the best meal she had yet had in her own new house and the next day, as if Isa's coming had been an omen of good, two new patients turned up at morning consulting. They arrived together, but one had been driven in a private cab and the other had walked up from the steam tram stop.

Isa, in her own old but clean dress and one of Annie's starched white aprons, showed the elder of the two ladies into the consulting room.

'I think you have been expecting me, Doctor Graham. I am Mrs Dryden.'

Mrs Dryden was as engaging as her nephew had painted her.

'How do you do, Mrs Dryden. How may I help you?'

'At my age, doctor, there are a dozen things going wrong, but nothing that we need worry about.'

Lucy was at a loss. Surely this was not a mere social call?

'Perhaps I should find at least one of the ailments, Mrs Dryden, and see if medicine can do anything to alleviate it.'

Mrs Dryden looked at her measuringly. 'Well, doctor,' she said at last, 'there's something that has been a bit of a nuisance over the last six months or so, perhaps even since last winter. Sometimes – I hope you don't think I'm stupid – but sometimes when I walk my right knee gives way.'

'Do you fall?'

'Stumble would be a better word. In fact I've taken to holding on to the banisters as I walk downstairs.'

Lucy nodded. 'Is the knee painful ... or any other joints?'

'Are thumbs joints, doctor? Sometimes my thumbs ache so much I can't hold a pen. I noticed it when I was writing to my daughter. She lives in Edinburgh,' she added as if that had some relevance. 'But sometimes a pain shoots right up my arm when I lift my heavy silver teapot. I've even spilled tea, once on my best linen cloth.'

Lucy smiled. Ruining the cloth was the tragedy. She held out her hands. 'May I look at your thumbs and then your knee?'

The thumbs were very slightly misshapen and the knee was slightly swollen.

Arthritis: a word that meant simply inflammation of the joints, one of the most common ailments known to man.

'I'm sure it's just normal ageing, doctor. My mother was just the same and that was what her physician said.'

'Ah, but medical science is rushing breathlessly into a new century, Mrs Dryden. We can make what is natural rather more comfortable. As yet we don't know what causes the various arthritic conditions,' she said, as she felt sure that Mrs Dryden would appreciate complete honesty. 'It may be a bacteria, or some disruption of the body chemistry. Tell me, do you feel more pain when the house is cold and perhaps even damp?'

Mrs Dryden agreed that this was in fact the case.

'You must strive to maintain a uniform body heat. Don't allow your shoulders to be caught in draughts.'

'Draughts. My dear girl. Have you not yet experienced the winds that blow across the Tay?'

'Uniform body heat, Mrs Dryden, twenty-four hours a day, and I should like you to pay attention to your diet.'

Mrs Dryden looked down at her solid, well-fed body in its tight casing of corsets. 'I have the best of everything, I assure you, doctor.'

'There is some . . . speculation . . . that the best of everything may not be good for us. I have read some interesting studies. Would you, perhaps, agree to monitoring your diet with particular reference to what and how much you eat and drink on days when your aches and pains are particularly severe?'

Mrs Dryden looked sceptical.

'I have heard that potatoes cause distress in some patients, while watercress and even parsley alleviate the condition.'

Mrs Dryden pulled on her gloves and rose to her dignified feet. 'I am to be a medical experiment then, doctor?'

Lucy felt flustered. Should she just have prescribed some drugs which would certainly ease the pain? 'I'm sorry, Mrs Dryden . . .' she began.

'Not at all, my dear. I am flattered and will send my coachman for a ruled notebook this very instant. Before the month is out, every matron with an aching back will be competing with me to find what triggers our pain.' The old eyes twinkled. 'I should be most unhappy if I should find that my dinner glass of claret affects me adversely.'

Lucy would not be drawn. Medical science might speculate that gout was caused by over-indulgence, but she would not insult this delightful old lady by comparing gout and arthritis, which surely were unconnected in any way.

'Well, Colin was right,' said Mrs Dryden. 'You are going to do very well in Dundee, Doctor Graham. I hope you will join us for luncheon some Sunday? My husband's nephew comes to us on Sundays. He's like my own son, and he admires you very greatly.'

To her dismay, Lucy found herself blushing. She had had dinner twice with Mrs Dryden's nephew and had found him a pleasant companion, no more.

'I'll see you out, Mrs Dryden,' she said, 'and I will come to luncheon one Sunday soon.' She rang the bell and Isa appeared. 'Show Mrs Dryden out, Mrs Murray.'

Isa opened the door for Mrs Dryden and returned a few minutes later with the second caller.

'Miss Bell, Doctor.'

Miss Bell was a tall, slim woman who looked as if she might be forty years of age. In fact, she was not quite thirty.

'I'm just that tired, doctor,' she said in answer to Lucy's first question. 'Perhaps you know of some new tonic?'

'I might, but first I have to find out why you are so tired, Miss Bell.'

Heather Bell – her parents had thought that a romantic name – was a dressmaker at Draffens, the big department store on the High Street. She lived with her elderly parents who were able to do very little for themselves. After working a full day in the shop she went home to cook and clean and nurse the old people and, if there was any spare time, she earned a little extra by taking sewing home with her. No wonder she was tired.

'My father had the tuberculosis, doctor, and he was in the fever hospital.'

'King's Cross?'

'Yes, but he's cured, doctor. We thought them as went into King's Cross never came out, and I'm sure it was the worry of that that brought my mother down so low. Her mind's gone, doctor, but Father is fine, well as fine as anybody can be who's had the tuberculosis. Wonderful doctors there, and nurses too, most of them, that is.'

'They do sterling work, Miss Bell, and . . .' Lucy had a feeling that Miss Bell herself was terrified that she too would be sent one day to the fever hospital, and set herself to ease the woman's mind. 'You know that all nurses who work in hospitals have to be properly trained now. The standard in

Dundee is first class. But I think, before we do anything else, that I should examine you, and perhaps do a blood test.'

'I can't be ill, doctor, else who would look efter meh fowk.' The broad Dundee dialect fell out by mistake and Miss Bell pushed it back soundly, thinking wrongly that this fine doctor with the high-faluting accent could not possibly understand her. 'Just a tonic, doctor, if you'll be so good.'

'Let's have a look first,' suggested Lucy and showed her patient to the screen behind which she could modestly shed her outer garments.

Without blood tests she could not be sure, but she was almost positive that exhaustion and worry were her patient's ailments. Worry she could not do much about. Exhaustion? Rest should cure that, if she could persuade Heather Bell to rest.

'Have you any other relatives who would help you with the care of your parents, Miss Bell, if I was able to arrange a little rest for you?'

'A rest?'

'There is a new hospital for women in Dundee. It has just opened and I might be able to get you . . .'

Heather Bell had jumped from the chair in alarm. 'You dinnae understand, Doctor. I need tae work and I need tae look after the old folk. There's nobody. I have a sister, but she's tied down with six bairns and forbye she lives up the Hilltown – and my brithers, they're dead.'

In the years to follow Lucy was to hear that terrible story again and again: a surviving unmarried daughter, or son, bravely caring for elderly parents in the face of appalling poverty and want. Even Mhairi Johnston, with her several small charges to care for twenty-four hours a day, had good food and a warm bed and surely a little rest when the children slept.

'I'll mix you up a tonic, Miss Bell, but I will approach the hospital authorities to see if there is a chance for even a week's rest for you.'

'I couldnae stop the weekend, doctor. I'll take the tonic and I'll thank you for your concern, but I couldnae leave them. Mither wanders if you're no watching her, and if he's worrit he sterts coughing.'

Lucy rang her bell.

'Mrs Murray, will you give Miss Bell a cup of tea in the kitchen while I make her up some medicine?'

Later, when the woman clutching her bottle of medicine had gone off to wait for a tram, Lucy stared into the garden and went over and over her day's work. One woman who could afford everything that would help her deal effectively with her medical condition, and one who could not and who would probably drop dead from exhaustion. A welfare service that would help the poor was necessary. But was that something for the politicians? Anyway, she would try to help both women. She would go to the Women's Hospital to see if there was a bed for poor, tired, undernourished Heather Bell. She could not, however, force her to get into it. What to do with the aged parents was the problem.

Doctor Graham, however, had miscalculated the strength of comradeship among the poor.

Two nights later Lucy was discussing with Donald Murray the future, if there was indeed to be a future, of several venerable apple trees along the back wall of her property.

'I wouldnae like tae mislead you, doctor, but I dinnae really know onything about fruit. My gut tells me never tae take doon a tree though. I think there's probably some pruning and maybe even some mulching as would help it. I seem to mind on my faither steeping sheep's dung in water and pitting that on his fruit trees. Gin it's right wi' you, I'll cut the affected bits off these trees and see what happens and, in the meantime, I'll ask them as kens more.'

'Good idea, Donald,' agreed Lucy, who was a great believer in asking information of those who knew more.

'Sorry to disturb you, Doctor Graham.' Isa had come out without their being aware of it, so engrossed were they in the fate of the trees. 'There's a person to see you, doctor. I've left her on the step.'

Lucy looked at her in some surprise. Usually Isa showed visitors into one of the waiting rooms, but this 'person' was obviously so disreputable that she had deemed it better to leave her outside the very door of the house.

'I hope she's not ill, Isa.'

'Not unless light fingers is a disease, doctor. She looks no better than she should, and I told her if she had to see you she could wait till I found if you were available. She's probably gone by now.'

Lucy was annoyed with her maid's officiousness. 'I sincerely hope not, Isa. This house is open to everyone. Bring her into the morning room and I'll see her there. Go ahead and do what you think best with the trees, Donald,' she said and hurried back into the house.

In a few minutes an unrepentant Isa was showing in a type of woman with whom her employer was only too familiar.

'How sheltered does Isa believe medical training to be?' thought Lucy with an inward laugh and went forward to put her frightened caller – for she was very frightened – at ease.

'Do sit down, Mrs . . .' she began.

'It's miss, miss. I mean I'm Miss Nesbitt, doctor. I'm fine, doctor, not ill. I've come about pair wee Heather. She telt her sister whae telt me, us being on the same stair.'

Lucy looked at her in bewilderment for a moment. Never would she have considered that there might be a social connection between a woman like Heather Bell and the sorry woman who stood before her now. Miss Bell was obviously from the working class, but in every way she was superior to this Miss Nesbitt.

'Miss Bell?' she asked.

'Aye, and I can see hoo you're wonderin' how me and Heather even kens one another. It's men, doctor, men that's the ruin o' us all. Janet's Heather's wee sister, and she lives up meh stair. Her man's useless. Never worked a day in his life, but he's that bonnie Janet fell for him, mair fool her. Onyway. E'll look after them, the auld ones, while Heather has a bit rest.' She lifted up a sad face and looked the doctor directly in the eye. 'You can tell my life history, I've nae doubt, doctor, but I'm clean in my person and in my cooking. I've had my lumps, same as everybody, but I have time tae help my neighbour if she'll let me.' The speech had obviously exhausted as much control over her nerves as Miss Nesbitt had, and she began to shake and Lucy was stirred with compassion. The woman's body and dress were, indeed, relatively clean. Neither met her standards and they obviously offended Isa's but they were respectable.

'If you can persuade Miss Bell to take up your offer, Miss Nesbitt, I will do my best to see that she has a place in the hospital. You are very kind.'

146

The woman blushed but she was in control again. 'Oh, we all help wir neighbours up the Hilltown. They'd do the same for me.'

When she had gone, Lucy went back to the garden and Elsie Nesbitt walked back up the town with a light step. What a lot she would have to tell Rosie! It had taken great courage to go to see the aristocratic young lady doctor in her beautiful house at the West End, not an area of Dundee that Elsie was in the habit of frequenting. She was walking to save the tram fare, but suddenly she decided to splurge. She went into a café and bought a buster, that delicious supper of peas and chipped potatoes that the Dundonians loved. As she walked along eating her chips, there was a new spring in her step. She had actually seen the new lady doctor, had sat down in the same room with her and they had talked. One day, at last she believed that it was possible. One day soon, Rosie would be just like her. She wouldn't talk so posh, but she'd be far prettier; they didn't come much prettier than Rosie. And would she have a maid, a frozen-faced woman like that Mrs Murray who had looked down her nose at Elsie Nesbitt? You bet she would. But her mother wouldn't see it.

'I'll never embarrass you, Rosie, love, not in places like that. Now I've seen it, I'll keep it in my mind and picture you in a gown like that, sitting in a chair like that, having old sour-face and everybody else call you doctor.'

Elsie felt good. Might as well earn a few bob since she was all dressed up and nowhere to go. She thought for a minute, finished her buster, and turned off the main street into one of the narrow streets that laced themselves like a spider-web behind the smart face of the town.

8

Dundee, 1897

'YOU MUST COME. Just think. A stately home, well almost, but more importantly, Rosie, glorious free food and lots of it.'

Rose Nesbitt had long ago trained her stomach not to expect too much food; she remained unimpressed. 'There's too much work to do.' She gestured towards the pile of books beside her under the tree.

Mary Black arched her back in an almost wanton gesture and held up her pale face to the sun. 'There will always be too much work to do. That's the profession we've chosen.' She sagged back against the trunk of the tree. 'Rosie, there's a man, an older man, just the way you like them.'

'Harmless,' laughed Rosie. 'In his dotage?'

'Gorgeous.'

Rose sighed. She was not interested in men; the only two she had ever liked were Frazer and old Wishy. She never stopped to analyse that she liked them because she felt completely safe with them. Frazer was her brother, and as for old Wishy? He was far too old for any of *that* nonsense. 'Who is this Kier Anderson-Howard?' she asked. 'Already I don't like him.'

'You don't like his name. It's the little hyphen that bothers you.'

'Utter pretension. He should be Anderson or Howard; not both.'

'Don't fight with me, Rosie,' laughed Mary. 'It has something to do with money. Either an Anderson or Howard heiress wouldn't marry unless they got to keep their name.'

'Then I shall marry him,' joked Rosie, 'and insist that Nesbitt be added too. Anderson-Howard-Nesbitt. Nesbitt-Anderson-Howard.' She played with the variations and then, serious again, asked, 'But why are they dispensing largesse to the women students?'

'His parents are rolling in money, absolutely amazingly rich, and his mother is on the board or something like that. They wanted to have annual garden parties but he got wounded or something; he's a soldier, or was. Now he's on the mend.'

'I've never met a soldier.'

'Then you'll come?'

But Rosie would not be drawn. Graduation with her first degree and matriculation into the medical faculty was so close, so very close that sometimes she woke from an exhausted sleep terrified that the struggle of the past ten years was all a nightmare and that she was not a student at the world-famous University of St Andrews but Rosie Nesbitt, mill-worker.

As usual Ma was waiting at the station to walk up the road with her, to share the load of books.

'Maybe somebody'll think I can read them,' she had joked and Rosie had laughed with her, but had understood that her mother really would like to have been able to read and understand the material in the heavy old volumes.

'And what did you learn the day, hen?'

'I had only one lecture today, Ma. Mary and I sat under a tree and studied.'

'Aye, you look the better for a wee bit sun. I bet Mary does tae. Awfie pasty-faced, that lassie.'

'She invited me to a party.'

'What like party could Mary Brown have?'

'Well, it's not her exactly, but she lives in, remember, and she hears everything that's going on. Seemingly some rich family near the town is giving a party for this graduating class.'

Elsie knew better than to say outright that Rosie should attend the party. That would make her daughter think of a dozen suitable excuses not to go.

'In their hoos, Rosie, a grand hoos. My, would I love to be invited to a grand hoos.'

'I don't really have much time for parties, Ma.' Rosie was weakening. 'There is so little time left before my finals. Besides, I have nothing to wear. I can hardly go in my gown.'

The red gown had saved the pride of many a St Andrews student through the years. Costly garments and the threadbare were equally hidden by the thick red wool.

Wisely Elsie said no more, but next afternoon she went up and down the Hilltown, stopping first at Gallagher's.

Gallagher was usually happy to have the attentions of someone reasonably clean. 'I've no the notion, Elsie, but I'll be bursting for it the nicht.'

'I'm needing money noo, Sandy.'

'One o' the bairns?'

'Aye.'

'Get yoursel' spayed, Elsie,' said the big man, reaching into his till. 'I'll want full value for that, after closing time.'

Closing time. She was too old to stay awake till the small hours. Clutching the coins, Elsie went out. If she could find what she needed, then she could sleep all afternoon and thus be ready to fulfil her part of the bargain.

She was at the station when the train from Leuchars pulled in but said nothing about her purchases. It was only after Rosie had eaten the simple supper of skirlie and mashed potatoes that she brought them into the front room.

'Look what I found up the Hilltown,' she said as she saw her daughter put the heavy books on the table when the meal had been cleared away. 'I thought you might like it for your graduation.' She did not add that the second-or-was-it-third-hand dress would be perfect for a party in a grand house.

Rosie's heart sank. She had innate good taste and everything in her told her that the dress was a disaster. At least it was not a flamboyant red; it was a demi-mourning gown, a lilac silk dress worn by the respectable in that period when good manners decreed that they might leave off their blacks but not return to flattering colour.

'It's a wee bit big and the colour's no' your best, but there's only the one darn in it, Rosie. Heather Bell would take it in for you. The material's bonny.'

And it was. It was pure silk and the feel of it as it caught in her rough hands was sensuous.

'Real silk,' breathed Rosie as she gently laid it aside. 'It's lovely, Ma.' She did not add that the dress was more suitable for her mother's age than her own, and she did not waste time wishing she had skill with a needle for she would certainly not bother her mother's friend Heather. Heather spent six days a week sewing. Leave her her evenings. Rose Nesbitt herself had always been too busy acquiring knowledge to acquire any domestic skills and, goodness knows, Ma had learned few of the arts that turn the simplest house into a welcoming home or a too-big dress into something suitable for a first party. She would go to the party, for it was only too obvious that Elsie needed the second-hand pleasure of hearing about a grand 'hoos'. Anyway, what did it matter? There would be no one at the party whose opinion Rosie valued.

Charabancs were hired to convey the parties of students to Laverock Rising, the house where the party was to be held. It was a fine summer day and the clouds that had hung threateningly over St Andrews all morning obligingly lifted to allow a rather weak sun to warm their spirits. Rosie was small and, pressed into the third row of seats facing the driver's broad green back, she saw very little of the Fife countryside and did not really care to sway so high above the ground. The carriages had stopped before the imposing Georgian front of the house before she was aware that they had reached their destination.

She stood on the gravel carriage sweep, her too-big hat slightly tipped over one eye by the proximity and exuberance of her companions, looking bewildered and, to Kier Anderson-Howard, totally adorable. Every protective instinct, long buried, came rushing to the surface and he hurried over to her as she stood, almost swaying, too close to the hind quarters of the rear horses.

'Stupid brutes, horses,' he said in the voice of one who loved them and accepted all their little foibles. 'They get very nervous when they feel something at their ... back ends.' He took her arm and quite naturally she clung to it for a moment as the world righted itself.

'I'm sorry,' she said in a soft voice. 'I'm not used to charabancs.'

'They do swing about a bit, don't they? Kier Anderson-Howard,' he introduced himself. 'May I get you some lemonade ... and you too, of course,' he smiled at Mary who had materialized behind Rosie.

'Mary Black,' said Mary. 'My friend is Miss Nesbitt, Rose Nesbitt.'

'Rose,' he said. 'Of course.'

'He's taken with you, Rosie,' said Mary as their host went off to fetch the lemonade. 'You've landed the biggest fish.'

Rosie shuddered in distaste. For someone who had grown up in a home owned and occupied by her family, Mary was sometimes amazingly coarse.

'You should have told him your name, Rosie,' said Mary. 'You don't mind my saying, do you, but when someone introduces themselves, you tell them your name.'

'Perhaps I didn't want him to know it,' lied Rosie. Mary smiled. 'You are clever,' she breathed and turned to their returned host. 'Oh, this is lovely,' she said. 'Isn't it, Rosie?'

Rose sipped from the glass and, completely unaware of the power of her eyes, looked at Kier over the brim. 'Thank you,' she said. 'I feel better now.'

'May I show you the gardens, Miss Nesbitt, and you too, Miss Black? I believe my mother is on the front lawn, and tea will be there later. I hope you'll feel like a little something.' He smiled down at Rosie. 'Mother's cook has been baking for days. She is so excited by the thought of all you wonderfully well-educated young women. What are you planning to do with your degree, Miss Nesbitt?'

As Rosie had dared to take a second sip from her glass just as he spoke, she was unable to answer and Mary spoke for them both.

'We're going to be doctors.'

Kier stopped walking. 'By all that's wonderful,' he said. 'Doctors! My best friend is a doctor. Jenny,' he called to a hurrying maidservant, 'has Doctor Graham arrived yet?'

'Doctor'll be later, Mister Kier. There's been an emergency.'

'You see the life you've chosen, ladies. Every minute at the beck and call of your profession.'

He led them to a garden seat and solicitously helped Rosie to sit down. He looked down at her with regret. How he wished she would raise those eyes to him again. Every atom of his being asked him to stay with her and to protect her. She was so small, so vulnerable; her frailty, and the colour and style of the too-big dress suggested that she was in mourning, for a father perhaps. Her voice, with the broad Scots words aching to get out, told him her social class. 'And yet, she's struggling to become a doctor,' he thought to himself in admiration.

'I'm afraid I must greet some of our other guests,' he told the girls, 'but I'll certainly look out for you both later. You must meet Doctor Graham.'

'We've landed on our feet here, Rosie,' said Mary as they watched the elegant figure move away. 'The son of the house for you, and it looks like a man for me as well.'

'A doctor in his dotage, Mary? You must be desperate.'

'He's not that old: must be early thirties. And just think how useful a fully qualified doctor could be.'

Rosie frowned. That thought had entered her head. She pushed it away. 'Come on, Mary. We're doing this all by ourselves. Rights for women: votes for women.' She stood up. 'Some tea on the lawn, Doctor Black?'

Mary laughed. 'How too, too thrilling, dear Doctor Nesbitt.'

* * *

Kier spent the next hour being the perfect host and neither his parents nor any of their excited guests realized that his mind was firmly fixed on a small figure smelling faintly of mothballs. Rose's nose was so full of the smells of the closie and of the jute-filled air of Dundee that she had not noticed the slight odour hanging on her gown.

'Either she is so poor that she had to buy the dress second-hand for her mourning period,' thought Kier, 'or she has been given it by some kindly neighbour.' Never could he have guessed that it had been bought with the sole aim of dazzling him, although poor Elsie had not known for sure but had only hoped that he might exist.

He looked for Rosie as soon as manners decently allowed. She was in the middle and yet somehow slightly apart from a large group of her fellow students, and he had time to admire her small profile. 'She's like a bird,' he thought and looked down at his hands. 'I could circle her waist with these. How can she ever withstand the rigours of medical school . . . the horrors of the wards?'

'Miss Nesbitt.' He drew her aside. 'Doctor Graham has not yet arrived but I should like to introduce you to my parents – and you too, of course, Miss Black.'

Mary at least went with him willingly enough, although Rosie would have preferred to stay safely on the lawn admiring the trees and the beautifully laid-out and well-stocked flower gardens. She had learned Latin and Greek and Mathematics and for the last three years she had read great literature and history, but no one had ever told her how to speak to someone who owned a house like this one, a house bigger by far than the entire closie where several families lived. Rosie had got into the habit of holding herself slightly apart, listening and saying little and trying,

trying hard to learn, stumbling sometimes as she struggled to develop taste. She could argue that such small matters were of little value, and of no value at all to a doctor who was going to work with the poor who would know no better than she, but, she realized as she walked by Kier Anderson-Howard's side on his family's immaculately cared for lawn, she wanted to feel at ease here, she wanted to belong. She held her chin up and straightened her spine and so, when she met Kier's parents, she did not look frail and helpless but hard and belligerent.

'How do you do, Miss Nesbitt, Miss Black.'

'How do you do, Mrs Anderson-Howard,' said Mary. 'How very kind of you to have us here.'

Rosie was tongue-tied. 'How do you do' sounded stupid – was that really what you were supposed to reply? – and she could think of nothing to say at all. She watched the easy and perhaps too familiar way in which Mary chatted to Kier's parents and she desperately tried to unlock her jaws. She walked with them to the huge marquee for tea, and here was another insurmountable problem. How do you eat a sandwich and hold a cup and saucer at the same time? She clung to the saucer and prayed that she would not drop it; only once before had she held such fine china. She could not believe that this was what they used in the garden. Rosie was not enjoying her first garden party.

And then she felt Kier stiffen beside her. She looked up at him, saw his eyes shining with joy and turned to see what he was seeing. A small dog-cart was being expertly wheeled in through the gates, and driving the horse was a woman in an incredibly smart bottle-green riding coat. She handed the reins to a groom who had hurried to her and stepped down from the cart. She chatted, laughing, to the groom for a moment and then she picked up her skirt over her arm and hurried towards them. Kier left Rosie and went to meet her and when he reached her he kissed her on the cheek, the gesture of one who had done the same thing a hundred times before. 'Oh, for such serenity,' thought Rose, 'for such ease.'

'Lucy, darling.' Kier's parents had gone forward too to greet the latecomer.

'Miss Nesbitt, Miss Black,' said Kier grandly as one does who is presenting a trophy, 'may I introduce Doctor Graham? Lucy, darling, you will never guess. The first two of our guests I met are medical students.'

There it was again, that odd response. 'How do you do?' This time Rosie was ready. 'How do you do, Doctor Graham,' she said and for the second time in her life was aware of the difference between the hardworking hands of the poor and the hardworked hands of the rich. Dr Graham's hands were beautifully shaped, long and slim and capable, but they were white and soft and the nails, cut short and blunt, were polished. Rosie almost snatched back her rough red hands with the bitten nails. 'Whatever else I have to do without I shall have that glycerine ointment for my hands, and this time I promise that I shall never bite my nails again,' she vowed as the conversation went on around her, Mary gamely holding up Rosie's side as well as her own.

Eventually Kier remembered his duties as a host and, with a look at Rosie that was almost regretful, he took Dr Graham's arm and steered her towards the tea tent.

'You are staying for dinner, Lucy?' Rosie heard him say.

'I'm spoiling myself and staying until Monday,' Dr Graham answered and then, before they drifted too far away for even Rosie's keen hearing she continued, 'Which one of us terrified your young friend, Kier? I do hope it was you and not me.'

Rosie felt herself blushing but no one else seemed to have heard. The Anderson-Howards excused themselves and went off to greet others and Rosie and Mary were left alone.

'I should have known the Doctor Graham was *the* Doctor Graham,' said Mary.

'Why the emphasis?'

'Rosie, where do you hide yourself? Doctor Graham is not only one of the first female doctors in the entire country but she is the only one in Dundee. She has a society practice at the West End. Could be very useful to an up-and-coming Dundonian doctor.'

Rose had heard once before of Doctor Graham but she had forgotten until today. Ma had said she was the one who got poor Heather into the women's hospital. Imagine Heather having the nerve to go to see a woman like that! Still, it proved what she had thought all along. Women needed women doctors. Heather would never have gone to a man to ask for a tonic. Now it suited Rose to ignore the poorer part of Doctor Graham's practice.

'I have no intention of working with the rich, Mary. I want to have a practice in my own street, right up the Hilltown among the tenements.'

Mary looked at her in amazement. 'You are incredibly naïve, Rose Nesbitt. Be so kind as to tell me how you are going to afford it.'

'Something will turn up. It always does if you work hard enough, and besides things will change. Perhaps the government will help with the medical care of the poor.'

'You shouldn't be out without your keeper. Thank God I am here to look after you. The son of the house is obviously smitten . . .'

'He's in love with Doctor Graham,' interrupted Rose.

'Maybe, but I don't think he knows how much; he's got used to loving her, and she treats him the way I treat my wee brother, hardly lover-like. The "daaalings" all over the place from the toffs don't mean a damn thing. What you should be thinking about, Rosie, is making sure that neither he nor Doctor Graham forget you're around.'

'I can't make friends with someone just so they'll be useful to me.'

'Rosie, you are a marvel; you've worked so hard against all the odds. You should be in a jute-mill, girl, not a world-famous university. Now you're a guest in the home of someone who obviously likes you and who has a friend who just happens to be the only female doctor in the entire area. You'd be mad not to encourage him and her to help you.'

'I've got this far on my own,' began Rosie and then realized that that was not true. There were the sacrifices of Frazer, Frazer who might have been able to marry, to become a father even, had he not given everything he earned to her; Wishy, who had spent hours coaching her; Elsie, who had somehow earned this dress. No, it was not tailored to fit like the green silk Dr Lucille Graham had been wearing, but it was beautiful, beautiful.

'Mr Anderson-hyphen-Howard won't give the likes of me another thought, Mary. Come on. It's almost time for the charabancs and I want to get a better seat this time.'

To give him his due, Kier did not forget Rose. Her pale face swam before his mind's eye quite often and he found more and more reasons for going into St Andrews, business that seemed quite often to take him near the university. He even went more often to Dundee for, when he had been able to prise a word out of the girl, she had told him she was a Dundonian. Kier, however, had not taken into consideration that a girl like Rosie would have to work during the long summer holiday, and he did not look for her in the Angus berry fields which is where she could easily have been found.

Lucy Graham did not immediately forget the frightened young girl in the ghastly dress either. She had ambivalent feelings about her. The child had been terrified and Lucy always felt sorry for things smaller and less able than herself, but Kier had been unable to hide his interest in the girl. He had talked of nothing but her courage and ability and ambition, until not only Lucy but Kier's parents were heartily sick of the sound of her.

'I have such a stupid prejudice against flower names for girls,' confessed Mrs Anderson-Howard when she and Lucy were having a quiet chat together in Kier's mother's own little sitting room, 'and besides, she looked to be a really aggressive young woman.'

'No, Auntie, she was terrified, totally out of her depth. Try to look at the afternoon from her point of view.'

'How like you and Kier to look out for the wounded of this world. Those girls will never make doctors, never. The blonde one couldn't even speak. And there's my silly son gazing at her as if he had found the holy grail.'

So Kier's mother had noticed it too. Well, the afternoon was over and the girl was gone and no doubt they would never see her again.

'If I had not had all my advantages, perhaps I would be rather like Rosie Nesbitt, or, more likely, I would have given up long ago.'

'Given up and married my son! You still can. We really do want grandchildren while we're still young enough, Lucy. Hasn't Kier asked you lately? Has he got out of the habit?'

'Am I a habit with him? Sometimes I think so, and when I see him looking at someone so young and so lovely . . .'

'Lovely? Lucy, you must be blind, my dear. That dress . . . and the smell . . .'

'That's poverty, Auntie. And Kier saw past it and saw the beauty of her face. He's never really been aware of clothes anyway.'

'Just like his father, my dear. They notice when their horses need new saddles, but I think their womenfolk could walk around in rags and they'd mutter charming, charming, which is all Archie ever seems to say about anything . . . But tell me, Lucy, how would a girl like Miss Nesbitt get into medical school?'

'Brains and hard work and determination and vocation, and endless sacrifices from many people. Exactly the way I did it myself, and every other female doctor, except that I had money to oil the wheels.'

'Oh, Lucy dear, your family was not wealthy.'

'To people like the Nesbitts of the world, Auntie, I must appear to be fabulously wealthy. Rose Nesbitt is a remarkable young woman and I wish her well.'

Mrs Anderson-Howard rose from her chaise longue as the dressing bell went. 'Go and make yourself beautiful, my dear. If you want him to, Kier will forget all about Miss Nesbitt.'

In her room Lucy slowly undressed and, for the first time in years, critically examined herself in the mirror. Too tall; Rosie Nesbitt was small and dainty. Too thin; Miss Nesbitt was thin too, but her body curved seductively in all the right places. Lucy did not admire her clear, guileless eyes or her firm, straight nose; she saw a cloud of yellow curls framing a pretty little face and eyes that glared at everyone but Kier.

I should have married him when he came back from Africa but no, no, I couldn't. There was poor Mrs Dryden so ill, and Donald's relapse.

Lucy had received two proposals of marriage within a month of the wounded Kier's return: one from Kier himself. *A habit, a habit,* her brain told her. The second was from Colin Dryden. *Gratitude for the way I looked after his aunt.* She had almost said 'Yes' to both proposals, and as she looked at herself in the mirror Lucy wondered why.

Is it because I am only too aware of the toll that time takes on the female body? Did I merely want a husband? Did I want children? Am I right to wait until one day I find I do not have to ask myself questions about my feelings? Is Auntie right? Can I make Kier forget the lovely little Nesbitt?

Thirty minutes later a sophisticated, elegant woman walked into the drawing room and instinctively responded to the admiration in the eyes of the men there. Not one of them could guess at the turmoil in her heart.

9

St Andrews, 1899

MRS ANDERSON-HOWARD WAS quite right: Mary Black never became a doctor. She never returned to St Andrews University, and Rosie had almost forgotten her by the time she learned much later that Mary had died of consumption. It wasn't that Rosie, by now trying hard to drop the diminutive and to be known as Rose, easily dismissed from her heart all those who had been her friends, but that the goal she had set herself was always to the forefront of her mind.

In 1898, at the age of nineteen, she had graduated with honours in Arts. She had looked down from the podium with her parchment in her hand and seen Elsie crying so hard with love and pride that the tears running down her old face were bringing with them the ghastly make-up that she had worn 'tae look ma best for ye, hen'.

'I've done it, Ma.' She sent the message silently down to the clown face. 'No, we've done it together, you and me and Frazer and old Wishy. A shame they didn't live to see this day.'

And now nothing and no one would be allowed to interfere with her ambitions. She was going to be a doctor, and none of these super-sarcastic male students who thronged the lecture rooms at St Andrews University and who enjoyed baiting the female students would be allowed to bother her hard-won serenity. Because Rosie was a street fighter, and when she walked into a room and found herself the butt of jokes and the object of cat-calls, her first impulse was to scream and kick, just as she had done on the streets of Dundee in her early childhood. From the age of ten when she had first walked all the way to the centre of Dundee to attend the Harris Academy, she had schooled herself and she had learned to appear to ignore the disparaging remarks of wealthier girls, and now she was able to appear unaware of the frightened malice of her fellow students.

'That's all it is,' she assured more delicate women students. 'They're afraid of us and so they say we are unfeminine. We will show them, ladies, that not only are we very feminine, but that we are also very, very clever, and we will win all the prizes.'

The first prize Rose won, she was not allowed to have, and its winning and subsequent non-award brought her to the attention of several of the professors including Sir James Donaldson, the principal of the University, and earned her admiration and respect.

There was a bursary of one hundred pounds per annum for two years. Rosie took the examination and won. She was elated: one hundred pounds each year for two years! Properly invested with a little interest added, and she could sail through medical school with nothing to worry about but passing exams, and she had never had to worry about *that*.

One hundred pounds! Rose and Elsie walked up from the station and made shopping lists as they passed the shops. What could you not buy for one hundred pounds?

'I cannae see that much siller in my mind, Rosie,' said Elsie. 'You could eat meat every day o'the week, twice on a Sunday if ye want to. You could have silk underwear. Look at those knickers. You could hae a clean pair every day fer a month. And look at that suite. Whit do ye think the neighbours would say if we took that posh furniture up the Hilltown? Goodness, you could get on a train and go ...' Elsie was at a loss. Where could one hundred pounds take her? She herself had only ever been to St Andrews and that had been an adventure. '. . . farther than London,' she finished off, not even sure that there *was* anywhere farther than London.

'It's going in a bank, Ma,' said Rose, ending the insubstantial dreams of silk underwear or upholstered furniture.

'A bank?' Elsie looked at her daughter in awe.

'If I open a bank account, Ma, the money will be safe and it will earn interest. I'll have all I need for textbooks, instruments, even some new knickers when I need them, but not silk,' said the practical Rose.

The grand plans went for nothing though because it seemed that it would take practically an Act of Parliament to award the bursary to a woman. When it had been set up, universities were not open to women, and the wording of the long legal document that talked about the awarding of such a magnificent sum showed that the money had been intended to benefit a poor *man*.

'You do understand, Miss Nesbitt; the grant was set up in a time when there was no thought that women would breach these portals.' (Was there a hint there that he too, sitting so comfortably in his silk gown, would prefer not to think of mere women within his sacred walls? He would not fight for her.) 'We must needs see to the rewording of the documents but, unfortunately, and I mean this sincerely, it will not be in time to aid you. The grant this year must be awarded to a man.'

Rose could taste the disappointment in her mouth. It stayed with her for days and she never forgave the university authorities for the injustice. No matter that the wording was changed so that subsequent female winners could be awarded the prize. In good faith she had been encouraged to enter the bursary competition, and she had won. She should have had the prize.

But now she sat stoically and listened to explanation after explanation, and not one of the council knew of the turmoil inside.

They stood up and so did she. The interview was at an end.

'Thank you, gentlemen,' she said quietly and they watched her leave the room, her small head held high.

Out in the street she wanted to run; she wanted to cry. But she would do neither of these things. She walked and walked and found herself miles along the beach. Then she turned around to see St Andrews.

'How could they do that to me?' she asked the great towers. She could almost hear Elsie. 'What ye've niver had, ye'll niver miss.'

'Oh, I'll miss it, Ma, but you're the only person who'll hear me moan.'

She went back into the town, for it wouldn't do to miss the train home.

'God does not make life easy fir the working classes, does he, lassie,' was all Elsie said, visions of silk knickers disappearing for ever.

'They're giving me thirty pounds a year for two years instead, Ma. That's an extra ten pounds.'

'Jist don't let it be a moneyed laddie that gets your bursary,' moaned Elsie.

'Come on, Ma. What you've . . .'

'. . . niver had, you'll niver miss,' finished Elsie obligingly but without her usual smile. 'God, lassie, do you no care? I'd be wantin' tae tear their hair oot.'

'I'll not give anyone the satisfaction of knowing what I feel, Ma. That's my revenge.'

She almost added, 'It always worked at the Harris,' but managed to stop the words. It would only hurt Elsie to be told that her daughter's poverty had been the object of ridicule. She remembered the dominie at her primary school: a nice, kind man who had been delighted that she was to attend the Harris Academy.

'My Niece Edith is a pupil there, Rosie. She's in the third year. Introduce yourself and she'll take care of you.'

Rose had promised to do so and had plucked up courage one day. She could still hear her quavering voice as she managed to force herself to approach the well-groomed young ladies with their beautiful ribbons in their shining hair.

'Are you Edith Morrison?' she had asked one tall, blonde, haughty beauty.

'No, I'm Queen Alexandra,' the girl had laughed and she and her friends had gone into paroxysms of mirth as Rose walked away, scarlet with embarrassment.

'No, keep your feelings to yourself, Rose,' she had told herself then and she told herself now. She took out her notebook and set herself to reading and memorizing the notes she had made on intermittent claudication. There was no point in worrying over injustice, she could do nothing about that, but she could help to eradicate disease.

She stayed later and later every night and often did not eat before going to the library from the lecture rooms. Elsie met her every night in whatever weather and walked with her from the station. Rosie found soup being kept warm on the fire, and for several years her diet consisted almost entirely of a bread roll in the morning and a bowl of soup at night, and tea, tea, and more tea.

Kier Anderson-Howard saw her one afternoon just before Christmas in her second year of medical school. Had it not been for the red gown that told the world her status, he would have thought that the slight little creature fighting against the wind on the way up Market Street was a child.

'Good heavens,' he thought delightedly, 'it's that young student. What was her name? Some flower, I seem to recall.' He began to hurry after her – he would not shout in the street to gain her attention – and when he caught up with her and her startled eyes looked up into his, he remembered. It could not be anything else.

'Rose,' he said and lifted his hat. 'I do beg your pardon, Miss . . . ah, Nesbitt, wasn't it?' and because she still looked puzzled or startled he added, 'Kier Anderson-Howard. We met at a garden-party.'

He saw recognition come into her eyes and then, well, he was not really a conceited man, but was it pleasure he saw there too?

The look, had it been there at all, was gone. 'Hello,' she said simply and moved as if to hurry on.

'Wait, Miss Nesbitt. Am I keeping you from some class?'

'No. I'm hurrying to get out of this wind.'

He laughed. Most of the girls of his acquaintance, except Lucy of course, would have been simpering up at him by this time.

'It is a cold one,' he agreed. 'Bringing snow, our shepherds say.'

She said nothing and he wished he hadn't said that. Obviously she wanted to go where she had been going when he stopped her.

'I'll walk with you if I may, Miss Nesbitt, steady you against this wind.'

She stopped then and laughed. 'But you don't know where I'm going.'

He laughed too. 'Oh, heavens, could be a lecture on the most unmentionable of subjects. I was hoping you were going to find a nice hot cup of tea.'

She blushed. Why on earth did she blush? Gosh, he'd done it again. Possibly she couldn't afford to eat in a restaurant. Could anyone be so poor that they could not afford a few shillings for a meal?

'I was,' he lied. He had been on his way to where his carriage waited. 'I was going to have tea; I'm starved. And it would be so pleasant to have some company. Would you join me, Miss Nesbitt, if you're not on your way to a lecture?'

Again he saw some battle in the beautiful eyes. 'I was going to the library, to read.' She blushed again.

How delightful. A woman who can still blush.

'I very rarely read in the library,' he said solemnly. 'Used to get into the most fearful trouble instead. There's a delightful hotel right here on the links, very respectable. Can you spare the time? My mother would love to hear how the first lady graduates are coming along.'

Mrs Anderson-Howard went to regular meetings to hear how the female students were surviving, but cheerfully Kier threw her into the fray. For some reason, he did not want to sever the tenuous connection with this young woman. Why? Why should he care what happened to Rose Nesbitt, who was so obviously from quite another world?

'I can spare the time,' Rose was saying.

'Wonderful,' he said. He tucked his hand under her elbow and fairly bowled her along to the majestic front of the hotel and up the broad stairs into a carpeted and lavishly furnished hall.

A hovering waiter gestured towards Rose's red gown.

'Madam's still a little chilly,' said Kier. 'Perhaps later. We'll have everything,' he added, 'and we'll have it here by the fire.'

The waiter bobbed his head and withdrew and Kier steered Rose, still in her red gown, to two plush seats beside the huge roaring fire. How quiet she was. Was she always quiet, or did he frighten her? Lucy had said that he had frightened her that long-ago summer day. What was it today here in the hotel? The waiter? The fire? Surely not the fire? Kier tried to imagine what it must be like to be cold and poor and to come into this luxury. 'But this is a bit shabby. It can't be the furniture. Is it the fire blazing merrily away in an empty room? Well, it's not empty now. We're here to enjoy it.' So his thoughts ran.

'Have you been shopping?' Rose asked, and he saw that she made an effort, that conversation was difficult for her. 'Christmas shopping, I mean.'

'Quite the reverse. I've been selling. Geese, you know, and hens. We supply one of the local poulterer's.' He tried to look as if he knew all there was to know about breeding poultry, that he had done more than merely agree to terms and sign his name on a piece of paper.

'I always believed . . .' She blushed again and he finished for her.

'That I was a soldier. I was.' His face darkened with sorrow. 'My father died. Fifty-two years old. Can you imagine? Never sick a day in his life, or so we thought, and then suddenly . . .'

'His heart?'

'No, they said it was a cancer. He was fine till the doctors started poking about. Seems it had been growing for some time . . . Ah, good, here's our tea.'

His face lightened. The waiter had put the heavy silver pots before Rose, who blushed again. Surely she knew she was supposed to pour? 'Shall I pour the first cups, Miss Nesbitt? That pot looks frightfully heavy.'

'Thank you,' she said quietly. 'It does look a big pot for two people.'

The hot tea and the warm scones dripping with butter made conversation easier. He was happy to see that she had a good appetite and he ate much more than he needed or wanted because he felt sure that if he stopped she would stop, and he had no idea when she would have her next meal.

'Are you in a residence, Miss Nesbitt?'

'No, I still live with my family in Dundee.'

'Gosh, that must make life a little difficult,' but she disagreed and made him laugh with her stories of running for the train and of the guard who had helped her until he found out that she was one of these dreadfully modern, unfeminine women who had more interest in the human body than a decent woman should have.

'You are a tonic, Miss Nesbitt,' he said finally when she had told him that now she really had to go because she would miss her train.

'Wait here. My horses are just round the corner and I'll drive you to the station.'

He hurried out of the hotel but he did not go straight to the waiting carriages. He sent the doorman for his phaeton and then ran back along Market Street to the poulterer where he bought back, at three times the price, a huge goose he had just arranged to sell that afternoon. Rose was waiting at the door, her red gown wrapped tightly around her. Again he felt that surge of protectiveness. He had never, ever experienced the feeling before and he liked it. Lucy had always protected and managed him; all the other girls, even Sally for whom he had really cared and who had married one of his classmates while he was in Africa, had mainly roused desire.

He kept to the other side of the street away from the lamps so that Rose would not see him and then he crossed the road and deposited the goose in the phaeton.

'Here we are,' he called to her. 'Your carriage awaits, madam.'

'I've never been in one of these,' said Rose, almost at ease with him.

'They're not really comfortable but they're fast. I shall certainly get you to the station in time.'

'I could walk to the station in time,' she said and he laughed.

He handed her into the phaeton. 'You are the most refreshing young woman, Miss Nesbitt.'

They waited four minutes for the train. He felt he could not let her go, could not let her just disappear again.

'Where do you live, Miss Nesbitt? Perhaps I could call some time, maybe during the holidays.' He thought swiftly. He dare not invite her to dinner. Whatever his mother thought about his ability to recognize anything other than the needs of his horses, he knew perfectly well that Rose's wardrobe was limited and he would not cause her embarrassment or distress. 'The theatre, perhaps; there are some fine productions in Dundee.'

'I . . . I have a job for the holidays. Here is my train.' He heard the relief in her voice. 'Thank you for the tea. It was lovely.'

'Another time, perhaps. I am often in St Andrews.'

She smiled at him then. She really had a lovely smile. He helped her climb into the train and then he ran back to the phaeton and lifted the goose.

'Here,' he said to the guard, handing the man the goose and a guinea.

'Well, thank you, sir,' said the man.

'Give the goose to the young lady who just got into the carriage. Say, "Merry Christmas from Kier". Go on, man. The train is about to leave.'

'Not without I tell it, yer honour,' laughed the guard, who had bitten the guinea to find that it really was the biggest tip he had ever had in his life.

Kier stepped back from the train and watched it pull out. He had a quick glimpse of Rose's startled face as the huge goose was put into her arms, and then she was swept away from him. He put out his hand as if to stop the train, for it had suddenly occurred to him that the goose was heavy and perhaps her home was miles from the station.

'What must she think of you, you idiot?' he scolded himself, but his heart was light as he bowled along the roads to Laverock Rising. It was only later that he realized that never once had she called him by his name.

Rose said his name over and over to herself in the train as she and her huge silent companion clattered over the new bridge across the Tay.

'Anderson-Howard, Anderson-Howard. Clickety-clack, Clickety-clack.'

Her second meal in a restaurant! She remembered how the long-dead Frazer had carefully counted out the pennies for the fish suppers in the rather dirty café. Kier Anderson-Howard had not even asked for the bill but had nonchalantly tossed a coin down on the table as he hurried for his phaeton – or really, as he hurried for the goose. She almost hugged the goose to stop it sliding off her small knees. What would Elsie say? How would they get it home and what would they do with it once they got it there?

She pictured her home and saw again in her mind Laverock Rising, the magnificent Georgian mansion in which Kier Anderson-Howard lived. She tried to picture the elegance of her afternoon's escort in the tiny rooms up the Hilltown. The image in her mind, the perfectly cut tweeds, the hand-made shoes, the open, friendly face would not transfer itself to the dingy tenement. Here Rose did Kier a disservice. Perhaps he did not expect her living conditions to be quite so poor as they were, but he did know a great deal about public housing, at least academically. Was he not on several committees that did practical work towards the alleviation of poverty?

Was she to say goodbye for ever to the chance of a friendship with Kier? Rose had enjoyed her afternoon. After her first cup of tea, as the blaze from the huge fire had warmed her chilled bones, she had relaxed. He was so friendly, so warm, had made her believe that he really was interested in her. She had talked and laughed with him as she had never talked with anyone in her life before, except perhaps Elsie, and with Elsie she had been unable to talk too seriously about her studies because, try as she might, Elsie did not understand. If she had enough courage to admit him further into her life ... but she did not want him, anyone, in her life, did she? There was no room for anything but study.

'A friend would be nice,' a little voice in her head teased.

'If I ever see him again, I'll ... well, I could agree to meet him at the theatre, say it was easier for me to go straight there from university. Why didn't I say that?' She saw herself arriving at the front of the theatre; she saw that look of ... what? pleasure, joy, light up Kier's face. How pleasant it was to see such a look.

The train pulled in and she forgot her lost chance when she saw the astonishment on Elsie's face.

'Whar the hell did ye get that?'

Rosie dropped the goose that she had clutched almost to her bosom all the way across the broad sweep of the Tay, and began to laugh, and Elsie lifted it up and began to laugh too as Rose tried to tell the story. She left out the effect that Kier had had on her and she left out the tentative invitation.

'We'll never get that up the Hilltown in one piece, lassie. It's bigger nor you and, onyway, I wouldnae ken where tae begin cooking it.'

They carried the goose between them to the nearest butcher where Elsie sold it for half what Kier had paid for it, plus a pound of best pork sausages – Rose's favourite food.

Despite the large tea she had consumed earlier, Rose was hungry by the time Elsie had the sausages spluttering and squeaking on the iron griddle over the fire. Rose raised her eyes from the book before her on the table and looked around the room. Last night, just last night, this room had looked cosy and friendly. Now she was seeing it with Kier Anderson-Howard's eyes and she did not like what she saw. The table was propped up with old papers to keep it steady, more as a convenience for Rose than for either of the other members of the by now small family. Donaldina, the only other one of the children who still lived at home, lay in exhausted sleep in a chair by the fire. She worked eight hours a day in a jute-mill and spent the time between coming home from work and going to bed dozing in that same chair.

Rose felt pity for her sister, too tired even to go out to dances with the other mill-girls.

'Look at her, night after night, Ma, lying there snoring.'

'Pair wean hasnae the strength for the mill, Rosie. The mills are like that fer some, juist working or sleeping.'

'That's no life.'

'Are they sausages ready, Ma? Ma belly thinks ma throat's been cut. You'll no mind me haein' a sausage, Your Majesty? It's my wages that bocht them.'

Rose almost recoiled from the venom in her sister's voice. Of course, it must look like that to Donaldina; it must look as if Rose contributed nothing to the family purse. She said nothing, but watched as the girl took a sausage from the griddle and blew on it before stuffing it into her mouth. Then she wiped the back of her hand across her face.

How often have I seen her do that? thought Rose. *And it's never really bothered me but if . . . if . . .* he *saw her. If he came here, what would he think of them and me?*

'I know you're hungry, but could you just wait a minute and I'll clear the table . . .'

'No, I cannae wait a bluidy minute, Lady Muck. Ma and me has our tea sittin' by the fire every night afore yer majesty gets hame.'

Rose said nothing. Every night that she could remember, Elsie had put a cloth on the table, and such dishes and cutlery as they had. She looked now and compared the cups with the one she had used that afternoon.

'Come on, lassies, we'll hae wir tea nice at the table. Come on, Donaldina, Rosie bought these sausages and we've ordered a chicken for Hogmanay. Think on it, the end of the century's coming.'

'So's my patience, Ma, if I dinnae get ma tea.'

Rose said nothing. She had lost her appetite. Oh, to be able to afford to live in Miss Lumsden's beautiful residence.

I like things to be nice, she thought, *and is that so wrong? I want us to live like civilized people, not like dogs.*

Again she contemplated the bottomless ravine that stretched between her and the young man she had had tea with that afternoon.

But he seems to like me. We have met twice and each time he has seemed to like me.

She forced such thoughts from her mind. There was only one thing in the whole world that was of any importance at all, and that was that she should continue with her studies. Men were a distraction she did not need and, besides, look where men had got Elsie.

There are men in the world like Frazer and old Wishy, her conscience told her, but she would not listen.

'I'm not hungry, Ma.' She smiled at Elsie. 'I'll go on with this.'

'What is it, hen?'

'Anatomy, Ma. Sort of, how we're put together.'

'You're that clever, lassie.' Satisfied, Elsie went off and sat beside Donaldina at the fire. Rose began to read but she was still conscious of them both sitting there and of the smell of the sausages. When in her life had she ever turned down the offer of a sausage? The words on the page danced in front of her eyes but she could not understand them for, unbidden, unwanted, *he* came into her mind. She did not realize how closely she had marked him. She saw again the way his hair just curled at the nape of his neck, the long fingers with the manicured fingernails. Oh, yes, they were manicured but they were not effeminate. His hands were strong. She pictured them holding the goose. She felt them holding her, caressing her. Her mind fled from the thought, from the feelings aroused.

Where on earth did the goose come from? she asked herself and she smiled and, somehow, the symbols on the pages became meaningful and she began to study and did not even notice when Elsie put a mug of hot tea on the table beside her hand.

10

Dundee, 1900–1905

THE EARLY YEARS of the century saw great changes in Rose Nesbitt's world and in the wider world around her. She moved to Dundee to finish her first degree and, instead of staying at home, she moved into lodgings nearer the university. She told herself, and Elsie, that it was to make running at all hours to the Dundee Royal Infirmary less of a burden on the family, especially Donaldina who certainly did not need to have her sleep disturbed. Had she not already once fallen asleep at her loom and almost lost her hand and her job?

Elsie seemed to accept her leaving with no apparent regrets, but still Rose found herself trying to justify the decision she had made. She told Elsie of the long hours spent visiting the sick.

'I'm studying midwifery and the diseases of women, Ma. There's this professor, a real smasher.' She decided to have a joke at her mother's expense. 'He had to get married.'

Elsie loved a bit of gossip and she heard constantly of people 'having' to get married. Rose laughed at her mother's expression.

'No, Ma. The university thought it unseemly that he, a bachelor, should be a specialist in women's troubles. We may be in the twentieth century, Ma, but in some ways our minds are still in the Middle Ages.'

'That's a shame, that he didnae have tae, I mean. I'd like fine tae prove that the rich are nae better nor the poor.'

'I'm quite sure they're not, Ma, but I was only joking. What I wanted to explain was that I'm taking cases in the district for practice in midwifery. I'm out at all hours. You know better than anyone about the times babies choose to arrive. Sometimes a qualified doctor goes; he gets one pound if he attends a birth; sometimes a nurse training as a midwife comes with me. The women like them but they like me better. Last night we were out. God, Ma, you kept us in luxury compared to how some exist in this city. Two o'clock in the morning. There's this lassie on a filthy rug on the floor; nothing else in the room but a rickety table and a chair with three legs and the stuffing and springs coming out of the seat. Oh, yes, there's some sacks on the table: that's what she does for a living, sews sacks. Everything is dirty, filthy. A neighbour comes in to help; she's dirtier than the lassie on the floor, so I don't let her touch anything. "Boil some water," I tell her and "Where's her man?" I ask, but she looks funny and says nothing. I cleaned a basin with turpentine and . . .' Rose looked at Elsie and tried to read the expression on her face. Better not to go into the details of the fairly straightforward birth. 'The baby was born and I washed him. Did you know it's thought unlucky for anyone but the doctor to wash a new-born baby? I washed him, wrapped him in newspaper – newspaper, Ma, not a wee frock in the place – and gave him to his mother. Her face, Ma, like there was a candle in her skull. "Is ma bairn a' a' richt?" she says. You know, Ma, every woman I've ever delivered has said exactly that. "Is ma bairn a' richt?" Then the neighbour made us some tea and I had to drink it for the lassie's talking to me. "Oh, doctor," she says, "I couldnae tell the ither doctors but I can tell you a' aboot it." It was her father, Ma: her own father, a drunken sot that abused her from the time she had any memory, and there's nothing I can do.'

Rose fell silent and Elsie looked at this daughter whose experiences she could barely fathom.

'She'll no be the last, lassie. It's a fact o' life. Now tell me whit else ye get up to.'

'There's a professor that's a real click, Ma. Professor D'Arcy Thomson. Everyone agrees he's devastatingly handsome.'

'Like one o' they stars in the melodramas,' breathed Elsie.

'Oh, ten times better, Ma. He's tall and broad and has a full beard like a lion. Very friendly but, well, you wouldn't take liberties. Then there's Professor Weymouth Reid. He teaches physiology and his particular interest is the study of insulin.' She stopped. Physiology and insulin were new words to Elsie.

'That's the stuff that controls the glucose in your blood, Ma. Glucose is sugar, and you've got to have just the right amount or you get sick. Well, there is nothing the professor doesn't know about sugar and last week he taught us all how to boil sugar to make sweeties: great fun. One day we'll have a fund-raiser for the new university, but the next time I'm home I'll make some for us . . .' When would she be home again? She thought of the peace and quiet of her room, the plain but unbroken furniture, the clean wallpaper, and admitted to herself but not to her mother that she never ever wanted to live in that room and kitchen again. Elsie's hard work could defeat dirt but it could not defeat poverty. *When I'm qualified, when I'm qualified, I'll make it all up to you, Ma,* she said over and over again inside her head.

'Then on Monday mornings I'm up at the Royal Infirmary to see surgical outpatients: all the cuts and bruises and broken bones from Saturday night. That can be funny sometimes. I had a big bruiser in this week. I doubt his own mother would recognize him, the mess he'd made of his face, but he says, "Aye, lassie, it hurts right enough, but aw it wis a grand fight." There's just something about the human spirit. Here, I'll let you have a listen through my stethoscope.'

Elsie wiped her hands down the sides of her dress before she took the instrument and inserted it in her ears. 'I cannae hear nothing.'

Rose waited and then saw the look of incredulity on her mother's face.

'I hear an awfie noise, lassie. Here, have them back. I wouldnae like them spoilt. Whit dae you hear?'

'Oh, I'm beginning to hear, Ma, with my understanding as well as my ears. That's what Professor Stather says we have to do, "listen with understanding". And I can administer chloroform. That's the thing, the anaesthetic, that makes you sleep so you don't have pain during surgery or childbirth. I don't really like doing that; it's scary.'

'Don't do it then, lassie. God meant women tae suffer in childbed.'

'Away you go, Elsie Nesbitt. You sound just like a man.'

It was good to laugh and joke with her mother away from Donaldina's sullen animosity. She ran from the university up through the wynds and parks to the infirmary. With her fellow students, men and women. They made her forget everything but medicine. Together they chanted the Dundee medical students' doggerel. 'Come in, come in, put out your tongue. Have you got a bottle? Next please.'

Their tired young voices rang in the clear air.

Rose was so busy that she barely noticed the announcement of the death of Queen Victoria or the wave of real grief and nostalgia that washed the country. She did not know that the new king had typhlitis and that his coronation had had to be postponed. She was more interested in applying for a summer job as an assistant dispenser at a chemist's shop on the Perth Road. At least two of the male students had applied for it and they, like Rose, were well qualified. She did not know that she got the job because she was a woman and could be paid less. Rose was thrilled to be out of the berry fields and earning one pound each week for, it seemed to her, nothing but measuring out ten grams of phenacitin into clean little papers and selling them to headache sufferers for a penny each.

She saved the summer money and bought herself a new costume made of soft golden-brown wool. It had a straight plain skirt and, the latest fashion, a three-quarter-length sac coat which just skimmed her knees. With it she wore a plain brown felt toreador hat trimmed with a quill. In the fitting room she looked at herself in the mirror and liked what she saw.

'New shoes and gloves,' she vowed, 'and even my mother wouldn't recognize me.' She ignored the glow of pleasure that told her that she was a very pretty girl.

The costume, wrapped in a sheet to keep it clean, hung behind her bedroom door. She was saving it for something special.

The university planned a fund-raising bazaar for October 1903. Rose and her classmates made their mouthwatering sweets and Rose herself worked on their stall. She loved every minute, not only of the camaraderie and fun of the bazaar itself but all the hours of work that she and other exhausted students, not just medical students, had put in before the event. Excitement added some colour to her usually pale face, and that was how Kier and Lucy saw her as they wandered from stall to stall.

Lucy saw Kier's eyes light up and at first she did not recognize the small golden-brown figure laughing and joking behind the table.

'Come on, Lucy, it's little Rose Nesbitt. I haven't seen her in years.' He pulled Lucy along and she went willingly enough.

'Have some of my delicious toffee, sir,' said Rose in her new persona. 'Dental students at the next stall will take care of any damage done – at a reasonable ... cost,' she finished lamely as she recognized her customer.

He laughed down at her rosy face, now red with embarrassment as well as excitement. 'We'll have a pound of whatever you made yourself, Miss Nesbitt, won't we, Lucy? You remember Miss Nesbitt, don't you, my dear?'

'Of course,' said Lucy, although she had not thought of Rose Nesbitt for years. 'How are you, Miss Nesbitt?'

Miss Nesbitt could feel her new-found confidence ebbing away under the eyes of this elegant, sophisticated woman, and Lucy saw it go and tried to make amends.

'What a wonderful occasion, Miss Nesbitt. I can't think how you have all managed to do so much. No sleep at all, I should imagine?'

Rose stammered something and Kier stepped in.

'You're right, Lucy, and probably no food either. A puff of wind will blow you away, Miss Nesbitt. We insist that you come and lunch with us, don't we, Lucy?'

If the suggestion was an unwelcome shock to Lucy, she recovered quickly. 'Absolutely,' she said.

Rose hesitated.

'Doctor's orders,' teased Lucy. 'Do come, Miss Nesbitt,' she coaxed. 'I should like to hear how the medical school has responded to the invention of the electro-cardiograph.'

'Oh, yes, doctor.' Rose was excited again. 'And pheno-barbitone . . .'

'Ladies, I refuse to lunch with pills and potions. Next you'll be talking about votes for women, and that I will *not* have.'

'Don't listen to him, Miss Nesbitt. He's a powerful advocate for the rights of women. Are you free for lunch?'

She checked the time on the delicate gold watch on her wrist while Rose looked at her own serviceable one.

'I'm free in ten minutes,' she said.

'We'll come back to fetch you,' said Kier and turned away. 'Come along, Lucy. I must just confirm that Mother is lunching with Lady Donaldson.'

His voice receded into the distance and Rose looked after him until a bag of toffee, pushed almost into her face by a grubby urchin, recalled her to her duties and she exchanged the sweets for a sticky coin.

'Well, you are a dark horse, Rose,' said Eddie Reid, the third-year student who was manning the stall with her. 'Here's me been trying for weeks to have you come for a buster with me. "You'll get nowhere with Rose," said the other lads. "Keeps herself to herself." That wouldn't be the Lady Donaldson who just happens to be married to the principal of St Andrews University, would it? No wonder you don't have time for us when you go around in that company. Must help . . . with lots of things.'

'Don't be sillier or nastier than you have to be, Eddie. I don't know Lady Donaldson . . .' Rose stopped. No, she would not justify or defend herself. She had nothing of which to be ashamed. Eddie was very young after all. 'I'm off to have lunch, Eddie. See you at the hospital on Monday.'

She pulled her lovely new brown hat with its jaunty feather down over her yellow curls, picked up her bag and smoothed her first pair of leather gloves over her almost soft hands.

Lucy saw her standing there, small and erect and very lovely. 'Well done, little Nesbitt,' she thought and she smiled and went towards her. 'Miss Nesbitt, what a charming hat.

Are you ready? Kier's gone off for a cab. The street is absolutely jammed.'

Rose felt herself almost pulled along by Lucy's personality, and she hurried along and tried to answer the questions that were raining down on her. Not that any of them were personal or difficult. She did not realize that, in a different way, Lucy was as nervous and ill at ease as she was herself, or that she was annoyed to be experiencing that same nervousness.

Was she not the daughter of a diplomat? Had she not been trained from earliest childhood to make people feel at ease? *I forget the lesson on being at ease myself*, Lucy thought wryly as they reached the doors of the crowded hall.

And there on the pavement was Kier.

'What a mad crush,' he said as he helped first Lucy and then Rose into the cab. 'The university coffers must be overflowing.'

'I was just telling Doctor Graham that we had taken almost seven pounds,' Rose managed to say.

'Gosh, and since you paid five pounds for that ghastly clock Mother's been trying to lose for twenty years … where is it, by the way?'

'I lost it,' said Lucy and together they dissolved into laughter and Rose watched them and envied the ease of their relationship.

Lucy recovered first. 'How awful you must think us, Miss Nesbitt, but it really was a most ugly clock.'

'And notoriously unreliable,' said Kier. 'Where did you put it?'

'Actually, I gave it to a little girl as a gift for her mother.'

'How unkind of you,' laughed Kier, 'but seriously, I've told the cabbie D.M. Brown's. Does that suit, ladies?'

'Five pounds,' thought Rose. 'More than the price of my costume and my hat, and she can afford to just give it away.'

'D.M. Brown's would be lovely,' she said. 'I believe they have started afternoon teas too.'

It was the new clothes, of course, and the gloves that covered the almost soft hands. They gave her confidence. She was able to smile, to chat, to relax, and Lucy saw her at her best and liked what she saw.

'We should stay for tea, too,' said Lucy. 'Certain people in this world, Miss Nesbitt,' she solemnly gestured towards Kier, 'will always find time for tea but others, like you and I, have to take our food when we find time.'

It was a delightful afternoon. Rose forgot, for once, the huge gulf that she always felt existed between her and people like these two, and she did not realize how hard they both worked to make her feel welcome. They did not speak of her career plans until they were in another cab on their way back along the Perth Road to Rose's lodgings.

'I'll give you my card, Miss Nesbitt,' said Lucy, reaching into her handbag. 'When you are qualified I should be happy to give you some experience in a general practice.'

'General, Doctor Graham? I had thought you had only female patients.'

'At first, yes, and still the bulk of my practice is female, but women have brought their children and now there are even one or two men. I can truthfully say "General Practitioner". Are you interested in general practice?'

'Yes, but I am mainly interested in the health of women, their pre-natal and ante-natal care.'

'Ah well, that is the least interesting part to me. I think, perhaps, I should have gone on to specialize in surgery but there were and are so many closed doors.'

'You are pioneers, Lucy, you and Miss Nesbitt. She will find it easier than you, because at least she has been allowed to enter a university.'

'Pioneers,' said Lucy, and her mind went back to an early autumn afternoon. She could almost hear the swish of Amos's broom against the leaves and a beloved voice: . . . 'butterflies in December'. Was Rose a butterfly too?

'When you graduate, Miss Nesbitt, do call on me. I would love to visit my father, who lives abroad, and a good locum would be worth her weight in gold.'

Kier walked Rose up the steps to the front door of her lodging house. 'I shall not lose you again, Miss Nesbitt. May I call on you sometime?'

'Yes, Mr Anderson-Howard,' said Rose, aware that it was the first time she had used his name.

He smiled. 'That wasn't too hard, was it? Keep in touch with Doctor Graham. She does mean to help you and help will be necessary. Qualifying, I think, may well be the easiest of the tasks before you.' He surprised Rose by quickly changing the subject. 'Do you enjoy the opera?'

'Yes,' said Rose rashly.

'Good. I'll get some tickets.'

He lifted his hat and was gone and Rose would have liked to watch him drive away, but felt that it would be better just to slip inside without gazing after him like a besotted little fool.

She was about to open the door when she heard someone call her name from the other side of the street, and she turned to see Donaldina running across.

'Eh wisnae sure it wis you, getting oot of a private cab and dressed like a dish o'fish. Nae wonder ye're niver hame wi' a bonnie click like thon.'

'I'm not allowed visitors,' Rose lied. 'What is it you want?'

'I'm no wantin' in yer fancy digs. I widnae be here at all if it wisnae for Ma.'

Rose felt cold suddenly. The beautiful glow caused by the afternoon left and never returned. 'Ma?'

'She's fell sick.'

Rose felt her stomach turn right over. Ma, Elsie, sick. It had never occurred to her that Elsie could be sick. Elsie was indestructible: she had always been there and would always be there, taking care of everyone else.

'Sick,' she said stupidly.

'Are ye deef tae? If ye'd been near us ye'd hiv seen fir yirsel. Ye've been that busy ye havnae seen her for months. Are ye comin?' Donaldina looked at her sister, at the elegant fashionable clothes, the jaunty hat. 'Ye'd maybe better change. Ye'll get jumped for that costume, or are all yer claes that guid noo?'

Rose shook her head in answer to that question. She understood the envy and anger in her sister's voice. 'How far I have come,' she thought, 'and all due to Elsie.' Oh to be Lucy Graham, and casually to order a private cab to take her to her mother.

'Let's hurry. There's a horse-bus due in a minute.'

Donaldina did not sit beside her sister in the bus, but whether from dislike or embarrassment, Rose could not tell. They changed buses in the centre of the city and again Rose sat in solitary state and saw nothing but visions of Elsie. Elsie telling her to whistle so that she could not eat the fresh young peas. Elsie crying her eyes out at her graduation and making a Greek mask of her face. Elsie listening in wonder to her own heart through her daughter's stethoscope.

The house smelled. Never before had Rose been so aware of the smell of poverty, but with the poverty there was a smell she knew only too well. It was the smell of death: a horrifying death from syphilis.

Elsie was lying in the box-bed and for a second her eyes lit up as the shining daffodil that was her daughter dispelled the darkness of the ugly room.

'Rosie.' The voice was a croak.

'It's me, Ma. I'm here to take care of you.' She turned to Donaldina. 'Boil some water. A wash will make her feel better, and these blankets are soiled. Could you not have washed them?' And all the time, against Elsie's feeble protests, she was probing, examining. *This disease-ridden body is not my mother,* her mind kept saying as the bile rose in her throat.

She turned in time to see her sister slip out of the room. 'Donaldina . . .' she began, but then she turned back to the dying woman on the bed. 'I'm going to get you to the hospital, Ma. I'll make you a wee bit more comfortable and then I'll go for an ambulance.'

There was no response and Rose set to work to get some water to wash her patient. She moistened the dry, cracked lips. 'I'll make us a nice cup of tea, Ma, when I get back with the doctor. Tea you can dance on, all right? Just wait for me, Ma.'

She hurried out, her mind still conversing with the woman on the bed. *You should have gone to the doctor. There's a women's hospital in Dundee. They can cure syphilis, but now there are so many complications. It's not too advanced: you'll get better, Ma. In the hospital with real doctors and real nurses, where it's clean and . . .* She was crying as she ran along, but the tears had dried by the time she had reached the hospital and had arranged for the horse-drawn ambulance to bring her mother back.

'Where are all the neighbours?' she asked herself angrily. 'Ma was always taking care of everyone else. I must find Murray's address. Ma must have it somewhere. Frazer's dead and Lindsay's dead and God knows where Donaldina's gone.'

Elsie was lying as Rose had left her. But she was dead. Her heart had stopped beating

'She's deid, lassie. Even I can tell that.'

'No. Let's get her into the ambulance.'

*   *   *

Doctor James Robertson was on duty. If only it had been anyone else. He looked down physically and mentally on all women, especially those pushing their way into what he believed to be the rightful place of men.

'There was a football match this afternoon, Miss Nesbitt. We have been busy enough without having to deal with this.'

'She has syphilis, doctor.'

He turned to the duty nurse. 'Take it away.'

Anger blazed through the tears in Rose's eyes and he saw it and looked again at the body on the table before him. Very gently he began to examine Elsie.

'I'm sorry, Miss Nesbitt. She's dead. Perhaps if she had come in weeks, even days ago ... She's lucky. The heart gave up before the worst.' He looked again at the intense young face before him. Good heavens, if she took the death of every patient so hard she would burn herself out before she was even properly qualified. 'We all lose patients. You'll have to face it if you're going to be any good, Miss Nesbitt, and they say you are going to be good, you know, but you're not God. None of us are, although sometimes our patients think so and adulation like that can go to one's head. I'm sure you did everything you could.'

Rose shook her head. 'I did nothing, nothing.'

'Good God, girl, don't be childish. I suppose it's your monthly time that makes you so irrational. Isn't there something in the rule book that says you are supposed to stay off the wards when you are unbalanced?'

Unbalanced! Rose began to laugh. She had almost been ready to like him: he had been so gentle. There had been no distaste on his face as he had dealt with what had been Elsie. Elsie with the hard hands, ready to slap, readier to cuddle and console. And now she was dead. Wishy was dead. Frazer was dead. Elsie should have gone on for ever. And then, unbidden, unwanted, a thought came into Rose's head that she condemned and loathed, and was unable to forget for the rest of her life. *I'll never have to introduce her to Kier.*

'The patient's name is Elsie Nesbitt, Doctor Robertson. She is my mother and I will take care of her burial.'

Again he surprised her. Did she expect him to look at her differently when he saw the stock from which she had come?

'Nurse,' he said, 'fetch Miss Nesbitt a cup of tea. I'm afraid she's had rather a bad shock.' He turned to Rose. 'Sit down, my dear, while I take care of the paperwork for you. A cup of tea is always the very best medicine.'

11

Dundee, 1905–1907

'HIGH TIME YOU got someone to help in the surgery, Doctor Graham.' Isa looked down at the thin slice of rare roast beef on the plate in front of her mistress. 'And when are you going to have a holiday? You've been talking about a holiday all the time I've known you.'

Lucy roused herself. 'Don't take it away, Isa. I'm sure it will be perfectly delicious.'

'No, doctor. It should be hot, and the gravy, and the vegetables. I'll warm up a plate, and you should have it with a nice glass of wine.'

'No. I'm rather worried about Mrs Dryden. I may be called out.'

'Young Mrs Dryden?'

'No, she's not due for a few weeks yet.'

Isa hurried out with the dishes and almost stomped down to her kitchen where Donald was sitting in his shirt-sleeves, cleaning the silver soup spoons.

'She hasn't eaten again,' he said, looking at the untouched plate.

'She got as far as cutting some meat. She's too tired. On the go all day, and then all night sometimes as well. If she's not going to marry Mr Kier, and God alone knows if she'll ever get round to that, she should at least take a business partner.'

Isa bustled about, arranging the cauliflower, carrots and potatoes as temptingly as possible around the meat.

'Don't overdo it, Isa. Too much food makes you tired just looking at it when you're already exhausted.'

Isa removed a floret of cauliflower and then, when Donald had turned to the sink with his spoons, popped it back on again, covered it with another plate and slipped it into the warming oven.

'I've been telling her she should take a partner, and it's about time she had a holiday.'

Lovingly Donald polished one of the beautiful spoons. 'She had a few days here and there with Sir John last summer.'

'A jaunt into the country for a picnic is not a holiday.'

'Wouldn't fancy them foreign places, but the rich are different.'

Isa agreed with her husband and then straightened up from the stove with annoyance as they heard the peal of the front door-bell. She pushed the plate back, whisked off her apron and hurried back upstairs tidying her hair as she did so.

Mr Colin Dryden stood on the doorstep.

'Hello, Isa. Is the doctor in? I'm afraid my aunt has had a turn for the worse.'

'Doctor hasn't eaten yet,' protested Isa, but she knew better than to keep a patient from her employer at any time, day or night. 'Come in, Mr Dryden, sir. She's in the dining room.'

Lucy was sitting at the window that looked out over a garden changed beyond measure from the one the young solicitor had first shown his client, now his friend and his beloved aunt's physician. She rose at once at the sight of Colin's face, papers scattering from her blue silk lap. 'Oh, my dear,' she said. 'I'll get my things and come at once.'

A few minutes later, Isa closed the door behind her mistress and returned to the dining room. She cleared the table of all evidence that dinner had been set there, but she left the papers on the floor. They were probably case notes, and therefore were not to be touched by any hand but the doctor's own.

'At least she died in her own bed. Thank you, Doctor Graham. I will always be grateful for that and, of course, all your care these past years.'

Mr Dryden Senior looked very much as he had always looked, but already the loss of his beloved wife was taking its toll.

'May I act in this instance as *your* physician too, and beg you to get some rest?'

'You're right, of course, my dear, but I would like a few minutes more with her.'

Lucy and Colin withdrew and left the old man with the body of his wife.

'You should go home to Sophie, Colin. I hope she will have gone to sleep, but she cares for your aunt very deeply.'

'Her mother, in fact her parents, are with us.' Colin poured himself a brandy and gestured with the decanter.

'No, I must get home. I have to call at the hospital first thing.' He made as if to stand. 'No, Colin, I'll go in a cab. Your wife will need you and I would prefer that you see your uncle to bed. Have Edith give him some warm milk and this powder.'

'She's left a great deal of money to the Women's Hospital, with the stipulation that you become a trustee.'

Lucy could barely speak. 'How very kind. She was such a good woman.' She set aside her own grief for a moment. Mrs Dryden had been a mother to Colin.

'Oh, my dear, I had forgotten . . .'

'I'll be all right, Lucy. We knew she was dying and it's almost a relief in a way that her suffering is over.' He swallowed painfully. 'We are grateful; no one could have worked harder than you to make her last days comfortable. I'm concerned about my uncle. You see, he always knew she bullied him. I didn't realize until I married Sophie. He said it was the secret of a happy marriage. "If she's a prudent and loving woman, give her her head and pretend that you think you're in control," he said. They would have been married fifty-two years in June.'

'The baby is coming in June, my dear. That will be your uncle's saving.'

'She wanted to hold this baby so much.' He set the glass down very carefully and stood up. 'Come, if you're sure, I'll put you into a cab. You really ought to have a companion, Lucy. You should not be going back to that big house alone.'

There it was again, even after all these years, this unspoken belief that a woman could not possibly manage on her own.

'Isa will have stayed downstairs. She's beginning to fuss as much as your dear aunt did.'

'A servant isn't the same thing.'

'Oh, I don't think of Isa and Donald as servants, Colin. Now, make sure Mr Dryden takes that powder and then you get off home. The next few days will be very stressful.'

They were, and for Lucy too. It threatened to rain on the day of the funeral but by afternoon the skies had cleared.

'She would have hated a dismal day,' said Mr Dryden as the mourners waited in the church garden for their carriages, the horses strutting proudly, their black plumes nodding. It was as if the whole of Dundee had come to bid farewell. 'Lucy, my dear, you will stay with us after tea, for the reading of the will?'

Lucy, who had intended to slip quietly away after the graveside service which she knew many of the family women would not attend, could only nod. Should she have told him that she already knew of Mrs Dryden's generous gift to the hospital? She went in the MacDonald family carriage. Mr MacDonald had not mellowed over the years; his wife would not attend the graveside, but would wait with the other family ladies at the family home. He had, however, given up trying to apply his values to Doctor Graham's life.

'I was once very rude to you, Doctor Graham . . .' He saw the slight smile she tried to hide. 'Perhaps I was rude more than once, but I have meant, often, to apologize. I cannot see that you have done anything a responsible male practitioner could not have done, but the women of our family are certainly happier, if not healthier . . . and who is to know the truth of that? I know Mrs Dryden has asked that you be put on the board of the new Women's Hospital. You will also be asked, soon, to take the Chair of Gynaecology at the university. I believe it is a two-year secondment, and several board members have put forward your name.'

Lucy was glad that they had arrived at the cemetery. And what was she supposed to do with her patients? Had these generous gentlemen, who finally half grudgingly admitted her capabilities, thought what would happen to her patients, to the practice she had laboured night and day to establish? *Keep your Chair of Gynaecology,* she thought angrily. *It's absolutely the last subject I would dream of teaching.*

The earth falling on the coffin brought her back shame-facedly to the day.

Oh, dearest Mrs Dryden, I'll miss your generosity of spirit. I'll miss your humour and I'll miss your warm friendship. The world is a colder place without you, but I would not keep you in such pain as you suffered these last few years. Say I helped, my dear, I pray I helped.

The minister was praying and the crowd around the grave had bowed their heads. Lucy lifted hers and felt the spring sun warm on her face.

And then suddenly she knew. *I'm saying goodbye to my own mother,* she thought and she smiled. There had been a memorial service in the wee church in Fife, but Lady Graham lay for ever under the parched dry soil of India, in a cemetery Lucy had never seen. *At last, at last, goodbye, beloved mother. I hope you're proud of me. Good-bye, dearest Mrs Dryden.*

Lucy's heart was light as she left the cemetery, not heavy as it had been when she stood in the church listening to a list of her patient's virtues. She saw Mr Dryden, eyes clear, back straight. *Father must have looked like that. Good men, both. I'll write to Father tonight and tell him. I know he'll understand.*

She sat through the interminable tea. Colin did not stay but went home to his wife who, of course, could not be seen in public in her condition.

And why ever not, thought Lucy. *In the midst of life we are in death and surely, surely, in the midst of death we are in life? I hope they have a little girl for Mr Dryden.*

Those mentioned in the will were shepherded into the drawing room, a dark and gloomy room at the best of times since it still wore all the trappings of Victoriana; today it was even more grim as the curtains were drawn against the pleasant early summer sun and black ribbons swagged the family portraits. Lucy felt cold. This room needed Mrs Dryden's cheery voice to warm it.

Mr MacDonald read the will, a straightforward enough document. There were a few sentimental bequests to her husband, the bulk of her jewellery to young Mrs Dryden, legacies to other relatives and to devoted servants, and then '*all monies left to me by my late father and invested for me by my dear husband, I leave to the Women's Hospital of Dundee for the succour of any indigent woman of this place and with the sole stipulation that Dr Lucille Graham be appointed to the executive board of the said hospital for her lifetime.'*

There were no ripples of surprise, no angry or offended glances. Mrs Dryden must surely have discussed her incredible generosity with her extended family. The lawyer was waiting once more for Lucy's attention.

'I read this as she dictated it,' he said. 'She had a most particular sense of humour.'

'I also ask Doctor Graham to choose one of the two paintings that I bought in Paris and to hang it in her consulting rooms so that her patients may, like me, be cheered and fascinated by it. The other is to go to my dearly beloved nephew, Colin, who, like Doctor Graham and unlike the bulk of my very worthy family, is possessed of an open and enquiring mind.'

Lucy saw a smile of genuine merriment cross the face of the elder Mr Dryden. How often had she caught them in loving battle over the two pictures.

'A child could have done them.'

'Don't be ridiculous; you know nothing of modern art.'

'There is nothing to know except that you have been robbed by an unscrupulous charlatan. He saw you coming, my dear.'

'You have an uneducated mind. In twenty years your thrifty Scots soul will be wishing that you had bought Monsieur Dufy's entire collection.'

'At least you need not look at that monstrosity in the peace of your home, Doctor Graham,' consoled the wife of one of Mrs Dryden's many nephews.

Lucy smiled but said nothing.

'I think when I miss her too much, Lucy, I may find myself in your consulting rooms,' said Mr Dryden as she was leaving. 'I still prefer a nice pastoral scene. I'm afraid my mind is quite closed to this so-called modern art, but she loved them and she loved you.'

Lucy knew she did not need to tell him what she felt about his wife.

'You are welcome at any time in my consulting rooms, Mr Dryden.'

'I'm too old to become a patient, my dear.'

'Why should you change from Doctor Bracewell? He is a fine doctor and he forgave me for stealing Mrs Dryden away from him.'

'Together with all the other women in this family.' There was a clatter of frenzied hooves in the street. 'Why, here is Colin . . .'

They both looked at the street where a horse-cab had lunged to a halt and Colin Dryden had almost fallen out on the pavement.

'Lucy, quick, quick, it's time! Oh, Uncle, what a time to intrude but Sophie . . . Lucy, quickly, the baby's coming.'

'Calm down, Colin. I must get my bag. Goodbye, Mr Dryden. I'm absolutely certain that Mrs Dryden, like young Sophie, is in excellent hands.'

The elderly man and the young doctor smiled at one another in perfect understanding and Lucy turned and led Colin back down to the cab.

'Stop at No. 4 Shore Terrace,' she ordered the driver, 'and see if you can do it without injuring me or this poor horse.'

'Do as the doctor says,' ordered Colin, since the cabbie looked belligerently at Lucy. 'To 4 Shore Terrace first, as safely as you can, and as quickly.'

'Try to calm down, Colin. Your nervousness will frighten your wife. Even if she in labour, and she is two weeks early you know, the baby will take some time.'

'You will make sure she suffers no pain: you have this chloroform?'

'I have it, yes.' She did not tell him that she would ease his wife's labour pains, not sedate her completely.

They fetched Lucy's bag and then drove on to Blackness Avenue where a frightened-looking maid-servant who had obviously been watching for them opened the door.

'Oh, Mr Dryden, sir, the mistress is suffering something awful,' she blurted out with some degree of pleasure.

To Lucy's surprise Colin turned as white as a sheet and, had it not been for her quick grip of his arm, would have fallen.

'My poor darling,' he breathed. 'I must go to her.'

'Oh,' thought Lucy, 'for a nice working-class home where I could set the expectant father to boiling water.'

There was a piteous cry from upstairs and Lucy hurried towards the staircase. 'No, Colin,' she ordered as he made to accompany her. 'Join your father-in-law and keep him from worrying. Sophie's mother and I will manage between us.'

Sophie's beautiful bedroom was at the top of the stairs and, when Lucy reached it, she found her patient lying back against the lace pillows, already exhausted – but more, she was sure, from fear than from effort. Her mother sat by her side holding her hand and attempting to quieten her.

'When did the labour begin?'

'She had a show this morning, doctor, but the pains didn't begin until this afternoon. They're quite strong now and about ten minutes apart.'

Lucy bent to examine her patient. 'Good girl, Sophie, everything is just fine. You and baby are doing very well.'

She straightened up. 'I think we'll make her more comfortable, Mrs Caird . . .'

'Chloroform?' Sophie's mother looked happily and expectantly at Lucy's open bag.

'No, if you'll help me, we'll change her nightgown. I can't see what I'm doing for all this lace. I know there are some plain cotton gowns in her dresser.'

'I made this gown myself.' Mrs Caird was offended. 'It's her favourite.'

Lucy had found a simple gown. 'Will you help me, please, Mrs Caird?' She ignored the anxious mother's annoyance. 'And if you could fetch a towel? Sophie is sweating, and we'll dry her off and make her much easier, won't we, Sophie dear?'

They worked together quietly, although Lucy could almost feel the resentment coming from the woman at her side. Mrs Caird had often told Lucy that she was not one of these terribly modern women who were rushing to change the established order of things. She had tried to persuade her daughter to stay with their own family physician, but although Sophie had been attended by Doctor Bracewell all through her childhood, she had been delighted to find a lady doctor when she married.

The change of clothing was effected just in time for the next contraction. Sophie screamed and her mother clutched at her hands. 'Oh, my poor baby,' she cried. 'Give her something, doctor.'

Lucy waited until the contraction was over and she had settled her patient back against her pillows, but lying on her side this time.

'There, Sophie, you will feel much more comfortable on your side. You are experiencing back labour; it's perfectly normal, and all that is happening is that the canal is widening so that your baby will soon be able to make the exciting voyage into the world. Think of your little baby, striving to reach you. You must help by being as relaxed as you can and by not fighting against the contraction but by going with it.' She straightened up and turned to her patient's mother. 'Mrs Caird, you are frightening my patient, and if you can't behave I will have to ask you to leave the room.'

'You see, darling, you see. She's trying to send Mamma away. Let me send Papa for dear Doctor Bracewell who . . .'

Another contraction prevented anyone in the room from knowing what Doctor Bracewell would have done. He would certainly, as Lucy well knew, not have come to the house.

Sophie remained on her side and Lucy exerted gentle pressure on the small of her back as the contraction took its course. 'Breathe, Sophie, that's it, don't hold your breath. There, dear, that's better, isn't it? Now lie back again and your mother will moisten your lips.' She gave Mrs Caird a simple task to do. There was no point in completely alienating the patient's mother, but she would do it if she had to in the interest of her patient.

The evening wore on; the contractions became more severe and at last Lucy decided to administer a little chloroform, enough to dull the pain but not so much that Sophie was unable to help her baby on the greatest and most hazardous journey it would ever undertake. The sickly sweet odour of the anaesthetic filled the air as Sophie inhaled.

'My husband is the dearest man, Doctor Graham, but Colin and I had to fight him every step of the way over the use of chloroform. He would suffer the pangs of childbirth for Sophie if he could but he is so set in the nineteenth century. "Women are supposed to suffer. It's God's law," he says, but I think he'll change his mind when he sees how you've helped Sophie.'

Lucy said nothing. She had no intention of becoming involved in a moral or philosophical argument, nor had she any intention of making her patient completely unconscious.

'Not long now, Sophie,' she said. 'Relax, relax, keep your strength for your baby. Go with the pain, that's it, that's it.'

'Auntie's dead, isn't she?' Sophie said suddenly.

'Yes.'

'I know she is, but I thought I smelled her perfume . . . it's the chloroform, isn't it? It does funny things to your mind.'

Lucy smiled but did not answer. During births, during deaths, sitting by the side of the very ill, she was often aware, like the patients themselves, of other forces, other presences. If it made Sophie happier to believe she could smell her aunt's perfume, then let her believe so.

Just before midnight, on the day when his great-aunt was buried, John Joseph Dryden slipped easily into the world and set up a bawl that had his father and grandfather, jacketless and tieless, racing one another up the splendid oak staircase.

When she had finished with her patients, Lucy walked slowly down the stairs to the library where a meal was waiting for her. She was too tired to eat, but she sat back in the chair and sipped a glass of wine while she waited for the coffee she had ordered. She was vaguely disappointed. It would have been so perfect if the baby had been the little girl she was sure Mrs Dryden had always wanted. Not that Sophie and Colin were disappointed; they were quietly and emotionally ecstatic over the birth of their little son. Presently Sophie's parents joined her. Mrs Caird had forgiven Lucy for threatening to remove her from her daughter's bedside and sang her praises to her husband.

'Easiest birth I ever saw,' she said. 'Muriel was right about you, Doctor Graham, and I shall tell everyone so. She was right about the baby too.'

Lucy was suddenly alert. 'The baby? She had so many nephews; I always thought she wanted a little girl to spoil.'

'Oh, no, my dear. The greatest tragedy of her life was that she was unable to give Alistair the son she thought he wanted. Colin was the nearest to her, and she would certainly have tried to usurp my place as little John's only grandmother. She would be absolutely thrilled if she knew the baby was a boy.'

'Perhaps she does,' thought Lucy. 'Perhaps she does.'

Not for the first time, Lucy fell asleep in the cab on the short drive home. Isa, watching from the hall, saw the cabbie waiting and went out to wake her mistress and to pay him.

'Mr Kier was here,' she said as she tucked Lucy up in bed. 'He had a young lady with him. He thought you might be upset after Mrs Dryden's funeral and he and Miss ... Napier was it, thought you might join them for supper. Seemingly they was at the opera. Can't think as how opera, with all those people singing at the tops of their voices, would calm anyone down after a bad day, but the young lady was having her finals ... did he say orals in all the subjects?' She waited for Lucy's answer and since it did not come, continued. 'The young lady is going to be a doctor. It's the new degree: MB, Ch.B, and the young lady is lovely, a very gentle manner. I bet she would be wonderful with our older patients and, of course, the younger ones, ones like young Mrs Dryden, would be pleased to have such a pretty young doctor in the practice. I bet she's snapped up right away, if those that know she's graduating don't take advantage and snap her up before it's in the papers. We could have a holiday then. Sir John plans to tour the western states, doesn't he, or we could have that holiday in Italy we always wanted?'

Isa had sown the seeds. She had been married to a gardener long enough to know that the same seeds had to be left to germinate. She turned down the light and left Lucy to sleep.

Lucy lay in a delicious half-awake half-asleep mood. Her mind was once more full of the knowledge of Mrs Dryden's generosity. Mrs Colin Dryden was there too, exhausted, but happier probably than she would ever be again in her life, her first child, her son, held securely in her arms. Lucy saw her face now as she had not seen it when she attended the birth, soft, glowing, vulnerable.

Will I ever look like that? Will anyone ever look at me as Colin looked at Sophie? Kier? He was here with Miss . . . Napier, no, Miss Nesbitt, who is about to graduate. He came because he felt that I would need him but he brought Miss Nesbitt. Did I need him? Be honest, Lucy. It is so important that you are honest with yourself. No, dearest Kier, I did not need you. Perhaps, just perhaps, the night Mrs Dryden died, it would have been . . . nice to share the burden of her death with someone.

Lucy thought of Isa who was becoming more and more motherly, more and more anxious that she eat well, sleep well, have a holiday. A holiday . . . with Father? She would think about it later.

Lucy slept and, not too far away, Rose Nesbitt lay awake. She could not sleep because she had been kissed and because she had been so careful, all her life, to make sure that such a thing never happened to her. Now she had let it happen, and she was not sure if she was changed or if life could go on the way that she planned. Perhaps it was the giver of the kiss who was the problem because Rose felt, correctly, that Kier Anderson-Howard had kissed quite a few girls in his time. Did it mean anything or was it just a gesture of admittance into the inner court, the women like Dr Graham who could be greeted with a kiss on the cheek and a 'Hello, darling, how lovely to see you.' Yes, that was all it meant, and it should be treated just as nonchalantly. Rose was quite, quite sure that she had no special feelings for Kier. She had even become used to having him around, to hearing his voice which had ceased to thrill her. When had that happened? When she had first known him, when she had first, so nervously, accepted an invitation to the theatre, she had listened to the music of that voice and been excited and happy and even amazed that it was directed at her. She had avoided him for months after her mother's death. It had been easy: she had been so busy, so tired. Had she also, unconsciously, been weaning herself farther and farther from the roots that were now well and truly pulled out of the soil that had nourished them? There was very little of Rosie Nesbitt left in the delicate, sophisticated young medical student who ran furiously between university and hospital, and hospital and home. Then in October of 1904 a Students' Union was opened in Dundee. Naturally, the president of the union was a man, but Rose had been overwhelmingly voted in as convener of social events. Mind you, the women could not go in the main entrance; they went down the basement steps and entered the union from there, but still they had achieved something.

Rose could hardly believe her first official function. She looked at herself in the mirror, admired the hard-earned pale olive silk suit, the carefully waved hair. 'This can't be real. This can't be me, wee Rosie Nesbitt, arranging a luncheon for Mrs Andrew Carnegie whose husband just happens to be Lord Rector and one of the richest men in the entire world.'

Not only did Lucy arrange the luncheon, she hosted it. Among her guests, besides Mrs Carnegie, were Mrs Woodrow Wilson, wife of a prominent American politician, and Lady Donaldson, wife of the university principal. It was to be a ladies' luncheon and the men had cheerfully given up all rights to the dining room for the afternoon. They themselves were giving a reception before the luncheon for all the ladies and their powerful husbands.

Rose was immediately aware of the unbelievable personal magnetism of Andrew Carnegie. As she shook his hand and smiled, 'How do you do, sir,' into those compelling eyes, she was aware of nothing and no one but the man himself.

'He has quite an effect, doesn't he?' The voice was one she had vowed would never overawe her, but she was overawed. Kier Anderson-Howard stood at her side, a sherry glass in his hand.

'Miss Nesbitt, I will not complain that you have been deliberately avoiding me if you will allow me to take you to the theatre this evening.'

Rose's hard-won sophistication flew right out of the union windows and disappeared somewhere beyond the Tay.

'At least you don't deny that you have been avoiding me. Come, Miss Nesbitt, we poor males are not bidden to your hen party. I will admit that Doctor Graham was to accompany me to the theatre, but she has a patient. Doctors always have a patient, Miss Nesbitt. Will you come to the theatre while you have a chance to sit through an entire performance?'

Rose laughed. It was that kind of day. 'Yes,' she said, her sophistication returning, 'to celebrate my meeting with the great man.'

'Oh, more than one, Miss Nesbitt.' He misinterpreted the look she gave him. 'Good heavens, not me. They say we will hear more of Mr Wilson.'

'Rose, Rose, Mrs Carnegie and Lady Donaldson are looking for you.' Sybil Anderson, another student, bustled up. 'I must tear our Rose away, sir,' she added to Kier. 'Quickly, Rose, Sir James has told Mr Carnegie of how wonderfully you behaved when you lost his award. I heard him say it would have to be made up to you.'

Rose stood for a second, unable to move. She wanted to go; she wanted to stay. Too much was happening all at once.

Kier smiled. 'Same address?'

She nodded.

'Seven?'

'Seven.'

And that had been the first of not many but several engagements with Mr Anderson-Howard. He had even asked her to a Christmas Ball at his home, that lovely, lovely house with the lovely, lovely name, Laverock Rising, but there was no money for a suitable gown and no Elsie to buy one in one of the second-hand shops in the Hilltown.

And soon she was to graduate and Kier Anderson-Howard had kissed her, not passionately, but gently on her unrouged lips.

'Next time I see you, you will be Rose Nesbitt, MB, Ch.B I shall be terrified to kiss Doctor Nesbitt.'

And then he had asked the question that was also keeping her awake.

'What do you plan to do, Rose?'

12

Dundee, 1905

THEY COULD NOT meet. Rose looked in her mirror and hated what she saw. She saw, not a girl who was going to become a doctor in a few weeks' time and who had worked and slaved and sacrificed for the opportunity, but the face of a girl who finally admitted to herself that she was ashamed of her family. For Kier was not the only visitor to the students' lodgings in the West End; Donaldina Nesbitt too had become a common visitor. She came, quite frankly, not because she loved or missed her older sister but because, in her perception, Rose was rich and she was definitely poor and so the balance must be redressed.

Rose had suffered badly when Elsie died. She had castigated herself for the neglect she felt her mother had suffered. *I could have done more. I could have helped. I should have stayed at home* – there, she still called that two-room flat up the closie, home – *during the summer holidays and given Ma my money instead of saving for a costume.*

Elsie was dead. Donaldina was alive and Rose tried to help. Donaldina knew about the approaching graduation and she hinted for an invitation.

At least Rose did not try to pretend that Donaldina would be ill at ease in the grand hall where the degrees would be awarded. It was quite simply that she, Rose Nesbitt, did not want her half-sister to meet Kier Anderson-Howard. For he too had hinted that he would like to attend.

Unlike Donaldina, he had not been subtle but almost direct. 'There's only this half-brother of yours in Australia, Rose . . .' (Rose had given him a carefuly edited version of her life story. She had never actually lied about Frazer – Frazer was too good, too noble not to be admitted into her life – but she had never told the whole truth either.) . . . 'and he'll never manage to come. Unless he's one of these fellows who suddenly finds gold. He's not an Australian millionaire, is he?'

'I doubt it. Murray is my half-brother, Kier. We're not really in touch. Men are notoriously bad correspondents.'

Kier, who had written letters religiously to and from many corners of the globe, did not deny this sweeping statement. 'You can't graduate alone, with no one to cheer madly,' was all he said.

'I'd like you to be there.'

'Good, and what are you doing with this hard-won medical qualification?'

Should she say something? Should she tell him? He could approach Dr Graham. Hadn't Dr Graham promised, hinted even, that she might help?

'I'm not sure yet. There are several possibilities.'

So far there were no offers of employment. No private doctor, no hospital, was rushing to hire the new female graduates.

'There's a further degree . . .' (My God, I've spent my entire life studying. Now I want to practise . . .) 'I'm not sure,' she finished lamely.

In the months before her graduation, Rose found herself worried more and more about the future. She was unconcerned about whether or not she would pass the examinations. Of course she would; quite simply, she was the best. She could not share her fears with Kier. He would speak to Dr Graham, and Rose had decided that she would rather starve than ask Dr Lucille Graham for a helping hand. If Dr Graham wanted Dr Nesbitt, she could jolly well come and ask her. Donaldina Nesbitt became her half-sister's only confidante.

'Whait will ye dae, hen?' Donaldina had asked, with a certain amount of relish as her sister became more and more dejected.

'I don't know. I can't believe it's happening. It's men, always men, with their wee small minds. They're terrified we'll beat them at their own game. Do you know that there are still professors in this very university who believe that if we were decent women we would find ourselves husbands and stay at home having children? Their knowledge has moved forward, but their petty little minds are still rooted in the Middle Ages. The law of the land says they have to educate us, but as yet it doesn't force them to employ us.'

'But the other lassies? Are no some of them getting jobs?'

'Yes, but not in Scotland. I want to stay in Dundee. I want to work right here, to help my own people.'

That much she could do. She could try to deny her own immediate family, but she would not deny her people.

And so the night before her graduation, which should have found her joyously looking forward to a glorious new dawn, found Rose Nesbitt biting her carefully nurtured fingernails and worrying herself sick about the future. She did not even try to sleep. She sat at her bedroom window wrapped in an old coat and went over and over again the interviews, the rejections. It was bizarre. It was insane. It could not be happening . . . but it was. Rose had applied for every opening in every hospital anywhere in Scotland, and had been rejected by every one. She was a woman and this authority and that authority did not hire women. Hospitals did not even want her on gynaecological wards, where one might have supposed there was a special need for a female physician. The other graduates in Rose's situation – that is those who had no money, no connections in the medical world, no fathers or brothers prepared to offer them a chance – were in the same position.

Rose re-read her letters of recommendation from her professors, from the dean of the university: '*outstanding diagnostic skills . . . eminently qualified . . . first-class honours . . .*

'This prize, that prize . . . this professor says, that professor says . . .' she muttered. But no one wanted to know. If a woman was poor, medicine was still a closed profession.

Rose got up from the window and moved restlessly around the room, her frustration mounting as she walked.

'It's so damned unfair. I'll be a doctor in a few hours and I can't work.'

Donaldina's voice echoed in her aching head.

'They cannae stop you, surely? Just hing a sign oot o' the windae and sharely the fowk'll come flocking.'

Rose stopped. Elsie too would have seen it as simply as that. A sign out of the window: 'Doctor Rose Nesbitt'. Consulting hours . . . any minute of the day or night. Oh, she'd be kept busy all right . . . eventually. Could she do it? What did she need apart from her skills? The list was endless. And how would she live while she waited for the first person who was brave enough or afraid enough to trust her? She looked around the simply furnished little room. She could not practise from here, from her lodgings, could she? The room was clean. One table, wooden. One overstuffed chair. A three-drawer chest. A wardrobe.

She remembered the handleless furniture in Elsie's wee place, the drawers that opened easily enough if a knife was stuck in just so; the curtain, heavily darned but clean, that hid the box-bed where Rosie and Ma slept. Suddenly she could see Elsie with her mug of tea. She was real; she could almost touch her.

'It wouldn't do, Ma,' she told the memory. 'It takes some money to start a practice and the folk up there, the ones I want to treat, couldn't afford to pay me anything. I have to find a job in a hospital or an opening with another doctor who needs a junior.'

As if in a dream, she saw Elsie reach over to put the kettle closer to the fire. 'Well, lassie, you could go on and do that other fancy degree you wis talkin' about.'

Rose felt an almost overwhelming feeling of love and gratitude well up inside her. 'Take still another degree. Don't hurry to pay us back. We were happy to help.' Was Elsie real? Was she a dream?

'I wish you were here, Ma.'

The dream Elsie emptied the cold tea into a bucket beside the fire and made a fresh pot. 'Ach, Rosie lassie. I'm that happy with whit ye've done. Look at yourself. Nae faither, yer ma nae better than she should hae been.' She held up her hand to still Rose's automatic protest. 'The good Lord kens fine whit I was, Rosie. I wisnae frightened tae meet Him wi' ma lassie there no' denying me. Lassie, lassie, yer a doctor. You can save life . . . you can . . . Ach niver mind. I cannae find the words, but I'm the proudest woman in the Hilltown, in the hale of Dundee. My lassie's a doctor. I'll be at your graduation, and our Frazer and auld Mr Wishart'll be there tae, never fear.'

Rose shivered. *Go to bed, Rose, or you'll look dreadful in the morning,* she told herself.

She slept, and the morning brought a huge bouquet of roses from Kier and a telegram from the university authorities. Miss Nesbitt was to be offered a Carnegie Research Fellowship at the instigation of Mr Carnegie himself. She was to become Assistant Professor of Obstetrics and Gynaecology for two years, at the end of which she would be offered the new degree MD. For Rose Nesbitt, MB, Ch.B, MD, there were to be no limits. Did Miss Nesbitt care to accept?

Miss Nesbitt sent a telegram of acceptance and cried with relief and happiness, but no one saw the weakness.

A very few streets away, Dr Lucille Graham sat over a breakfast of freshly squeezed orange juice, poached eggs on toast, and hot fresh coffee. She read her letters; one from her father from Washington, D.C.:

> . . . I plan to see one or two places before I return permanently to Scotland. Once at home with you, my dearest child, I know I shall not want to wander far from my pipe and slippers. I have long wanted to see the Rockies and the deep South. The du Pays have invited me on a little jaunt to Georgia. By the way, you do remember the du Pays? They are incredibly powerful and have the wealth that goes with such power, but there is something about Max that is so innocent, so naïve. I think perhaps he would have found life easier had he been born in a different century . . .

Lucy tried to conjure up a picture of Maximilian du Pay, but it was horses she saw; splendid, perfectly matched horses.

'Well, thank you for being so sweet to my dear father.' She sent the thought-wave three thousand miles and returned to the enjoyment of perfectly made coffee.

'Mr Kier, doctor.' Isa was at the door and there behind her was Kier.

'Oh, that coffee smells wonderful. May I have some?'

'Good morning, Kier,' said Lucy and waited while Isa carried a cup and saucer from the sideboard.

'I'll fetch some brown sugar, Mr Kier.'

'Don't bother, Isa. Mr Anderson-Howard wasn't invited for coffee.'

Kier smiled at Lucy and then, meltingly, at Isa. 'She doesn't mean it, Isa. She knows well the rigours of an early ferry from Fife. I am in need of a restorative, no longer being in the first flush of youth as you might say. Lucy, darling, all that is needed to make today perfect is for you to say you'll marry me.' He stopped clowning as if he, like Lucy, was taken by surprise by his levity. 'Please, Lucy. I want to be married. My house is so big and so empty.'

'An excellent reason for marrying,' said Lucy tartly, although her heart was pounding.

He sat down and stirred the sugarless coffee and, not for the first time, Lucy wondered if she had said the wrong thing. 'When is a woman old enough to know when she is saying and doing the right thing?' she thought.

'Father is in Washington. He's having a splendid time with all his old "buddies".'

He leaned across the table and put his strong brown hand over her equally strong pale fingers. 'Rose graduates today, Lucy. I had hoped you might hire her; you need a junior. You could go on holiday, visit your father, get married.'

There it was again. But was it now a joke?

'Can you come with me to the capping?'

Lucy looked at him in amazement. He had made no secret of his interest in Miss Nesbitt. What had been impossible to gauge was the depth or quality of his interest.

'I have met Miss Nesbitt twice, Kier. She would be extremely surprised to see me there.'

'But, Lucy darling. Think of our graduations. All the old toothless aunties; lovely presents, lashings of food and gallons of champagne. This poor little thing has no family. Her brother, who kept her alive until she was almost old enough to fend for herself, was captain of a whaling vessel which went down with all hands when she was scarcely sixteen. Her half-brother, her only other relative, is in Australia and seldom corresponds. Medical school was hard for you, Lucy, because of the climate of the time. Think of what it was like for her and come to cheer her.'

'I have an afternoon clinic.'

'Just this once, for me, can't you postpone, or get someone to help? Old Bracewell thinks the sun rises and sets on your head. Won't he take your overfed old biddies, just for today?'

Lucy folded her napkin primly, a gesture that should have told him, had he been in a mood to read signals, that she was angry; usually she tossed the napkin beside her plate.

'That was an uncalled-for remark. I can't think why you should think either Miss Nesbitt or myself would be cheered by an afternoon in the other's company. Now, if you have finished your coffee, I suggest you leave, so that one of us at least can do a decent day's work.'

He looked after her. That last had also been an uncalled-for remark. He was wealthy enough never to have to work but he worked very hard, not only in the management of his estate but in every charity or good cause that she herself laid before him.

'Women,' he muttered under his breath as he stood watching her furious departure from her elegant dining room.

Kier could not know, of course, for Lucy had taken great care that he should not, of the many hours of correspondence that lay between one Doctor Lucille Graham and those in charge of the future of his protégée, Miss Rose – so soon to be Dr Rose – Nesbitt.

Lucy had thought of offering Rose a job. She needed a junior; the girl was superbly qualified and trained. But between them stood Kier. Not for a second did Lucy think that Kier loved Rose. She had known him all her life; she had nursed him through illness and through Camillas,

Claires, Carolines and sundry other females. Rose was different, she was so obviously not of his milieu. But Lucy could not like her and she knew herself well enough to realize that she liked her less because of Kier.

Am I a frustrated old woman who doesn't want him herself but doesn't want anyone else to have him either? I don't think so. If he loved, really loved, and was loved in return I could cut the knots, but I'm still being weak in not taking Miss Nesbitt into my home. It's not because of Kier; it's because of my patients. This is my consulting room but it's also my home. I want to be happy here. I want the atmosphere happy. I cannot like Miss Nesbitt.

And then at one of her committee meetings of the Women's Hospital Board, the possibility of the offer of the Chair of Gynaecology had come up.

Lucy had thought long and hard, and eventually rejected the offer. 'I am sensible of the honour, gentlemen, but am forced to admit to you that I have no deep interest in the subject. I would suggest to you that Doctor Wentzell is far more qualified.'

'We thought that, since you are a woman, Doctor Graham . . .'

Lucy smiled. It really was the only thing to do when men pointed out something she had known for nearly thirty years. She spoke boldly, the weight of dear Mrs Dryden's money behind her.

'I have a proposition ... Lady Donaldson is particularly interested in a young female student ...'

'Mr Carnegie's protégée? Miss Nesbitt?'

Lucy had not heard of the great philanthropist's interest in Rose, but it proved surely that she was right that Rose was a suitable candidate. She agreed readily enough.

'In 1907 the degree MD, Doctor of Medicine, will be introduced from this university.' (Oh, that I could take it myself. You can't, Lucy, you can't. Too many depend on you.) 'If the university were to offer the chair to Doctor Wentzell, who is gaining a worldwide reputation in the field, and a two-year research fellowship to Miss Nesbitt as his assistant ...'

'Mr Carnegie will be satisfied. We gain a world-renowned professor and, in two years' time, our first female MD.'

And I don't feel that, because of Kier, I have to offer a job to Miss Nesbitt, thought Lucy.

There had been times when Lucy thought of submitting her own name as assistant to Dr Wentzell. She had even thought of offering Rose a partnership so that she would have time to study for the degree herself. Lucille Graham, MD, Lucille Graham, Doctor of Medicine.

Had it been Surgery, you would have jumped, Lucy Graham, she told herself. *But this is ideal. They say Miss Nesbitt is superbly qualified and, according to her record, she has a particular interest in Obstetrics. She should be the one to assist Doctor Wentzell.*

Lucy tried not to dwell on the knowledge that a two-year research scholarship would keep Miss Nesbitt very busy. By 1907 the world could have changed. Practices all over Scotland would be lining up to hire female doctors. Therefore she, Lucille Graham, would not feel that she had to ask Miss Nesbitt to join her.

I could have taken her as a locum and seen whether or not we could jog along together. Or I could have taken a holiday, joined Father on his little jaunt to Georgia or his trek through the Rockies. How wonderful that would be . . .

Patients and their well-being came first. The Rockies would stand until she had time to visit them.

She did not attend Doctor Nesbitt's graduation, and so she did not know that the day had been spoiled for Rose by the action of a half-demented drunken woman who had begged to be allowed into the hall where the capping was taking place.

'We're no good enough fer her now, but whae worked in the mills tae keep her ladyship at the skill. Yer mother wis a whore, Rosie, bluidy doctor Nesbitt, same as mine, and don't you forget it.'

Kier saw and heard the woman. He saw Rose, her face ashen, and then he saw Dr James Robertson gently lead the woman from the hall.

Rose saw him and felt the sudden bile in her throat. He knew, he knew, he had attended Elsie. Kier would find out, the dream was ended.

Her classmates were at her side, chafing her hands, begging her to take no notice, to remain calm.

'Doctor Robertson says there's an old drunk turns up at almost every graduation in Dundee. Part of the festivities.'

Rose could not enjoy her celebratory meal with Kier. Her trembling hands could not open his gift. Her mind was too full of Donaldina and the action of Dr Robertson. She had seen him often since the night when Elsie had died, and he had been his usual aloof self. Never, in any way, had he referred to the night, the patient, or the disease from which the patient had died. Why not? And once again he had rescued her. Why? What did he want? He had to want something. No one did anything for nothing, did they?

Had there been any phantoms at the capping, phantoms of long-dead lovers who had given everything they had for nothing, surely they would sadly have slipped away.

'Let me,' smiled Kier and he took the jeweller's box from Rose. There was a delicate gold watch inside. 'You see, not a personal gift, just something an old friend can give . . .'

Rose winced at its beauty. 'Rose Nesbitt, MB, Ch.B' was engraved in fine script on the back.

'It's lovely,' she said.

'There's just room to add MD.'

A little colour flowed into Rose's face. 'It all seems like a dream,' she said.

'It's not a dream; it's very real. You're a doctor, Rose. In fact, you're Assistant Professor of Gynaecology at the University of Dundee. Where are you going to live?'

'Live?' The thought had obviously not occurred to her.

'You can't stay in student lodgings. Have they told you there is accommodation at the university? I'm sure there must be.'

'I'm afraid I'm not taking anything in. It's all too wonderful.'

He smiled at her. 'It's going to be even more wonderful. Come along. You're dead on your feet; I'll take you home.' He saw the sudden look of panic in her eyes. 'I must catch the last ferry so I shall dump you out, Doctor Nesbitt, very unceremoniously, on your doorstep.'

She laughed and a few minutes later he did almost exactly that. He had gone before Donaldina staggered out of the bushes in the basement.

'Well, well, Doctor Nesbitt, too good fer yer ain blood.'

'I'm not working yet, Donaldina. I'll give you what I have, but I won't be able to help much for another two years.'

She emptied the shillings in her purse on to her sister's dirty, calloused hand. First thing in the morning, she vowed, first thing, she would find somewhere else to live, and she would leave the university as a forwarding address. She looked down at the dainty gold watch.

'I'm a doctor. I've done it and no one is going to spoil it.'

13

Dundee, 1907

DUNDEE HAD MANY philanthropists and among the most generous were the Cairds. In 1899 J.K. Caird, LLD, together with the Forfarshire Medical Association, had built a maternity hospital in Dundee. The need for maternity beds very quickly outgrew the new facilities, and in 1907 an extension was opened. There were six beautiful new spacious wards, each one holding twenty beds.

Dr Lucille Graham was one of the many doctors at the official opening. Dr Rose Nesbitt, Assistant Professor of Obstetrics and Gynaecology at the university, was the only other practising female medical practitioner present.

The younger woman bowed politely to the slim, elegant figure in the soft grey silk gown. Lucy smiled and held out her hand.

'Dr Nesbitt, how very nice to see you. I hoped you would be here; I hear such exciting things about you.'

Rose had learned to school her features but still a little surprise showed, while at the same time she strove to sound sophisticated and blasé. 'You terrify me, doctor. Surely not from Mr Anderson-Howard?'

'From Professor Wentzell and from other members of the faculty. I have been asked to attend your graduation, and will be most happy to be there.'

'How very kind,' said Rose quietly. She wished she could have bitten back that stupid remark about Kier. Now Dr Graham would think her guilty of bad taste, and it was so important to make a good impression – even after this, after nearly two years of research. Her findings had been published in the prestigious *British Empire Journal of Obstetrics*, and yet, and yet . . . She smiled at Lucy. Surely it was not too late to make friends.

Lucy made it easy for her. 'You must be very proud of yourself, doctor. I would give anything to be in your shoes, to be the first female medical graduate of St Andrews University, the first to be able to call herself MD.'

Rose was surprised out of her usual challenging, defensive mood and, if she only knew it, was for a moment at her likeable best. 'I can't believe it's all happening,' she confessed excitedly. 'I pinch myself sometimes. It's as if, suddenly, I'm looking over my own shoulder and I see myself practising medicine. I see someone look at me and take courage from my presence . . .' She stopped and blushed furiously. 'I'm sorry.'

Lucy felt a stirring of genuine liking. 'No, it's like that for me too; it has to be, hasn't it, or it makes everything else, the . . . little sacrifices . . . meaningless.'

Rose looked at her as if she could not see what sacrifices a woman like Lucille Graham could possibly have made. *Perhaps she's right*, thought Lucy. *Perhaps I have made no sacrifices. Marriage, children, Kier? Did I really want them? Do I still?*

'Tell me about the graduation, Doctor Nesbitt. I believe it is to be quite splendid?'

'I will find it difficult to be the centre of all eyes, Doctor Graham,' answered Rose truthfully. 'A new hood has had to be designed. It is to be magenta silk lined with white satin. The department has paid for it – two pounds ten shillings, can you believe! And so they would like it back for the museum.' She laughed at the carefulness of the department.

Lucy laughed with her and then spoke seriously. 'You have made a mark on the world, doctor.'

'I never meant to . . . make a mark. I wanted to make a difference . . . to the poor, to my own people . . .' Perhaps she could talk to this elegant, sophisticated woman who never in her life had had to wonder if there would be food on the table, who certainly never had to save for a year for the ten pounds needed to pay for the degree.

'And Mr Anderson-Howard is to host a dinner-party at the Faculty Club?'

She had to explain. 'He is a good friend, Doctor Graham, so unfailingly kind.' She could not add, 'It's no more than that. I do not want more, I fear more, and he is still confused by you, by the hold your shared memories have over him.'

Perhaps that was not true, completely true, either. The two women sat in nervous silence and, at last, the ceremonies began and they were able to stop thinking, analysing, and to give themselves up to the speeches, the rhetoric, the music, and then the interminable luncheon with more speeches washed down by, to Lucy if not to Rose, indifferent wines.

Lucy left before coffee was served. 'I was unable to get a locum and have had to delay my hospital visits, and then there is my evening surgery.' She held out her hand, now encased in the softest of soft grey leathers to match her exquisitely cut, deceptively simple gown. 'I have enjoyed today, Doctor Nesbitt, and look forward to – what would Kier say? – cheering wildly at your graduation?'

Rose watched her go, saw the heads bow as she passed, the lanes of frock-coated barrel-chested men separate to make passage for her, respect and admiration in their eyes.

She did not ask and I could not say, but I must, I must if I am to have a chance of staying here.

For the truth was that the men who controlled the hospitals, the practices, were no more amenable to Rose Nesbitt, MD, than they had been to Rose Nesbitt, MB, Ch.B Rose, who was about to leave her two-year secondment, had received but two offers of employment. The first was in Rhodesia and the second was in Australia.

'I suppose they are desperate in those countries and will take anything with a qualification,' Kier had said when Rose laughingly told him of her predicament, and she had laughed at his confusion.

'I know, I know you did not mean that I am better than nothing but, Kier, it is so bizarre. I had thought, in all modesty, that all doors would fly open before me at the end of this two years, but we are still as locked in the Dark Ages as ever we were. The very hospital where I lecture and do my research says there is no place for me in its wards. I am even unwanted in Gynaecology, my speciality. I have written to every authority in the country and even the inhabitants of the remote isles, it seems, would prefer to die rather than to be treated by a woman.'

'You must speak to Lucy, or let me. She needs a junior desperately.'

She leaned closer to him, and he was aware as always of the slight scent of Erasmic Violet soap that she used, and which he was still able to contrast with that faint musty smell that used to hang on her clothes. This new pleasing scent always made him feel protective.

'Don't, please, Kier. I couldn't bear it. Doctor Graham hasn't asked me to work with her; she must know I will soon be free.'

'But Lucy wouldn't intrude. She will have assumed you are ploughing your way through offers. You must let her know you are available. There's been so much on her mind this past year.'

Rose thought of Donaldina, whom she had managed to avoid but whom she still expected to pop up suddenly one day to burst her carefully blown-up little bubble. Perhaps it would be good to go to Rhodesia, not Australia where she might encounter Murray, or worse still Nancy, and be made aware again that her career had stolen Nancy's future.

'They say Africa is very hot, and I do like the sun.'

'No.' He was quite adamant and she was surprised at the violence of his reaction. 'You can't go to Africa. My God, I've been there. It's no place for a white woman, and especially a beautiful young one on her own.'

Rose blushed. Beautiful, he thought her beautiful. No, Doctor Graham was beautiful with the kind of looks that stay. She herself was pretty, like an advertisement for soap, all curls and innocence, and neither would last.

'I won't be on my own, Kier. It's a hospital. There are Catholic nuns and priests and at least one grizzled old doctor . . . and his wife.'

'Sounds a heaven on earth,' he said drily. 'Look, can we make a pact? I'll have this little party for you when you're capped and if Lucy hasn't spoken to you before then, you must ask her for at least a temporary contract, you know, to see if you would rub along together. I can't see that you couldn't. She's the dearest thing and as hard-working as you could like. You'd make a perfect partnership. She hates Gynae and you loathe Surgery. Do you know she's talking about putting her name down for a motor-car? The electric tram is a boon, but a car! There was a fellow had a little two-seater in 1899, used to watch him tootle down Reform Street. I'd have given my commission for that car. But anyway, Lucy needs a car. She can't be in two places at once, but a car would make it almost possible. She needs an automobile, but more than that she needs a junior and you are ideal. Will you speak to her?'

Rose thought carefully. Yes, to work for Doctor Graham would be the ideal solution. She could take care of the poorer end of the practice while Lucy dealt with the malingerers among the idle rich, but Lucy hadn't asked her and probably wouldn't ask. She doesn't like me. Oh, Kier, you poor fool. She'll hate us both if you ask her.

'I may approach Doctor Graham if I have received no other offers, but you must promise that you won't ask.'

He had promised and he kept his promise, but Lucy would have had to be extremely stupid not to be aware of the seeds he was planting.

Lucy sat whenever she had a chance to sit and watched the white blossoms drift down from the gean trees outside on the pavements. They were glorious, beautiful trees. In spring they were a mass of flurry, as Donald had called the cherry blossom, in summer they were cool and green, in autumn again they were spectacularly beautiful in their crimson and yellow gowns, and in winter they held their naked branches up against the bleak sky like some examples of primitive sculpture.

Dr Nesbitt, I find I need a junior.

Doctor Nesbitt, if you have not yet accepted an offer, I wonder if you would care to work for me.

She had to hire a junior. Perhaps it should be a man? Many of her patients' husbands, fathers, sons, still preferred a male practitioner. There were several capable boys graduating this summer. Hire one, check that he could handle the practice and then a three-month holiday; Italy, the Gulf of the Poets . . . You're daydreaming, Lucy. Your practice is ninety-nine per cent female. You will lose them all if you hire a boy and then go off for a . . . she had been about to say 'jaunt' but that was still too painful a word to use. Hire the little Rose and earn Kier's undying gratitude.

'Most men marry for security, for children ...' The words came back to her and angrily she pushed them away.

'If you love, when you love, really love, then nothing will stop you from marrying, not all the patients in the world.'

Who had said that? When? Oh, it was nothing. She would sleep on the problem. It really was the only thing to do.

14

Dundee, 1907

It was surprisingly easy to sleep once the decision had been made. Lucy had lain, gritting her teeth, demanding that sleep come. She had a long day ahead; consulting hours, home visits, hospital visits, the paper to prepare on the health of working-class children in the local schools, and Rose ... oh, yes, Rose. Doctor Nesbitt had said that she might call in, that she had something she wanted to discuss. Lucy knew the subject of the discussion. She had to be fully rested and alert to deal with Rose; not only Rose's life but Lucy's own future hinged on what she said to her. She had no real choice, only one decision could be made. Lucy made it and was asleep before she even had time to feel satified with herself.

Was there even a dent made in her pillow by the time Isa was there with her morning tea?

'It's half-past five and you said not to let you lie a minute longer,' said Isa, plumping up the pillows behind her mistress.

'Oh, I've just closed my eyes,' groaned Lucy. 'How do you always wake so fresh, Isa?'

'Sleep's a matter of a clear conscience,' said Isa, pouring the tea. 'You were an awfie time walking up and down afore you put your head on the pillow.'

If she hoped that her mistress would allow her into the causes of her insomnia she was disappointed.

'I'll be down in a minute, Isa. I have a visit to make to the Infirmary before my morning surgery.'

'You'll be the better for a boiled egg. That gives you three minutes from the time I get down the stair.'

Lucy smiled to herself. 'Oh, Isa, live for ever, and keep me sane with your boiled eggs,' she whispered to herself as she scurried around. 'I should definitely cut you off,' she told her hair as it defiantly swirled around her head, pushing the hairpins out as if the hair and the pins had lives over which they alone were in control, but at last she saw reflected in the mirror, Lucille Graham, MB, CM. If the eyes were not quite so sparkling as usual and the face was perhaps a little paler, no one would notice. Dr Graham was in control.

It was two-thirty before she had time to stop again.

'You look tired out,' scolded Isa. 'You'll have chicken soup; it's always good for whatever ails you, except lack of sleep. Come on, Miss Lucy. There's time before your evening surgery, and you'll do your patients no good if you faint from lack of nourishment.'

Lucy was sitting in solitary state at the top of her mother's cherished Jacobean dining-room table when she heard the front door-bell and Isa's voice as she muttered about the utter selfishness of those folk who would not leave a poor overworked woman to get a bite to eat. Lucy smiled and finished her soup.

'It's Doctor Nesbitt, Miss Lucy.' Isa was at the door, half in, half out.

'I was expecting her, Isa.' True enough. Rose had had to come, but she had thought tonight, surely, after her lectures.

'I've put her, them, in the morning room, doctor.'

Alarmed, Lucy half rose from the table. Isa only called her doctor when there were patients within hearing or if she was seriously disturbed. 'What is it, Isa? Has Doctor Nesbitt brought a patient, a slum child to dirty your chairs? You will have to learn to . . .'

'Mr Kier's with her.'

Kier! Lucy's heart rose. How lovely! It had been an exhausting day; it was only half over but seeing Kier, letting him hear her decision, that would be a joy.

She hurried past Isa and went to the small morning room. She had time to wonder at the beauty of the blossoming gean tree as it filled the window.

'Kier, my dear, how nice of you to bring Rose.' She went to him, her hands outstretched in welcome.

'Lucy.' He grasped her hands and held her there at arm's length. 'Lucy,' he said again.

Lucy turned to Rose. How delicate she was, how dainty. Rose had moved to the window and now stood, haloed by white blossom – an indescribably lovely picture. Lucy looked down at her plain black gown and contrasted it with Rose's pink silk. She wished she had tidied her hair.

Rose made as if to speak, but Kier caught her hand and at the look in his eyes, the smile on his face, Lucy sighed. *A medical fact, dear Doctor Graham. When you are about to receive bad news your blood does indeed run cold,'* she told herself.

'I'll tell her, Rose; it's only right. Lucy, my dear, I found I could not bear the thought of Rose leaving us for the vast uncharted wastes of Rhodesia. This morning she has done me the great honour of promising to become my wife.'

It does indeed feel like a sharp blow. Words hurt; they cut deeply, cleanly. Lucy heard herself utter all the right things, was aware that she was doing all the right things.

'You must come back for champagne, after my evening surgery. I do insist. You see, you now have two things to celebrate. I had planned to offer you a place here, Rose. I need a second good doctor. For Isa's sake if not for mine, you must accept, unless of course your . . . husband would not wish his wife to practise after the wedding.'

Was there a slight look of guilt on the achingly young, lovely, face? It was fleeting, a trick of the light perhaps, as it played among the cherry blossoms.

'Heavens, I thought only to keep Rose from emigration. What do you think, darling? Shall you accept? Shall I become a patient? And which of my two favourite doctors shall attend to my every ache and pain?'

'I have nursed you enough, malingerer.' Lucy was almost able to speak normally. 'When is the wedding to be, Rose? Your family . . . ?'

'My poor Rose is quite alone in the world, Lucy. It was the typhoid epidemic that took your parents, wasn't it, darling?' He did not wait for an answer. 'My mother, as you well know, Lucy, will be only too delighted to have me married as quickly as possible.' He looked at Rose. 'You don't intend to keep me waiting long, do you, my dear?' He turned again to Lucy. 'I shall take her over on the first train. Picture my mother's face, Lucy, when this time I tell her that her dinner guest will stay for ever.'

'After the wedding, Kier dear,' said Rose, a little archly. 'Do you mean it, Doctor Graham, Lucy? Do you want me?'

'There is more than enough work in Dundee for the two of us, Rose.' She could not lie in reply to the second part of the question, but Rose seemed happy enough with her answer. 'And I have promised Isa a holiday. We have lost so much this past year . . .'

'Then I accept and thank you.'

Lucy shook hands with her new partner and all the time her mind raced. 'Could she not have acknowledged our losses? No, Lucy, be kind; she's young and in love and she has just become engaged to be married.' At last, at last they were gone and there was Isa to tell her that her first patient had arrived, had been there for some time in fact. It was Mrs Brady, wife of a local councillor, and as usual she was worried about the condition of her heart. Lucy examined the woman, her face showing no distaste at the smell of unwashed flesh that fled from the tight encasings once Mrs Brady had been persuaded to – modestly – remove the top of her dress.

'Eat less and get a little exercise.' Lucy almost heard herself say the words. The practice had grown a thousand-fold since Mrs MacDonald and Mrs Dryden had taken up the new young lady doctor. Now there was more money to enable Lucy to practise in a less salubrious area of the city where the women desperately needed medical attention. Rose would enjoy that part of the practice, the Hilltown, the back streets of central Dundee. Lucy smiled at Mrs Brady, whose money made a partner possible.

'Your heart's sound as a bell, Mrs Brady,' she said and saw the disappointment on the fat face. 'I expect you are allowing yourself to worry too much about your family.' She coated the bitter pill of truth with sugar. 'I'll give you a little something to steady your nerves.'

The woman sighed with gratitude and relief. 'Thank you, Doctor Graham, I knew I could rely on you.'

Lucy showed her out, thinking, *Be kind, Lucy, be kind. Perhaps there is some dark reason why she haunts your surgery.*

The afternoon wore into evening, and still they came, and her mind had to deal with real people and real illness, but at last they were gone and she had to go upstairs and dress – to please Isa – for dinner. She had to sit at the table and toy with her glass of wine and face the fact that Kier would never sit at the end of it as her husband and now that it was too late, now that he had promised to marry someone else, Rose, she had to admit that always, always, every day of her life there had been the belief that one day, some day when she had achieved what she needed to achieve, when she had done what needed to be done for her own fulfilment as a woman, as a doctor, he would be there, smiling at her, holding out his arms to her, and she would run into them and . . .

Isa heard the crash of the door and her steps as she fled upstairs.

'Ach, have a bit greet, lassie, and maybe you'll learn what every fisherman kens. There's far better fish still in the sea than ever came out of it.'

Lucy had herself well in hand when Isa brought the early-morning tea next morning. She had cried – but more, she admitted, for the end of a dream than because her heart was broken. She had cried too because now there was no one in the world to whom she could tell her tale of woe. She could hardly tell Kier how she felt, if she could indeed work out exactly how she felt herself, and Sir John was dead, and Kier's defection had brought that appalling tragedy back. Sir John had gone from his 'jaunt' to the deep South on a 'jaunt' to the Rocky Mountain region of the western states. His last letter postmarked Portland, Oregon, April 10th 1906, had spoken of the majesty of the country, and had said that:

> after a tour of San Francisco, where I go tomorrow, I plan to return to Scotland. I have had enough of wandering and feel that I will be most happy never to have to venture farther than Fife. Can you house a crusty old soldier?

She had not worried when April newspapers spoke of an earthquake in San Francisco. After all, she still thought him to be among the magnolias and gardenias he so admired in Georgia. Max du Pay's letter had come in a diplomatic bag and so was faster than her father's last letter.

> When we heard of the devastation in San Francisco, I was able to go at once. We knew Sir John was to stay there and it distresses me to have to tell you, Miss Lucy, that the authorities do list as missing, assumed dead, one Colonel Sir John Graham. The center of the city was practically razed to the ground

and the chaos from the continuing explosions from burst gas mains and the ensuing fires had to be experienced to be believed. Sir John's hotel was totally destroyed and I will repeat, verbatim, the story told me by a waiter, a lad of about fourteen:

'The building just collapsed around us like one of them card houses the real good gamblers can make. We were in the dining room and lots of folk got killed as the chandelier crashed to the ground. There was dust thicker than a desert wind and I couldn't see nothing, nor hear nothing but the screaming of people, me mostly, I think, and the groaning of timbers. Then this thing appears, this great tall man comes out of the dust and he's carrying these two little girls and he's leading their momma and then, oh God, it was awful but the floor opened up right under us. There's this chasm in the floor and there's nothing below, not the laundry rooms which shoulda been there, just nothing but smoke and this dust that got everywhere so you couldn't breathe or see, and it gets wider and wider and then it closes up a little again and then it opens and then it kinda stays in one place. The guy sets down the little kids and he smiles at me and he says – and he talks real funny – "I do believe I can see what must pass for safety on the other side of this ravine," and I says, "That was the smoking room

but I think we just made us another garden room."
He was smiling so he made you pretend not to be
scared, you know. And he looks down at the girls and
he says, "Ladies, we are going to have an adventure. I am going to be a bridge and you are going
to walk across the bridge to my young friend's new
garden room. Can you jump the crater?" he asks me
and I say, "Yessir" although I never jumped nothing
that wide before, and he says, "Good chap." Good
chap. But I can't. I'm no athlete and it's wider than
me and he says, "Try the bridge" and he lays down –
Blessed Saviour, he lays down with his hands on one
side and his feet on the other – and I run across his
body, quick and light as I can, and the lady nudges the
little girls on his back and she's sorta pushing them
from one side and I'm reaching for them from the other
and they make it and he calls her to go and she's crying and he says, "Your children" 'cause he can't really
speak, and she stands on him and he shifts a bit and
then, dear God, it's getting wider and he gasps, "Your
children" again and she sorta runs across him and we
both turn to reach for him – and he's gone.'

Sir John was the only British resident of the
hotel at that time, Miss Lucy, and the actions of that
brave man just tell me this was the last deed of your
father and my friend.

The letter had gone on to talk about gallantry awards, but Lucy had read it again and again and hugged it to her. She had cried and then she had laughed because Sir John had saved four people and one was a waiter and she could almost hear her mother's voice: 'Your father just does not know how to handle staff.'

His body had never been recovered, and once again there had been a sad little ceremony in the churchyard in Fife. No bodies lay under that hallowed soil.

'I'll be the first,' thought Lucy, and had given herself a shake and told herself not to be morbid but to think of having a nice holiday with Isa who, after all, had lost Donald to pneumonia last winter. 'We'll go somewhere warm, just as soon as they're back from their honeymoon and Rose has proved that she can do justice to my patients.'

Dr Nesbitt did not face the dawn of her wedding morning with any of the feverish excitement experienced by most young girls. She had come to the conclusion during the long night that she had made a grave mistake. Had she waited one more day, just one more, Lucy Graham would have offered her a job. She did not want to marry Kier Anderson-Howard. She did not want to marry anyone, and certainly not now, not just at the beginning of her real career. And it was too late to tell him so. Today she was going to marry him, and tonight she would have to sleep with him. He had been so good, so patient. She did love him, she did, and she would do her best to be a good wife, but his restrained love-making frightened her and what it would be like when his passions were allowed full rein . . . oh God, it did not bear thinking about. All that *stuff* led to babies, no matter that early man had thought it led only to disease, and she wanted no squalling brats around her. She was no Elsie to take them all in her stride, no Leslie to die in her own blood giving birth to them. Oh, doctor, doctor, scratch an insecure woman and all the book-learning flows out with the blood.

'I'll get used to it, and it will mean nothing, and anyway, men want only satisfaction and once they have it, and that takes but a few moments, they sleep.' Rose had learned all these inalienable facts in her childhood and in her years of study among the poor and downtrodden – and yes, among the rich too. Men had the best of everything. Damn them all! Had they given her the job she had earned by right, then she would not now be lying in a cold sweat waiting for the dawn she did not wish to see. If only it could be just the way these last few weeks had been, the only cloud the patent dissatisfaction of Kier's mother. Kier was a gentleman and when told that his fiancée had not been brought up to 'indulge' her fiancée's baser instincts, he had coloured furiously and been a perfect angel ever since. Lucy was a splendid, generous and helpful employer. She had encouraged Rose to increase their list of poorer women, but had coaxed her into meeting the richer ones like Mrs MacDonald and her lovely young daughters. They liked having such a pretty new doctor. The oldest daughter, like Doctor Nesbitt, was also engaged, but how differently she approached the marriage bed.

'I can hardly wait, Rose. I may call you Rose. Frank and I are modern; we do not expect that I shall be, like my dearest mother, in an *interesting* condition every year. I could not have this conversation with dear Doctor Graham. Ma adores her but, *entre nous*, she is such an old fuddy-duddy.'

Miss MacDonald found that, like Doctor Graham, Doctor Nesbitt too was an old fuddy-duddy. She confessed to knowing all that there was to know about, well, you know . . . making sure that . . .

'Contraception,' Rose had said, taking great pleasure from seeing the effect that calling a spade a spade had on the pert young woman. 'I will be happy to give you the sum total of my knowledge . . . as soon as you are married.'

'Mother fell with me on her wedding night,' had argued the thoroughly up-to-date young woman.

'A risk all well-brought-up young women have to take. I will see you when you return from your wedding trip.'

'Please, could I not see you before, the day before? Even if I wanted to, I couldn't possibly commit a sin on the night before my wedding. The house will be packed to the ceiling with decaying relatives.'

Rose had promised to see her . . . and the embarrassed Frank.

Oh, yes, she liked being a doctor. She could spend the rest of her life quite happily just doing her job. And Kier? Could she do without Kier?

Kier was sweet; he was gentle, although every now and again she thought she saw a glimpse of steel, and he was kind. He was also very, very rich, and he owned Laverock Rising. Rose was honest enough to admit that she would love to live in that house, that its very name stirred her. As soon as Kier's mother moved out – she had bought a town house in St Andrews, bless her – Rose would have the house redecorated. Kier wanted her to change everything, to put her own stamp on the place. My God, to go from the Hilltown, to lodgings, to Laverock Rising. If she had to pinch herself to believe she was really a doctor, what would she have to do to convince herself that she owned that house?

Rose groaned and, turning over, buried her head in her pillow. She knew what she would have to do, and she hated the very thought.

15

Venice, 1908

AT FIRST, VENICE was a disappointment. Where was the light, the colour, the play of the reflections of the buildings on the waters of the canals? It rained the whole of the first day. Lucy sat at the window of her little hotel, La Colombera, and looked out across the waters of the canal to the Jewish quarter.

'I might as well be in Scotland,' she thought as countless tourists must have thought before her. 'At least there I could understand what is going on.'

She rang the bell for the maid and, with much laughter and gesticulation on both sides and referral by both women to Lucy's phrase book, managed to order water for a bath.

La Colombera, she wrote in her diary, for she could not write to Kier, not now that he was married to Rose, has the prettiest name, the prettiest maids and the hottest water in the whole of Italy. Her love affair had begun.

They took a gondola to St Mark's Square.

'You have to come, Isa. Heaven knows what the Italians would think if I travelled about alone.'

Isa had proved an enthusiastic traveller. She had, after all, never been anywhere before, but she had her standards. 'I'm not going in there,' she protested as they approached the doors of the great Basilica.

'No one is asking you to convert, but merely to see the architecture. It's reputed to be quite magnificent inside.'

But Isa would not compromise and stood outside under her umbrella while Lucy explored.

Even in the rain, in early April, the building was busy with worshippers and sightseers. It was very, very dark, and Lucy stood for a while until her eyes became accustomed to it and it was then that she became aware of a low sound, a voice at prayer. At a side altar a priest knelt. Aware only of his God, he was singing, and his voice, Lucy knew in wonder, could have graced any of the world's great stages. He was singing quietly, communicating only with God; his prayer was not meant for the world to hear, but Lucy moved over and stood behind him, listening, and as she listened she was filled with a tremendous feeling of peace and relief. It was as if her sadness and sense of loss were pouring out of her and joining the glorious voice as it rose to heaven. She felt that she could have stayed there for ever.

'Well, as I live and breathe,' said a voice directly behind her and Lucy turned and saw Maximilian du Pay.

He had hardly changed – tall, sun-bronzed, arrogant, his dark eyes smiling down at her.

Her heart leaped, her stomach churned. My God, after all these years, could his very presence have this effect on her?

'Max. What on earth are you doing here?' She did not wait for an answer but went on, 'Oh, Max, how very nice to see you.'

She had never answered his letter that told her of her father's last moments. She had meant to: she had sat, often, pen in hand, but the words had refused to put themselves down on the paper.

He smiled again, the smile that told her that he knew exactly what was going on in her mind.

'Good voice,' he said. 'Wasted, don't you think?'

'How can you say such a thing?' They were back in Washington, D.C., fighting with one another.

'To make you mad, Miss Lucy, or must I call you doctor now?'

She blushed at her gaucheness. She had not seen him for, dear God, was it fifteen, sixteen – no, seventeen years! His last act to her had been one of immense kindness and yet she was prepared to squabble.

'Max.' She looked around. There was no one who was obviously with him. 'I can hardly believe that you are really here. Your wife?'

'No wife,' he said. 'Not yet. Foot-loose and fancy-free, Miss Lucy.' In his turn he looked around. 'And you? Married to medicine?'

He did not make it sound attractive. Again she bristled. 'As it happens, that's exactly the situation.'

'It's so easy to make you mad. Where's your group, or shall I be your guide? I know everything about this church, since it has rained every day I've been here and it's the nicest place to shelter. Are you one of the faithful? Not that it matters in St Mark's which isn't really Roman Catholic. That's why that loss to the world of grand opera is singing at a side altar – the centre aisles belong to the Orthodox lot. Five denominations are represented here, even our Jewish brethren round the back.'

'Herr Colner.' For the first time in many years Lucy thought of her old tutor. 'I'd like to see the Jewish part, if it's true.'

'Now, why would I lie? This church wasn't built for the greater glory of God, Lucy' – he had dropped the miss, but there was no point in saying anything, she knew he would pay no attention – 'but for the greater safety of man. It's a centre of wordly power, a defence against the infidels pouring in from the north. Religion is incidental, but nice, when it's sincere like the boy with the voice over there.'

First Lucy had to marvel at the magnificent marble screen with its statues of the Virgin, St Mark and the

Apostles, and to stop, dazzled by the Pala D'Oro, the golden jewel-encrusted altar-piece of the Presbytery. But at last they reached the Jewish part of the Basilica.

'I don't know which way to look. It's all so overwhelming, overpowering, so unbelievably beautiful.'

'Here you are. Say prayers for your Jewish friends here. Basilica means, or was, the Roman centre of administration. Crafty Venetians added the religious element so that they had a place of sanctuary big enough to take the population. Jews were very welcome; they were the money-makers, and Venice even had at least one Jewish Doge. Why have you never married, Lucy?'

She had not remembered that Americans were quite so direct; she found herself answering honestly. 'I was never sure whether I loved the man I loved enough to marry him. And then he married someone else.'

'And are you sad?'

'Sad for me, yes, because time is rushing past, and I'm confused too.'

Even in the semi-darkness of the church she could see that he smiled.

'Then you can dine with me tonight and we'll talk about old times.'

What arrogance! He took her acceptance for granted. He led her through the church and out on to St Mark's Square where Isa still stood under her umbrella.

'Where are you staying? I'm at the Gritti Palace. Say you're there.'

'I'll say it, but it wouldn't be true. We're at a little hotel on one of the side canals, La Colombera.'

'I'll find it.'

'I haven't said I'll come.'

He smiled again. 'You have to take pity on a lonesome old friend. Eight o'clock.'

'Miss Lucy.'

Perhaps it was the note of warning in Isa's voice, but Lucy found herself agreeing.

'I'm not a young girl, Isa,' she justified herself on the way back to the hotel in the gondola, 'and besides, I've known Mr du Pay for years. His father was a good friend of my father. It was Mr du Pay, remember, who wrote to me about Father's death.'

She had nothing festive to wear. Every dress in the wardrobe said 'professional woman'. She threw them on the bed in a despairing heap.

'I need something frivolous to wear when dining with Maximilian du Pay.'

Desperately she took her scissors and unpicked the lace inserted into the neckline of her dark blue silk.

'Miss Lucy?'

Lucy ignored the shocked voice of censure. 'Good heavens, Isa! I could wear this gown at a medical consultation. All Mr du Pay will see is three inches of skin, well, maybe four.' She laughed, the laughter of a young carefree girl. 'I've missed this, Isa, this dressing-up and going out. I didn't realize how much. When my father was alive, I dined out almost every night, and danced and listened to beautiful music in lovely rooms full of hothouse flowers.'

She stopped, for suddenly a picture of the very young Lucy Graham had come into her mind. She was in the Russian Embassy in Washington, D.C., and she was wearing a white lace gown and her first, her only, string of pearls.

'I'm old, Isa. He'll see how changed I am.'

Since the death of her husband in the same month as that of Lucy's father, Isa had become more maternal, more proprietorial. She sprang now to Lucy's defence. 'Nonsense, Miss Lucy. He'll see a beautiful, elegant woman who has dedicated her life to others. He'll be honoured to take you to dinner.'

But Lucy looked at herself in the mirror and could see no shadow of the girl she had been.

'Has it stopped raining yet?' she asked calmly, for what did it matter? She was dining with ... she could hardly call him an old friend, someone she had once known and whom she had met by accident and would no doubt never see again.

The rain had stopped and Max had arranged for a private gondola. He helped her in as if she were a piece of exquisitely delicate Venetian glass, and for the first time in her life Lucy felt small and vulnerable.

'I thought it best to dine at the Gritti Palace, Lucy. Should any of your family connections see you, your reputation would come to no harm in such a public place.'

'Good gracious Max. I'm not a young girl.'

He laughed, a full-throated laugh that echoed over the waters of the canal.

'Bravo, Miss Lucy, for a horrible moment I thought you'd changed.'

They smiled and gave their attention to enjoying the journey as they turned into the Grand Canal. Churches and palaces stood shimmering in the waters, lights streaming from every window. The mooring poles for private gondolas stood, their family flags blowing in the evening breeze. Liveried gondoliers handed jewelled women on to sumptuous cushions and, everywhere, there were reflections.

They caught glimpses of inviting little side streets. 'Oh, wouldn't you love to explore up there, Max?'

'I have. The gondolas take so long to get anywhere because the canal twists and turns, but actually it's quite easy to get from here to there if you walk, crossing the bridges. I've found churches with paintings by Canaletto just hanging on the walls, exquisite little gardens. The entire city is a living, breathing art gallery.'

Lucy clapped her hands like a child, her face still turned to the wonders on either side. 'I must take a tour. It's a dream city.'

They arrived at the small dock outside Venice's grandest hotel and the gondolier handed Lucy out. She looked back at the canal.

'It's so ethereal, I almost expect it to disappear.'

'I don't want to disillusion you, but sometimes you might wish it would disappear. They're not always too careful about hygiene.'

'Oh, don't, Max.'

He tucked her gloved hand into his arm as they walked into the hotel. 'Tonight, I promise you, only Venice's glorious surface.'

It was pleasant to bask in the unexpected admiration in a man's eyes.

'You grew up, Miss Lucy,' said Max in his soft Southern voice as Lucy handed over her cape. 'We won't have champagne. Italians, very sensibly, see wine as an accompaniment to good food – the two together, very rarely alone. Shall I order for you? You would be sensible to have fish; or do you know Italian food?'

The meal was exquisite. Because of her father's career and her own long training, Lucy had travelled extensively and was used to different cuisines, but Italy was new and she revelled in it, protesting only at the array of sweets that finished the meal.

'I can't, Max. I've eaten vegetables, and pasta, and such delicious fish. I've had soup and bread and . . . was that really rice with the fish, and so much wine . . .'

'Let's dance then. I've never danced with a doctor before. I met one once, a lady doctor, that is . . .'

'You make it sound like a bug, Max.' Lucy laughed and deepened her already throaty voice. 'I met one once. Shot it and had it stuffed.'

He held her more tightly and they moved together on the terrace to the sound of violins.

'We could have champagne now, or more wine?'

'Coffee,' said Lucy firmly.

He laughed and led her back to their table. 'Now tell me more about why you haven't combined matrimony with your career?'

It was an impertinent question, but tonight was a special magic night and she answered without thinking.

'It's as I told you, Max – and almost every minute since we last met, I've been studying or working. That doesn't leave much time for love.' How easily she could speak to him. 'Can you understand how important medicine was, is to me? I had to do something with my own life to make things better for those less well-off. Everywhere I went with

Father it seemed to me that the poor really had little chance of a decent life, and women almost none at all, and there I sat in my lovely home with my lovely gowns and everything was so easy and my parents, my mother, expected that it would go on. I would come out, marry the right man . . .' Her voice broke a little and Max squeezed her hand. When had she given him possession of her hand? '. . . and have the right number of children, but I couldn't. Oh, Max, if you could see some of my patients . . .'

'You work with the poor?'

'No, not really. My parents weren't wealthy. I have no private income and so I have two practices, one supports the other. My . . . my colleague, to her credit, works mainly with the poor, but . . . she is married now, and no doubt things will change. She will have children . . .'

Her voice wobbled again. Rose would have children, Kier's children. Lucy shivered.

'Let me get your cloak. We'll walk back across the bridges of Venice, and tomorrow I will take you to the Bridge of Sighs and I'll show you a church where paintings by Canaletto hang for everyone to see.'

She was outside, and somehow it seemed right that he should hold her hand, and she trusted herself to him completely as he crossed one bridge and walked past sleeping buildings, and then crossed another little bridge and they stood and looked at their reflections quivering on those of Venice in the waters.

Did Venice work its magic or was it Max? She could have walked for ever. She forgot Kier and Rose and her patients and was, once again, carefree. They were outside La Colombera, where Lucy lifted her head to look at the carved doves that flew permanently among the flowered vines that hung over the door and Max kissed her, softly, very gently, on her lips.

'Tomorrow, I'll show you paintings, Veronese, Tintoretto . . .'

'And Canaletto.'

'Better bring the dragon lady, although I'm quite sure she'll find Veronese's voluptuous women quite decadent.' He kissed her again and this time she lifted one hand, rather tentatively, to his neck.

He smiled. 'Yes, better bring Isa. Goodnight, little doctor. I've never kissed a doctor before.'

He turned and she stood watching him until he crossed the last little bridge and disappeared up a side street.

An old lady, disapproving like Isa, handed Lucy her key.

'It's only an interlude, a magic interlude,' she told herself as she prepared for bed.

'And so sensible, Isa, to go with Mr du Pay who knows Venice so well,' she told Isa next morning as they ate their delicious breakfast of coffee and warm, crusty bread straight from the oven.

For three days they went everywhere with Max. He was a knowledgeable and charming guide and even Isa relaxed and admitted, somewhat grudgingly, that Venice had its points and only some decent roads could improve it. Rice, however, would always remain something with which to make a pudding and should have absolutely nothing to do with fish or meat.

Max did not kiss Lucy again.

'It was the wine,' she told herself. 'We had too much wine.'

For their last dinner together, she bought a new gown.

Signor Bico, the owner of the little hotel, told her how to get to a shop where she could find a reasonable gown, Italian in design and cut but not Venetian in price. That price still made Lucy gasp, but, oh, she turned this way and that and knew that somehow the dress had been designed for her alone.

She dressed for dinner, put on her pearls and took them off again.

The admiration in Max's eyes was unmistakable. 'You should have rubies with that gown, Lucy. May I buy you rubies, a souvenir of Venice?'

'Don't be silly.'

The dinner was superb and the orchestra in the little restaurant played the same Italian serenades as the musicians in the Gritti had done. They danced and Lucy relaxed in his arms and willed the night to go on for ever.

'Shall we walk back through the streets, one last walk?'

Of course, how silly. It was over. It had to end but she had not expected it to hurt so much. They put Isa into a gondola; she now trusted Max completely and apart from a, 'Don't stay out too late, Miss Lucy,' she said nothing.

'I'm leaving tomorrow, Lucy.' They had reached the little bridge. She looked down into the water and saw his reflection as he moved closer and tilted up her face for her kiss.

'Come with me, Lucy.' His voice was almost desperate. 'I'm going north to Tuscany . . . to paint. There's so much I have to . . . we have to decide.'

He kissed her again.

'It's Venice, it's Venice,' she tried to tell herself as her pulses raced and she pushed herself even closer to him, responding with every fibre of her being.

Drowning in her own senses, she pulled away from him. 'Don't, Max. I can't think.'

'You think too much, Lucy,' he said breathlessly. 'Sometimes it's better just to *do*.'

'No, no, I can't go to Tuscany.'

'You're not a child, Lucy. I won't deny that I have designs on your virtue, but I am, I hope, a gentleman. Bring Isa. I have hired a woman to live in and cook and clean; she has her husband with her to drive the cab. I'll tell her to bring her cousins and aunts if that makes you feel better, but we can't just decide, "that was a real nice little holiday," and go back to everything the way it was before. At least I can't, Lucy. You've come to mean so much. I can't tell at this point if it's love or lust, not with you standing there shimmering in the moonlight. I'm in Italy to decide what I want to do with the rest of my life: I think I want you to be a part of it.'

She heard a small, trembling voice say, 'We'll come.' The voice was stilled by his kiss. She saw Venice reflected in the water and then she could see and hear and feel nothing but Max. He gained control first.

'If your patients could see you now,' he said somewhat shakily. 'Don't change your mind, Lucy of the red dress. You have thinking to do too, I know. Let's think together in Tuscany.'

And that was why she found herself on a train with Isa, a thoroughly disapproving Isa who sat tight-lipped as they crossed one after another of Italy's wonders of engineering.

'Look, a bird's-eye view of Italy,' Lucy would say as she peered out of the window and looked down at the valley hundreds of feet below. She tried hard not to think of what would happen should the train fall off the track.

'It's not my place to say, doctor . . .' Isa would begin.

'No, it's not.'

'But it's not what Sir John wanted for you.'

Ah, that silenced Lucy's protests.

'It's perfectly correct, Isa. We are going together to stay with a friend. There are servants in the house.'

Lucy sat, pulses racing, feeling a little sick. What had she promised on that magical Venetian night?

'I'm not a child, I'm not a child,' she kept telling herself, 'and Max is a gentleman.'

Just thinking of him seemed to conjure him up in the carriage, although he had gone ahead the day before leaving Lucy perfectly free to change her mind. At the station, before leaving Venice, she had almost done so when she had to telegraph Rose to let her know of the change of plan.

Venice was wonderful. Going on to Tuscany to compare Florence. Returning one week. Lucy.

'I'm insane,' she had chastised herself. 'I'm a respected Dundee doctor; I've worked so hard to be where I am. What am I doing here?'

And all the feelings of hurt and despair came flooding back. She was here because all her life she had loved Kier Anderson-Howard and he had married Rose and for the rest of her life she would have to watch them, day after day, unless, unless . . .

She sent the telegraph but the doubts did not fly away with it. How can I go to one man while I love another? What do I feel for Max? Do my pulses race whenever I see him because I love him, or am I a desperate woman snatching at a chance for happiness, a chance to experience what Rose has experienced? I'm thirty-six years old. Am I flattered because a handsome man desires me? Oh, God, does he desire me, Lucy, or just the body?

Dusty and tired, she climbed from the train when it finally stopped at the station at Aulla, and there was Max. He shook her hand, friends who were meeting to tour a delightful region of a delightful country.

'Look,' he pointed behind him. 'There's still snow on the mountains but the valleys think the spring is here: Mauro will take your bags, ladies.' An incredibly bent and wrinkled old man, rather like a splendid vine, smiled broadly at Lucy through blackened teeth and, picking up all the bags in one massive sweep, loaded them into the back of the little trap. 'We're heading up there.' Again Max pointed to the mountains. 'Can't you just see why Italy produced Titian and Michelangelo? I've already set up my humble easel in an overgrown orchard.'

He talked and talked and the nervousness fell away; even Isa seemed to succumb again to his charm and more than once pointed out clumps of wild irises waving at them from the roadside.

'You'd pay a penny or two for flowers like that in Dundee,' she said.

'I did explain this was no luxurious villa I've rented?' asked Max anxiously as the sure-footed pony pulled the loaded trap up winding roadways. It's a maze of little rooms added as the family expanded. It was a farmhouse, but as far as I can make out everyone in the village owns a bit of the land now.' He became very quiet as the trap pulled further and further into the mountains and into the village of Montale. To Lucy it seemed as though the streets were too narrow for more than one human being, never mind a trap loaded with four people and luggage, and several times she could have touched the walls or picked flowers from a garden, but at last they stopped. Mauro jumped down and held the pony's head – in case we slip back down the mountain, thought Lucy.

'Welcome to Casata d'Aurora, Lucy.'

The house was long and low and built of whitewashed stone. There was a courtyard in front where a yellow cat dozed on a terracotta pot full of blue blossoms that Lucy did not recognize. The courtyard supported several ancient vines which laced together overhead to form a roof.

'In summer, they say, the leaves and grapes give shelter from the sun.'

In late spring the sun chased its own beams through the tracery of bursting young leaves. The house itself was held in the arms of the mountain slopes and seemed to rise out of a cloud of white and pink blossoms.

'Cherries,' said Max, 'and peaches, apples of course, and pears.'

'Casata d'Aurora?' asked Lucy in a voice so quiet that it could not break the spell.

'The little house of the dawn.'

'Ven, ven, ven …' The raucous voice disturbed the moment and out of the door burst a little woman as gnarled and wrinkled as Mauro.

'This is Stella, my housekeeper, and she has hot water ready for you to refresh yourselves, and a meal fit for a king.'

16

Tuscany, 1908

CHURCH BELLS WOKE Lucy at 5 a.m. She counted them and then smiled and tried to go back to sleep. Almost five minutes later the church on the other side of the Tavernelle told the sleeping village that it was 5 o'clock. Lucy smiled again but gave up all thought of sleep. Five hours was a good night for a doctor. She would lie and rest and wait for the dawn.

It came and, forewarned by bird-song, Lucy sat wrapped in her dressing gown and watched the sun appear over the mountains. Sentinels of pink and gold and blue painted the mountains and the trees and the old churches. They reached the orchard and Lucy saw the blossoms quiver as they saluted the arrival of the Sun God. The valley shimmered in a blue haze. And then Max appeared, a Max that Lucy had never seen before. He wore no collar and his shirt was unbuttoned and, unaware that he was being watched, he stretched his arms above his head as if he too showed obeisance to a deity. How tall he was, and how masculine. The peasant shirt was moulded to his body and Lucy hugged herself, why she did not know. Max set up the easel and after several minutes while he watched the mountains and Lucy watched him, he began to paint. He was totally absorbed in what he was doing. She could not stay and watch him secretly; that was almost like spying. She would dress and go out to him.

Lucy winced as her bare feet touched the tile floor. Quickly she washed, using the cold water in the ewer, and dressed. She thought for a moment of leaving her hair down, but then quickly coiled it and pinned it securely to the top of her head.

So engrossed was Max in what he was doing that he did not hear the swish of her skirts through the long grass of the orchard. He was painting a picture of the mountain-side. There was the rough outline of the first church which towered above the house, the trees, even the blossoms.

He had to decide about the rest of his life. Was this the decision that had to be made?

'Are you trying to decide whether or not you have enough talent to become a painter?'

He made as if to stand up and she put her hand on his shoulder to keep him down. 'No, don't get up. I didn't mean to disturb you.' Her fingers stayed lightly on his shoulder and she could feel the strength of him through the thin fabric of the shirt. When she lifted her hand and held it tightly against her, she could still feel the heat in her fingers.

'No.' He answered the question. 'I'm a mere dilettante.'

'Well, now that I have become such an expert on Italian artists, I would go so far as to say that you are very talented.'

'Why, thank you, ma'am.' He looked at her and smiled, and it was she who dropped her eyes and moved away. Something was happening to her. She could feel Dr Lucille Graham slipping further and further away. It was the magic of Italy, of course, nothing more.

He had followed her. 'I cannot paint the mountain with you standing there against the cherry trees, Lucy.'

'They're quite beautiful, aren't they?'

'Yes, very beautiful.' But he was not looking at the trees.

'Why, there's Stella,' said Lucy almost breathlessly. His size was so overpowering in the small orchard, and yet she was not a small woman.

'She has coffee ready and fresh bread.'

They went back to the dining room with its bare white-washed walls and heavy oak table.

'What an absolutely divine smell,' said Lucy. 'I'm hungry, would you believe? After that dinner last night, I felt sure I could never eat again.'

The moment of tension was over as they drank large mugs of coffee and ate bread still warm and steaming inside.

'Shall we go to Florence today, or shall we explore the valley?'

'Oh, the valley please, Max. I'm still digesting the magnificence of Venice.'

For the next few days, with Isa, they meandered along winding lanes. Bird-song accompanied them, and the tinkling of the bells worn by goats and sheep and the occasional cow. They met very few people, and those they did meet were shy but friendly.

'They are so poor, Max, and they work so hard, but they seem to have no jealousy. And the children we see look healthy.'

'Country living, Lucy. The back streets of the cities will teem with disease and squalor, just like every place else.'

'I suppose you're right. I must make notes, though. The chestnut flour for bread and their pastas, eggs, goat's milk, and cheese.'

'And a long summer of vine-ripened tomatoes, and countless other vegetables and fruits, but think of this paradise in the winter when the snows come down from the mountains.'

'They must preserve food. I shall ask Stella.'

'That will be an interesting conversation,' laughed Max.

'I meant, you will ask her for me, won't you Max?'

'I am clay in your hands, Lucy, not marble.' He looked towards the mountains. 'Carrara is over there. Carrara, where Michelangelo got his marble. I wonder if we could get there in a day?'

They never got to Carrara; neither did they see Florence.

'I'd like to paint the house from the top of the mountain. Let's take a picnic up there.'

Isa preferred not to go. 'What am I supposed to do with myself while he sits for hours painting flowers and you get lost in a book? I'll stay and work with Stella.'

'Analyse that friendship, doctor,' laughed Max as he encouraged the pony to trot up the mountain path. 'One speaks not a word of English and the other no Italian, yet they laugh and chatter by the hour together.'

'Perhaps they're saying perfectly dreadful things to one another.'

It was a glorious day, the warmest they had had so far. The air was soft and clean and clear. They reached a glade in the shadow of the ruined church that towered above the valley and unharnessed the pony.

'I hope I can catch the little rascal this afternoon or we'll have a long walk and some explaining to do to Mauro.'

Max set up his easel and Lucy spread a blanket on the grass and sat beside him. She did not read, but closed her eyes to enjoy the feel of the warm sun on her face. The sounds of the valley floated up to join those of the mountain; bird-song, bells, the dull but rhythmic sound of a woodcutter, running water. Lucy slept.

'*Una biquieri di vino rosso, Signora?*' Max's voice disturbed her. He was sitting beside her on the blanket, two glasses of Mauro's raw red wine in his hands. 'You hold the glasses and I'll get the bread and cheese.'

The food tasted as Lucy had never tasted simple bread and cheese before.

'It's the air,' said Max, and then he kissed her and it was the most natural thing in the world. She was lost in his kiss; she knew nothing, thought nothing. All she could do was feel. His hand was on the buttons of her blouse and, for a second, Lucy's eyes flew open and she could have said no. But her senses, so long repressed, were surging and seething and her whole body was on fire with longing. His fingers touched her breast, his lips found her nipples and she moaned with a desire for fulfilment. He moved away from her and she groaned and pulled him closer. She could not bear it; he must not leave her. She was dying.

And then his body blotted out the sun and she knew nothing, nothing but the wonder of Max du Pay . . .

She opened her eyes to a snowfall of white apple blossoms. They were on Max's hair, his back, her breast. She laughed and Max opened his eyes.

'Veronese,' he said and kissed her again.

'Canaletto,' she answered and allowed her hand to slide with proud ownership over his bare broad shoulders. 'But I'm too skinny for a Veronese portrait.'

'You are magnificent,' he said.

Lucy shivered.

'The sun has gone behind a cloud,' he said and helped her to her feet. 'Well, ma'am, I have come to a decision today. I love Lucy Graham and I want to stay here and paint for the rest of our lives.'

Lucy turned away from him as she fastened her skirt. Her mind was racing. Stay here for ever? He loved her. She had to love him. She could not have responded to him so eagerly and fully if she did not. But stay here? What about her patients? Isa?

He smiled down at her, a smile tinged with sadness. Had he expected her to say something? Of course he had. But what could she say?

'Come along, Miss Modesty. Help me catch General-issimo.'

The pony was only too happy to be harnessed and Max seemed to be totally occupied in harnessing him and loading the little cart. Lucy reached for the picnic basket just as he did and their hands met. He tightened his hold on her fingers and Lucy trembled as the fire that had consumed her began again to glow.

'Oh no, please, Max, don't touch me. I can't think.'

'I know. I don't want you to think, Lucy.'

'It's not fair.'

He bowed; there were still blossoms in his hair and her hand ached to reach out and touch them.

'We'll talk at the table. You at one end, me at the other.'

'We'll have to shout,' said Lucy and he smiled.

Isa and Stella watched them arrive back at the house. Stella smiled and shrugged as if to say, 'Of course it has happened. They are in love.'

Isa did not shrug with the calm easy acceptance of the Italian. She shook her head and went back to washing the vegetables. Vegetables were the same in Scotland or Italy; they came out of the ground dirty and you washed them.

Lucy wore the red dress at dinner.

It seemed as if Stella had lit every candle she could find in Tuscany and the sombre dining room was bright as day. The candlelight glowed on Lucy's white shoulders; it revealed highlights in her dark hair and it showed her eyes sparkling and shimmering.

Max stood behind her to pour the wine. He did not touch her but still she felt as if his hands caressed her shoulders as they had caressed her body a few hours before. They did not shout, they did not even speak. They sipped the sparkling Italian wine and their eyes talked across the table.

Stella placed the food before them and they made an attempt to eat. Lucy tasted nothing, she did not know what she ate. When Stella came to remove the plates of antipasto Max stood up and Lucy watched him as he came to her. She gave him her hand and he pulled her to him. He did not kiss her but stood for a moment looking down at her, and the desire in her rose to meet his. His arm went around her waist and, unafraid, she went with him.

Stella found the room empty when she returned with the steaming vegetables. She shrugged and smiled.

'Well, well,' she said. 'The chickens will feast tomorrow.'

For three days they lived in a world where nothing mattered but their love. All day they talked and said nothing that was significant, content to live for the moment in the world of their senses. They took huge picnics with them to local beauty spots and while Lucy ate – she could not believe her appetite – Max painted. He painted furiously as if he had already wasted too much time, or perhaps as if he knew that it would be years before he painted again. All night they loved and Lucy thought of nothing but Max and her need for his hands, his mouth, his body.

On the fourth day they went once more to the orchard above the Casata, and Max painted Lucy as she lay among the blossoms. They returned to the house to find the telegram which had followed him from Venice and lay on the table. All her life Lucy was to hate telegrams.

'They're never good news, are they, Max?' she said.

'It's my father.' His face was grim. 'I have to leave at once, Lucy. I may be too late already.'

Less than an hour later, she said 'Goodbye' to him.

'Oh, dear God, if only it wasn't so far,' he groaned into her hair as he held her close.

'You'll write, Max, when you can? I'll wait for your letter.'

She stood in the soft Italian dusk for a long time and watched the progress of the pony and trap as it went off down the mountain. Even after she could no longer see it, she stood on the terrace under the great vine and looked down into the valley.

'*Caffè, Signora?*' Stella was there and Isa, an Isa with eyes full of sadness.

'*Si, Stella. Grazie.*' She took the coffee. How hot it was. How good.

'We'll leave tomorrow, Isa. We really shouldn't have stayed so long. Mrs Anderson-Howard – (somehow the name didn't hurt) – has held the practice together too long on her own.'

They took a cab from the station when they finally arrived in Dundee. Isa was white with exhaustion and Lucy felt guilty. Isa was too old to be trundling around Europe like this.

'I told Donald I'd aye bide with you to look after you, Miss Lucy, and that's what I'm going to do,' she had insisted.

'You can have a good sleep in your own bed tonight, Isa, and a lovely long rest tomorrow.'

'A rest . . . with my kitchen not scrubbed for weeks?' The jute-filled air of Dundee had revived Isa as the clear air of Tuscany had rejuvenated Lucy. For the first time since the telegram, Lucy was able to smile.

'It was sensible to come back before I'd made any irrevocable decisions,' Lucy told herself as she stood in front of her mirror brushing her hair, hair that Max had admired as it tumbled down over her bare shoulders.

'You should always wear blossoms.' She could almost hear his soft warm Southern voice.

She trembled and was suddenly filled with an agonizing sense of loss. *Max, Max,* her body whispered across the miles. She ached for him. If only, if only. 'Selfish,' she scolded herself and tried to think of Max's father and of Max's unhappiness. Had he really made the decision to stay in Italy? Could she have, would she have stayed with him?

She hardly slept and welcomed the bracing effect of the cold water she splashed over her face and neck next morning. When she had finished dressing she looked again in the mirror. Tall, thin, almost sallow. Brown hair pulled back tightly into a coil. A high-buttoned, plainly cut dark blue dress. This was the woman who had gone to Italy to nurse a broken heart. Of the naked girl in the apple orchard there was no sign.

When Rose arrived for her morning consultations, Lucy was already seated at her desk going through the accumulation of letters and notes on cases that awaited her. Rose was conscientious and thorough and her notations were copious and detailed. They made it easy for Lucy to greet Kier's wife.

'And how is Kier?' she was able to ask as they finished the coffee Isa brought for them.

'Thoroughly happy,' said Rose. 'He is taking a real interest in finding us a house in Dundee. This daily travelling across the Tay is really not very sensible for me.'

'No, you're right. It does make for a tiring day. Where are you looking?'

'Kier likes Broughty Ferry, but I think a small flat in this area. Kier thinks he'll want to stay in town during the week but really, it would be more sensible for him to stay at home. We don't need two large houses.'

Lucy looked at her and heard the deliberately light tone. Six months' married, and already Rose was talking of separate living arrangements. Of course it was sensible. She was seeing a problem where none existed, she told herself as she stood up.

'You have had to work so hard while I was away, Rose. I don't know how you managed it. Perhaps you would enjoy a few days at home, or to go house-hunting?'

'I've loved every minute, Lucy,' protested Rose. 'I don't mean that I haven't missed you ... the practice hasn't missed you, I mean, but I've relished it, being responsible. At last, at last I am a real doctor and you trusted me enough to leave me in charge. I hope I haven't made any mistakes.'

'It's unlikely that the best diagnostician of her year has made any mistakes,' said Lucy drily, 'but we ought to start seeing our patients. I have a paper to write on the health of Dundee school-children, and I would like to do as many home visits as I can today. If you'll send in my first patient on your way out . . .'

Eczema, ecthyma, strumous sores, psoriasis, scabies, warts; Mrs Campbell to be assured that her first pregnancy was progressing perfectly naturally; polite and encouraging words to tell Mrs Hartley without offence that there was nothing wrong with her that less rich food and more exercise wouldn't cure; Mrs McLeod to be told that, yes, she had a tubercular disease and that it had gone too far for there to be much her doctor could do for her except make her more comfortable.

There was no time for lunch, not that day nor the next nor the next. How had Rose managed on her own? Hospital visits had to be made – not many, only to her wealthy patients in their private rooms. Oh, the frustration of not being allowed into the general wards to see the women there, to see anyone, man, woman or child. Overworked, underpaid male doctors struggled along in the wards because too many still believed that women were too delicate and pure to be subjected to the sights they would see in a hospital.

Rose raged. Lucy accepted.

'It's changing, Rose, but things move slowly and we will only hold up the changes that are bound to come if we antagonize everyone in power. You are a doctor. Isn't that enough for now?'

Rose's answer was almost a groan. 'No, no, no. It isn't. I have to admit that I long to change the world.'

Lucy smiled. This was the Rose she liked and admired. 'You have changed it, doctor. Now go home. You have a husband to look after now too, and I have my paper still to finish.'

'I shall be anxious to see your paper, if I may. Remember I have first-hand experience of both the Harris and the city centre schools.'

Lucy looked up from her notes. Rose was standing in the doorway. Where had she come from, the beautifully groomed and dressed woman who stood there, a diamond and ruby brooch glittering amongst the lace at her throat?

'Rubies, let me buy you rubies.' She heard Max's voice so clearly that she almost answered him again: 'Don't be foolish.' She had packed away the red dress carefully. When would she ever wear it again? Italy. Italy. Just a few days ago I was in Italy in an orchard and Max . . .

'Are you all right, Lucy?' Rose's voice was concerned.

'Tired, as you must be.'

'I'll say goodnight then. You must visit and tell us all about Italy, Lucy. Kier is especially keen to hear all about Venice.'

Venice. Casata d'Aurora. In the busy days that followed Lucy began to feel almost as if it had never happened. She prepared her paper:

I have examined 539 girls. Among these were six mentally defective twelve-year-olds who are being dealt with in the infant classes. They have learned nothing.

There are appalling differences between children from various schools. In good schools, and I mention particularly the Harris Academy, girls and boys seem equal in their intelligence and ability, but in the poorer areas girls are much brighter.

Lucy stopped writing and looked again at her notes. Bodies very dirty. The boy with honeycombed teeth. Rickets. Lice. Enlarged hearts. St Vitus' dance. Bowed legs, flat feet, spinal curvatures, knock-knees, pigeon breasts, rickets, rickets and more rickets, wryneck, cleft palates, anaemia ... oh, God, would the list of the sufferings of children never end? If they could only get better food; if there could be cleaner air in the classrooms. Surely opening windows would be a good start? Could there be some way that they could remove outdoor clothing indoors? Cloakrooms of some kind? Sometimes it appeared that the ones without shoes and coats were healthier than those well wrapped up. Perhaps it was because wet feet dry much faster than wet shoes.

> In the poorer schools, the older girls are usually quite clean, but the bodies of the smaller children are very dirty and their heads are lousy . . .

It was then that Lucy realized that for the first time since she had begun to menstruate she had missed a flow.

17

Dundee

IT WAS IMPOSSIBLE to expect a letter from Max so soon and yet Lucy found herself feverishly turning the letters on the breakfast table over and over, half hoping that somehow she had missed an envelope with Max's distinctive thick black writing on the front.

'I will not panic,' she told herself a million times a day while she dealt with other women's wanted and unwanted pregnancies.

'Shall I write to him?' She did not. If she wrote she would be forcing him into a decision which he had to make for himself. Instinctively Lucy knew that, if she were to tell Maximilian du Pay that she was expecting his child, he would move mountains to marry her.

'He has to want me, just for me,' Lucy whispered as she lay night after night in sweat-soaked sheets, and tried to work out how long it would take a letter from Max to reach her.

'He needs to write it first, and if his father is ill he will be too worried and too busy, and if his father has died then he will have the funeral to arrange and the family business to re-organize. He will have no time to write to me until everything is settled. It could take months. I must be patient.'

Lucy remembered that Max's father had been a member of the United States Senate, and she tried hard to recall everything her mother had said about the family, but try as she would nothing came back. The young Lucy Graham had been too interested in flirting with a Russian count – or had he been French? She could not remember. He had mattered so little and Max du Pay mattered so much. How had he come to mean so much and in so short a time?

I didn't even like him, she told herself in anguish. *He was so arrogant, so sure of himself.* And then she turned her head into her pillow and wept. 'I must have been so young: too young to realize, to see how really wonderful he was.'

And still no letter came.

'Are you all right, Lucy?'

It would be impossible to hide from the trained eyes of another doctor, a doctor bursting with youth and beauty.

'You have been working so hard since you came back. You must come and dine with us on Saturday,' Rose went on. 'I have made a few changes to the house, just a few, and I would like to hear what you think of them. And then there's Venice. You promised to tell us all about Venice.'

She went to dinner and she sat at the Anderson-Howard table where the young Lucy had sat so often and where she had imagined herself as Kier's wife. She saw the candlelight dancing in Rose's eyes and Kier's mother's diamonds sparkling around Rose's white young neck, and she told them about Venice and Canaletto and Veronese, and she gave them their Venetian glass candlesticks, and she did not mention Maximilian du Pay. She did not tell them about Tuscany either, and certainly said nothing about an orchard and a man and a woman with blossoms in their hair.

Kier was happy. He followed Rose's every movement and listened avidly to everything she said.

'Do you approve of my changes, Lucy?' asked Rose as they sat in the drawing room after dinner.

Lucy had noticed the different wallpaper and the new upholstery in Kier's mother's little sitting room. To her the newness had been like a raw wound, but she had tried to see it with a stranger's eyes and she had to admit that the selections of bright new materials were charming.

'I have no right to approve or disapprove, Rose.'

'Oh, I know that, but you have such excellent taste and I wanted to know if you agree with my choices.'

Of course she would need to change the furnishings; she had to stamp her personality on to this house that had sheltered Charlotte Anderson-Howard for nearly half a century.

'Mother thinks it lovely, Lucy. She says she was always much too lazy to change anything,' said Kier, his eyes noting his wife's skill as she poured the coffee from the Georgian coffee pot that had belonged to his great-grandmother.

'It's charming, Rose, and a perfect foil for you.'

That was when the cramp struck and she bit back a gasp of pain and surprise. She excused herself and hurried along the corridor to the room set aside for her use.

'Not in this house,' she prayed. 'Not in this house.'

Another ferocious cramp gripped her stomach and she felt the warm, sticky wetness on the insides of her thighs, but she was a doctor and had dealt with the symptoms so often. There was pain and relief mixed with sadness in the white face that stared back at her out of the mirror.

Did you merely hope to be pregnant, Doctor Graham? she whispered to herself. *Travel, change of food, of climate ... of living conditions, all upset the harmony of normal bodily functions. You need never write to Max du Pay. There is nothing he needs to know.* She wanted to get home, to weep for the end of a dream, for the end of a nightmare.

There was still the evening to be got through, and she was glad she had not accepted the invitation to stay for the night.

'Are you unwell, Lucy?' Rose was outside in the corridor.

'No, thank you. Merely "the curse of Eve".'

'Oh, won't you change your mind and stay? Bed and a nice hot water bottle on your stomach . . .' Rose blushed. 'How dare I prescribe for you?'

'Dear Rose,' smiled Lucy. 'It sounds delightful, but I'm perfectly well and will catch the Aberdeen train. Isa would worry.'

And when the evening was over and she had said all the right things and admired all Rose's changes, Kier took her to Leuchars and she got on the train and sat down with relief in a first-class carriage where she was the only passenger. She put her hands on her stomach and hated its flatness, its barrenness. 'Poor unconceived little baby,' she thought. 'If you had existed, what price to pay for a marriage that your father surely does not want. For him I was part of the romantic dream of Italy, nothing more.'

There Lucy wronged Max. He had laughed at the young British miss he had watched flirting so admirably with the Russian Count at the Embassy in Washington. He had thought then that she was too young for him. She should have her head for a while; she should be allowed, even encouraged to break the hearts of a dozen Washington beaux, and then when she had reaped the field – and if she had not herself been harvested – he would make his play. Max du Pay well knew what a catch he was on the marriage market; he had been told often enough.

When circumstances changed and the flibberty-gibbet young socialite had shown the depth of character he had only suspected and remained in Britain to attend a university, he had sighed a little over his wasted opportunity but wished her well. There were, he thought, a thousand Lucy Grahams. But he had never found one . . .

And then he had reached the age when even he told himself that it was time to settle down, time to decide whether politics or managing the family's considerable business interests was to be the life for him, time indeed to marry. But Max was a romantic and wanted to marry a woman he could not possibly live without, and not just one who would be a perfect hostess in the du Pays' magnificent Southern mansion house or who would properly spend a large proportion of the du Pay money.

He had been seeing a great deal of Ammabelle Redmond.

'That girl's chitter-chatter is like water on a stone, Mister Max,' his old nurse, Florrie, told him time and time again. 'If you don't come to a decision, she and her mammy are going to do it for you. They'll wear you down and you'll find yourself hogtied before you can say it don't make no never-mind.'

Max did not at that time appreciate the incredible power of dripping water.

His father wanted him to assume control of du Pay Chemicals and du Pay Engineering, and his mother wanted him to marry Miss Redmond and to stand for the soon-to-be-vacated local Congressional seat. Max could just as easily have done one as the other, and had decided to travel in Europe for a while before deciding. And there in Venice he had met again Lucy Graham and, being a romantic, had recognized his twin soul, and the intensity of his feelings had almost frightened him and had made him shout out with laughter and relief as he walked back to the Gritti Palace from the little hotel where Lucy was staying.

'What a woman,' he had told a black Venetian cat as it looked at the strange, tall man who was not drunk but who sang out like a drunk across the Venetian waters.

He could have told her of his feelings that first night in Venice but as he had held back in Washington, so he held back now. In Tuscany, in the apple orchard there had been no need to hold anything back for she had held nothing back from him. She was tall and strong; she was a doctor. Yet she had made him feel like a giant whose sole aim in life was to protect her. The telegram, so unexpected as are most of life's blows, had spoiled everything. He had to get back to his father, to his mother who would surely crumble like a building that has lost its foundations should anything happen to Henri Jacques du Pay, 'Senator Hank' as the Southern press called him. They were already publicizing his death when his only son reached Georgia, and his mother, who for years had ruled a huge staff with an iron will, sat crumpled in a chair like a heap of faded flowers and held up a devastated face to her son.

When had he promised to marry Ammabelle? She and her mother had been there in the cool, quiet room with his mother when he arrived. They seemed to have been there every time he turned around since – at the funeral, at the interminable reception afterwards where he had to smile and say all the right things when he wanted to cry like a little boy, on the verandah beside him when he waved goodbye to the last house-guest. His mother said that he had promised, and that the marriage would have made his father very happy. The pictures in his mind of Lucy, shyly smiling at him in the gondola, devastating in the red dinner gown, naked in the orchard with apple blossom in her hair and on her breast, began to fade or at least were superseded by other more immediate pictures and sounds – the dull thud of wet mud falling on his father's coffin, and Ammabelle's soft Southern voice like dripping honey. He felt tired and listless; he had no energy. One month since he had left Lucy, two months, three. Surely she would have written if he had meant as much to her as she had to him? Surely she would have expressed regret at the death of his father? The announcement had to have been in the British press.

The British press had covered the death of the eminent Southern politician, but it did not cover the engagement of his son to Miss Ammabelle Redmond of Sea Island, Georgia and Philadelphia, Pennsylvania, nor publicize the society wedding of the year.

On the morning before his wedding day Max had left the house at dawn and saddled the tall, raw-boned horse that was his favourite. He had ridden until he and the horse were exhausted, and then he had lain down under a tree and slept. It was late afternoon when he awakened, and he had sat up and leaned back against the tree and tried to sort out his thoughts.

'I am marrying Ammabelle and I love Lucy. This is crazy. How did it happen? If I told her yes, if I asked Ammabelle to be my wife, I cannot turn my back on her. Was I mad with grief? I thought I was rational. I did everything that had to be done. I talked to Ammabelle of marriage, at least she talked to me, but that was before I went to Europe, why I went to Europe, because I could not make up my mind. Or was it just about working for the family? I can't think, I can't think.'

Max beat his fists against the hard ground in frustration and remembered that the last time he had lain on the ground he had lain with Lucy.

'Oh, Lucy, my heart! What have I done?'

His horse stood patiently at his side, reins trailing. He caught them up and vaulted into the saddle, his body and his heart for the first time in months as light as thistledown.

And there on the verandah was his mother, as pale and frail as a moth.

'Oh, Max, my dearest boy,' she whispered in her pale, frail voice. 'I was so worried, you were gone so long. We have to get ready for your bachelor party, my dear.' She clung, light as a burr, to his arm and led him along the verandah to the door of his room. 'Oh, Max, I have always wanted you to marry dear Ammabelle, the daughter of my very dearest friend. You have given me something to live for. Your father would be so proud of you. I wasn't going to tell you this yet, it's a kind of wedding present, but the Party wants you to fill Daddy's place. What a truly good son you have been to me all my life, and especially now in my time of grief. I wanted to die with Daddy, Max, but now you and Ammabelle will fill this sad house with music and laughter again.'

Her hands clung, her voice clung, sweet sweet as honey, till he felt he was drowning. He could not get his head out from under.

18

Dundee, 1914–1916

'DON'T BE RIDICULOUS.' Rose was angry but also, and later she would try to analyse why, a little frightened.

She pushed back her chair and stood up. 'I'm going to bed, Kier. Have your coffee here or in the drawing room.'

'But wherever you have it, don't bother me. Is that what you are trying to say, Rose?'

The years had not been so kind to Kier Anderson-Howard as they had been to his wife. He looked his age, although he was fit and healthy and carried no spare weight on his tall, lean frame. Rose was still slim and, to Kier, even more lovely. He had long since forgotten the waif in the too-big dress. No one could possibly recognize Rosie Nesbitt with her rough red hands and the badly bitten fingernails in the delightful creature staring angrily at him from the door.

'You always have to equate everything with sex, don't you, Kier? I would prefer to sleep alone tonight because I have to get up very early tomorrow – Lucy and I have an important consultation at the infirmary – but I have never denied you and if you must have sex . . .'

'Sex? I might have felt like making love, Rose, but not now. You're quite safe.'

He turned away and reached for the claret jug that still stood, almost full, on the table.

'Perhaps I won't bother with coffee. Good night, Rose. I'll sleep in my dressing room.'

'And you won't do anything silly?'

'As usual you are right, my dear. The British Army wouldn't want such an ancient recruit.'

Rose stood for a moment watching him. She wasn't worried that he would drink too much – no, not Kier. He was as disciplined in his way as she was in hers. Perhaps if he wasn't . . . But at least he was not going to contact old friends at the War Office and ask their help in enlisting. Enlisting? At his age? Blast the Germans! Life was so pleasant, and they were spoiling everything.

The practice had grown. They had even hired a male colleague, and so Lucy had begun to fulfil her dream of taking a further degree at the university. Now the decision as to whether or not she should specialize in surgery was being taken out of her hands. War had been declared and young Doctor Thomson, like too many other young men, was anxious to leave everything for which he had worked so hard, to join the Army. And there too was Kier, Kier who had willingly resigned his commission to take over his estate, aching to 'have a go at the Hun'.

Rose undressed angrily. Men were so stupid! If they were not, if they were as rational and as level-headed as women, there would not be this war that was raging out of control all over Europe. Stupid men with their hearty 'over by Christmas, lads'.

'I can't see it being over until they've all blown one another to bits,' thought Rose, 'and where does that leave me? They wouldn't take him; surely they wouldn't.'

Rose liked being Dr Rose Nesbitt very well. She admitted too that she liked being Mrs Kier Anderson-Howard very well too. Kier was an attentive, even an adoring husband, although sometimes in the last year or two she had found him looking at her in a questioning way. She knew he was distressed that there had been no children. He did not know that there were no children because Rose was taking great care that there should be none. At the beginning of her marriage she had said, 'In a year or two,' but now, she admitted to herself – and Rose was almost always truthful to herself – that she had no intention of ever having a child. Because she knew more about birth control than probably any other doctor in Britain, it was quite easy for her to adhere to this decision.

'I don't want a child because it would obviously inter-fere with my career. Kier even complains about having a working wife. If I had a child he would really put his foot down.' She tried not to admit that, even though she was a doctor and had been at countless live births, the thought of having a baby terrified her. She had watched women in labour, women powerless to control what was happening to their own bodies. 'No, no, I must always be in control. I know it's safer now than when my sister died, safer than when my mother was producing rapidly and, in her case, easily, but it's not for me. I'm needed where I am.'

She heard Kier's firm tread as he reached the door of their bedroom and she sighed resignedly and threw down the covers in welcome; she would never deny him. But when the footsteps died away towards his dressing room, she pulled the covers back up and turned over into the pillows. No, he would not change his mind. He had said she would sleep alone and he always kept his word. The sheets were cold. Kier always lay on her side to warm it before he slid over to his own side. It would have been quite nice to have had his arms around her. She had not been home for a week, and before that she had had her period.

'If he'd just do it and get it over with, I'd call him,' but of course he wouldn't because for him it wasn't just sex but love, and he would do his utmost to see that his wife was pleasured too.

'Damn all men,' thought Mrs Kier Anderson-Howard, and eventually fell asleep in the cold bed that could so easily have been warmed.

'I have your anniversary gift at the house, Rose,' Lucy said next morning as they drove to the hospital in Lucy's splendid new Bentley.

'Oh, how kind, Lucy,' said Rose. 'After all these years, you shouldn't have bothered.' But inside she was realizing why Kier had been just a little difficult at the weekend. She had forgotten again and this was the second year in a row. To keep Kier happy she should have been delivering and receiving unsubtle hints about gifts, but she found that difficult. Kier had given her so much in the last seven years that there was nothing to want, nothing to desire, and what *he* wanted she could not, would not give.

'Can you and Andy handle surgery tonight, Lucy? I wanted to surprise Kier by going home for dinner.' She would do what she could.

It was worth the trouble. He was like a child on Christmas morning when he came out of the musty old estate office she never entered and found his lovely wife sitting in a swirl of yellow silk in her drawing room.

He stood at the door for a moment, joy leaping in his eyes. 'Rose, my dear. I hardly hoped . . .'

She stood up gracefully and walked towards him. 'Silly, did you think I would miss our anniversary?'

'Surgery?'

'Lucy and Andy will manage.' She said it lightly, as if he was much more important than the evening consultations. 'Lucy has sent us a gift. You can open it after dinner and come in with me tomorrow, if you're not too busy, to thank her.'

'Tomorrow?'

'I must catch an early train, but I couldn't not be with you on our sixth wedding anniversary.'

'Seventh, darling.'

Rose coloured delicately and raised her lovely face to his. 'Sixth, seventh? I can't remember life before you, you silly old thing. Don't you realize that?'

And it was true, of course. She had become both Rose Nesbitt, MD, and Mrs Kier Anderson-Howard within the same three months and she had had no time to think of the hard years of struggle before then. If a photograph had existed of Rosie Nesbitt, she would not have recognized her; she would not have *wanted* to recognize her. Sometimes, in the mean bedroom of a simple house, she would find memories tugging. She would look at a wee girl in a patched frock sitting by the side of her mother as the woman struggled for the seventh, eighth, ninth time to bring new life into the world, and she would remember Rosie, more often Elsie, and double, if possible, her attempts to ease and help. Her work done, she would return to her spacious modern flat. She would have a hot bath in her beautifully appointed bathroom; she would make herself some tea and some toast; she would remember Kier and his constant worries over her health, and she would boil an egg, and then she would sit and in the peace and quiet of her home, gather strength again for the next day. Life was good.

There were the odd niggles. Kier's mother had never really wanted her as a daughter-in-law. She was unfailingly polite, but she had wanted Lucy, poor Lucy who obviously still loved Kier. Clever Lucy, she managed to treat him like a favourite brother but, poor thing, she had made no attempt to find anyone else. The servants, too, made Rose uneasy. They were never insolent, for then Kier would have dismissed them, but there was a certain something, too many . . . 'Mister Kier said . . .' She was 'madam', very rarely even 'Mrs Anderson-Howard'. Kier's mother, in her lovely town house in St Andrews, was Mrs Anderson-Howard. No, this was where she belonged, in this lovely renovated flat, and alone. She was happier alone. She was so tired after a day and sometimes an evening of medicine.

'You're not strong enough for the life of a doctor, Rose.' That was Kier. 'No woman is . . . well, there are exceptions, like Lucy. She's physically strong. But you're such a delicate little woman.'

Remarks like that brought back memories too, memories of running from the Hilltown to the Harris, a fresh bap in her hand, another in her bag for dinner.

'Of course I'm strong, much stronger than I look. I've never been sick a day in my life.'

Andy Thomson enlisted: silly young fool. There was no need for him to enlist; as a doctor he would have been quite safe.

'We'll have a place for you when you get back, Andy,' said Lucy. 'We'll even be thinking of a partnership, won't we, Rose?'

Rose smiled at the joy in the boy's eyes. Yes, he had good reasons for coming back: a partnership, and a young teacher at the high school who was no doubt promising to write.

* * *

'You didn't tell me Andy had enlisted. I met Lucy for lunch this morning when I was in town and she told me.'

Rose had not expected to find her husband in her flat when she returned home from the hospital. She liked to keep the flat as a sanctuary, just for herself. 'I didn't think it very important,' she said lightly.

'Rose? Your junior decides to go to war and you don't think that important?'

'Of course it's important, but we don't see one another every day and it wasn't ... vital. I mean he hasn't gone yet. For heaven's sake, Kier, did you come here to fight? I would have told you when I remembered.'

He came over and put his arms around her. 'I'm sorry, darling.' He kissed her gently, tenderly, softly, until she relaxed against him. 'Do you mind if I stay? I miss you.'

'You own this flat.' Her voice was calm but there was no excited welcome.

He moved away from her. 'Rose, I bought the flat for you. The deeds are in your name.'

She went after him, put her hand on his arm. 'Did you have a decent lunch with Lucy? I have eggs and perhaps some cheese . . .'

His face lit up. He was so sweet, so like a child. 'You can't cook, can you? I thought we might go out.'

'I can't cook, darling, but I can scramble eggs. We could have a light supper here, just the two of us.'

He followed her into the tiny kitchen. 'I have never seen anyone cook anything in my entire life, you clever little thing. Nanny used to make cocoa. My mother doesn't know where the kitchen is.'

Rose tied a sensible apron around her trim waist. 'I'm quite sure she does. Mrs Potter is forever telling me how much better the real Mrs Anderson-Howard does things.'

He looked ill at ease. 'Old family retainers are . . . difficult, but one word from you and they go, my darling, every one, lock, stock and barrel.'

Rose laughed and handed him a bowl. 'Here, take your vehemence out on these eggs.' She took another apron from the drawer and tied it around his waist. 'Now, aren't we the domesticated old married couple? I understand Mrs Potter. Don't worry. It's difficult for them, I know.'

'Perhaps Mother should have taken the old ones with her to St Andrews. It's just that Laverock Rising is their home.'

'I understand.'

He put down the bowl. 'Lucy, let's go to bed. If you had a baby, if you stayed at home all day, things would be different.'

She turned off the gas burner and went with him. What could she say? 'Even if I did have a baby I would still want to work. I couldn't give up medicine, I couldn't.'

Later, as Kier slept, she poured the beaten eggs into the sink and washed up the dishes. She did everything else she had to do too; there would be no baby. In the bedroom she looked down at her husband. Curious how young and vulnerable he looked while he slept. She felt a rush of almost maternal warmth as she bent down and kissed him lightly, and he smiled and stirred in his sleep.

Andy Thomson went off to the Front, but to his dismay – and much to Lucy's joy – his Front was a hospital near London. Lucy bought him a copy of a book that had just been privately printed and which was setting the literary world afire, James Joyce's *Dubliners*, and sent it off in a box with shortbread – Rose never used her sugar ration and had willingly handed over a supply for Christmas baking – and some of Isa's best oatcakes.

The year 1915 started badly with Clydeside armament workers striking for more pay, and got steadily worse. In May a train crash at Gretna Green in the south of Scotland killed 158 people, many of them soldiers. In July, 200,000 miners in Wales went on strike, and on December 30th a U-boat sank the liner *Persia* with a loss of 400 lives.

In October, the Germans had executed the nurse Edith Cavell, and not only Kier but Rose herself began to mutter about 'helping put an end to all this madness'.

Lucy remained calm and sensible.

'How could they shoot a nurse, Lucy, someone who was there to help?' Kier Anderson-Howard was a decent man who could not understand or accept unreasoning, ferocious brutality.

'To them she was not a nurse; she was merely someone who broke martial law. It was a particularly stupid thing to do because they have created a lovely young martyr for the Allies.'

'Will her death help to end this abominable war?'

'Would yours, Kier? Miss Cavell did what she did because she knew that, for her, it was the only way to behave. You have a huge estate to run, an estate that feeds hundreds. That is viable war work.'

'My grieve can run the farms, Lucy. I am a crack shot and a trained soldier; perhaps I would be better employed in the Army in some capacity.'

In the end Kier and Rose decided to turn Laverock Rising over to the Ministry of Defence for use as a convalescent home, and Kier moved permanently into the small flat in Dundee. Their marriage had been shaky for some time, but while they had maintained the custom of Rose working in town all week and going over to Fife at the weekend, the cracks had not grown or even, to the unobservant, been particularly visible.

'Sometimes I wish he would join the Army,' Rose confessed in exasperation to Lucy one day as they found a few moments to sit and enjoy the soup that Isa had made for them.

'Good gracious, Rose! You can't mean that; he's too old to start all over again.'

Rose sighed. 'Of course I don't really mean it but, Lucy, I can't breathe in the flat with Kier there. He's so big and when I come home at night, he wants me to sit with him, talk to him, listen to music. I want to be alone, to unwind, to rewind. I usually eat a boiled egg, have a bath and go to bed. Kier wants Mrs Kier Anderson-Howard at his beck and call. And that dratted woman is driving me mad.'

Lucy hesitated. She had worried about the marriage for a long time. She had watched Kier change from being the sunniest of men to one who was withdrawn and even moody. He was her oldest friend, but her partner was his wife and she could not take sides.

'It must be difficult with Mrs Potter in such a tiny flat.'

'I seem to be the only one making adjustments. They invade my home . . .' She stopped as if she was aware how odd that must sound. 'I mean, it's the huge meals, every night, dressing for dinner . . . Mrs Potter didn't even pass on a message last week. "Madam is at dinner", says she. I was so angry I could hardly speak.'

'Yes, that was unforgivable, but understandable. Why don't you buy a bigger house?'

'I suggested that but Kier says that it would be wrong. Surely you must have noticed how diffident he is about having so much money, and to spend hundreds of pounds on a new house when people are starving all over Europe . . .'

Lucy could see his point, but she could see Rose's position too. A pity that they had got into the habit of being part-time man and wife.

'Be patient, Rose. Kier will change his mind if he sees how difficult such cramped living is for you.'

But by their eighth wedding anniversary Mr and Mrs Kier Anderson-Howard were barely speaking to one another, and Rose was finding more and more work to do and more and more reasons to stay overnight in the quarters made available to her in the hospital.

19

Dundee, 1915–1916

AN OUTRAGED ISA was at the door to meet her. Lucy registered the fact that she was still wearing the old dressing gown that she had first worn all those years ago, that she had even taken to Venice, that had gone to Tuscany. Tuscany . . .

My God, Isa is old, old and tired.

'It's Mr Kier; he insists on seeing you. I told him you were out at a confinement and would need your sleep as soon as you got home, but will he listen? And' – and Isa was outraged – 'he's been . . . drinking and he—'

'Go to bed, Isa, dear. I'll speak to Mr Kier.'

'I'll go when I've given you your supper and watched you eat it, and not a minute before.'

'Where's your new dressing gown?' asked Lucy, knowing the answer but vainly trying to deflect the old woman's ire.

'Oh, that's far too good for the house. It's for the hospital when my time comes. I'll not have you ashamed of me.' She turned towards the door. 'He's in the morning room and I redded up the fire. If he's not too drunk, he'll have put a log on.'

The firelight danced around the little room as years ago the sunlight had danced through the window, turning Rose into a fairy-tale creature. Now it showed Rose's husband lying in her father's chair by the fire, his long legs stretched out before him. He looked young and vulnerable, fourteen again.

Oh, dear God, what happened to us? her heart cried.

She shook him. 'Kier, wake up.'

He groaned and stirred and then opened his eyes and he no longer looked a child. He was a man, a sad, unhappy man who, for once in his adult life, had had too much to drink. He stumbled to his feet.

'Lucy, forgive me, what a time to be calling, but I had to tell you. You had to know first.'

Lucy turned up the gas-light and he turned away from her. She went to him. 'What is it, Kier?' She grasped his arm. 'Turn around and face me, man. I've seen and heard worse than you can ever tell me.' She felt a sudden fear. 'Is Rose all right?'

He laughed, a singularly unpleasant sound. 'All right? Rose is always all right.' He was quiet for a moment as he leaned on the black marble mantelpiece and then had to push himself up from it. He obeyed the urging of her arm and turned to face her. 'I raped her, Lucy, raped my own wife, but that's not what I've come to tell you.'

'Your tea, doctor, and there's coffee for him.'

How much had Isa heard? Her face registered nothing.

'Put it on the table, Isa, and go to bed.' Lucy spoke sharply, more sharply than she had intended, and the old woman walked stiffly from the room.

'I'll worry about her hurt feelings tomorrow,' thought Lucy as she handed Kier a cup of scalding coffee.

'I'm not drunk, Lucy.'

'I know. Sit down and tell me what it is.'

He stopped, the cup poised near his face. The steam hid his eyes. 'I've enlisted in the Black Watch,' he said simply. 'I'm off tomorrow, today. It wasn't over by Christmas, was it?'

Whatever she had expected, it was not this. 'But you're a married man, and you're far too old.'

How like a man: his vanity was offended. 'Good heavens, Lucy. I'm fitter than half these boys they're taking.' He sipped his coffee and smiled at her, the old charming smile that made her heart turn over. 'It's who you know in this insane world.'

Still she said nothing.

'Rose doesn't need me; she's never needed me. You would have given her a job so that she would never have had to emigrate.' So he knew he had been used then, but he was not angry, unless he had worked off his anger. What had he done to Rose? He put the cup down and stood up, his tall, slim frame filling the small room. 'Poor little Rose. We can't really understand what it was like for her, growing up in poverty. She did, you know. She thought she had hidden it but there was a sister, a half-sister; she got in touch with me and I made her an allowance until she died. I don't blame Rose for being hard. She only wanted to better the conditions of her class, and you can't blame her for that. You'll be kind to her, Lucy, won't you, if anything happens to me? She'll inherit, of course, probably turn it into a children's home after the war. Not a bad idea. I wanted children. So did Rose. If she'd had an easier life, maybe . . . That's all by the by.' He turned away from her. 'I said some hard things and I . . . well, I'm not too pleased with myself. Always felt deep down that Rose didn't really love me. Maybe, when this mess is over, maybe if tonight has cleared the air a bit, we can start again. You will look after her for me? She's not like us, Lucy, not . . . secure . . . yes, that's the word, secure. Every child should be given security. If I'd had a child, I'd have made her feel secure.'

What could she say? To her dismay she found that tears were rolling down her cheeks. A knight in shining armour should not go to war with his heart broken. It unarmed him.

'Oh, what have you done, Kier? Whatever has happened between you and Rose, surely you don't have to run away like this? Go back home and talk to her.'

'I've talked, Lucy. Perhaps too much. I don't want to see Rose again; I can't see her again, not for a while. If there's anything for me to forgive, I forgive her and I hope she'll forgive me for tonight.' He stretched out his hand and imprisoned a tear on the end of a finger. 'She said I'd always loved you, you see,' he said gently, 'and that I'd been unfair to her too. I suppose she's right.' He moved to the door, leaving her standing there with tears streaming unchecked down her face. 'Make it better, doctor,' he said, and then he was gone and the door had closed behind him, and a moment later she heard the sound of the front door being shut.

Lucy stood there for some time looking at the door. The fire had died down and the room was growing colder, and she began to tremble, but whether from cold or from shock the doctor could not tell. Like an old woman she turned to the fire and put up the guard, not that the few embers in the grate could cause any damage. She turned off the lamps and went softly out, closing the door behind her. Methodically she locked and bolted the front door and then she went upstairs, leaving the hall lights hissing gently on. Isa found them still lit in the morning, sighed for the sinful waste, and said nothing.

Lucy had not slept; she had not even undressed. She had no energy. It all seemed to have gone with Kier. All night she sat by the window watching countless ghostly phantoms passing in the snowy lamplight below her. Kier at fourteen, ill and fretful; at fifteen, scoffing at her lack of education; at nineteen, telling her for the first time that he loved her. Later, telling her that he was going to marry Rose. She saw Rose too. Rose, at the garden party in the ridiculous dress which had made her look so helpless and vulnerable; Rose, the secret smile of triumph when they had announced their engagement, the look – was it of chagrin? – when she had offered her a post. She saw her, a vision in her wedding dress, and then the older, sophisticated, harder Rose.

Kier said he had raped his wife. He could not have hurt her, not Kier, could he? Rose did not need medical attention, surely? If she did the last doctor she would want to see would be Dr Lucille Graham. Because she was so tired, Lucy allowed Max to walk out there in the snow, and at the thought of him she cried out in pleasant pain.

Oh, Max, my love, my love. Everything has gone wrong, for me, for Kier, for Rose . . . for you? But we were right, Rose and I, we were right to fight for our place in the world. We have made a difference to countless others, haven't we, Max? Butterflies in December. Did I ever tell you that my father called me that? No. I told you so little and oh, dear God, what am I supposed to say to Rose in the morning?

Rose herself forestalled everything. She arrived at the office on time and looking just as lovely and untouched as ever. It must all have been a dream; this ethereal creature had never been raped in the early hours of the morning, by her own husband. She had not lain awake seeing the ghosts of the past, the frightening visions of a desolate future.

'I'd better tell you, Lucy, because you'll have to know sooner or later,' she said, her beautiful soft leather bag held almost defensively in her gloved hands. 'Kier is being absolutely silly; he met some old chum from Sandhurst at a party and the bloody fool has enlisted . . . gone . . . "having a go", he says.' She half turned from Lucy as if she did not really wish to look directly into her eyes and laughed, a bitter, unnatural little laugh. 'I'm sure the War Office will send him home with a telling-off about food supplies and being there for our women and children, but . . .' and for a moment her schooled face was bleak '. . . in the meantime he's playing soldier. Black Watch. If he hasn't scuttled home by the weekend . . .' She stopped. 'I'm off. I have a million calls to make.'

She was gone. Lucy sat looking at the door for some time.

'Are you having a surgery or are you not this morning, doctor? There are children with snotty noses and dirty shoes in my front room.' Isa could always be depended upon.

'Send in my first patient, Isa.'

The morning wore on, and the afternoon, and three weeks, and still Kier had not returned. Had he been accepted? Rose said nothing and Lucy dared not ask. If he had been dismissed would he tell them, tell his wife?

'They've reinstated him and promoted him.' Rose was paler than usual, and was she even thinner? She looked drained, tired. She must, thought Lucy, be under enormous strain. 'Nearly all the young officers are dead. Hardly worth having a child, is it, to watch them grow and see them go off to be blown to bits? Do you think the bullets will know that Major Anderson-Howard was decorated in the Boer War and is therefore too senior to be obliterated?'

'Sit down, Rose, and I'll have Isa bring us some coffee.'

'No coffee, Lucy. I can't face it these days.' She stopped and for a moment Lucy felt that she was about to say something real, something important. 'It's all such a mess, isn't it?' was all she said, and then she turned and began to walk into her own office.

Lucy jumped up and followed her. 'Rose, please. Where is he? When did you hear? Is he well?' She stopped, angry at her show of emotion. She saw too that Rose had misinterpreted her interest.

Rose laughed, an ugly laugh. 'So we're both spurned, neglected women, are we, Lucy? I was almost sure I'd find him here that morning, you know. I thought he would run to you to tell you what a bad wife I'd been.'

'He came . . . to say goodbye. Never, *ever* has he said one word against you. He was always your champion, Rose.'

'My champion? I never needed a champion. Was he rescuing me? From what? What conceited arrogance, Doctor Graham. I may not have had your advantages growing up, but I certainly needed no knight in shining armour to rescue me from the gutter.' She threw off Lucy's restraining hand. 'I have patients to see. We'll discuss this intolerable situation later.'

20

Dundee, 1916

DECISIONS THAT CHANGED one's life were often easy to make in the lonely dark stretches of the night. In the morning the spring sunshine was calling all tired, old, even dead things back to life. The blossoms on Dundee's ethereally beautiful cherry trees seemed to hang dazzled in the air as Rose walked the few streets to Lucy's offices. They called to her highly charged mind, assaulted her quivering senses.

'I'll think about it,' Rose found herself saying. 'My God, I'm having a conversation with a tree. Is this what being pregnant does to you?' But she was almost happy as she reached Shore Terrace and the new day of satisfying work that lay ahead of her.

Lucy did not ask about Kier and Rose found that odd.

She should ask if I've heard from him. Wouldn't it be normal for an old friend to ask, for my partner to ask about my husband? Unless she has had a letter.

'I have an address for Kier if you would like to have it,' she said brusquely. 'I heard yesterday.'

Lucy looked up from her desk and, for the first time, Rose was aware of the dark shadows under her eyes, of the fact that Lucy, always slim, was even thinner.

'Oh, I'm so glad, Rose. Is he well? Did he say where he is?'

Rose answered the second question; she did not know the answer to the first. 'No, and the address doesn't tell anything but I'll give it to you.' She turned to leave the office and then stopped. 'He hasn't written to you, then? Dreadful correspondents, men.'

When the door closed behind her Lucy sighed with relief. 'Dreadful correspondents? Men? Kier?' She thought of all the letters she had received over the years. 'Poor Rose. Poor Kier, but at least he has written. They will work this dreadful thing out. I hope he's not in France. Surely to God, he's too old to be sent to France.'

The telegram waited all day for Rose to return. Mrs Potter put it down on a silver tray and carried it into the drawing room at Laverock Rising. The room was soft and mellow in the warm summer sunshine. As she put the tray down beside a crystal bowl of Rose's favourite yellow roses, she did not notice the teardrop that beaded on the polished wood beside it.

'Thank God she'll find out here. Thank God! Poor lassie.'

*

Rose waited for the train. She was anxious to get to Fife for the weekend and she desperately needed to loosen her corsets. *What a fool I am, what an utter fool! I can't go on like this much longer.*

At last she was able to sit down in the first-class carriage and she relaxed. Soon she would be at Leuchars. Someone would be there with the car. She must learn to drive. *I was right to ask for the use of a flat,* Rose smiled. At Laverock Rising she had come to terms with what had happened to her. She had drifted, like the cherry blossom, until the decision was taken out of her hand. Was it that or a gut feeling that abortion was wrong, that she, who strove so hard to maintain life, should be the last person in the world to end it? Or was it merely a bargaining tool in her battle with Kier? Whatever it was, she was now six months' pregnant. 'Why can't I bring myself to tell Lucy? I can't hide it any longer. How have I hidden it from her? Surely she suspects; some doctor!' Rose smiled. Lucy preferred bones to babies. 'Half my patients are making cosy remarks. If I don't get this bloody corset off I won't have to tell her, I'll abort anyway.' And suddenly, suddenly Rose felt cold and very frightened. She put her hands for the first time protectively over her stomach where tight corsets and the fashion of the day had allowed her to conceal the fact that she was most definitely pregnant.

'I'll admit you're there on Monday, little person. I'll need your Aunt Lucy. I certainly don't want your grandmother around.' The relationship with Kier's mother, never good, was now non-existent.

She was home. Laverock Rising. Everything would be all right.

'This came this morning, madam.'

Rose stood still. She did not turn but slowly eased her kid gloves off her long slim fingers, as always having difficulty sliding the material over the huge diamond Kier had given her on their engagement. She knew. She had had that cold feeling in the train. Or was it the housekeeper's tone, the voice low and almost breaking? She laid the gloves down on the polished rosewood table. Ma would have admired that table. The right glove, then the left glove. Turning, she saw the small buff envelope and stretched out a hand that would not be allowed to tremble.

'Thank you, Mrs Potter. That will be all.'

She did not notice that, for the first time ever, Mrs Potter bobbed a slight curtsey before she withdrew.

How long did letters take to get to the Front, for that was where he had been, some damned place in France. This would be so much easier to bear if she could be certain that he had had the letter, that he had known.

Kier looked through the smoke. What was it? Mars, Flaming God of War. It was not Mars. Surely a God, if there was a God, would be a noble being. If He brought death and destruction, would there not be some beauty in that death, some justice at least?

It was a dragon. He could see it, them. Sweet Jesus, there was more than one. He could see them advancing towards the trench where he stood. He could hear them. Yes, that was the sound he had made all those years ago when he had played St George and the Dragon. Lucy had been better though. Darling Lucy, she had been better at everything. He smiled. Did she know? How happy she would be for him.

Someone was pulling him; voices were screaming at him. He was so tired of noise, interminable noise.

'Bird-song,' he said quite seriously. 'Bird-song is the best sound. I used to think it was the sound of a violin, properly played of course, or a tenor. Yes, a tenor: Caruso. The most beautiful sound in the world.'

'Christ, major. Them's flame-throwers. The bloody Krauts are going to incinerate what they haven't blown to bits.'

Kier looked again. He echoed the soldier. 'Christ.' he said.

He could feel the heat.

'Run,' he yelled. 'Run!'

He shook off the hands and climbed out of the trench. Which way, which way? Any way but forward. That's where the dragons were making their slow, deadly and inexorable progress. 'And more inexorable far, Than empty tigers or the roaring sea.' Shakespeare; he was quoting Shakespeare. Was it because part of his mind refused to believe what his eyes were telling him, that this could not be happening?

'Major?'

He came to himself, sensible, articulate, trained.

'That way, lads. Run.' He looked around. Easy enough to find a weapon later if they escaped. The ground was littered with the debris of the dead. 'Throw away everything that will hold you back.'

A man went up beside him like a bonfire at Hallowe'en. The screams threatened sanity. No time to think, to plan. The terrified soldiers ran tossing rifles, even masks, aside in their mad need to get away from the advancing horror. The mud grabbed at their feet, clung to them like a lover, loath to release them. They slipped, stumbled, fell and, sobbing desperately for their wives, their mothers, they tried either to rise or to bury themselves under the mud, to do anything that would help.

Kier fell and a rat popped up from the mud in which he lay. He could see its little eyes, terrified, insane. 'Just like mine,' he thought as the most excruciating pain enveloped his entire body.

'No, please,' he said and his prayer was answered. His agony, everything, was blotted out . . .

It was impossible that anyone could be left alive. Kier regained consciousness to find himself lying against the wall of the trench into which he had fallen. Gradually he became aware of silence. When had the pounding stopped, that relentless pounding that had gone on and on, and roared around in his brain until he could do nothing but beg for a respite, beg even for death in order to escape it?

'Am I dead too?'

The air was full of smoke from the flame-throwers but no gas: they hadn't used gas this time. Kier straightened up slowly and that's when the pain started, pain that made him cry out. The sound startled him.

'I'm not dead if I can feel pain,' he said.

'Help me . . . somebody help me.'

There was someone else. Thank God, thank God, he was not alone.

Kier tried desperately to focus his eyes. The voice came again.

'Who's there? Is that you, Joe? Major, is that you?'

He should answer; he was the major. He knew that, but his tongue refused to obey the commands his brain was sending. The voice stopped and the moaning started.

'I'm here,' he said desperately, but no sound came. He was confused. There was the pain that clawed at him, and the groaning of dying men that was almost as hard to bear as the pain. But from somewhere there was the scent of violets. Who wore violets? Lucy? No, no, it was Rose.

'Rose?' he said but the sound of her name, the smell of her flowers, they were in his head. He tried to smile. 'Rose,' he said it again and this time he could see her. He was in the nursery at Laverock Rising; he was with Rose. The pain ebbed away. There was no moaning, no sound but the sweet Scottish voice.

'Kier,' she said, so clearly that he lifted his head to smile into her lovely, smiling, happy, eyes. 'Kier,' she said again and held out her hands to him.

The officer found them . . . at least he thought that the blackened remains had once been men. He looked and he retched.

'In the name of the Father,' he began, 'and of the Son, and of . . .' But the prayers refused to come. He tried again. 'Into Thy hands, oh Lord.' The tears were running unchecked down his cheeks.

'Lieutenant? Are you all right?' The boy soldier was very young.

The officer looked at him, at his frightened young face.

'How will the world remember us?' he asked. 'Will they think of Germany and say Goethe, will they say Wagner? Will they say Beethoven . . . or will they say . . . savages?'

He looked down at his feet. 'Rest in peace,' he said softly. 'I pray that I could.'

Dr Rose Nesbitt, Mrs Kier Anderson-Howard, widow, was extremely drunk. She was still sober enough to know that she was drunk and she was very ashamed of herself. She had ordered a bottle of Kier's best claret to be sent up from the cellar just because she felt that old Baxter did not really want her to have it. It belonged to Kier, to the master, the laird, and now that he was dead it was to be kept inviolate. Rose had always known that the staff did not like her. She thought it was because they could strip away the veneer of expensive clothes and see the frightened slum lassie underneath.

'Why couldn't they accept me?' she raged. 'I never pretended to be anything other than what I am. I'm proud of my fight out of the gutter.'

Then she remembered all the people who had helped her struggle, especially Frazer and Ma, and she cried maudlin drunken tears.

'Ma would have understood why I would never have introduced her to Kier. I didn't know a thing about my husband. I was never really interested. He was Lucy's, and I took him away from her and made him miserable and I didn't even need to do it. Oh, Lucy, why didn't you ask me to work for you when I first qualified? Why did I have to go through all those applications? Why did I have to threaten to go to Africa? I could have had a practice and you could have had Kier. No, not Lucy's fault. Rosie's. Rosie uses people. She used Frazer and old Wishy and Ma . . . and Lucy and Kier. But I'm being punished now. Oh, God, I'm being punished.'

Rose lurched across the room and violently closed the curtains. Kier's gardens were so beautiful. She did not want to see them

When had she ordered a second bottle? When had she drunk it? She staggered across the room to find the door. When she had negotiated the beautiful oak staircase she found her bedroom, their bedroom, and fell across the bed. Rose slept.

It was dark when she woke up and she was glad. She never wanted to see sunlight again. She would stay in the bedroom for ever and she would draw the curtains to make sure the light stayed out.

Rose moaned as she tried to rise from the bed. Her head was aching and swimming and her stomach . . . she barely managed to reach the bathroom.

When the retching was over she was unable to rise from the floor and lay for some time beside the lavatory. At last the top of her head seemed to have settled itself where it belonged, and she managed to push herself up by holding on to the lavatory and then the hand-basin. She did not recognize the ravaged face that stared back at her with frightened eyes from the mirror.

She splashed cold water on her face and into her mouth and then managed to undress by pulling at the buttons so skilfully and expensively sewn down the front. She managed to get back to the bed and this time to throw off the counterpane and to crawl tremblingly under the blankets. Rose slept, but the nightmare was still with her when she woke up.

'Doctor Graham sent a messenger to see how you are, Mrs Anderson-Howard,' Mrs Potter came in answer to her bell. 'Baxter told him to say that you would prefer to be alone, that we would take care of you.'

'I'd like some tea, please, Mrs Potter.'

'I'll fetch something else as you'll be the better for it. First we'll get you into a nice fresh nightie.'

Rose tried to protest but found herself, for the first time in her life, being undressed and tidied up.

'There, doesn't that feel better? I'll be back with your tea.'

Rose barely had time to realize how much better she felt before her housekeeper returned with a tray of tea and a bowl of a strange-smelling brown liquid.

'It's just a bit of bread and a little Worcester sauce. I know, smells awful when you're hungover but it'll cure you. Come on, eat up.'

With a barely suppressed shudder, Rosie put a morsel of the foul-smelling mess into her mouth.

'There, now. Doesn't that feel better?' Mrs Potter spoke as if Rose was a child. Was that how she dealt with her own grief, looking after Kier's . . . widow? 'Here,' her voice was motherly, almost loving, 'have a nice hot cup of tea. Then you can sleep again and you'll feel better in the morning.'

But in the morning Kier was still dead and nothing would make her feel better. How could she feel better when he would never feel again? He lay dead somewhere in the mud of a river called the Somme. They had strolled near there on their honeymoon. The banks of the river had been ablaze with wild flowers; the sky had been reflected with the flowers in the clear water. Kier had pulled her down among the flowers and . . . 'Oh, God, don't let it be the same place. They don't even know, they can't even tell me . . . his mother will never get over this, ever. There's no body, nothing. "The officers made a pact to lie with their men." Was that supposed to make me feel better? Would it make his mother feel better? Would this? I should tell her. Had he known? Was he pleased? Oh, please God, please let him have known.'

She took two days to recover from what Lucy called 'grieving' and Rose knew was merely a hangover. She returned to the offices on Shore Terrace to find Lucy looking almost worse than she did herself. She had had the extra burden of her own real grief and Rose's patients but, as usual, she angered Rose by being solicitous.

'You shouldn't have come back, Rose. People won't expect you to carry on like this.'

'I want to come back, Lucy.' Rose reached for the file with the names of the patients she was to see that day. 'I need to be back. I'm sorry that you've had extra work.'

'I was happy to do it. It's understandable. You should have taken some time as soon as you heard the news. I feel that perhaps you still need time. Two days . . .'

'For God's sake, Lucy. You always have to see the best in people, don't you? I had a hangover, a simple hangover because I drank too much. I wasn't weeping a widow's tears.'

'We all grieve in our own—'

'Oh, no platitudes, doctor, please. Have you grieved yet? For my husband, your lover?' She hadn't meant to say that, she knew Lucy and Kier had never been lovers. But Lucy had loved him and, oh yes, Kier had really loved Lucy.

'Poor Rose,' said Lucy. 'Poor Kier,' she whispered. 'We were never lovers, Rose. I loved Kier and once, a long long time ago, I thought I was in love with him too, but I wasn't, Rose, and he was never *in love* with me. He loved you, or he would have if you had let him.'

'Oh, excuse me. Now you're the great psychiatrist too. Well, I did let him love me,' said Rose, deliberately misunderstanding the sense of what Lucy was saying, 'so much so that I'm going to have his child.'

There, she had said it. The words hung in the air between them as they stared at one another. Lucy recovered first.

'Oh, Rose, that's wonderful; that's the best of all good news.' She started up from her chair, her hands outstretched.

Rose ignored the gesture and leafed through her file. 'Is it?' She had not meant to be so blunt, so unnecessarily cruel. What devil got into her sometimes? 'I'm glad you're pleased, Lucy. I hope Kier's mother will be . . .'

Lucy stared at her incredulously. 'You haven't told her . . . but this will . . .'

'Make her accept me . . .'

'Make it easier to bear, Rose.'

'I have ambivalent feelings, Lucy. I almost aborted, you know. A baby, the result of . . . Then, I thought, it might help . . . but that's hardly fair to the baby. Let's just say that I left it too long and now it's too late. A child has no real place in my life, my career. How can I go on with my work with a child? Every day I see or hear of more people who need us. I shall have this child . . . but as soon as I am physically able, I shall be back at work.'

She left the room and went to her own office, calling to their receptionist on the way.

As usual the morning passed so quickly that she had no time to think of anything but the needs of others. At lunchtime she found herself walking smartly along the High Street to Draffens where she bought a coat. It was a lovely coat, soft blue wool beautifully cut into a body-skimming line; it was not a widow's coat.

'Would madam like to try it?' asked the puzzled assistant.

'No, thank you. Wrap it, please. I'll take it with me.'

Outside in the street she waited patiently in the line for the tram and, carrying her parcel, made her way to the Hilltown.

She stood in the street outside the closie where Ma and Frazer and Lindsay and Murray and the others had all lived. People looked at her strangely – she was so very well dressed – but passed on. She held on to the coat, Ma's coat, a much better one than the coat Frazer had bought . . . oh, so many years ago. But Ma was dead, dead from too much work and too little food and from damp and, oh yes, from her way of life, but most especially from despair.

A woman approached her. 'Can I help ye, missus?' The voice was quiet and solicitous; obviously the speaker wanted only to help.

Even in the depths of despair Rose recognized the qualities in the voice. 'Typical Dundee,' she thought. 'Why have I abandoned my own people for so long?' She looked at the stranger with a doctor's eyes. 'Yes,' she said. 'Yes, you can help me, you can accept this coat.' The woman looked at her warily. 'I bought it for someone who lived up that closie – Elsie Nesbitt, but she's been dead for years.'

'Elsie?' The woman's face was an artist's study of joy, but still she did not hold out her hands to receive the parcel. 'Hell, I kent Elsie fine. Grand woman. One o' her bairns took to the doctoring, would you believe? There was a big joke wi' Elsie. All her bairns was cried efter the faither, Frazer, Lindsay ... except for that wan. She was Rose. Never kent why. Maybe Elsie liked roses.'

'Perhaps,' said Rose. 'Will you take this?'

The woman took the parcel. It would probably never be worn by her; it might change hands in a pub up the Hilltown or be sold in a pawnshop – there were plenty of them on the very street where they stood – but that didn't matter. Somehow a little of the debt was paid, but there was still so much to pay and the safe birth of this baby was the first step.

'You had better be a boy,' said Rose as she hailed a cab.

Frazer Lucille Anderson-Howard was born in her godmother's private room at the Dundee Royal Infirmary.

'It's a beautiful name for a beautiful baby,' sighed Lucy as she gazed in rapture at the perfection of the tiny hands. 'Frazer?' She dared not ask, but allowed her voice to rise a little.

Rose lay back against the white pillows. She had been surprised at the powerful feelings that had surged through her when the tiny scrap was put into her arms. Never demonstrative, she had felt an almost uncontrollable desire to cover the tiny face with kisses; almost, but not quite.

'Kier would have wanted a boy,' she said.

Lucy wanted to protest, to say that Kier would have been delighted with his daughter, but she said nothing.

'Not Frazer,' said Rose.

'Not Lucille, but something nice, a good name to grow up with.'

'Frazer Lucille, on papers, but I'm going to call her . . . Robin.'

Lucy looked down at her face. 'Welcome, Robin,' she said and she held out her hand and touched the tiny infant. To her delight, Miss Anderson-Howard gripped the finger held out to her and, though she did not know it, in that spontaneous action she had forged a bond with Lucy that nothing would ever break.

Rose laughed. 'You look positively maternal, Lucy. You should have had her, not me.'

Lucy's thoughts went back to the awful panic of the days following her Italian holiday. A baby. Max's baby. Kier's baby.

'I would have liked to have had a child,' she admitted. 'I can only hope you will let me share your daughter a little.'

'You may share with pleasure, Godmama, you and her besotted grandmother.' She hesitated, just a fraction.

'I have already engaged a competent nursemaid . . . They'll stay in the flat at Laverock Rising. Kier's mother will be there constantly and we . . . well, there are weekends.'

'Oh, Rose,' Lucy began to protest and then thought better of it. She had no right to tell Rose how to bring up her own child. 'You won't be able to give her up to a nanny, Rose.'

But Rose *was* able. Within the month she was back in her consulting rooms and her daughter was safely ensconced in the light, airy nursery where her father had spent his infancy and where the young Kier and the young Lucy had forged their friendship. Lucy asked as often as she dared about the baby's progress.

'You must visit her for yourself, Lucy. She is, after all, your goddaughter.'

And so began the Sunday afternoons, the times that were to become for Lucy the highlight of her busy week. She took the train from Dundee to Leuchars where Rose's smart new car met her to take her to the house. She lunched with Rose in the dining room where she had so often sat with Kier and his parents and then Miss Robin was brought down, starched and laced, to see her adoring public. It did not seem to Lucy that Rose adored the baby – she rather laughed at Lucy's infatuation – but Lucy was content to admire the child and to talk to her and even sometimes in fine weather to take her out in the gardens.

Kier's mother was almost always there. She seemed to have called a truce with her daughter-in-law, for nothing would keep her from her granddaughter.

'Stupid name, Frazer,' she told Lucy. 'Why Frazer? If she had to give the child a man's name . . .'

'It's a family name, I think, and really it's not important, darling.'

'Why not Kier?'

They were silent, and Lucy looked at Kier's mother and saw that the baby's coming had not worked the miracle for which she had hoped. She was trying hard and she adored the baby, but her heart was broken.

'I'm beginning to see him everywhere, Lucy, especially here. I turn round and he's teasing me from behind a hedge, or I hear him calling from the stables. Why did he go? He was too old. Different if he'd stayed in, but suddenly to enlist like that and then . . . the Somme, . . . so many, Lucy, so many. You'll see that things are done . . . our way, Kier's way, won't you?'

Lucy was embarrassed. 'Her mother knows what Kier would have wanted, and you'll be here . . .'

'I won't. God knows I want to watch this baby, but I'll never see 1918.'

She caught a cold in October 1917. She had been playing with her granddaughter in the garden, which was so lovely in its autumn colours, so lovely but so cold. The cold developed into pneumonia.

'She didn't even try to fight,' wept old Baxter. 'I never knew an Anderson-Howard that wouldn't fight.'

21

France, 1918

ROSE THOUGHT IT might have been easier to bear if Robin had not looked quite so much like Kier. The little girl became more and more like her father as she changed from mewling infant to rounded baby. By the time she was eight months old she was crawling around the floor, lifting a gummy grin to her mother on Rose's infrequent visits, and by her first birthday she was hauling herself upright by whatever means she could and taking brave steps into the unknown. She attempted to use her first Christmas tree, ablaze with flickering candles and bedecked with gaily wrapped parcels, as an aid to walking, but luckily the faithful Sarah was there to rescue and to scold her and to tell Dr Nesbitt, Mrs Anderson-Howard, that they could not possibly have a lit Christmas tree this year, not with Miss Robin trying to walk.

Rose, who had never experienced Christmas until she married Kier, had shocked Sarah by ordering the Christmas tree to be set up instead in her private sitting room where no one and certainly not – and this according to Mrs Anderson-Howard's strict orders – Miss Robin was ever allowed.

Sarah, of course, turned a blind eye to the number of times Dr Nesbitt lifted the sleeping child from her crib in the beautifully appointed nursery and carried her off. It was hardly a nurserymaid's place to reprove her mistress for waking her own child from her sleep. And so Robin's first real Christmas found her sitting, as midnight and Father Christmas approached, on her mother's exquisitely tailored tweed lap in Mummy's sitting room, watching the candlelight dancing on the tree.

'Your father was such an idiot about Christmas,' Rose whispered into the child's black curls. 'He told me he believed in Santa Claus and he said that if I was a good girl I should have everything I asked Santa to bring. I asked for diamond bracelets and they were there, every Christmas, and Daddy asked for a fat little baby with black curls and Santa Claus never brought him his present. But now you're here, Miss Anderson-Howard, and Daddy is singing carols lustily with all the other angels. Can you hear him? He sings so dreadfully, but he played the piano beautifully. Perhaps a nice old angel has taught him to play Christmas carols on a celestial harp. I doubt that even an angel could teach him to sing.'

Robin nuzzled against her mother's blouse and, half asleep and half awake, listened to the soft Scottish voice.

'I was not a good wife to your daddy, little lambie. He really loved Aunt Lucy' – Robin smiled at the only word she recognized – 'but he was so gallant, he thought I was a poor little frail creature to be cherished and he mistook that for love . . . And I? Oh, Robin, did I lose the ability to love in the closies up the Hilltown? No, I loved him. How could I not love someone so good and kind? Your Uncle Frazer was just such a man; he sacrificed everything for me. And then there was this old classics teacher. I called him Wishy. He taught me Latin and Greek and never asked a thing in return, and that's why we're having this wee chat, lambie. I need to pay a debt, Robin, to Daddy and Uncle Frazer and Aunt Lucy – poor Aunt Lucy. She never married, Robin, because I stole her love. He should have married Aunt Lucy years ago, and they should have had half a dozen bairns to fill this house.'

The baby yawned and then slept and Rose looked down at the little face with the dark curling lashes. 'If I'd known what joy a bairn could bring, I'd have had you long ago, but you did get in the way, Robin. You see, I'm a doctor. I take care of the sick; that's all I ever wanted to do. It was like the visions the knights in armour are supposed to have had, me – wee Rosie Nesbitt from a closie up the Hilltown – caring for the sick. And I did it. I've made a difference. If I died today I could say, "My life made a difference." I'm going away, Robin. There's a horrid war going on. It killed your daddy and it's killing other people every day and every night. There's a lovely old convent in France. Daddy and I went there on our honeymoon. What's left of it is a hospital, and I am going there to work until the war is over. You will stay with Sarah, and Aunt Lucy will come to see you often. Won't that be nice?'

Aunt Lucy did not think so. She was aghast at the thought of a young mother going off to work at the Front.

'How can you leave her, Rose? It's totally unsuitable. A baby needs her mother.'

'Robin needs Sarah, who feeds her and keeps her clean.'

'And loves her? Who could love her like a mother?'

'You, Lucy. And Sarah.'

'Oh, Rose, it's not the same thing.' For the first time she broke her self-imposed rule. 'Kier would never have approved.'

Rose laughed. 'You must feel really strongly. I have to do it, Lucy, and it's done: I leave for France on Friday. And I'm not an angel of mercy; it's miles from any battlefield, but it's just more immediate help than I'm giving here, more . . .' She wanted to say reparation, but she couldn't say that to Lucy, to anyone but her small daughter who could not understand.

'I signed over the estate to Kier's daughter as soon as she was born,' she went on, 'and so, should anything happen, there will be no problems.' She got up abruptly and began to pace the room. The first flush of enthusiasm was over and the reality of what she had decided to do was making itself felt. She was going into a war zone, she could be killed. 'I want you to take care of Robin if anything goes wrong. Make the decisions for her future that Kier would have made.' She stopped as Lucy made a gesture towards her and she turned away from the desk. 'I see dirt and disease every day. This should not be very much different.'

But it was. Rose had seen mangled bodies before, but usually one at a time. And it had not been huge pieces of flying metal that ripped flesh from bone or limb from body. She had listened before to the groans or screams of injured men, women in advanced stages of difficult delivery, abused children – but this noise, this constant screaming of men, of shells, the staccato drumbeat of death dealing bullets . . .

'I can't think in this noise,' she said to a French nun, Mère Dolle.

'The silence is more frightening. In the convent silence was welcome, a chance to offer up the whole mind and heart. Here, if there is silence, I see evil as a huge bat gathering itself up to throw more death at these poor boys. And they are only boys, Madame Médecin. Look at this *pauvre bébé* here.'

The soldier was almost no more than a child. Had a beard ever grown on that almost grey skin?

'Why, he's German,' exclaimed Rose.

'Le bon Dieu looks only at the soul, madame,' chided the old nun gently.

'I didn't mean ...' began Rose and stopped as she looked into Mère Dolle's eyes. Around her was war and hatred and fear, and in those eyes was unquestioning love and acceptance. Oh, for such serenity, thought Rose and bent over the German youth.

The boy opened his eyes and, seeing Rose, began to cry and plead in German.

'What is he saying?' she asked the nun who was soothing the boy in his own tongue. Not for the first time, she wished she had had more classes in French and German.

'He is afraid you will cut off his arm.'

Rose almost fainted at the smell from the wound as she uncovered it, and she had to turn away for a moment to discipline her heaving stomach.

'I may have to,' she said when she could speak. 'There's little left to save.'

The boy soldier had lost consciousness and they worked over him in the poor light.

'I need another nurse, sister. Is there anyone else?' She looked at the nun, who was now almost as grey as the boy. 'Don't faint on me,' she pleaded silently and, as if she could hear, the nun smiled. 'I am well, doctor, only tired.'

They were all tired, hideously tired. How old was Mère Dolle? Better not to ask. She was not young; the few wisps of hair that stole out from under the wimple were quite white. The capable hands were marked with age spots and yet she stood hour after hour, day after day, and often long into the night, and did everything that had to be done. Rose had never seen her eat or drink. Once she had been given a mug of hot soup and had turned modestly away to drink it.

Strange creatures, nuns, thought Rose, who had never met one before. The older ones were unfailingly cheerful; only the very young occasionally broke down under strain and then, when they had recovered, worked twice as hard as if to expiate the sin of being merely mortal.

'Have you had much medical training, Mère Dolle?' she asked as they finally sat down to rest. A young nun brought them soup. Oh, the power of a bowl of delicious soup! Mère Dolle again turned away so that Rose could not see her but, back to back on the old bench, they chatted.

'None at all, Madame Médecin. I spent my days until the war teaching fat little girls to sing, and playing the chapel organ like that boy there, the German. He is a student of music. That is why he fears the loss of his arm. There is little piano music for a one-handed pianist.'

'Oh, God, war is hell,' said Rose.

'*D'accord*,' said the nun as countless others had agreed before her.

Rose sat drinking her soup and looking at the slim black shape before her: a musician with no medical training, a life of prayer and penitence devoted to the service of God, and yet she did the most intimate and, to some eyes, demeaning things for these men without a murmur or whimper of complaint. Why? How? Too difficult to tell if she had been pretty when she was young. Had she ever had a lover? Had she ever wanted one? She herself would have been content without a lover, except that there was now Robin. Robin . . .

'I have a little girl, Mère Dolle.'

'You miss her?'

'I did not expect to miss her. I have spent very little time with her because medicine always came first.'

'It was Bach with me . . . or Beethoven. I have been blessed because I gave them up to the Saviour and He has given them back to me. Your sacrifice will not go unnoticed, Madame.'

'My husband died in France in 1916. He didn't even know about her.'

'He does now.'

'You really believe that?'

'*Bien sûr*, madame.'

The strange conversation came to an end as Mère Dolle finished her soup and straightened her back. 'Why don't you have a . . .' she began. Rose was never to know what she had wanted her to have . . . a bath . . . a rest . . . a walk in the Convent gardens?

'We have two more field ambulances coming in, doctor.' An ambulatory patient had come in to the ward. 'Doctor Mutton wants you in theatre if you're not doing nothing.'

Dr Mouton was an elderly French doctor who headed the medical team at the convent. Like Mère Dolle, he seemed possessed of extraordinary strength. Rose only learned much later that his shame that so many French troops at the Front had mutinied on May 4th had caused him to come out of retirement, leaving his gardens to the weeds he had fought assiduously and successfully for five years. He spoke no English and Rose was only beginning, thanks to Mère Dolle, to really learn any French, but with the nun's help the two doctors understood one another well enough.

At 3 o'clock the next morning Rose fell fully dressed on to her bed and slept. She had been on her feet for twenty-five hours. When she awoke she found that she was dressed in a cool white broderie anglaise nightgown and that she was inside the crisp white sheets. Even her hair was brushed.

'Can I come in, doctor?'

'Come in, nurse.'

'Look at this,' said the girl, pointing to the plain white china as if Rose might not recognize the object that sat in the middle of it. 'It's an egg. We've got one each.'

Rose did not look at the egg, welcome stranger though it was. She looked instead at the round cheery face of Nurse Jeanette McDonald. The eyes were twinkling – had she stolen the eggs? – and the perpetual dimples in her cheeks were dancing with suppressed laughter.

'How did I get undressed?'

'Ach, that was me and Mother Dolly. She was worried aboot you, you being such a wee bit thing, and there is nothing of you. Mind you, my mither aye said it was the skinny ones had the strength. You've had twelve hours. Everything's quiet and there are smells coming oot of the kitchen . . . I can hardly wait for my dinner. It's the garlic, doctor. Did you ever use fancy things in your cooking? I never used onything but a wee bit salt myself, but Sister Anthony Joseph says add an onion, a tomato and garlic and you have a meal fit for a king. Roll on the end of the war. Wait till Glasgow tastes my mince!'

'Have you a big family waiting for you, nurse?'

The cheery face clouded for a moment and then the sun shone again. 'Not really, no. My mither sort of just gave up and died when wee Jimmy got killed at Verdun.

Five boys, and every one deid. No fair, is it, doctor, but two of them was married with bairns and I'll cook the new mince for them.'

'The young German, nurse?'

'We've had to send him up to the big hospital at Le Tréport; the arm has to come off if we want to save his life. I doubt he'll even survive the trip. The road's no' there at all now. Well, I'll leave you tae get dressed. Mother Dolly told me tae watch you eat every bite.' She walked to the door as Rosie slipped out of the bed. 'We're going to have a bit sing-song for the laddies the nicht. Have you heard her play a polka? She's fabulous, she can even play "Loch Lomond". You hum it, Mother Dolly'll play it.'

The door closed behind her and, apart from the clack of her heels as she walked quickly along the polished corridor, there was a welcome silence. Rosie hurried to dress. When had Nurse McDonald rested, or Mère Dolle or, even more importantly, Doctor Mouton?

The wards were quiet apart from the moaning of wounded men for whom they did not have enough painkilling medicines. A young nun was washing the floor. The Mother Superior obviously believed in the old dictum that cleanliness is nearest to godliness. In Rose's book it was certainly nearest to 'good chance of survival'.

'Nurse, nurse, give me something, can't you?'

It was not the first time the mistake had been made and it would not be the last. Rose walked across to the patient and looked first at him and then at his chart.

'I'm sorry,' she said gently. 'There is nothing I can do for you. Your wound is healing nicely.'

'Get the Froggie doctor. He'll give me something.'

Rose tried not to let her distaste show on her face. 'Doctor Mouton is not on the wards at the moment.'

'Get him then . . .'

'Glad to hear you are almost back to normal, corporal.'

Rosie had not heard the dressing-gowned figure enter the ward.

'I'm Captain Drummond,' he said, 'and you must be Doctor Nesbitt. What an honour to meet you when I'm awake, doctor.'

Rose laughed and took the hand held out to her. Captain Drummond had been unconscious the last time she had seen him.

'A woman doctor! No bloody wonder I'm still lying here.'

'Mind your tongue if you don't want to be put on a charge, corporal. It's thanks to Doctor Nesbitt that you're even alive.'

'Thank you, but that's not quite true,' said Rose as they moved away from the bed. 'The corporal's wound is minor compared to some of the injuries, your own for instance. Who gave you permission to get out of bed?' She was a doctor, and as a doctor found it easy to speak naturally to this gaunt young man whose voice and manner told her that he was just such another as Kier.

'I dreamed I was at the Usher Hall with my best girl who looked very like you, if I may be so bold, doctor, and an angel was playing Bach.'

'It wasn't an angel – or maybe it was: it was Mère Dolle.'

'The old nun? My God, what a waste!'

'She would not agree with you, captain.'

'Andrew, call me Andrew.'

She smiled. 'Back to bed, Captain Drummond.' *Oh, Kier, what a lot you taught me,* she found herself thinking, *or is it just that I now wear a mask labelled doctor and no one can believe in the lassie from the slums who is still underneath? Or is she still there? Have several years of marriage to a* gentleman *turned me into a* lady?

Captain Drummond was not so easily put off by the young doctor's sternness. He had himself wheeled into the recreation room at the convent where the concert for the invalids was being held and even against Doctor Mouton's wishes, took a turn on the piano. He did not have Mère Dolle's classical training nor Kier's delicate touch, but he could certainly thump out the rousing choruses the soldiers wanted to hear.

'You will open your wound, Captain Drummond.'

He looked up at her from the piano stool; he was laughing, but the eyes were strained with denied pain.

'If a beautiful Scottish doctor was to say, "Go to bed at once, Andrew", I would probably obey.'

'Captain Drummond,' she began, and then she too laughed and capitulated. 'Andrew, you must give your stitches a chance to heal.'

He got up slowly. 'Has anyone ever told you that you are very beautiful? I can't call you doctor . . . I won't.' He stood demanding an answer.

'Rose. And yes, my husband, quite often.'

He looked down at her ringless hands.

'I left them for my daughter, just in case; they were heirlooms.'

'Your husband?'

'Good night, Captain Drummond.' She turned as if to leave him there in the middle of the corridor.

'I'm sorry, Rose. You know you can't abandon me, but I promise not to ask any more. It's just so strange. I have a feeling that there is so much to know and so little time left. I was aware of you, you know, through the pain and the anaesthetic . . .'

She interrupted. 'Medical school. Lesson No. 24. Your male patients will all "be aware" of you.'

'Not Corporal Dempsey,' he teased and she had to join in his laughter. When had anyone ever made her laugh so easily?

Thus began two of the happiest months Rose had ever known. When the horrors of daily life became almost too much to bear, there was Andrew with his ready smile and his humour. It was not that he did not take life seriously. He did, but he had an amazing capacity for finding humour in the strangest situations, and he could explain it in his execrable schoolboy French well enough to raise a smile from even Doctor Mouton.

Rose always spent her free time in the convent garden. She would love to have been allowed to kneel down and work in the soil with the two nuns who seemed to spend their lives weeding and hoeing, but they would not allow it. It would not be suitable, but Madame Médecin was welcome to sit there and watch while they worked. Captain Drummond found her there and often they would sit saying nothing, but allowing the peace of the garden to wash away the stress of the moment. Rose no longer noticed the constant roll of guns from just over the fields; it was Andrew who told her that the war was relentlessly coming closer and closer.

'We are going to have to evacuate our walking wounded, Rose. We're smack in the way of a German retreat. Our lads will follow them but . . .'

She wanted to cry out, 'No,' but she said nothing for she could not tell him what she felt. How could she say that her first thought had been that she would miss him, Andrew Drummond? For the first time ever, she had thought of herself before her patients. Then she laughed, a wry little laugh. Andrew was a patient still.

'I will travel with my patients then.'

'I'm trying to decide what would be safer for you. The nuns will stay, and Monsieur Mouton and those who cannot be transported. I doubt that they will be in any real danger from a retreating army. Mother Superior will be happy to hide you and Miss McDonald in the cloisters.'

'That's a very funny thought, Andrew. Wee Rosie Nesbitt from the Hilltown in Dundee hiding in a convent.'

He turned to her then. 'Oh, Rose, I always felt there was so litle time. There's so much I want to know about you . . . important things like, "Do you like Christmas pudding with custard or brandy sauce?" '

'I hate Christmas pudding.'

'Do you prefer Bach to Beethoven?'

'I'm a Mozart lover.'

'Do you like John Buchan?'

'I don't know him.'

'Shame on you! He's an exciting Scottish writer.'

'I haven't read a real book in . . . a hundred years.'

'I have some Sassoon in my kit.'

Rose smiled. 'I've read him.' She looked at his anxious face and laughed. 'I liked the poems. Is that what you wanted me to say?'

'There, you see; we've got lots in common, apart from Christmas pudding . . . and I would find myself with no appetite anyway with you at the table.'

She moved as if to get up, but he grasped her hand and pulled her down.

'It's too soon, Andrew . . .'

'It's too late, Rose; for me it was too late when I saw your lovely face through the mists of ether or whatever it was that put me out.' He saw tears start in her eyes and impetuously kissed first one and then the other and she sat unmoving, but trembling, and the tears slipped down her cheeks. 'What is it, Rose? Your husband? The professional oath? Asclepius, ancient God of healing, is that it? He said doctors can't be kissed by their patients?'

'Hippocrates. He was a doctor.' Rose looked up at him, at his gaunt face almost wavering before her as she tried to stem the tears. There was a strange but pleasant feeling in the pit of her stomach, she felt as light as a feather. A defeated army was approaching rapidly and she could not fear, she could not worry, because of this young man. She forgot Kier; she forgot Robin. 'Oh, Andrew,' she said and leaned towards him, and in a second she was in his arms and kissing him as she had never kissed Kier.

They did not hear the two soldiers approach. The voice that spoke was educated and apologetic.

'How charming. I am so sorry to put an end to this idyll . . . for the moment, of course, captain.'

Rose and Andrew looked up at the two soldiers. Rose was still dazed from the enormity of what had just happened to her, and it was a few moments before she realized that the men were German.

'You are the senior officer here, captain. I am Major Heinrich Von Kesserling of the German Army. I regret that we find ourselves in need of some supplies.'

Then Rose noticed that both men held guns and that the weapons were pointing at them. She clutched Andrew's arm protectively.

'You are in no danger, nurse. I have some men who will be grateful for your help perhaps.'

'This lady is a doctor, major, and you must speak to Mother Superior if you need supplies. We are merely guests here.'

'Then we must find this lady, captain. You will take us to her?'

It was couched as a question, but with two guns trained on them there was nothing they could do. The second German soldier said something and the officer answered angrily. Andrew too spoke in German.

'What is it? What is he saying?'

'Nothing,' said Andrew shortly. 'Uncouth fool!'

Rose walked beside him quickly through the gardens towards the convent. It was unreal, it could not be happening. A few minutes ago the gardens had been the most beautiful place in the world, and now they were contaminated, soiled. As if he sensed her thoughts, Andrew smiled down at her.

'They won't stay, Rose. They are anxious to get away. Our boys have licked them and now they are right behind the retreating glorious army. Isn't that right, major?'

'We will not impose on the good sisters' hospitality longer than we need, captain. And please, captain, it is not wise to try to provoke. Not all my men have had my advantages. No doubt it is the same in the British Army: there are some with, how would you say, a nervous finger on the trigger? Ah, *bon soir, ma soeur . . .*'

Mère Dolle had come out of the Convent at their approach. She answered the officer in fluent German and then returned to English . . . 'for the sake of Madame Médecin' and she smiled at Rose.

'This is a house of prayer and peace, major. I would ask you to put away those weapons.'

'In good time, sister. I must inspect first. You understand?'

How did it happen? How *did* it happen? For the rest of her life Rose went over and over those few minutes. As Mère Dolle and Major Von Kesserling spoke, the other German soldier moved nearer to her. She made as if to move closer to the nun, and he followed. He grabbed her arm and said something, and then everything happened at once. The nun and the German officer turned and spoke in rapid German, and at the same time Andrew pushed the soldier as hard as he could. He was not strong; he had been badly wounded, and the blow was not severe. A light of madness was lit in the soldier's eyes and he fired

377

once and then turned the gun towards Rose. There was a second shot . . .

Major Von Kesserling put his gun away. 'I regret, sister,' he began but Rose heard no more. She was on the ground beside Andrew, desperately feeling for a pulse. The German soldier lay spreadeagled beside him.

Happiness is such an ephemeral substance. Rose knelt in helpless anguish on the dusty pathway. Mère Dolle knelt beside her and prayed the prayers for the dead, both English and German, and for the living who had to watch their happiness slip away.

Rose considered returning to Britain after Andrew's death. For a while it seemed to her that everything she had ever touched was doomed to end in disaster. Had her education cost Frazer his life? Even old Wishy had not lived long enough to receive the free medical attention that he had claimed as his payment for the hours and hours of tuition he had given her. She stood in the garden beside the grave that held the mortal remains of Captain Andrew Drummond who had died, not in glorious battle, but because he had objected to what an uneducated lout had said about her.

I'm sorry, Andrew. We hadn't time to . . . To do what? To learn from and to accept the lessons of the past . . . to fall in love?

Had he parents? If he had, should she write to them and tell them how their son had lost his life? Would they be proud of how and why he had died? Would they sit in a gracious drawing room somewhere and say, 'We brought the boy up to be a gentleman and he never let us down'? Or would they scream and cry and rail against fate as she wanted to do?

She knelt down in the dust beside the grave. She was so tired, so very tired. The visiting American congressmen had been exhausting in their kindness, in their repeated reassurances that the war could last only a few more weeks. Were they right? She remembered the tall Southern one: she had liked his soft, warm voice. It had made her feel protected – easy to believe what he said.

'Robin. I must get back to Robin, to Kier's daughter. Kier. Oh, Kier, I wish I knew that you had my letter. She is so like you in so many ways.'

More regrets. He had died for her too, in a way.

Doctor Rose Nesbitt pulled herself to her feet. There were still patients to see and the Americans had brought supplies.

'I have a dispensary now,' said Rose and laughed. 'At last I have a dispensary and there's medicine in it.'

Mère Dolle was in the ward.

'You look exhausted, doctor,' she said. 'Why don't you finish your rounds and go to bed? Do you know the Americans left us a ham? Can you imagine? We shall have a feast, and then I shall go to the chapel and play for you . . . Bach, I think.'

'Bach? Someone once told me that the angels play Bach's music in heaven.'

'A good choice. Go to bed, little doctor. I shall bring you food myself.'

Doctor Nesbitt was asleep when the nun arrived with the tray. Mère Dolle stood looking down at her, at her blonde hair tumbling in damp curls around her face. The skin was so white, and under the eyelids she could see the blue tracings of the veins.

'Sleep is better than food,' she said.

Rose heard the music in her sleep, but she did not recognize it. Kier or Andrew could have told her that it was part of the first Brandenburg Concerto. She sighed, not with grief but with contentment. It was so warm and peaceful, and the faint notes of the organ caressed her wounded spirit. Mère Dolle would have said that music caressed the soul. Rose sank once more into a deep sleep and in the morning, when she did not appear as usual in the wards, it was Mère Dolle who went to find her.

At first she was not too worried. A rest, complete rest, that was surely all that was required. She hurried out, no panic, just efficient speed, and found another nun to help her lift Rose from the bed. Together they changed the sheets, but it was Mère Dolle's loving hands that washed the damp body, replaced the soaking nightgown.

Doctor Mouton diagnosed pneumonia.

'Thanks to the Americans we have medicine, sister,' he said. 'Our little Rose has exhausted herself in our service.'

'We'll give her round-the-clock care, doctor.'

Did Mère Dolle sleep at all for the next few days? She was there when the climax came, when Rose's fevered body tossed and turned to try to get away from the heat that was consuming it.

'The fever will break,' the doctor said. In all the cases of pneumonia he had ever treated where the patient was young and well fed and well nursed, this had been the pattern.

Mère Dolle replaced the damp cloth with which she was attempting to cool the delirious woman. She held Rose's hot hands and talked to her, sang to her, tried to keep the wandering attention firmly attached to a world which had not treated her too well.

Doctor Nesbitt talked to many people whom she seemed to see around her. Some she smiled and laughed to greet, others made her cry . . . tragic tears which further weakened her. There were Ma and Frazer and Wishy, Lucy, and Kier. Lucy calmed her, and the nun welcomed her presence as if she was indeed there in the darkened room.

Rose lay quiet and Mère Dolle rose to adjust the light. The climax had arrived: the fever was breaking.

'Kier.'

She heard her patient say the name so clearly and the voice was light and happy. Rose was lying on the bed, her eyes were open and she was smiling, a smile of such intense love and beauty that the nun was moved almost to tears.

Rose closed her eyes with a soft sigh.

'Robin,' she whispered, and the voice held regret. 'My little Robin.'

22

Dundee–London, 1921

ON THE 15TH of March 1921, an African country called Ruanda was ceded to the British by the Belgians. Lucy and Robin did not notice this latest piece of world news. Robin was too interested in the mysteries of penmanship as revealed to her at the High School of Dundee, where she sat every morning in a grey skirt that she hated but accepted as the price she had to pay for education. Lucy treasured Robin's days at school in Dundee and she enjoyed to the full the job of surrogate mother, for early in 1919 a letter had come from France. The writer was of course unaware that Lucy was a fluent French speaker and the letter, in English, was short and rather stilted. Doctor Nesbitt had caught pneumonia in the winter and had died of endocarditis. She had asked to be buried in the convent grounds beside Allied personnel who had also died as a result of the conflict. She had been much loved by the community and would be greatly mourned.

Endocarditis, a heart disease for which there was no cure, and which had probably been lying latent, waiting to strike down Rose's overworked body. Kier had intuitively worried about the strength of his wife. Lucy sighed and reapplied herself to caring for their child.

Robin had not grieved, as she did not grieve for her father, but Auntie Lucy worked hard to paint a picture of her parents for the little girl. At five years of age, however, all that was real to Robin was Lucy and Sarah, weekly visits to Laverock Rising, and now the world unfolded by education. Lucy watched her as she sat hunched over the table, a strand of curly hair and her pencil clenched between her teeth, and she sighed for all too soon she was going to send the little girl to the boarding school in the south of England which was to have been the scene of her own formative years. Robin accepted the news of her future departure as she accepted twice-yearly visits to the dentist or hot baths in front of the nursery fire every Wednesday and Saturday whether she was dirty or not. She was always dirty on Saturday. Saturday they went to Laverock Rising, and Robin gloried in her pony and the dogs and, in season, the lambs and the calves, for Lucy was determined that the young laird should grow up familiar with her home and known by her tenants. She knew many of them too well and was spoiled atrociously. Every baker in that beloved corner of Fife outdid herself to provide home baking, 'in case Miss Robin should stop by'. And Miss Robin did. She rode her pony, not only over the huge estate which she had inherited from her father but over the surrounding countryside, and she stayed longest with those who had known her father or her grandparents. Unfortunately, as far as Aunt Lucy was concerned, many of these old acquaintances vied with one another for the little girl's favour, and she had to be very strict about Robin's diet during the week. Apart from writing and reading and a weekly piano lesson, Robin hated weekdays.

Another important reason for Lucy – who, as the daughter of a diplomat, would have been intensely interested – to miss the Ruanda news was the announcement – with much invective – that a Doctor Marie Stopes had opened a birth control clinic in London.

'Good heavens,' she exclaimed as she sat at breakfast, 'she's only forty and she's making such a mark. Rose would have welcomed her. I must visit.'

She wrote to Doctor Stopes and was invited down to see the clinic. Doctor Hendry agreed to give emergency care and Lucy planned her visit carefully.

'We will go to London together soon, Robin,' she told the little girl as she towelled her dry – on Wednesday – 'and we will see the Tower of London . . .'

'And Wendy's home?'

'Oh, yes, of course, dear.' Robin, like every other child in Britain, knew all about Wendy Darling and her friend Peter Pan who had been delighting children since 1904.

It was not of Peter Pan or Wendy or even the Lost Boys – although probably they were nearer her heart than the very secure Wendy and Peter – that Lucy was thinking as she checked into the brand-new home of the Overseas Club, Vernon House on Park Place, just off St James's Street. As always, when she travelled, Sir John and his terrifying but heroic death were on her mind. She had joined the Overseas Club, now the Overseas League, almost in memory of her father. Like that other more famous John, John Evelyn Wrench, who had founded the Overseas League, Lucy's father had believed in a 'world society', a brotherhood of widely different men and women in every corner of the globe. She looked around the lobby on this, her first visit, and admired the Edwardian panelling which lined the lovely wooden stair-well. She did not see the man who was descending that very stair.

'Why, as I live and breathe. Lucy?' The voice was hesitant, doubtful of its welcome, but recognizable.

Lucy concentrated on writing her address to give herself time and then turned, nothing on her schooled face showing the unutterable consternation raging inside her. Once before he had appeared in her life after years of mutual neglect, and he had turned her carefully developed existence into glorious chaos. He would never ever know how much she had loved him, how much she had mourned him and their never-to-be-born child, how much she had suffered at his too casual rejection of her. 'Max, good heavens, the proverbial bad penny; you do get around. I can't say that it's a joy to see you.'

He was older, of course he was. The hair was grey but still thick, and the eyes were as keen and full of humour as ever. He was so obviously American that she wondered why she had never noticed that about him before.

'Because he means nothing,' her head said, while her blood told her something very different.

'One meets every foreign acquaintance one has ever made at the Overseas Club, eventually,' she said, more for the benefit of the interested clerk than to hurt Max.

He was gazing at her as if he had been struck by a vision. 'My God, Lucy.' He pulled her almost fiercely away from the desk. 'Of course you must hate me, but give me a chance to explain,' he whispered. 'Take tea with me, Lucy, please,' he asked pleasantly, again for the benefit of the clerk. 'You must be ready for tea. Aren't the British always ready to drink tea after a journey?'

'I need to go to my room and unpack.'

After a cup of tea. Oh, take pity on . . . an old acquaintance. There's so much I want to say, need to say.'

Lucy was in full control of herself. 'I don't think there's anything for us to say, Max. Now, if you'll excuse me . . .'

'Dad, would you believe, there's a box for the . . .' The boy stopped talking as he saw Lucy. 'I'm so sorry, ma'am,' he went on. 'I didn't see you there.'

'This is Doctor Graham, Brook, one of the very first lady doctors in Scotland and an old and dear friend. Lucy, my son, Brook.'

The sight and sound of the boy hit her like the killing blow of a sledgehammer. She felt almost faint, a mist clouded her eyes.

'Ma'am,' the boy said anxiously, 'are you OK?' There was no way of avoiding the du Pay men. Their charm, their personality, their sheer size made it impossible for Lucy, herself a tall woman, to do anything other than be guided by Max to a table in an alcove.

'Come join us for tea, Brook. Doctor Graham needs tea after her long journey, and Mother's . . . resting.'

'She'a always resting,' said the boy in a matter-of-fact tone, 'but she'll be thrilled about the ballet. Do you like ballet, ma'am . . . I mean . . . doctor?'

Years of discipline came to her aid. 'Yes, I like it very much, Brook,' Lucy said as she watched the boy's face and listened to his voice, so like his father's. 'I prefer opera, though.'

'Crikey, no way! All those Italians screaming at one another.' He laughed and Lucy smiled at him. How assured well-brought-up American children were, friendly but not forward. She liked it.

'You can come with us if you like, ma'am. I got the whole box, Dad; I didn't quite understand what I was buying.'

They all laughed and Max looked at her, a question in his eyes.

'I couldn't, Brook. I'm sorry. I'm here on business and brought no clothes suitable for the theatre.'

'Why, you look just fine to me. Wow, look at all these tea-cakes. Wasn't I right, Dad? You have to try everything a country has to offer, don't you, Doctor? Sadler's Wells. Afternoon tea.'

There was something so infectiously likeable about the American boy – How old was he? He was tall, but oh so young, twelve, perhaps? – that Lucy found the tea-party almost enjoyable. She devoted herself to introducing Brook to the intricacies of scones with cream and jam, to crumpets – which she assured him ought really to be hot – and to the wonders of shortbread. Because he was so open she discovered that his mother was an invalid – 'I don't remember her ever being well, poor Mother' – and that they were on a trip to some of the spas in Germany so that she could take the waters.

'One day, if Mother gets a little bit stronger, Dad and I are going to tour all the art galleries in Europe. I want to study art in London, you have such fine schools here. But when I finish school I have to go to Yale first, to please Mother.' He blushed as if he was ashamed that he might have sounded just a little disloyal. 'I mean, I want to go. I think she's so right. Everyone should have a really broad education, don't you agree, doctor?'

'Yes, of course, Brook.' What a lovely and unusual name. He could be mine; he *should* be mine. She could bear no more.

'I really must go and unpack. I have an early appointment.'

They stood up. 'You're still practising, Lucy?' Max did not ask about marriage; he had seen her ringless hands.

'Oh, I could never give up medicine, Max,' she answered lightly. 'You know that it always meant everything to me.' There, she had told him he meant nothing. 'Enjoy the ballet, Brook, and the rest of your stay in London.'

She managed to get across the foyer and into the lift, aware that they stood watching her as she walked away from them. She found her room and sat down on the edge of the bed to steady her legs. His voice, his eyes, his hands.

How had she ever told herself that she had forgotten the feel of his hands, the demands of his lips?

She waited until they would have left for the theatre before she went down for dinner, and felt quite sure that she would have breakfasted and gone to her meeting before they were even awake in the morning . . .

Max was waiting in a car as she stepped out into the early spring sunshine.

'Why call a cab when I can easily drive you, Lucy?'

'I have ordered a taxi. Here it is now.'

'Sorry, the lady made a mistake,' said Max and handed the taxi driver a note which earned him a, 'Crikey, ta very much, sir.'

'You had no right to do that,' Lucy said stiffly as, aware of the doorman, she allowed Max to hand her into the beautiful car.

'We have to talk . . .'

'There is nothing to talk about. We had, what, a passing affair fourteen years ago? You must have an incredible conceit about your charms, senator.'

'I love you, Lucy. I have never stopped loving you, and I have thought of you with longing every day of my life.'

Lucy looked down at her clenched hands where the knuckles strove to push themselves up through the soft kid of her gloves. 'Stop this car and let me out. How dare you! If you think for one moment that you can come back into my life after abandoning me . . .' She turned to look at him, her face showing for the first time in years the despair that had tortured her. 'I thought, I prayed, that I might be pregnant. I waited for letters . . . and nothing, *nothing*. Let me out or I shall start screaming . . .'

'Please, Lucy. I apologize if I have insulted and embarrassed you, but you can't get out in the middle of the street. I'll say no more but I'll drop you off . . . where?'

'The Marie Stopes Clinic. It's on . . .'

'I know. I helped . . . family money helped . . . fund it. What a wonderful woman she is. You know of the pioneering work on birth control by . . .'

The awkwardness over, he drove surely and safely to the clinic and let her out. 'I won't offer to come in with you; I was here yesterday. You know how we Americans like to know we're getting value for money. I can't offer to come back either; I'm taking Brook to the Tate.'

'He's a nice boy, Max.'

He smiled, that remembered smile that lit up his face from the inside. 'He's about the only thing in my . . .' he began. 'We must talk again before I leave, Lucy. Please?'

'Thanks for the lift,' she said and walked into the clinic. Her heart was pounding and she doubted that she could speak rationally to the doctors. His wife was an invalid. No doubt an ailing woman found *that* side of marriage tiring. Lucy could name a dozen such invalids, real or imagined, from her own practice. He could not still love her. Had he ever loved her? He was a virile man and the intimate side of marriage would be important to him. For years she had told herself that in those, to her, idyllic days in Italy, he had wanted only sexual release. She had taught herself to dislike him, to forget – no, never to forget, to ignore the memories, the longings, and here he was overturning her carefully nurtured life as easily as easily as he had done all those years ago. *No, no, senator, no willing frustrated woman to toy with as an extra on your London jaunt.* Was there one in Paris, in Rome? Why had they not visited Venice? What had the boy said? 'Dad says the lagoon waters would be bad for Mother's health.' She was talking to Doctor Stopes; was she herself making any sense? Would she remember one word of this conversation? Lucy took herself firmly in hand and thrust Maximilian du Pay back into her subconscious.

He was not so easy to dispose of physically however. Having spent the day in the clinic, Lucy returned late to the Overseas Club. She could see his long legs stretched out in the foyer as she came through the entrance. He was not alone; a woman like a decaying flower sat across from him in a pink chair that could just have been chosen to suit her soft fragility.

'Doctor Graham, if you're not too tired, my wife would love the honour of meeting you.'

He had no right to do this. He should get out of her life. He had his wife and the boy. She had Robin; it was enough. But she could not ignore him without being deliberately rude.

She avoided his outstretched hand and went over to his wife.

'How do you do, Mrs du Pay.'

'Doctor,' Ammabelle du Pay raised a languid hand, 'I am honoured to meet you. Had I had a tenth of your strength' – immediately Lucy felt like a veritable Amazon – 'I should have liked to do something for my fellow man. As it is, I give of my money and my time, I do admit, to many charitable causes, and none dearer to me than birth control. Max, the champagne. You British have your afternoon tea, but I have one glass of champagne; it refreshes me and gives me strength for my evening duties. You will join us, Doctor Graham, or may I too call you Lucy? Such a charming name.'

She stopped for a second while Lucy murmured all the polite things and wondered why Max and Brook were not the exhausted ones. Surely that clinging voice would suck the very life-blood from anyone on whom it fastened? She looked with trained eyes at the woman in front of her. 'One glass in public,' she thought. 'How much in private?' She looked at Max, who seemed unable to meet her eyes, and sadness for all the wasted lives overwhelmed her. 'Poor Max,' she thought.

The champagne came and Max himself opened it expertly. He would be an expert, supposed Lucy, if he had opened a bottle every single afternoon for the last fourteen years.

'Come the recession, I can get a job as a wine waiter.' He laughed as he poured.

'A recession? Surely America is leading the world.'

'There's a great big bubble blowing in the States, Lucy, and bubbles burst.'

'Don't be silly, Max,' said Ammabelle shortly.

'Does she always dismiss her husband so readily, and in public?' thought Lucy, but she smiled as Max's wife turned to her.

'He's made millions, Lucy. He's every bit as fine a business-man as even my dear late father was. And, would you believe, we had to coax him to take his father's Senate seat.'

'But you don't go into the Senate to make money, do you?' Lucy asked before she could stop herself.

'Touché,' laughed Max and his eyes smiled at her across the rim of the glass.

Mrs du Pay, Ammabelle, was annoyed. 'Of course not. I just meant that we need men with brains in government and Max has brains.'

'Government needs men with hearts too, Mother, and that's why Daddy's successful.'

'I've ordered you some fruit juice, Son,' said Max quickly.

Was there an undertone there? The boy said nothing but poured himself a glass of juice. Silently and solemnly he toasted the adults and then he flopped down beside Lucy, almost spilling her drink.

'Gosh, I'm sorry, ma'am,' said Brook, but he was looking at his mother. 'Sometimes I can't handle my legs – like a colt, you know, all legs and no body.'

'You just need to think of others, Brook,' said Mrs du Pay, 'and don't interrupt. His father spoils him abominably, Lucy. You were telling us all about your visit to Dr Stopes' clinic?'

'Was I?' thought Lucy.

'There are no clinics such as this anywhere else in Britain at the moment,' she said. 'I shall be pleased to learn more from Doctor Stopes and to pass the information on to my patients.'

'Bravo, Lucy. What men fail to understand is that a child not only drains a woman's body of all strength and vigour for nine months, but continues to make demands of his poor mother every minute of every day and often night, too, until he is quite grown up. If only the agonies were over with the birth pangs.'

'What an unutterably selfish woman,' thought Lucy as she looked at Brook's young, fresh face. It registered nothing. Had he heard it so often before that he no longer listened or no longer minded? Max's lean brown hand was on the boy's knee.

'I've never had the joys or the pains of a child myself, Ammabelle, and so I can't really agree or disagree, but even the poorest of my patients in the meanest of circumstances seems to feel that the joys of motherhood far outweigh the pain.'

'Even those with nine, ten or even more children whom they cannot afford to feed or clothe?'

'Well, they don't want them when they're carrying them, and too many resort to unbelievable methods to rid themselves of unwanted pregnancies, but once that child is in their arms ...' She stopped and looked at the boy, and the bleakest moment of her entire life came back to her. It was not the day she realized that she had lost Max, but that awful moment in Rose's bathroom when she knew that there was to be no baby, no baby to grow into this beautiful, sensitive boy. 'He should be mine ...' her thoughts repeated.

'What are your professional feelings about legalized abortion, Lucy?' asked Max across the darkness and she was glad to answer.

'I went into medicine to save life, and so to deliberately take life would hardly be acceptable, but there have been cases, even in my experience, where it is necessary to think of the greater good, to sacrifice the child to save the mother. I welcome Doctor Stopes and her teaching. To prevent conception is surely the answer, for the duchess or the mill-girl.'

'Bravo, Lucy! You are a shining light in your profession. Too many doctors mumble platitudes about woman's natural function. Let them try it.' Ammabelle stood up. 'Now I hope you will take pity on my family and dine with them. I was dragged to the ballet last night when all I really needed was rest, and today I have trailed all over London looking at pictures, some of them quite ghastly, and I shall go to bed and have a little toast and soup. I am exhausted. No, don't come with me, Max. I want you and Brook to have a nice evening and I am too tired to be gay.'

She held up her cheek to be kissed, gave Lucy a hand that felt like paper, and drifted away to the stairs.

'Will you dine with us, Doctor Lucy?'

Brook sounded as if her really wanted her company and she wanted to be with them, just once. 'I'd love to dine with you, Brook,' she said; Max was not to think she wanted to be with him. She followed Ammabelle upstairs and washed and changed as quickly as possible. As always, she found herself remembering the dress she had bought in Venice. She had never had another occasion to wear it and now, of course, it was a museum piece. 'Face it, Lucy. You are an old woman and life has passed you by. You are not going down there to pretend you are a family.' But still she had to admit that she was glad, glad that Ammabelle had been too . . . *tired* to dine with her husband and son.

'But there's no need for me to be quite so dowdy,' she decided as she walked downstairs in a serviceable wool dress that she had brightened up with pearls and her grandmother's amethyst brooch.

Max and his son greeted her with obvious pleasure. 'Americans are so polite,' thought Lucy, not for the first time. 'They would never let me know they think they're dining with a frumpy old maid.'

'I thought the Dorchester,' said Max, taking Lucy's arm and leading her outside. 'We can dance after dinner the way . . . well, we can remember our youth.'

'You don't dance, Dad,' said Brook. 'You and Mother sit out all the time back home. But I learned to do the waltz at school, Doctor Lucy . . .' The boy blushed at his audacity and subsided into silence.

'How can you refuse such a charming invitation, Lucy? I will hobble in after Rudolph Valentino here, and maybe you have a pill I could use if it all gets too exciting for me . . .'

'Aw, Dad.' The boy was embarrassed and suddenly looked his age. 'Doctor Lucy knows what I mean.'

'Of course I do, Brook, my dear, and if you're sure you would like to dance, I would be honoured to be your partner.'

'I don't really want to,' the boy answered honestly, 'but I have to at home, at family parties and such. Everybody wants to dance with me, but they know Dad's a senator and they know he's rich and I sometimes think I could be bowlegged and have adenoids . . . you know. Things like that never seemed to bother Dad.'

Lucy remembered the young Max. No, it would never have occurred to him that he was popular because he was rich, but this boy was a more sensitive soul.

Max was smiling. He understood his son more than the boy knew, and that he loved him was so obvious. No, she must not find herself wishing, wishing . . .

'I feel guilty eating all this wonderful food while Ammabelle eats toast alone,' she said later as a sumptuous dessert was placed reverently before her. Did Max and his son look at one another quickly before laughing off the remark and devoting themselves to their own puddings?

Later, they sat drinking coffee and watching the dancers. Brook excused himself and went off to find the gentlemen's room.

And then Max said, 'This feels good, Lucy, feels right.'

'Please, Max. If you say anything, I'll leave.'

'You won't run out on the boy. He likes you.'

'He's a puppy; he likes everyone.'

'No, he doesn't like everyone.' His voice was cold and tired and he leaned across the table, his face inches from her own. She could not get away from him, she had to hear his explanation and she wanted to hear it, no matter how much she told herself that it did not matter to her. 'I couldn't write at first, Lucy. My father had already died when I reached home, and I spent every moment arranging the funeral, comforting my mother and dealing with all the business affairs. It was to escape . . . it was to make up my mind about marriage and career that I went to Europe, and there I found you again.' He laughed, for a moment as young as his son. 'I should have hauled you off on a white charger that night at the Russian embassy, but I had this fool idea I had to let you grow a little, experiment a little. God, you were lovely, and you didn't know it, or at least acted like you didn't – and that was so refreshing, and then I was so much older.'

'Please, Max. I can't listen to this.'

'I loved you, love you more than I have ever loved any woman. Even now in that silly old-lady frock. Hell, Lucy, are you forty yet?'

'I'm fifty, as you well know. I must go, Max,' She half rose from her chair and he stood beside her, and she was as aware of him as she had ever been. She could smell his strength, his vulnerability – God help her, his masculinity. Knees weak, she sank back into her chair and with trembling hands sipped at the glass of champagne that stood, all its bubbles long gone, beside her coffee.

'When my father died I was devastated.' That was all he would ever say to excuse himself, but Lucy had met many women like Ammabelle du Pay. She was only too aware of the fragile ropes that bind the strongest men, the unvoiced blackmail, the feelings of unwarranted guilt. There had been one tonight. 'Why, you all go and enjoy yourselves and poor little exhausted me (exhausted from the birth of one child twelve years before) will just stay here with a little hot soup.' But still she must not listen.

'I don't know when I asked Ammabelle to honour me by becoming my wife, but I must have done and I could not back out and embarrass her and her family and hurt my own sorely grieving mother. She died happy, just after Brook was born.'

He believed all this, he really believed it. There was nothing devious about Max du Pay. He was just a century behind his time. Lucy could just hear the weak echoes of those soft Southern voices that had trapped him in a loveless marriage. No, she must stop this thinking. He was an international statesman, a world traveller. She knew enough to know that a sexual relationship went on in marriages where there was no real affection. And if Ammabelle du Pay pleaded exhaustion, no doubt her husband found physical consolation outside the bonds of holy matrimony. She thought of Isa: 'You've made your bed, noo lie on it.' By marrying Ammabelle he had effectively made Lucy's bed too, and she was quite happy. She had medicine and she had Robin, and she could not live without either.

'You could have written, Max, to explain, just even to let me know that you were alive.'

He bowed his head in shame. 'I have no excuse. But you didn't write either, Lucy. I hoped and prayed, and then decided your first love had won.'

'Well, it did win and I have Robin.'

'Robin?'

'My goddaughter. Her parents both died in the war; her mother was my partner.'

'Were you bombed? I didn't think Dundee, the bridge maybe . . .'

'She went to France to work in a hospital, really a convent where she and Kier had spent part of their honeymoon. Why, what's wrong?'

'This is unbelievable, but I must have met her. As you know, we didn't come in to the war until near the end,

April 1917. We lost a lot of men around the Argonne area, and in 1918 the president asked several of us – senators, congressmen – to tour the war zones, see our boys had supplies. We found the convent near this little town called Le Tréport just a day or two after some Germans had arrived. There was an old French doctor, and a young Scotch girl who looked like a Georgia breeze would blow her away. We gave them supplies – heck, they had everybody's walking wounded in there, Brits, Canadians, French, Germans, and not so much as an aspirin. I asked this old nun what language they communicated in and she said, "The language of love." Pretty soppy, maybe, but old nuns can get away with stuff like that. But you say your partner died there? What a waste! They thought the world of her.'

'I'm glad. I'll tell her daughter.'

He was gazing at her with such intensity that she stopped. 'What is it, Max?'

'I was so close to you. I could have spoken about you and I didn't even know.'

'And Rose? We know so little of her last days.' Speak about Rose, about anything except themselves, except the longing to hold him in her arms, to be held by him.

'Like I said . . . looked like a puff of wind would blow her over, but she worked all the hours God gave her and then some.'

'Her daughter will want to know.'

'Well, she looked happy. They all did. There was this incredible atmosphere there, you could just feel it.'

They sat quietly. Anyone watching would have thought them absorbed in the music, but they were each thinking of Rose Nesbitt, Max with nostalgia and Lucy with a mixture of sadness and love.

Brook came back and Lucy and Max laughed as he tried to stifle a yawn.

'I think we should go?' suggested Lucy.

Brook looked relieved; he would not have to dance. It was impossible to read the expression on Max's face.

The doorman summoned a cab and they sat in silence as the famous buildings of the world's most famous city slipped by in the moonlight.

'You go on up to your room, Brook,' said Max at the door of the club. 'I think we'll walk a while.'

Lucy could not speak. She was not tired and she wanted to walk with him through the starlit streets of London, just once, just once.

They did not talk but walked companionably for a while. Lucy had no real idea of where she was but it did not matter, nothing really mattered. After a while he felt for her hand, and she tensed a little and then relaxed. Was there any harm, just once, in pretending that there was no Ammabelle, no Brook, no Robin?

They were on a bridge crossing the river. Above them they could see the carved front of the abbey soaring into the heavens.

'A beautiful sight,' said Max and his voice was husky. It was inevitable: Lucy turned into his arms with a sigh and for a while they stood and she relaxed against his heart, at ease, at home. When he bent his head she turned her face to him like a flower to the sun that gives it life. Her heart soared higher than the façade of the beautiful building behind them. She was a girl again, on a bridge over the Grand Canal. No, no, she was not. Feverishly she pulled herself away.

'Max, no, this is madness.'

He stopped her protestations with his lips and for a moment she fought, and then gave herself up to the feelings that were overwhelming her, feelings that had not abated in fourteen years but had lain, disciplined, just under her control. This time it was Max who stopped.

'Oh, God, Lucy, what a bloody mess I have made of everything.'

'We made it together.'

'Let's walk some more or, so help me, I won't be responsible.'

'I can't lose you again, Lucy,' he went on. 'I fought the yearning for fourteen years and one sight of you at that desk with that silly little hat . . . You're wearing it again; it's a doctory litle hat!'

She unpinned the hat and threw it into the Thames and then she unpinned her hair and let the pins fall unheeded to the ground.

'My God, don't do that.' His voice was harsh and rough. 'You're such an innnocent, Doctor Lucy, or is that something they teach in medical school – "Let down your hair when you want to entice a man." '

'No, but they do teach how to blow out the fire if it's started.'

He laughed and hugged her, the spontaneous gesture of a brother, not a lover.

'Time to get a cab. Come on.' He tucked her arm into his and they walked towards a busier street. 'I can't divorce my wife, Lucy. I wish I could. It's not that she loves me . . . you see, she's . . .' He stopped; he would not be even more disloyal. 'Can we, at least, write one another, even maybe call when they get these transatlantic lines in, see one another when I'm in Europe? I could send the boy to school here; I could come over every year . . .'

She said nothing, for she could not speak. Her heart was breaking for the despair and anguish in his voice. She wished they had not met . . . No, she didn't. Oh God, oh God, it was an impossibility. What good could come of it? Better to make a clean break, to cut out the heartache.'

She heard her voice. 'I'll write, as a friend, at Christmas time.'

407

He had hailed a cab and, to her surprise, handed her in and gave the driver the address and the fare.

His voice was calm but his eyes were unutterably sad.

'Until Christmas, friend of my heart,' he said and stepped back into the shadows.

23

Dundee, 1921

LUCY LEFT EARLY next morning, or that morning, for Dundee, and therefore did not see Max or any member of his family again. She had not slept but had packed her few clothes and the toys bought for Robin into her small overnight bag and then, fully dressed, had lain down on the bed to wait for her early morning tea. Over and over again she had relived those moments with Max by the river. Her feelings for him had not died as, for fourteen years, she had fought to convince herself that they had. Instead they had grown and matured like the fine wines of which he was fond, but he would not divorce his wife and Lucy would not – when she was rational and the blood was not raging through her fevered veins – have wanted him to take such a drastic step.

By the time the chambermaid arrived with the tray, she was going over and over the things she had learned in Doctor Stopes' clinic, and which she intended to utilize as soon as she returned to her practice. There was a parcel on the tray – from one of London's finest jewellers, and beautifully wrapped. Max's card, in a small envelope, was beside it.

The box contained a small gold brooch in the shape of an exquisitely formed butterfly; the body of the butterfly was a perfect ruby.

'Merry Christmas past' was the inscription on the card.

'I can't accept jewellery from a man,' said Lucy to herself as she pinned the brooch to the front of her dress.

An hour later she was on the train north.

Robin was sitting on the dining-room table when Isa welcomed Lucy home. She jumped from the table into Lucy's arms.

'Ladies do not sit on dining-room tables,' said Lucy, kissing the child's tumbled curls.

'Isa has told me all day that I am not a lady.'

'And so, you decided to prove that she was right. You are a naughty girl and should not be given the parcel that's at the bottom of my bag.'

It was good to be home. Already it felt as if she had never been away.

The brooch caught in Robin's hair as she slid out of Lucy's arms.

'Pretty,' she said.

'Robin, I almost forgot. The friend who gave me this brooch knew Mummy in the war. He said she was beautiful and brave and saved the lives of lots and lots of soldiers.'

Robin forgot about the parcel waiting for her in Lucy's bag while she heard over and over again about the meeting of Dr Rose Nesbitt and an American senator. Some things Lucy had to realistically invent. 'What was Mummy wearing? How many British soldiers did she save? Did she save German soldiers too? I hope she didn't.'

'But of course she did, Robin, for Mummy was a doctor and the poor German soldiers didn't want to fight any more than the Scottish ones did.'

'That's stupid. If no one wanted to fight, then why was there a war?'

Lucy looked down at the five-year-old child who had lost both her parents to a war neither had wanted. She did not know the answer and so avoided the question. 'It was so awful, Robin, that there will never ever be a war again.'

'Good. Did you bring me a book?'

'I thought little girls liked dolls.'

'Not so much as books.'

'Wherever I go from now on, I shall buy you a book.'

Robin nodded emphatically. 'Good.'

'Time for bed. I'll bath you.'

'I haven't done my homework and you haven't sharpened my pencils. Get a scalpel. Mine have to be the very, very sharpest. Miss Blair likes Fiona best 'cause she has the best pencils.'

Lucy sighed. Robin adored her teacher, an ironclad maiden lady, and wanted to please her in every way. Miss Blair demanded four sharp pencils every day, and so every evening they went through the ritual of sharpening Robin's pencils to danger point.

'You are trying to make me forget that you have not yet done your homework, madam.'

'It's just to read, Aunt Lucy, and to learn three words and I already know them anyway, but if you hear me say them, then you can sign my jotter and Miss Blair will love me as much as she loves Fiona.'

Was it her lack of parents that made Robin so insecure, or did all little girls want to be loved by their first teacher? Lucy could not remember, but vowed to have a word with the, to her, formidable Miss Blair. She listened to Robin read, signed the jotter to show that BELL, WELL, and SPELL could be correctly spelled by Miss Anderson-Howard, and an hour later managed to sit down to go over the accumulated letters.

'A doctor should ken not to read while she's eating,' fussed Isa. 'It's very bad for the digestion and not a good example for Miss Robin.'

'She's sound asleep, Isa, and this halibut is wonderful.'

Somewhat mollified, Isa went off and Lucy finished her meal and went through her letters. She went into her office and began to go through her notes on birth control and then somehow, all by itself, the pencil wrote 'Merry Christmas past'. She had promised to write to him, once a year at Christmas. She would send it once a year, but there could be no harm in writing little bits all year round. Having no real idea of the length of time it would take for a letter posted in Dundee to reach Washington, D.C., she posted her first letter to Max on the 1st of October 1921.

Max laughed with pleasure when the strange letter arrived a full month before Christmas and sat down to answer it immediately. He had never been to Dundee and he had certainly never seen her home, but he imagined her fairly accurately as she sat before a roaring fire in her elegantly furnished sitting room, scribbling away everything except what was really in her heart. He took his tone from her letter. Brook was a joy. Ammabelle was rather unwell – he did not give her illness a name and Lucy sighed for him. He had hoped that the trip to Europe, new sights, new sounds, would help, but if anything it seemed to have made things worse. She could not bear to have Brook near her and was somewhat less fond of his father.

I refuse to leave her though, for I feel that she does draw some strength from my presence although she denies it and says my very size tires her. The doctors agree with me but suggest I do send Brook to a board school. It is not merely with my own interests at heart that I have decided on one of your fine Scottish institutions.

In August 1922 Brook du Pay arrived at Lucy's front door just as she drove up with Robin. Lucy's heart leaped like a spawning salmon trying to jump up a waterfall and then settled somewhere at the bottom of her stomach. At thirteen the boy was tall and slim; it was Max she saw there, Max. 'Brook!' Her voice whispered and then recovered. 'Brook!' Her voice was much stronger. 'How lovely to see you.'

'I guess the letter didn't reach you.' His voice had changed in a year; low and strong, it uncannily resembled the mellow tones of his father. 'Dad sent me over with a tutor. Mother is . . . well, she's kinda sick, Doctor Lucy, and I really get in her hair.' He broke off and looked at Robin who was staring at them with both her eyes and mouth wide. Lucy laughed. 'Brook, this is my goddaughter Robin Anderson-Howard.'

'How do you do, Miss Robin Anderson-Howard,' said Brook and held out his hand.

Robin shook hands formally and Lucy was proud of her training. Then the child spoiled the effect by adding, 'You are a very pretty boy.'

'Robin, "how do you do" is enough.'

'Heck no, Doctor Lucy, no one ever told me I was pretty before.'

'Where are your cases,' – no, what did Americans say? – 'your bags, Brook?'

'Oh, we checked into a hotel and Mr Van Doeren let me take a cab over. We're only here a few days. I have to get to Edinburgh to buy the outfit.'

Isa had opened the door and was standing waiting. 'Are you coming in or are you going to stay out there all night?'

'We have a guest for tea, Isa.' For the moment Lucy had forgotten that Isa had been with her in Venice, with her in Tuscany.

'Oh, no,' breathed Isa as she looked at the boy's face, so like that of his father. 'It can't be.'

'This is Brook du Pay, Isa.'

'I'll get the tea,' Isa muttered, ignoring Brook's out-stretched hands.

'Please forgive her, Brook,' said Lucy angrily. 'She's a rude, bad-tempered old woman.'

'She isn't usually,' said Robin, 'but it doesn't matter. She makes lovely biscuits.'

There was no opportunity to talk to Brook until he was seated beside her in the car driving back to his hotel. Robin had demanded his full attention to her school-books and Lucy had enjoyed watching them. They were very alike, tall for their ages, slender and dark-haired, 'almost brother and sister', she thought and tore her mind away from that path.

'I'm sorry that your mother is no better, Brook.' She did not want to pry, to make the boy unhappy by forcing him to face a situation that his father had obviously encouraged him, in public at least, to avoid.

'She's never been very strong, Doctor Lucy, and she gets real exhausted when there's any kind of pressure, I guess you'd say. She used to love our house in Washington and all the parties, but now she never goes and Dad has to go himself . . . but this year he has decided to stay in Georgia, just until she gets a little better.'

'And he has decided to send his much-loved son away from him,' thought Lucy. She had been a doctor for a long time; she had many patients who shared Ammabelle's symptoms, but she could not tell the fragile boy that she knew. She muttered something encouraging and then talked of the adventure of going to a new school in a new country.

'And you can come to me for exeats, Brook. You must never stay in school when you have permission to have a weekend away.'

Later, in her bedroom as she sat at the mirror, she regretted those words.

'Oh, Max, am I to be content with being a surrogate mother for your child as well as Kier's? I should be content;

my child-bearing years are over. I should have forgotten the anticipation, the uncontrollable leaping passion. I should have forgotten Italy, forgotten those desperate words in London. Better far to say you never meant it, to hate you, to put you out of my mind. Better not to encourage your son, Ammabelle's son, to make himself welcome in my retreat. This house is for Robin. And it's a doctor's house, a place where people come to get well, to find hope and joy and courage in despair.'

She glared in the mirror at the dark eyes, the tumbling brown hair that had – yes, it did – flecks of grey. 'You're too old to still want Max, too old to have your heart dance with joy at the sound of his name, at a glance from his son that reminds you of Washington and, oh, dear God, how he reminds you of Tuscany. Why do I torture myself with longing? Max belongs to Ammabelle and I can't hope, can't . . . must not pray.'

24

1923

ALTHOUGH LUCY HAD sent her yearly letter, she received no Christmas letter from Max, but in early December a card arrived from Brook. He was on his way home for Christmas: he hoped to resume his studies in the New Year. What did it mean? Lucy refused to speculate – she could not, must not. A few days later a small packet arrived for Miss Anderson-Howard and, when opened on Christmas morning, was found to contain a silver propelling pencil ... 'to make your jotters tidier ...' Robin practised all day.

'When he comes he'll see I'm neater than Fiona.'

Lucy tried delicately to prepare her to be hurt. 'He might not be able to come back for a while. America is a long way away.'

Robin wrote a superbly beautiful 'B' on her paper. She decorated it with flowers. 'He'll be back, Auntie Lucy.'

The New Year came. The spring followed, but there was no communication from Georgia or Washington, D.C. Lucy accepted an invitation to a conference in Paris.

'Paris? Can I come?'

'Not this time, Robin. I'm working. One day, I promise.'

'But you will go, won't you? You'll go to see my father's grave?'

Lucy faced that that was what had been in the back of her mind since she heard about the conference. The first war graves had been officially prepared in 1920. Why had she not gone then? 'Robin was too small,' she answered herself. Now there was no excuse, no excuse not to find and visit both graves.

'I'll go, sweetheart, and I'll put some flowers there.'

'I'll pay for them,' said Robin, and fished a rather sticky sixpence out of the pocket in her knickers.

The conference in Paris went very well. On the first Friday evening Lucy took the train to Amiens, which was relatively close to everywhere she wanted to go and where she could at least find taxis, if not a car for hire. It was late and dark when she arrived, and so she went straight to her hotel. Even on the trains she had been aware of the cemeteries; it was impossible not to be aware of them. They stretched, in silent witness to the stupidity of man, for miles into the distance. She had

Robin's sixpence. Tomorrow she would take the equivalent amount in francs and see what flowers a little girl could buy for the father she had never known and who had probably never even known of her existence.

The hotel was comfortable and clean and, thanks both to Herr Colner and to her year in Rouen, she was able to order a delicious meal.

'I'll bring Robin here one day,' she thought.

There were few other guests in the hotel, and the others in the dining room were obviously local people who appreciated Madame Viseux's superb cooking. Madame took pity on her foreign guest – perhaps because that foreigner had enough sense to try the local speciality of Queues de Boeufs aux Olives Noirs and not to stick to the familiar Coq au Vin that all other foreigners ordered – and stood beside her while she drank her second cup of excellent coffee.

'You are on holiday, madame?'

'No. I was in Paris on business . . .'

Madame Viseux was interested. A woman alone and on business.

'Business, madame?'

'I am a doctor and I am attending a conference.' Lucy realized there was no reason not to tell her; the woman was interested, not nosy.

'Médecin. This is undoubtedly an honour, madame.'

'You are a superb cook, madame.' It was time to share the glory.

Madame was complacent. She shrugged, a typically Gallic shrug, and Lucy smiled to see it. 'We all use the talents le bon Dieu gives us, Madame Medecin. You have come for the graves?'

'Yes.'

'Few come but we are thinking, Jean Luc and I, we are thinking that a trickle is becoming a tide and we should expand our hotel.'

'Very wise, Madame.'

'The good food eases the heartache, no?'

'Indeed.'

'Your husband, madame?'

'A friend.'

Well satisfied, Madame Viseux took herself off to the kitchen where Lucy became a woman who had lost her lover to war and who had become a doctor to cure the ills of the surviving world. Unaware of the halo she was wearing, Lucy went to her comfortable room to write to Robin and to sleep.

. . . Now I am in Amiens and tomorrow I will find Daddy's grave in Louvencourt. The War Graves Commission have worked so hard to make a list of where every brave soldier is buried. It is very beautiful and peaceful. I have your sixpence, dear Robin, and I am sure I will find some lovely flowers.

This hotel is small, very comfortable, and the food is, you will be glad to hear, absolutely superb. It is a perfect place for a little girl to practise her French, and one day soon, we shall have a holiday, a *vacance*, here.

The next morning a solicitous and sympathetic maid brought croissants light as air and the coffee Lucy had ordered although she had been offered tea. The tea in Paris had cured her of ever making that mistake again.

'No doubt madame could make a decent cup of tea, but in Rome etc. etc.,' she told herself. 'Who knows, tomorrow I may be brave enough to try chocolate in the morning.' She could imagine Annie as clearly as if she were in the room. 'Chocolate, for breakfast? You have your cocoa afore you go to your bed.'

But Annie was dead, had been dead for years. Lucy shivered. She had not thought much about it before but, apart from Isa, only Robin was left, a tiny thread connecting her to everyone who had gone before.

She left the hotel and her taxi driver escorted her to the cemeteries.

'You should have seen them just a few years ago, madame: wild flowers everywhere, scarlet poppies, blue cornflowers, white camomile, perfect for French and English dead, no? But, like you English we French are good gardeners and we have worked hard to grow the flowers of the countries these children left behind. Unfortunately the giant maples of Canada do not grow well here, or some of the flowers of India. You have forget-me-nots for your husband, Madame?'

'No.'

'Your king came in 1922 . . . to Passchendaele. At Etaples he asked the gardener to take him to a grave, not one of the ones he was being shown. The King of England, madame, he stood by this little grave and he took an envelope from his pocket. There were forget-me-nots in it, sent by the soldier's mother, a simple woman, to the queen. He bent over the grave and carefully put the little bouquet upon it. Then he turned to the gardener: "See you keep them watered as long as possible," he said. I hope his maman knows how hard we try.'

Her heart too full for speech, Lucy lay back and watched the rows and rows of headstones go by. How many mothers would be unable to put flowers on these graves? They reached Louvencourt and she asked the driver to wait. She would not be long.

She had already contacted the authorities and knew the number of the cross and the line it was in. Her arms were full of the flowers for which France was justly famous. She stopped on a path and looked around and remembered Wordsworth's poem about the daffodils. But it was not gaily dancing flowers that stretched as far as the eye could see here, but little headstones marching in solemn witness towards Blomfield's magnificent cross of remembrance. The silence crushed her eardrums, her brain. Thousands and thousands of mute appeals. Lucy knew the figures. She had read them every day in the newspapers but eight thousand, eleven thousand, nineteen thousand in one day meant nothing, nothing until now.

Her eyes misty with unshed tears, she started walking again to the section that sheltered Major Kier Anderson-Howard. Private _____ aged nineteen; Gunner _____ aged seventeen, Fusilier _____ aged nineteen. 'My God, they are children. We fought a war with children.'

No, not all were children. Here lay husbands and fathers. How many, like Kier, had never known that they were to live on in the gift of an unborn child?

Her feet had found his grave, but her knees refused to support her legs and she sank down on the neatly mown grass.

Almost four years. Did it make it easier to accept death if one could take part in its rituals? Had she really realized the finality of death? 'The War Office regrets . . .' Had they really accepted it? Now she saw with painful lucidity that it had taken seeing this plain little white stone with his name and rank and the simple cross carved on it and the date of his death. She looked around again. How many of the wives, mothers, sweethearts of all the men buried under these crosses could ever afford the luxury of seeing the grave, of attending it as she was doing, of putting a floral tribute on the sad mound? The war was not over – the fighting perhaps, but for too many women the war would never end.

Lucy looked in her handbag and found her nail file; it was all she could find with a sharp point. She began to dig, and when she had a little hole she dropped Robin's sixpence in it and covered it up.

She's giving you all she had, Kier. You would love her; she's very like you, in looks but in nature too. I'll have to watch her as she gets older, make sure no one tries to take advantage of her soft heart. You should see her on her pony, fearless. Suddenly she made up her mind. 'I wasn't going to, but if the conference finishes early I'll try to see Rosie for you too, Kier, and for Robin.

That night she finished her letter to Kier's daughter.

The graves are very peaceful. There is an atmosphere – a feeling, a peacefulness. I gave Daddy your flowers and I have taken a photograph. (*She was no expert with the unfamiliar equipment and prayed it would turn out.*) There are gardeners, old soldiers,

who drive around in a dreadful old car but they keep
everything quite beautiful. There are flowers all year.
The French are so good at flowers, and Daddy did
love the gardens at Laverock Rising. I go back to
Paris tomorrow and I shall buy you a new frock – and
a book . . . in French!

I may be a day or two late – I will send a telegram
– but I will have lots to tell you when I meet you in
London.

Lots of love,

Aunt Lucy

The next morning, after a second visit to the cemetery, she
went back to Paris. On the train she looked at and revised
the notes she had made for her paper on community welfare
and found herself drafting a letter to Colin Dryden, still a
valued friend, who might just start a fund that would allow
impoverished relatives to visit, at least once, the graves of
their dead. She would call it the Anderson-Howard Memorial Fund. Did not both of the Anderson-Howards lie in
graves in rural France marked only by small white stones?
Four days later, her paper delivered and well received – the
French had Madame Curie after all; they easily accepted a
woman – she was on a train to Ste Antoine sur Somme. No
lines of crosses here. She hoped there would be an hotel, and
made enquiries.

'There are fine hotels at Le Tréport, Madame, or Dieppe itself,' she was told, 'but the convent sometimes takes guests. At least they used to, before the war.'

The Mother Superior welcomed her with coffee in a room that should have been gloomy but was not. The heavy oak furniture was lovingly polished and there was a glorious arrangement of roses in a silver bowl set in the middle of a round table. Reverend Mother spoke excellent English.

'We have not had an English guest for some time, madame. The coming of the motor car . . .' She shrugged her shoulders. No one needed to stop at the convent now.

Lucy, who found her Bentley a necessary and welcome replacement for her old pony and trap at home, commiserated with her.

'But we must not stand in the way of progress, Sister.' She bit into a biscuit that dissolved like snow on a child's tongue. 'The new idea is to advertise. These biscuits would bring hungry guests from all over Britain.'

Reverend Mother laughed and threw up her hands in mock horror.

'What a truly terrifying thought! We are a contemplative order, madame. Our hospitality was originally a gesture of goodwill, charity if you like, to the benighted traveller. But you have come deliberately to see us, Sister Antoine says.' Her voice rose a little, questioningly. She would never ask outright, but if madame chose to honour her with a confidence . . .

'I am not Madame Graham, Sister, but Doctor Graham. I wrote to the convent in 1918 . . .' She stopped. As soon as she had said the word doctor, a warmth had come into the old nun's eyes. 'Did I write to you, Sister?'

'No, madame. I was not Superior then, but I was told about your letter. You have come about La Petite, the little doctor?'

'Yes. Doctor Nesbitt was my partner, and I am guardian of her daughter.'

'You will wish to see her grave. It is marked like the others and I tend it myself. Unfortunately, it is too dark now, but tomorrow morning . . .'

'Then I may stay for a day or two?'

'But of course, and now you are doubly welcome.' Reaching behind her, she took a photograph in a silver frame from the bookshelf and handed it to Lucy. It was a group picture and the photographer had not been very skilled. The figures were blurred, but she recognized Rose. She had changed from the elegant and sophisticated woman who had gone to France. Always slight, she was almost emaciated, but even the poor quality of the photograph could not hide the happiness in the face.

'She was happy here, Sister. I am so glad. She had not been happy for some time.'

'Ah, the death of her husband. I understand. We worked together. There are sisters here and even people in the village who remember her with gratitude; she was a good doctor.'

The old nun's hand was held out. Lucy was embarrassed that she had stared so long at the photograph, at Rose surrounded by recovering patients, she supposed, and one or two nuns.

She handed it back. 'You are not in the photograph, Sister?'

'She liked music, La Petite, and so did Captain Drummond.' She pointed at a tall, thin soldier beside Rose. 'When we were not too busy I played the piano. The patients liked to hear it when they rested in the garden.'

'It's a lovely garden.'

'Ah, tomorrow you will see. It is back to the splendour of before the war. The other doctor, Doctor Mouton, weeded when he had the chance. Not much opportunity to garden in a war and, besides, it is well known that the soil of the Somme is heavy with chalk, is it not?'

'Rose stayed here on her honeymoon in 1907, Sister.'

'I wondered, but I was not here until the war and we never knew her married name.'

'Anderson-Howard.'

'Come in, Sister.' Lucy had not heard the soft footsteps.

'Sister Antoine will show you to your room, Madame. Dinner will be served to you there. If there is anything at all that you want, please ask.' She hesitated. 'You speak French very well, I think.'

'I studied in Rouen for a year.'

'Forgive me, Madame. Usually the British . . .'

'I am rusty, Sister, and will enjoy being oiled by conversation with Sister Antoine.'

'And if I may continue to practise my English . . .'

Lucy smiled. The nun's English was stilted but very good.

The guest room was simply furnished and reminded Lucy with a pang of her bedroom at Casata d'Aurora. In the morning she found that the view was not of mountains but of the garden, and as soon as she was ready she hurried out to see it in all its glory. She walked briskly down a path, trying to see everything as Rose had seen it, and came to a small gate. The graveyard: so unlike the serried rows in Louvencourt and Le Tréport. There were a few stones to commemorate members of the community who had died and then, against a wall of pear trees, the graves of the Allied servicemen, and of the Scottish and French doctors who had died as a result of the war.

'You wish to change the inscription?' The reverend mother had joined her from another pathway.

Lucy shook her head. 'I don't think so. One day her daughter will decide, but as Rose Anderson-Howard she is commemorated on her husband's family crypt. I like "Rose Nesbitt, Médecin".'

'We had begun to pray that she might find new happiness with the young officer. He died saving her, you know, from a German. He lies here too, the German, but in another part. His commander shot him. They were not all bad, the Germans.'

Lucy had wondered about the serenity in Rose's face in the photograph, and had decided to ask no questions about Captain Drummond.

'Were you taken by the Germans, Sister?'

'No, they were retreating and wanted only food. The Americans came after them – a day or two, no more – but one day too late to save the gallant captain.'

'And Rose?'

'She worked too hard and, I think – though perhaps you will say I am a romantic old woman living vicariously – I think she lost heart.'

Perhaps she did, thought Lucy, but the photograph had told her that Rose, as she had expected, was already ill.

'I nursed her myself as well as I could. We had no trained medical personnel at all by that time. Our recovering patients returned to their armies and, her job done, La Petite released her hold on life.'

'Did she speak about her daughter?' She could not tell Robin that her mother had seemed to have forgotten about her completely.

'She did not speak very much at all, madame. I knew she had a child – she told me, but she was a very private person. She liked birds, though; she was very fond of birds.'

'Birds?'

'Ah, the ubiquitous little robin. Madame's mind wandered at the end and always she said, "My robin, my lovely little robin." '

25

1923

It was raining when Lucy arrived in London. After the sunny skies of France that fact should have been guaranteed to dampen the spirits, but for some reason she felt happy. She would see Robin; she would tell her about her mother and about the bravery of Captain Andrew Drummond. She would not tell the child that at last her mother had been falling really in love, but she would tell her Rose's last soft words. Looking out of the taxi windows at the sheets of rain, she became more practical. It would be very nice if the rain would go before morning. Tomorrow they were shopping.

The Overseas League was as warm and as welcoming as ever. Lucy signed in and looked automatically for Robin's name. She and Isa should have arrived yesterday:

Miss Anderson-Howard
Mrs Isa Murray

There was another name written in large, proud letters at the top of the page, just above Robin's. Lucy gazed at it, her heart doing remarkable, very unmedical things inside her body.

Maximilian du Pay

She should not be surprised. Thousands of people used the club as a home from home. He was an international statesman, and the Overseas League was more intimate than a hotel; probably he was here on Senate business, and was not even going to tell her. Well, she would dine in her room. Robin would like that. They would make it a party; she need not even see Max.

He was alone. Ammabelle? Brook? Yes, Ammabelle was better and he had decided to see his son's school for himself. That was all.

He doesn't mean to see you, Lucy, to raise hopes. Oh, stop your heart leaping, the way it leaped all those years . . . all those wasted years . . . It should be schooled by now. The fires should be dead.

She turned to the porter. 'Send up some tea, please, and milk for my ward.'

'There's a note, ma'am – I'd almost forgotten. Mrs Bell has taken the children to the opera.'

How dare he? Isa would never have contemplated such a thing. He had sent them off to leave the way clear . . . for what?

She smiled at the porter. 'Tea for one, then, please,' and went off up the lovely wood staircase to her room.

There were roses in her bedroom; their scent filled the air. They were everywhere: on the table by the window, in the fireplace, on the bedside table. Lucy's heart leaped again. No, no, it was stupid. This was the action of a romantic young man. She had been given the wrong room, a honeymooner's room. She would complain at once . . . her hand reached for the bell to summon a chambermaid.

It was Max who stood there when she opened the door. She could say nothing, do nothing.

'I couldn't quite match your red dress,' he said at last, and then she was in his arms. There were tears on her face. Were they hers? Were they his? She could not see him through the haze. There was nothing and no one in the whole world but Max du Pay . . . another woman's husband. She wrenched herself out of his arms, turned away from him and stepped back into her room.

He stood in the corridor and waited. A thousand thoughts were rushing through Lucy's head. She was a young girl again and she had no idea what to do or what to say.

'We Southerners don't compromise our women,' said Max from the safety of the corridor, and she turned and saw that he was laughing at her gently, understandingly. 'I guess the red dress is long gone?'

She nodded.

'We'll buy a new one tomorrow. Tonight, you look just beautiful the way you are. Will you have dinner here in the restaurant with an old friend?'

Why did she hesitate?

'We have to talk, Lucy.'

She was filled with panic. 'I've ordered tea . . . I'm tired, Max . . . the conference . . . the boat-train.'

'I cancelled your dratted tea.'

He straightened his shoulders and she looked at him. He had changed, he looked like a man who had . . . suffered.

'Ammabelle is gone, Lucy,' he said quietly, 'and I deeply regret any part I played in her death. She had cancer of the liver; too many years of too much champagne, maybe because a rich husband who didn't really love her wasn't enough for her. I'm fifty-five years old, Lucy. I've wasted half my life, more. I don't regret it all; there's Brook, and I think I can be proud of some of the work I've done . . .'

He stopped as an interested chambermaid hurried past the open door. Lucy laughed and pulled him inside. 'I'm too old to be compromised,' she said and, without thinking, she put her arms around his neck.

Max bent his head, but he did not kiss her. He held her gently as if she was a butterfly that must not be crushed, and buried his face in her hair. As they stood together without speaking, in a silence that said more than a thousand conversations, Lucy felt all the doubts and worries and regrets of thirty-four years grow lighter and lighter and eventually fly away.

'We'll have dinner,' he said at last, his mouth still against her hair, 'and we'll talk. Come with me now, because if I leave you here you'll start thinking about age and your patients and Robin . . .'

'And the fact that you live on one continent and I on another . . .'

'Little things, little things,' he said. 'Come on, before I change my mind.'

She laughed and they went downstairs hand-in-hand, but said nothing until they were at a table in the dining room. Words did not seem to be necessary. The waiters came and Max ordered for them both.

When the wine steward had poured the glasses of champagne, Max lifted his glass and toasted her silently. Then he spoke.

'I wish I could say I loved you from the moment I first saw you, Lucy. I sure . . . fell in like with you . . . that evening in Washington . . . you flitted like a butterfly among all those old iron-clad people.' He stopped for a moment, remembering. 'And then, when I was drifting so aimlessly, I found you again . . . in Venice. Venice and the Casata d'Aurora . . .'

He stopped and they looked at one another, and the lost years of pain melted away.

She blushed. 'It must be changed,' she said to hide her confusion.

'No,' he said, 'nothing's changed. I bought it that winter, you see – for us, Lucy. One of Mauro's sons looks after it for me. His kids play in the orchard where I still see you . . . the blossoms in your hair . . . on your breast. I've carried that picture in my head all these years . . . He stopped and Lucy smiled at the look on his face. 'You're wearing my brooch.'

'Every day,' she told him.

He stretched out his hand and lightly touched the brooch and then her mouth.

'I've got it all worked out,' he said at last. 'I've resigned my Senate seat. The businesses have good managers. You want to keep on working, I'll . . .'

'One day you'll meet a man and you'll know. Nothing else will be important.'

'I do,' she said. 'You've never asked, Max, but I do. I love you, and nothing else is important.' She hesitated. 'Well, that's not quite true. I can't leave Robin. Otherwise I would go with you tonight, anywhere, to Washington, to Georgia, to Italy . . .'

'You'll go nowhere until you're married, you hussy,' he said and his voice was low with suppressed passion.

Married? Married? How? There was Robin, and there was Brook, and there were patients – always, always her patients.

'You will marry me?' he asked anxiously. The obstacles disappeared. How could he doubt?

'Yes,' she said simply and her hand reached for his across the table, and all the years fell away and they were young again.

'I'll establish residency,' he said, his voice choked with emotion. 'December?' he suggested.

'December,' she said.

'*Women like you are rare, Lucy, like butterflies in December.*'

Acknowledgements

With thanks to: Fiona Scharlau, archivist; Ian Flett, archivist; L. Ball of the Commonwealth War Graves Commission; Robert F. Newell, director general of the Royal Overseas League; Dr Gary Colner; Dr Jim Inglis; Dundee and Angus librarians; Mrs Jo Currie, Special Collections, Edinburgh University Library.

Welcome to the world of *Eileen Ramsay*!

Keep reading for more from Eileen Ramsay, to discover a recipe that features in this novel and a sneak peek at Eileen's next book . . .

We'd also like to introduce you to MEMORY LANE, our special community for the very best of saga writing from authors you know and love and new ones we simply can't wait for you to meet. Read on and join our club!

www.MemoryLane.club

Dear Friends,

I hope you enjoyed my story, which was first published as *Butterflies in December*. I thought you might like to know how I came to write it. We lived in the U.S. for almost twenty years and both our sons were born there. Both loved animals and wanted a dog. Because we were considering returning to Scotland and none of us could consider putting a pet into quarantine, they settled for a cat.

Once back in Scotland we began to look for a house, one with a garden big enough for a dog. Every weekend we were house-hunting and, yes, dog-hunting. How did it happen that we bought the dog, a deerhound puppy, before we finalised our house purchase? Isla, the deerhound, remained in the kennels until we moved into the house but, of course, we visited her every weekend. The boys attended a school in the nearby town and a few months later our younger son invited his school friends to his birthday party. It was a perfect autumn day and so rugby was played on the lawn by children, the puppy and some of the parents who had driven their children to the house.

As it happened several of them were doctors and as I passed with the umpteenth laden tray I heard one say, 'I think this was Dr Thomson's house.'

My antennae zoomed out. Who was Dr Thomson and why was he – or she – so important that all the parents knew the name?

Writer does research. I started by questioning farming neighbours and discovered that Dr Emily Thomson, one of the first female doctors in Scotland and the very first in our area, had lived in the house early in the twentieth century. The garden still tells of her. There's a paddock with a small stable for the horse she owned to pull her dog cart. In the paddock too is the gate through which doctor and pony would trot on their way to work in Dundee, useless now since a tall wall denies exit onto the road. At the back of the lawn is a summer house which we renovated but which still contains the antique fire which kept the summerhouse warm when her niece and nephew were visiting on school holidays.

Another neighbour told us that Dr Thomson had put up the wall when she started being driven into Dundee and had realised that the pathway though the paddock was too small for her 'automobile'. A thoroughly modern woman, another told us that she was actually seen smoking a cigarette as she flew past.

The old logs of the small local school told me that she gave a party for the children every Christmas. More and more fascinated by this incredible pioneering woman, I went to Edinburgh University where she studied originally and, for £15, the wonderful archivists in the Medical Library discovered that she was born in India in 1863 and graduated from The Edinburgh School of Medicine for Women in 1899. They also sent me a copy of her course of study – fascinating, especially when I found that Emily had studied midwifery and practical pharmacy under the famous Dr Jex Blake.

My first impulse was to attempt to write a biography but I decided instead to write a novel inspired by the career of this remarkable woman. I hope you've enjoyed her story.

Please join my readers club by emailing me at Eileen.ramsay@bonnierzaffre.co.uk, where you can sign up to receive exclusive news about my next book along with updates of other authors in our Memory Lane community.

Fondest,
Eileen

Eileen's Recipe for Cranachan

Cranachan is a very old Scottish pudding, it's easy to make and is absolutely delicious. I like to think of it being made for the first time on a wee croft in the Highlands by a crofter's wife who had some extra milk from her cow, wild raspberries growing against her stone dykes, honey her own bees had made and maybe a wee dram – for medicinal purposes – in the kitchen cupboard. The first ingredients were probably some whipped cream cheese, a large handful of oatmeal, a spoonful or two of heather honey, as many raspberries as she had picked, and a tablespoon of whisky.

Today there are possibly as many recipes for cranachan as there are cooks. I'd like to share with you mine:

You will need:

85g porridge oats
570ml double cream
3 tbs honey
7 tbs whisky/white wine/fruit juice
450g raspberries

Dessert glasses for serving

How to make my cranachan:

- As always the oats are toasted on a metal skillet over heat and the cream is lightly whipped.
- The host's best dessert glasses are put on the table and assembly begins.
- When the toasted oats are cool the honey is poured over them and they are lightly mixed. Then the whisky is poured over them and again they are mixed. (When we have non-whisky fans visiting we use white wine and when our grandchildren are at table with us, we simply have two large bowls, one with whisky and another with a few tablespoons of someone's favourite fruit juice.)
- At the bottom of each glass we spoon some oats, then some cream, then raspberries, more cream and – if there any – more raspberries, a last spoon of cream and a sprinkling of oats.
- Enjoy.

If you enjoyed *Rich Girl, Poor Girl* you'll love this sneak peek at Eileen Ramsay's next book *The Farm Girl's Dream*

Prologue

Paris, 24th May 1900

HE HAD LEFT THE WINDOW open and the sound of the fruit sellers' carts, as they rattled along the cobblestones, woke him. The early-morning scents of Paris – baking bread and cold, damp, sickly sweet river water – drifted through the windows and mixed with Genevieve's perfume, the bouquet of the remainder of that second bottle of very good claret and the pleasing, masculine smell of an excellent cigar.

He smiled and stretched, remembering the assorted pleasures of the night. France was a most civilized country. Great food, fine wine, wonderfully seductive and enchanting women; too much to expect the cigars to be French. He should buy a box or two before he caught the boat train: couldn't get tobacco like that at home.

Genevieve woke, her glorious eyes focusing slowly.

'Jean,' she breathed, in that so French way she had of caressing his very ordinary Scottish name, the way that turned his legs to water. 'Jean,' she said again, and she stretched out her white hand with the scarlet fingernails towards him and he almost yielded.

'Must go, my darling,' he said, kissing her lightly but keeping out of the way of those nails, nails that could caress so softly but could scratch so deeply. 'I have to catch the steamer train.'

'Oh no,' she said, her hands gripping him. 'You said two whole days in Paris.'

He laughed. 'It *has* been two days, *ma belle*, the most beautiful two days . . .'

'Of our lives, my Jean.'

She was so desirable; he had never met a woman like her. He groaned and forced himself to move away from the rumpled bed. How easy it would be, and how very, very pleasurable, to slip back into the warm bed, into Genevieve's arms. 'I have something to attend to in Scotland, Genevieve. I'll come back just as soon as I can.'

Genevieve was not a woman to beg. She shrugged a shoulder in a very French way. *Très bien*, her shoulders said. Who cares? I am just as content if you go. What does it matter?

For a moment he looked down at her creamy back and toyed with the idea of making her change her mind. He could do it. They were all the same, *n'est-ce pas*? And then he remembered Scotland and his responsibilities. He echoed her shrug and began to dress.

Less than half an hour later, he was whistling merrily as he sauntered down the plushly carpeted staircase to the foyer, where two maids were already angrily scrubbing and polishing unseen dirt. He strolled past them and reached the door.

'Monsieur, Monsieur, the bill?'

John Cameron tipped his hat lightly back on his handsome head. He stared boldly at the hotel manager out of his grey-blue eyes and laughed.

'Don't fret, my man. Madame will take care of it.' And, once more whistling gaily, he was gone.

Priory Farm, Angus, 24th May 1900

Pain gripped Catriona. It tore at her angrily, as if punishing her for some unknown crime. Sweat broke out on her forehead and she tried desperately not to scream. She had never believed it would be like this, never. Was she not the daughter of farmers? Had she not seen birth a dozen times a year – a thing done privately, causing as little trouble as possible.

'Ach, lassie, let it oot. There's no one tae hear but me and auld Jock out there and he'd bear it for ye, if he could.' The voice was that of Maggie, employed by Jock Cameron as dairy maid and now midwife.

Catriona's scream tore through the air and died to a gasping whimper. Maggie held her hand and, outside, Jock stopped his pacing and listened.

'Dear God, help the lassie, as I've never been able to help.'

She was quiet. Was that it? Was it over? Was he a grandfather?

There was another scream, cut short by the simple expedient of biting as hard as Catriona could on the rolled-up towel that old Maggie had put into her open mouth. Catriona's eyes rolled in agony; there was a name she wanted to call out, but she would not. She would not beg and she would not hurt the old man any more by having him hear it.

The pain receded and she took the towel away. 'It's cold for May, Maggie, so cold.'

The midwife looked at the girl for a moment. Cold? It was a perfect May day. This morning the sweat had been rolling down between her ample breasts as she had sat milking in the parlour, and now her newly washed cotton frock was damp with perspiration. But the lassie was cold. 'Dear Lord, shock.' She ran to the airing cupboard for clean, warm blankets. Everything was to hand, meticulously prepared by Catriona herself.

'Let me wrap you up a bit more, lassie: you've lost a wheen too much blood but it'll soon be over. In a moment, the next push will bring us the head and your bonnie wee bairn will slip out like a boat bein' launched intae the Tay.'

Catriona could hear Maggie's voice but she could not make out the words. She seemed to be floating. It was such a lovely feeling. She had been so cold, and now she was wrapped up the way her own mother had bundled her up against the cold of an Angus winter. So safe, so secure. Nothing hurt, nothing mattered – nothing, nothing. She would drift away, oh so slowly, like a leaf tossed into a quiet stream.

But Maggie would not let her slip away into that peace and contentment. She shook the girl, she cajoled, she wheedled. 'Catriona, Catriona, fight, lassie, fight. The bairn's crowning. He's coming, lass. I can see his head. What a crown of dark hair, jist like his daddy.'

His daddy. John. John with his grey-blue eyes, his devastating smile, his hands that could . . . For a moment she struggled but no, it was so warm here, so peaceful – no pain, no tears, no wondering why. She would stay here where it was warm, where nothing hurt, where sound was blurred and hazy and soft. 'Oh, John, why?' Had she said the words or just thought them? She had no time to wonder, for the pain struck again and instinct took over her exhausted body.

'Work with the pains, lassie, dinnae fight them. That's it, that's it. Jist a wee breath there, a wee rest tae get ready for the next one.'

In the passageway outside, Jock Cameron paced as he waited. It was his fault, all of it. That lassie had been in there for fourteen hours trying to birth her baby, and the man who should have been here, either by himself or marching side by side with Jock, was God alone knew where.

'I spoilt him, Mattie,' he told his long-dead wife. 'He was that bonnie and winning though, and aye minded me of you. I couldnae hit you, Mattie, that's whit it would have felt like and he knew it, the wee rascal, but he's a grown man now, Mattie. I'll never forgive him for this and if the good Lord spares me my daughter-in-law and my grandchild, I'll make it up to them.'

He walked on, backwards and forwards, sometimes praying to the Almighty, at other times justifying himself to his Mattie. Then he would work out how best to reward Catriona for her patience, her friendliness, her charm. He would bypass John, hurt him in his pocket – that would teach him. He would see the lawyer fellow and write the babe in and John out.

The door of the best bedroom opened and Maggie stood there, drying her hands on one of Catriona's best towels. She was smiling – well, as near as auld Maggie could get to a smile for a man. 'You can stop your tramping, Jock Cameron. You've near worn a hole in that good rug and it's the mistress will have to be on her knees darning it, and her with more than enough to do.'

'Catriona? The bairn?' He could barely speak, so anxious was he.

'Mistress Cameron's fine. A bit tired, and who's to wonder at that after what she's been through. The bairn's a bonnie fechter. She'll lead you a dance, you auld fool.'

'A lassie?' The relief was so great that he felt his knees buckle and he forced them to stay straight. A wee girl. What a comfort to an auld man a wee lassie would be. He felt humble and grateful.

'Can I see them?' he asked.

She stood back to let him enter the dark, low-roofed room. Catriona, her face pale in the cloud of her red hair, was lying back against the pillows, but she opened her eyes as if she sensed his presence and smiled tiredly at him. In her arms rested a tiny shawl-wrapped bundle, no bigger, he thought, than one of her own clootie dumplings.

'I'm sorry it's no a laddie, Faither.'

'A laddie?' His heart swelled within him with love and he put out a hard, calloused, work-worn finger and gently touched the bundle. 'Ach, Catriona Cameron, was it not a lassie like you and my Mattie that this house needed?'

The baby lay snug in her mother's arms, and as her grandfather leaned over she yawned heartily in his face. Then she opened her eyes and stared at him measuringly, as if she found him wanting. He was captivated.

'You'll have thought of a name, lass.'

Catriona was quiet, as if summoning up her strength. She had been through so much, one way and another, in the past nine months. At last she said, 'I prayed for a boy, another John.'

Mattie, he thought, it should be Mattie. Then he turned from his study of the baby's face and looked at the serene expression of his daughter-in-law, after all she had been through. Women were amazing creatures. He would never understand them.

'Do you know what day it is today, lass? It's the auld Queen's birthday. Can you believe she's eighty-one years old and most of that spent on the throne? Victoria. Is that no a name for a bonnie bairn?'

'Victoria. It's perfect. Welcome, Victoria Cameron.'

Miss Cameron yawned again and thus dismissed her court.

'I'll leave you to sleep, lass. I'm sorry my son's no at your side where he belongs, Catriona. If I could change him I would, but I promise you this, lass. Everything I have is yours and the bairn's and I'll no allow John to gie you ony more pain.'

She tried to argue, to talk, to tell him that a halfpenny-worth of love from John Cameron was worth more to her than anything.

'It has to be my fault,' she tried to say. But how can you tell your father-in-law that in some essential way you must have failed his son? Otherwise John would be here, wouldn't he? She knew well that they did no real business in France. John's business trips to see stock, to see crops – she forced herself to admit that he had to be seeing other women. 'But, dear God, dear God, I have no pride. I want him. I need him.'

She closed her eyes and the old man tiptoed out and left her to sleep.

John Cameron arrived home from his latest business trip in France to be met by the barrel of his father's shotgun.

'You shouldnae hae dismissed your cabbie, lad. It's a long walk tae the toon in your fancy shoes.'

'Father, are you crazy, man? It's me, John.' He made to move closer to the house, but the rock-steady hands of the old man gestured backwards with the gun – the gun that John knew could be used to deadly effect against foxes and other predators. Jock Cameron never wasted a shot. He would not waste any now.

'I ken fine who you are. Isn't it me that's ashamed of fathering you.'

'Come on, Father, it was business. Wasn't I looking at French cattle? I want tae see my wife and my bairn. You cannae deny me my ain child. A boy it'll be – a grand, healthy John Cameron tae carry on the farm.'

'And whit do you care aboot the child or the farm? What were you doing the night your wife lay in there near bleeding tae death tae bring your daughter intae the world? You're nae good, John. Ye never were, and for your mother's sake I wouldnae let myself admit whit I saw, but that's over. I should hae belted ye years ago, and as God's my witness, ye come one step nearer this house and I'll blow yer head aff and swing fer you.'

John started to shout then. 'Ye crazy auld fool. I'll get the bobbies in. Catriona, Catriona, come out here and tell that auld devil tae let me in my ain house.'

'It's my house, John Cameron,' Old Jock said, 'and one day it'll be the lassie's. Take yersell back tae yer French whoor, and see if she'll keep ye warm when she finds out the landed gentleman has lost his land. Not a penny more do ye get from me. I'll be at Boatman's office first thing in the morning tae change my will.'

He wouldn't shoot him, he wouldn't. John moved closer and the gun spoke. John jumped as the dust flew from the ground exactly in front of his right foot.

'You're crazy, you old fool.' He was crying with fear and anger, and with fatigue. 'Catriona,' he called out desperately, 'Catriona.' But he did not see the weeping figure at the window, and he turned from the gun and stumbled blindly into the night.

Introducing a new place for story lovers – somewhere to share memories, photographs, recipes and reminiscences, and discover the very best of saga writing from authors you know and love, and new ones we simply can't wait for you to meet.

A new address for story lovers

www.MemoryLane.club

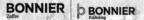